Deborah Wright graduated from Oxford University in 1997 with a degree in English and did voluntary charity work before becoming a full-time writer. Her first novel, *Olivia's Bliss*, was published in 2000 and won the Poolbeg 'Write A Bestseller' competition. When she's not writing, Deborah enjoys painting, watching movies and travelling. Her favourite trip was a visit to India in 2006, which partly inspired *Swimming With Dolphins*.

By Deborah Wright

Olivia's Bliss
The Rebel Fairy
Under My Spell
Love Eternally
The History of Lucy's Love Life in 10.5 Chapters
The Celebrity Mother
Swimming With Dolphins

DEBORAH WRIGHT

Swimming with Dolphins

headline
review

First published in 2010 by HEADLINE REVIEW
An imprint of HEADLINE PUBLISHING GROUP

1

Cataloguing in Publication Data is available from the British Library

ISBN 978 0 7553 5114 5

Typeset in Sabon by Ellipsis Books Limited, Glasgow

Printed and bound in Great Britain by
Clays Ltd, St Ives plc

Headline's policy is to use papers that are natural,
renewable and recyclable products and made from wood grown
in sustainable forests. The logging and manufacturing processes
are expected to conform to the environmental regulations
of the country of origin.

HEADLINE PUBLISHING GROUP
An Hachette UK company
338 Euston Road
London NW1 3BH

www.headline.co.uk
www.hachette.co.uk

For S.L.K.
With love, always

Acknowledgements

Thank you to Clare Foss for being a wonderful editor and thinking up my title (which I love)! Thanks to all the team at Headline, especially Emily Griffin and Georgina Moore.

Thanks to my agent, Simon Trewin, and to Ariella Feiner and Jessica Craig at United Agents.

Thanks to friends and family – to Alexander for HD and all; Diyar, for your amusing US anecdote; to Victoria for being an email buddy and always inspiring; Kate for our trip to Japan which inspired part 4; to David for the trip to Italy and being rude about my cooking; to Tom for PE in Cheam; to Mum for thoughts and tips on Sicily; to Julie Cohen for putting me in touch with Elizabeth Kerri Mahon for NY advice; to Lyra for sitting on my lap and purring whilst I wrote.

Prologue

Do you ever wish that you could change your life?

There. I've started my story like some kind of cheesy self-help book, but I promise that I'm not about to start suggesting you tell the mirror how much you love yourself, or indulge in mental aerobics. I just want you, dear reader, to consider whether you are happy. Do you go into your office at 9 a.m. and wish it was 5 p.m.? Do you dream of wild, passionate love affairs? Do you ever see an exotic beach on the TV and wish you could go there someday? Do you keep hoping that something exciting is just around the corner, that magical twist of Fate that will change your existence for good?

Once upon a time, a voice inside me whispered all these things, but I was in a state of denial: I wanted to pretend that everything in my life was hunky-dory. Let's face it: change is a frightening thing. It's necessary to destroy before you can create. The process from dull routine to dreams fulfilled involves eruptions in life's crust, followed by the lava flow of difficult emotions.

Which is why, at the start of this story, I, Julia Rothwell – a deeply unhappy woman, a woman who was terrified of change – was setting off to explore the world.

I'm in an airport lounge in Stansted. *How did it all come to this?* I ask myself. What am I doing, sitting here at five in the morning on a tatty beige seat, waiting for my flight to Venice, which has been delayed for two hours, wishing desperately that I was anywhere but here?

The answer is simple. I'm doing this, in order to fulfil number one on my list of *Ten Things To Do Before I Die*.

1. *Sleep with an Italian man.*

The list was something Reece and I thought up last year. I was drunk and she was just being herself.

Reece and I grew up together. We've been best friends from primary to high school to the degrees we took at University College, London – and now we share a flat together. But we're very different people. At university, I got a first in Economics and was voted the Person Most Likely to Achieve, whilst Reece was nearly thrown out for smoking pot and keeping a pet Jack Russell terrier in her room. And now we're so-called adults, I had a responsible job as a hedge-fund manager, while Reece is 'looking for work' – which seems to involve surfing the net all day.

One evening last Christmas, I came in from work at 10 p.m. – which was normal for me. As I passed by Reece's bedroom the door was slightly ajar and I saw the yellow flicker of potential danger. I'm always fretting that Reece will light a candle, fall asleep and burn the flat down, so I poked my head around the door. Reece was sitting cross-legged on the floor, surrounded by tea-lights, scribbling in a notebook.

'Julia!' she cried, beckoning me in. 'You have to do this! Kick off your shoes and sit down. I'm making a list of all the things I want to do before I die. I saw a TV programme about it.'

I feigned grumpy dismay, but I was smiling inside. Moments like this reminded me why I loved living with Reece. Everyone at work spent all day stabbing each other in the back. It was always refreshing to come home to my flat in Hampstead and find Reece watching *EastEnders* whilst knitting a pair of pink and purple striped tights, or offering me some of the horrendous, homemade ginger wine she'd just cooked up.

I sat down, accepting a pen, paper and a glass of Baileys.

'How many do you have to put on the list?' I asked, glancing over her shoulder at the page she had already filled with her large, babyish scrawl, Some of her choices were decidedly weird. *Shake hands with a Yeti, Go swimming with dolphins, Meet the Dalai Lama, Learn to crochet . . .*

'You can do as many as you like – twenty, fifty, a

hundred.' She saw my face and said, 'Well, if it's easier, then maybe just stick with ten.'

The first one came easily:

1. Sleep with an Italian man.

'Nice one!' Reece laughed.

The rest of the list took a little more thought.

You see, I wanted my list to be a rainbow of delights – places I'd longed to travel to but only ever seen in films, skills I needed to learn, special people I wanted to meet or find.

'How are you doing?' Reece asked. 'Oh, let me see, let me see!'

'But it's secret,' I cried. As Reece tried to peek, I folded over my list, shielding it from her.

'Oh, but Julia, you saw mine,' she protested. 'Honestly, you're so secretive.'

'I'm not. It's just ... *personal*,' I said, flushing slightly. 'OK, maybe when I've finished it, you can see. I've got nine so far ...'

'... so you just need one more.'

I gazed at Reece. When we were little, she got to play the angel in nativity plays at school, whilst I always had to go down on all fours with a rug on my back as a token sheep, or if I was really, really lucky, I might get to swap the rug for a tea-towel and be upgraded to a shepherd. Reece's hair was the colour of butter, her eyes were blue and her skin soft as a peach. When she smiled, she showed off her gappy teeth but she radiated sweetness.

She was smiling at me now – a smile bright with affection and warmth. Reece was a wonderful friend to me, I reminded myself for the hundredth time. She never lost her temper. She didn't mind when I got grouchy from overwork or moaned about my boss.

So she was sometimes late paying the rent to her landlady – me, since I owned the flat. She was terrible at remembering phone messages, which drove me mad, and she filled the fridge with all sorts of pills and potions from Holland & Barrett which she then forgot to take. She could be bitchy about other people, and laughed at those she thought were boring – being 'boring' was the biggest sin a person could commit, in Reece's eyes. She was also allergic to work and excelled in getting fired. Jobs were just temporary novelties to her anyway, things she applied for on a whim and then lost interest in. Her father, Edmund Wentworth-Jones, was stonkingly rich, despite the credit crunch, and was always giving her stashes of money. This helped Reece to enjoy a carefree, breezy attitude to life but it had possibly delayed a certain emotional maturity.

But: she was a great friend.

I lowered my eyes, glad she didn't notice my tears. I'm very good at crying without people noticing.

'You still need one more. What about . . . I don't know – eating the biggest chocolate bar in the world whilst bungee-jumping?' Reece suggested.

But I already knew what number ten on my list was. I just didn't dare write it down.

I feigned a yawn, said I'd sleep on it, and gave Reece a hug good night.

I lay in bed in the darkness, listening to the sounds of London revellers below. I had to get up early for work in the morning, but found it hard to drop off; the Baileys had left me feeling blurry with emotion. I suddenly switched on the light, picked up a pen and wrote:

10. Tell Ciaran O'Hare that I love him.

There.

But I found no therapy in writing it down. Turning my abstract sin into concrete words made me feel afraid. I scribbled the words out ferociously and turned off the light. Reece must never, *ever* know about my number ten. For Ciaran O'Hare was, unfortunately, her boyfriend.

The list.

I could never have imagined that I would find myself pursuing it. At the time I wrote it, I was very happy working seventy hours a week and practically camping in my office. Losing my job in the credit-crunch madness was the main trigger in getting me to take it seriously.

Fantasies really ought to *stay* fantasies – reality only ruins them. For example, it's much nicer thinking about getting on a plane in pursuit of a handsome Italian than actually doing it.

When I used to work in the City, I travelled a lot, but I always flew Business Class. I used to sit in the VIP lounge and sip champagne. But now, as I'm paying for it all myself, I need to economise. This is the first time I've ever used a no-frills airline, and it really isn't much fun. In my dreams, I saw the plane soaring through skies of frilly clouds, saw myself stepping out of the airport into a gold Venetian morning, a handsome Italian appearing out of nowhere and offering to carry my bags for me. He would ask me to have dinner with him later that evening, when he would tell me all about the *palazzo* in Tuscany that he owned, before ravishing me in my five-star hotel room.

But this is reality: an extremely bored kid opposite me, pretending he's a dog, barking ferociously at our suitcases whilst his haggard parents try to restrain him. Our plane has been delayed by two and a half hours.

By now, I'm actually beginning to fantasise about giving up on this whole silly idea and going back home. I think of how comforting it would be to make coffee in my kitchen. To sink into my bath and then slip back under my duvet.

But I know if I give up on the list this early, Reece will rant and rave. At work I was always quite bossy and headed up my own team, so people often assume that Reece is the dippy one and that I organise her life. But in a funny way, it's the reverse; she's often looked after me.

'You really *need* to do this,' she had coaxed me last night, when I was having doubts. 'I mean, you're thirty-two years old and you've spent the last decade trapped in an office. It's not really a list about Ten Things To Do Before You Die, it's Ten Things To Do Before You *Live*. Because I reckon you've never really lived.'

I check my watch. The kid stops barking and starts bawling. I sigh.

'For passengers awaiting flight 1667 to Venice, I'm pleased to announce that this flight is now boarding at Gate Twenty-Two and I apologise for the delay.'

It's as though sunshine has broken through a cloud of gloom. Everyone cheers and the cabin crew smile as we all jostle to queue up for the plane.

And here I was, half-hoping they'd cancel it. I join the end of the queue, still wondering, Am I really going to go through with this?

As I sit down in Seat 14 A and fasten my belt, I realise that I am. But there is no way I'm going to follow Reece's advice and spend a whole year working my way through all ten things.

Just the Italian. Then I'll go home, tell her I had some fun and then I'll start applying for new jobs.

After all, sleeping with an Italian man can't be too difficult to pull off, can it?

1. Sleep with an Italian man

1

My plane seat is horrible. When I used to travel in Business Class, I never noticed the shape of the clouds or the countries and oceans we were passing over. I always had so much work to do I just saw decimal points and memos.

However, I used to appreciate the leg-room. This seat feels so cramped. My knees are knocking the safety instructions, and there's nowhere for my elbows to go.

Then a guy strolls up, shoves a duffel bag into the overhead locker and sits down next to me.

I imagine these seats aren't much fun for him, either. He looks about six foot, with very, very long legs.

He looks interesting, as a matter of fact. He's wearing jeans and a brown suede jacket over a yellow T-shirt with a picture of Bob Marley's face on it. His own face is slender, with delicate cheekbones accentuated by cute fuzzy sideburns. His eyes are the colour of conkers; his brown hair is slightly messy. He's got an earring in his left lobe, which normally I'd hate on a guy, but it kind of suits him.

I'm just spying the tattoo on his wrist, snaking out from under his sleeve, when he catches me looking. I quickly glance out of the window, my cheeks warm.

It's a long time since I've been on a date with a guy. Or even been chatted up by someone. I'd put that down to working such long hours that I never even got a chance to hang out in a bar. And being in love with Ciaran.

Sometimes I'm afraid that my secret Ciaran obsession is so overwhelming that I'll never love anyone else, just spend the next fifty years never having sex and die a spinster. It's quite empowering to be distracted by another guy – even if just for a few seconds.

'Sorry for the delay to this flight,' our Captain says cheerfully, and then proceeds to warn us that there may be turbulence ahead.

The plane roars down the runway and soars into the sky. I look out of the window, eager for a view so that I can take my first mental snapshot to store in my memory. But all I can see are thick grey clouds.

I feel restless – keep wanting to reach for a copy of the *Financial Times*. I wish I'd brought a novel or something. I'm used to doing things, using my mind, being on the go.

A man starts pushing a trolley down the aisle. I sit up, realising how thirsty I am.

'Would you like anything?' he asks me.

'A white coffee, thanks.'

He pours me one from his jug.

'That'll be two pounds.'

'What? I have to pay?'

'Yes.' He looks apologetic. 'This is a no-frills airline, you see.'

'Sorry.' I pass over the money and take my coffee. I don't even get any proper milk, just that fake stuff in a little pot that splats everywhere when you finally succeed in tugging off the foil top, then hangs in my coffee in miserable swirls.

The guy next to me catches my eye, then we both look away quickly. I start fighting a fresh blush. Then he says: 'Given how late this stupid plane was, you'd think you'd get a free coffee, right? I mean, it's real stingy.' His accent is American.

'Yes, it is really mean.' I hear nerves catch in my laughter. It's weird. Normally when I do business I'm confident and project an image of toughness. I'm rusty at this man stuff, though. I think how relaxed Reece is around guys and try to pretend I'm her. 'If I want to go to the loo, d'you reckon I'll have to pay two pounds for that too?'

My neighbour chuckles, and I feel chuffed that he liked my joke.

'So, are you going on holiday to Venice?' I ask him shyly. 'I'm Julia, by the way.'

'Hi, I'm Luke. Pleased to meet you. In answer to your question, yeah, kind of. I've been in England for a while, and I'm glad to escape. I mean, England sucks.'

'What! Oh – gee, thanks. It's not so bad really, you

know,' I tell him, feeling unusually patriotic now I'm on the defensive. 'I mean, we have James Bond and Judi Dench. And London is magnificent, and though I'm not a big royalist I do think our Queen is pretty cool. After all, what have you got? Lindsay Lohan. Jerry Springer. And you – you started Iraq!'

I realise I sound like a petulant fifteen year old, but he laughs.

'True. But we have Obama now. I'm sorry, but that beats you guys hands down.'

Well, I can't argue with that one.

'As a matter of fact, my mum lives in New York,' I say. 'And she has very bad taste – so it can't be a great place to live.'

'You just don't like to lose an argument, do you?' Luke teases.

'Nope,' I admit, laughing.

'So why are you going to Italy?' he asks. 'Don't tell me – you want to sleep with an Italian.'

I nearly spit my coffee out. How the hell did he know that? Did he look at my list with X-ray eyes?

'I— no, no, no,' I object.

'Oh come on,' he says, nudging me. 'I travel a lot and I've seen it all the time – a single girl, going to Italy for fun – and to meet a guy.'

I can't believe how upfront he is. I might be offended, if it weren't for the teasing sparkle in his brown eyes and the charm of his carefree manner.

14

'Actually, I'm not going for fun, I'm there on business,' I reply quickly.

'Oh really?' He looks almost disappointed. 'Who do you work for?'

Worked for, I think miserably.

'Charlton Cross. I'm a hedge-fund manager.'

'Wow. So how come your firm is sending you on such a cruddy airline with plebs like me?'

'The credit crunch. We're all cutting back,' I lie hastily. 'And well – I'm not just going entirely for business. I will have some fun too.'

He looks at me quizzically.

'So is this some sort of healing, repairing-yourself-after-a-burnout type of trip?' he asks.

'You're very eager to define my trip – you haven't said why you're travelling,' I point out.

'It's a bit like that ad,' he goes on, ignoring my question. 'You know the one, it's really cheesy – the one advertising Australia. Mrs K. Whatever had a job with long hours and her boyfriend left her – sob sob, cue violins. Then she went to Oz, swam with an Aborigine, was miraculously healed and came back Kate.'

'Oh God, yes – I *hate* that ad,' I agree. 'Actually, I hate the way career women in commercials and films always have to have something wrong with them. They have to find a man and learn to *soften* and be nice, because of course, all career women are really hard bitches who need a man to show them work isn't everything. A woman

15

can't actually have a high-powered job and enjoy it.' I realise that I'm beginning to sound as though I belong at Speaker's Corner, Feminist Special Hour. But Luke is looking amused.

'Imagine the equivalent ad for England,' he says. 'It'd be the reverse of the Aussie one. "Kate came to England a fulfilled, happy human being, but after sampling the soggy chips, dodging late-night drunks and getting mugged by an eleven year old in the park, she left a much more uptight and unhappy Mrs K. Whatever".'

'Oh, you *really* don't like my country, do you?' I sigh. 'What happened? Did you get mugged by an eleven year old?'

'As a matter of fact, that was one of my better moments. I was jogging in Regent's Park and the little bastard said could he borrow my phone to call 999, it was an emergency. And then the fucker ran off with it.'

'I'm sorry. I almost feel I should apologise.'

He smiles and holds my gaze for a few seconds.

'I forgive you,' he says lightly.

I'm surprised to feel a lick of desire in my stomach. It's immediately followed by confusion as Ciaran's face springs to mind. Ciaran's got long eyelashes like my neighbour's, but his gorgeous Irish eyes are a piercing blue. What am I doing, being 'unfaithful' to Ciaran, let alone to the Italian lover – whom I haven't even met yet. Luke is seriously throwing my plans into disarray.

2

I suddenly become aware that the plane is landing – the flight went by so quickly. I've enjoyed chatting with Luke so much that I don't even feel tired any more. He's kept me entertained with stories of his backpacking travels around the world. Every anecdote seems to involve him narrowly escaping with his life. I would have had a nervous breakdown by now if I'd suffered all that, but he relates his stories with a breezy cheerfulness.

Now we're standing waiting for our luggage. A self-consciousness has risen between us. We're both aware that this is the full-stop of our flight. I wonder what will happen next. Will we exchange email addresses and phone numbers, and wish each other a happy trip? Or will we end up leaving the airport together and spending a few days in Venice with each other as friends? I almost feel relieved. Then I can forget about the Italian and just relax and enjoy myself. Luke is such fun company, we'd be sure to have a good time. But I can hear Reece hissing disapproval in my head.

And I have to admit, I hate the thought of falling at the very first hurdle. I was always addicted to making lists of things to do at work; I couldn't bear it if I reached the end of the day without ticking everything off.

'Hey, here's mine.' Luke yanks a guitar case and a large rucksack off the conveyor belt.

'I was one of the first to check in, so mine'll probably be last.' I glance at his guitar case. It's scrawled over with signatures, a rainbow of languages and marker pens.

'Wherever I've travelled, I've always got someone to sign it,' he grins.

I notice quite a few flamboyant hearts drawn under names like *Marie-Françoise* or *Helena-Z*. Hmm. Maybe Luke is a charmer. Maybe he just intends to seduce me, get me to sign his guitar case and be off without saying goodbye.

'I like that Madonna sticker,' I remark, noticing a vintage one of Madonna when she used to wear black lace and sport a mole on her upper lip. 'I idolised her when I was a kid.'

'You did?' Luke raises an eyebrow, then frowns.

We fall silent as the luggage comes round yet again. The leftover bags are becoming familiar: a pink rucksack ... a large khaki shoulder-bag ... a big brown suitcase with *Mr Amble* on a sticky label on its side.

'So,' Luke concludes, 'that means you grew up in the eighties?'

I realise he's fishing for my age.

'Did you?' I ask cautiously.

'Well, I'm twenty-five, so I kind of grew up with techno and dance and that kind of thing.'

Twenty-five! I thought he was older than that.

'I'm thirty-two,' I say.

I can tell from the look on his face that he thought I was younger than that.

I haven't bothered with make-up in years and I tend to pull my hair back in a ponytail, which does make me look younger.

'Seven years,' he remarks. 'That's quite an age gap between us.'

I flush. That's rather a presumptuous thing to say, isn't it? And is he implying that I'm ... *old*? Thirty-two isn't old! Forty is old. I've always thought that forty would be like crossing a line, at which point I'd have to accept that I could only ever be an affectionate mother figure to men and knit them condoms etc. But – thirty-two?

The trouble is, when I was twenty-five, I thought thirty-two was completely past it. When I'm forty, I'll probably redefine 'old' as when I retire. Age is all relative – that's the painful thing about it.

It's not even as though I was *that* interested in Luke romantically, but now I've had the subtlest hint of rejection, my interest is piqued. I've never been with a younger guy before. Maybe I should swap number one on my list with *1. Date a toyboy.*

I glance over at Luke, who's staring hard at the conveyor belt. There's nothing on it now except for the pink rucksack.

'I'm getting sick of seeing that pink thing!' I snap.

Luke gazes at me, looking worried. 'I think you've lost your luggage.'

At this point, Luke switches from bohemian traveller mode to perfect-gentleman mode. At least one advantage of losing my case is that I've stopped worrying about looking old. I'm spitting with fury and worry, but he calms me down and leads me over to the help desk. A middle-aged Italian with a moustache gives me a languid glance when I cry that I've lost my luggage. Then Luke takes over. To my surprise, he's fluent in Italian. It brings out another side to him. When he was speaking English, his voice had a slightly lazy drawl. Now, speaking Italian, he becomes animated and passionate; he even starts gesticulating wildly. It's pretty sexy.

The man with the moustache raises his voice in reply. Good – it means Luke is pushing hard. I feel shaky with hope and relief. Luke will get my case back. He has to. It contains nearly all my worldly possessions.

Luke turns to me, pulling a face.

'Sorry. They can't find it. You're going to have to fill in a form and put down the details of your hotel, then wait it out.'

'You – you mean I'm going to have to go off to my hotel with no clothes?' My stomach clenches in horror. My pyjamas are in there. My wash bag. My tooth-brush.

'What am I going to do about underwear?' I cry, thinking aloud.

'I'd offer to lend you a pair of my boxers, but I don't think they'd fit.'

'You really can't get them to . . .' I trail off in despair. I know Luke has done his best. There's nothing more I can do.

Luke and I stand outside the airport, looking awkward. It's already very hot and Luke has pulled on his sunglasses, so I can't see the expression in his eyes.

'So what hotel are you staying in?' I ask.

'Fuck, I don't know,' he admits. 'I just land in a country and find some place to stay.'

I'd hate that, I think. I spent weeks in advance picking out the hotel I wanted to stay in and making sure it had the correct amenities.

'You can come and stay at *La Calcina*,' I say lightly, wondering if that sounds like a come-on. The *Pensione Calcina*, or Lime House, as it is translated, is an ancient and famous hotel that I found on the internet.

Luke smiles enigmatically and shakes his head.

'Hey, Career Girl, that's way out of my price range. I'm thinking more of *La Youth Hostella*.' He puts on a mock Italian accent.

'So . . .'

21

'We should swap numbers,' Luke says. 'You know – maybe later in the week if you're still about and I'm still about we could hook up for a beer.'

'OK.' I reel off my number and he logs it in his phone, then he rings me so that I have his number.

'Well . . .' he says.

'Well . . .' I reply.

'Well, so long,' says Luke. Words that, later on, I find myself analysing over and over, wondering if I will ever see him again.

3

When I get to the hotel, the full horror of my lost luggage hits me. Luigi, the charming receptionist, asks me if I have anything to check in and I feel myself go hot, then cold in swift succession. I tell him what's happened and he gives me a consoling look.

'I'm sure it will turn up in a few days,' he says kindly.

Luigi's manner is very comforting, and he's really quite handsome. Then my eyes drop to his left hand. Wedding ring.

Upstairs in my room, I automatically go to unpack – only for the shock to hit me again. *It's all gone.* My iPod. My favourite dress. My mobile phone charger. A new pair of sandals.

Yes, I do have travel insurance from the Post Office, but that won't replace my favourite pin-striped trouser-suit from Karen Millen, a one-off I bought in a sale. And what about the old photos in my purse? Another wave of anguish comes over me as I recall that my suitcase also contained a copy of *The Lost Princess* by Herbie French, my favourite childhood author – who I'm meant to be pursuing if I ever make it to number five on my list. It's dog-eared, with a cracked cover, but I've always treasured its particular scent. I've had the book since I was five years old and whenever I open it up, I breathe in the memories stained like a watermark in its pages – a lingering essence of childhood, of gingerbread and *Doctor Who* and blue skies and playing in the garden.

All gone.

I try to cheer myself up by sitting down and making a list of essentials I need to buy to replace them:

1. Toothpaste, moisturiser, toothbrush
2. Pyjamas
3. Underwear
4. Clothes

The trouble is, after all the stress of the early start and the delayed flight and the lost luggage, I'm feeling completely knackered.

I lie down for about half an hour, drifting in and out of consciousness, the sounds of Venice weaving into my dreams. Then I wake up feeling a little better and go into the bathroom to freshen up. I open up the toothpaste supplied by the hotel and rub it over my teeth using my forefinger.

I examine my reflection. It's a strange sensation. I'm used to glancing at myself for no more than a few seconds. Now I take a good look – and it becomes apparent that I've let my appearance slip over the last few years. My hair is dark and quite fine. I used to spend a fortune on thickening shampoos as a teenager. Its only asset is that it's very shiny. In my early twenties, I grew it long and it was probably my most attractive feature. But it started to irritate me, and when I went to work in the testosterone-fuelled bank, it wasn't a good look. I remember going to one meeting where a guy from Carlton Bank looked me up and down, said I had lovely hair and asked when my boss was going to turn up. When I pointed out that *I* was the one with whom he had to discuss the sale of a small German bank, he repressed a smile that seemed to hover on his lips throughout the meeting like the Cheshire Cat.

The next day, I went and got my hair chopped into a functional bob. It was a little severe to really suit me, so I let it grow a tad longer and then got into the habit of pulling it into a low ponytail.

I once overhead two secretaries on their lunch-break, discussing magazine article about your 'true face' versus your 'mirror face'. The article said how important it was to let your face fall slack and see what your true reflection told you about your character. At the time I thought it sounded moronic. Now I find myself taking the test. I stare into my eyes. They look tired – and, if I'm honest, a little sad. I swallow. Since losing my job, this year has probably been the worst of my life, so it's no wonder if some of that pain has fossilised in my pupils.

I have to admit it: I hardly look attractive. My face is so pale that Reece used to tease me about being a vampire. My lips turn downward and my skin is pasty, with a few spots on my chin. I look as though I ought to be attending a business meeting – serious and sharp around the edges. No wonder Luke dismissed me. The thought irritates me. I don't like the idea of basing my sense of identity on how I look, and I thoroughly resent the concept that my happiness depends on the judgement of how men view me. And yet . . . looks *are* important and anyone who says that men are more fascinated by the personality underneath is delusional.

I came to Italy naïvely assuming that an Italian would automatically want to woo me. But what if I'm not up to scratch? Especially if loads of women come over here looking for love and all dolled up? It's been so, so long since I was with a guy and Luke served as a litmus test. His verdict on me was that I'm some kind of premature OAP – what if Italians feel the same way? I'll have to return home and tell Reece I didn't sleep with an Italian man because I . . . er . . . suddenly decided I'm a lesbian or something.

Then I decide to stop worrying, head for the city and jolly well buy some brand new knickers.

4

I've been searching for some underwear for an hour now and I've discovered two things:

1. Venice is beautiful.

2. It doesn't seem to sell much beyond pizza, postcards and masks.

I must have passed about a hundred restaurants. Their tables fight for space on the piazzas or jostle in the narrow side-streets, and their shiny plastic menus all seem to advertise the same seven types of pizza. Several times, a handsome waiter has sashayed past me carrying a tray of Cokes and given me a flirtatious smile. I've blushed but been too embarrassed to smile back. Italian men really are different from Englishmen. They've got a naughty zing in their eyes, an invitation in their smiles. They look as though briefcases and spreadsheets could never be of interest to them; they positively gleam with *la dolce vita*.

It's given me a little boost of confidence, though I'm

still not sure how I'll manage to get into a situation where I feel comfortable going to bed with one of them.

I've passed through St Mark's Square and now I'm wandering through little cobbled streets. The houses are so pretty, with stucco fronts and window-boxes spilling over with red and yellow flowers. I cross a few little bridges arching over the canal and spot a gondola, the gondolier wearing a red and black suit with a straw hat. The couple inside are staring at each other dreamily and I feel a little ache, wishing I could be in a boat with a man looking at me like that.

I shake myself, realising that I'm losing track of time. I set off at a brisk pace, determined to tick off everything on my list. Time seems slowed down. It wouldn't surprise me if I looked at my watch and discovered it had fallen asleep.

I consult my list once more, but it's no good: I find myself drifting, lingering at a shop window containing a display of beautifully painted masks.

I wander inside.

'*Ciao*,' the girl says, smiling.

I smile back. I wonder if I ought to buy a mask as a present to take back to Reece. Then I notice the price: 28 euros. Since the pound is approximately the same as the euro at the moment, it's rather a pricy item for a girl who's unemployed.

Reece says that people fall into two categories: spenders or savers. She tends to spend her wages in a day, but I'm fond of ISAs and good interest rates. I'm using up pretty much all of my savings for this trip – which is scary when I don't have a job to go back to.

There are a few dresses hanging on a rack, so beautiful and opulent they look as though they could belong in a fancy dress shop. There are no tracksuits to be seen around here; Italians definitely are more elegant in their tastes.

'You like?' the assistant helps me. 'Look. Look. *This*. Bella!' She points to a mannequin, clothed in a scarlet dress with a halter neck and a tulle skirt that falls in swishy folds.

'Yes – you try, you try,' she insists, sensing weakness.

'OK,' I laugh. Clothes are on the list, after all.

In the changing-room, I take off my blue trouser-suit and cream blouse and I pull on the dress.

Wow. My eyes widen. The dress is one of those magical creations that conceals and clings in all the right places, so that my waist looks narrow and there's a hint of cleavage, and the pretty folds kiss my knees.

I look as though I ought to be dancing at a ball, holding a mask to my face, opposite a dashing man.

'You like?' the assistant calls.

When I emerge, she shrills in Italian and flutters her hands around me. I can feel that there is a big grin on my face.

'OK – I'll buy it. How much is it?'

'Seventy euros,' she says merrily.

Back in the changing-room, I pull off the dress with a sad heart, knowing I'll be dreaming about it tonight. There's simply no way I can afford it.

When I pull on my trouser-suit, I realise how drab I look. I used to wear this all the time in the office. It's not really holiday wear. I remember my lost case with a sigh.

I take the red dress back to the assistant, saying, 'Sorry – too expensive.'

From the way her face crumples, you would have thought I'd just confessed to murdering her pizza-making grandmother. I know she'll only pressurise me so I make a hasty exit, trilling some polite *ciao*s.

Another mask shop catches my eye. Oh God, there's another gorgeous dress in the window. A voice inside my head cries, *Why didn't you just buy the red one? You've got savings. You can afford it.*

But I've got nine more things to do on my list, I argue back, and I ought to save as much of that money as possible. Who knows when the credit crunch will ever improve. Who knows if I'll ever even get another job . . .

But you're on a mission to break free, the voice insists. *You may as well use that money to enjoy yourself. You spent years saving it, why let it just sit there in your account . . . ?*

I find myself turning back. Re-entering the shop. The assistant is so overjoyed to see me that I burst into laughter with delight. She wraps up the dress in crisp tissue, chattering away and suggesting I buy a mask to go with it. I give her a fierce smile and tell her I think I've spent quite enough already; she grins and winks at me.

As I walk out of the shop clutching a smart carrier bag, I suddenly have an insight into shopaholics. I've never been one for browsing in stores because I've never really had time to do it. I was very disapproving when the credit crunch came and I read about people who had stacked up huge sums on plastic. But this deep flicker of pleasure surprises me. This really has to be a treat, I tell myself, and not be the start of an addiction – or I'll be broke by the end of the week.

Back at the hotel, there's no sign of my case but I don't care.

As I put on my new dress and brush my hair, I feel sparkly. I feel ready to meet an Italian . . .

5

I can't decide where to eat. I'm torn between pizza near the Doge's Palace, pizza by the canal or pizza at St Mark's Square.

There are actually loads of interesting restaurants that I researched and ringed in my guidebook – I just feel nervous about venturing out and finding them alone. Whenever I travelled abroad for work, a car would be sent to pick me up and take me home. A restaurant was always booked for me. It feels strange, organising it all myself. I'm scared I might get lost, so I decide to play it safe. I'll go and eat pizza in the piazza at St Mark's.

It's a glorious evening. Twilight is smoking blue across the canals, imbuing everything with a dreamy, romantic hue. I sit down at a table under a large red umbrella. A few pigeons peck at the cobbles by my feet. The air is sweet with sounds of pleasure: lapping water, laughter, glasses chinking, the distant music of a waltz.

I wait for my food, feeling self-consciously alone. I wish Luke was here. I pick up my mobile, tempted to call him – but then I remember, with a wince, the 'seven-year age gap' remark. I mean, with me being so *old*, he'd probably have to cut up my pizza for me, feed it to me and wipe the drool off my mouth, right?

I notice a missed call on my mobile: Reece 6.43 p.m. I decide to phone her back when I've finished eating. My nutritionist gave me instructions to chew my food carefully and not eat too much. I hope that doesn't make me sound like a crazy diet-freak. It's just that in the last few months of my job, I was so worried about being made redundant, I had killer stomach-aches all day. Everything I ate just sat in my stomach like a lump of cardboard and I lost two stone. So I'm still trying to get my appetite back to normal.

She used to tell me off for eating and working at the same time. I'd barely notice what I was eating, for I'd be too busy shoving things into my mouth whilst staring at my paperwork spread out across the table. Now I try to focus single-mindedly on my pizza.

'*Signorina*, may I join you?'

I look up and nearly fall off my chair. An utterly gorgeous Italian guy is standing in front of me. A few feet behind him is a pack of his giggling friends.

'Why not?' I say, trying not to leap up, punch the air, whisk out the chair and tell him he's a dream come true. Instead, I smile pleasantly and offer him my hand.

Naturally, being an Italian, he doesn't shake it, just brushes his lips against my knuckles. It's all very smooth but I admit it – I'm turned on.

Just as he sits down, my mobile buzzes. It's Reece. I flash him an apologetic glance.

'Er – excuse me just one minute.'

'*Bellissima* . . .' He rattles off something in Italian, but he nods.

'Reece, I'm just with – er – an *Italian guy*,' I say in a low voice. I glance over at my companion and he gives me a look of naked impatience. 'Can I call you back?'

'Oh my God!' I can hear her addressing Ciaran in wild excitement. 'Julia's in bed with an Italian!'

I wonder what Ciaran thinks about that.

'Well, not exactly,' I say quickly. 'I'll – I'll call you back.'

I switch off my phone and smile at my Italian. He leans forward, smiling back. He really is rather yummy – though not the cliché dark-haired, dark-eyed man I saw in my fantasies. His hair is fair, gold-streaked with sun, and his eyes are a vivid, intense blue. His skin is tanned and very lustrous, as though it's soaked up the sun and is reflecting it back in joy.

'*Que bella ragazza*. You are very, very pretty lady!'

It's all very charming, but he doesn't seem to speak much English. And I don't speak Italian.

'You?' He gives up and points at me.

'Er – my name? I'm Julia.'

'Ah, Giulia. *Bella* Giulia.' The way he pronounces my

name, rolling the 'J' and stretching it into three syllables, is so sumptuous; he makes it sound as though my name belongs on a chocolate-bar wrapper, '*Io* – me Piero.'

'Piero,' I repeat.

'Giulia,' he repeats.

We beam at each other, wondering what topic to struggle through next.

'You American?' he asks.

'No, no, no.' I smile, thinking how Luke would be laughing and painting a 'one' in the air. 'English.'

'Ah. *Inglesa.*'

I can still see his friends in the distance, watching us, whispering and pointing. They make me feel uneasy – I wish he'd tell them to go away.

Another silence. I reach into my bag and pull out my Italian-English language guide. I flip through to the section at the back entitled *Helpful Phrases*. He leans over eagerly, running his finger down the list, a crease in his brow. The closeness of his presence is electrifying. I have a sudden vision of us in a bedroom, smudged with erotic purple darkness, his mouth hot on mine. An excited voice whispers: *It's going to happen, you're going to sleep with him, it's really going to happen!*

'*Allora.*' He alights upon a phrase that appeals to him. 'How – old – are – you?'

I'm not going to fall into that trap again.

'How old are *you*?' I ask.

'Me?' He pauses, then skips a few pages to find the list

of numbers, his fingers slipping down the digits. His hands are very beautiful – long, tanned and slender. 'Twenty . . . six.'

'Oh wow. I'm twenty-seven,' I say brightly.

'Oh.' He looks a little disturbed and I freak inside. Does he think I'm lying? My temper is just beginning to fray with the possibility that twenty-seven might be too old, when I see him reassessing the list and announcing triumphantly, 'I am twenty-nine.'

I repress a smile at his obvious piece of spin, glad we're past the stupid issue of age. He peers at my guidebook again.

'Do – you – have – brother – or – sister?' he manages, with some effort.

I can't repress a flicker of frustration. He is so lovely, so charming, so handsome . . . but it doesn't look as though this is going to make for an evening of scintillating conversation.

It takes us five minutes to ascertain that I have one brother, Alexander, currently living in America near to my mother, who relocated there with her second husband. Piero has three sisters and two brothers (Catholic family, I'm guessing). Then ten minutes for him to explain that he's a student and me to explain that I was a hedge-fund manager – the word 'hedge' is fatal, leading to a labyrinth of conversational confusion when he thinks that I'm a gardener. By the time we've spent another ten minutes verifying that I'm single and definitely don't have an

'Engleesh' boyfriend or husband back home, we both look a bit frazzled.

There's a long silence. He bites his lip. I flick back my hair.

'Er – we go to *la mia casa*?' he says, scanning the book again. 'To me – my 'ouse.' When he looks at me, his eyes speak far more fluently than his stumbling sentences.

'Er – OK. Yes.'

I ask the waiter for the bill. Whilst we're waiting, Piero stands up and stares into the distance, whistling faintly.

When we get up to leave, I feel a fluttering in my stomach, somewhere between fear and desire. We cross St Mark's Square and he takes my hand in his. It feels warm. It feels good. But when I glance back, I see his friends following at a distance.

'They're coming too?' I wince.

'They OK. They friends.'

'Yes, but – it's just … I mean, I feel it might be a bit strange if they're there too in the flat.' I stop. 'I mean,' I say laughing awkwardly, 'I'm not really up for some kind of gang bang.'

Piero stares at me. He might not have understood all my words but he seems to understand my fears, for his eyes are full of sympathy and reassurance. He signals to them. They laugh and wave back, disappearing down an alleyway. Phew, thank goodness for that. Piero touches my cheek, then curls his hand around the back of my neck and pulls me in for a kiss.

I haven't been kissed in such a long time. Fireworks of joy explode in my stomach. Then he becomes more insistent, his mouth fierce. I pull away. He takes my hand and leads me on with an impatient tug. I frown, sparks of bliss still drifting inside, rapidly extinguished by my worries. I can't help feeling that though the kiss was very nice, it was also a bit aggressive. As though he feels he's got me in his net and now he's going to hurry me along as quickly as possible to his lair so he can eat me.

Isn't that the point? a voice asks. *After all, why waste time? You wanted to sleep with an Italian man!*

It just doesn't feel quite right. I want to sit down with him for at least another hour and *discuss* things . . . except we tried that and language became a wall between us that got higher and higher with each attempt.

I've been feeling so mixed up that I haven't even noticed that Piero has stopped. We're standing outside a stucco house: his place. It looks nice. I feel slightly more reassured. Surely an axe murderer wouldn't live in a house with clouds of red flowers in window-boxes at the front?

I may sound naïve, but I'm just trying to enjoy being spontaneous for once – and gosh, it is hard work.

He unlocks the door, pauses and calls something into the hallway. Then he beckons me in.

The hallway is cool and elegant, rugs sprawling over wooden floors. Piero is clearly proud of his pad, for he takes me on a guided tour, pointing at the odd urn or picture. It strikes me then that he must be pretty loaded to own a house like this in a plush part of Venice. For all I know, he's a high-flying lawyer or banker.

We enter the living room. There's a girl sitting on the sofa, eating an apple, an artist's sketchpad propped up on her knee. Piero suddenly drops my hand and turns pale.

I feel indignation bristle inside me. Clearly Piero thought his wife was out.

He addresses her in vehement Italian. She brushes a lock of dark hair from her eyes and flicks him a 'V' sign. Then she carries on with her sketching.

'My sister,' he says to me apologetically.

'You live together?'

'No, no, she – how you say? She invade. She little.' He sighs, then grabs my hand, tugging me to the foot of the stairs, an invitation in his eyes. My smile replies with a 'yes'.

His bedroom is clear and white, with an exquisite balcony. We stand on it for a while, gazing out at the view, and a wave of happiness tumbles over me. I can't stop my imagination from leap-frogging into the future. I can see myself coming back to Venice on a regular basis for passionate weekends, where we'll hole ourselves up in this bedroom and make wonderful love for forty-eight hours straight. I imagine Reece and Ciaran gossiping about my fabulous Italian boyfriend; I imagine showing them his photo with a smug, loved-up smile.

For so long I've been waiting for someone to cure me of Ciaran. And I think Piero could be the one.

As he leans over and kisses me, I wonder, Why didn't I come to Venice years ago?

His arms are tight around my waist; his kisses soon become aggressive. Within seconds, he starts pulling up my red dress. I hear a few threads tear and I wince as he chucks it on to the floor, but it feels churlish to break the spell by folding it up neatly and asking if he has a sewing-kit. Conscious of the bright light, I immediately fold my arms with a flush of paranoia, worried that I have pale skin and a flat chest.

'*Bellissima*,' he mutters, though by now he's used the word so often it feels tatty and frayed. He pushes me down on the bed and tears off my bra. Then he gets up and removes his shirt. Wow, his body's yummy. But isn't this all going a bit too fast? He's already unbuttoning his jeans. I wanted to take them off, to savour his mounting excitement as I popped each button out of its hole. As he climbs back on to the bed, I feel like a kid who's woken up disappointed on Christmas Day; I want to cry out, '*So there's not going to be any foreplay?*' My desire leaks away; anticipation was better than the reality. Then, as he lies down and starts to kiss me again, I feel the promise of its return. Pleasure begins to creep over me, but I'm just hotting up when he breaks off and hunts about for a condom. I stare at his erection in panic. I feel much too dry and tense; I have a feeling this is going to hurt. I could be a nervy teenager losing her virginity all over again.

'*Ecco!*' He brandishes a silvery square.

He's just succeeded in rolling it on when we hear the slam of the front door, a muttered conversation and then a voice shrieks up, 'Piero!'

The condom drops to the floor in a limp squiggle.

'*Figlio mio!*' Footsteps thunder up the stairs.

Piero is in such a state of panic, he can't seem to move; saliva glistens on his lips. 'Ah – you go – under bed.'

'No!' I cry. His wife can bloody well see me and know the truth. Then I hear that rasping voice again – '*Piero!*' – and wonder if I can escape this place alive. I fumble my bra back on, gathering up my red dress.

The door opens.

My mouth becomes an 'O' of shock – and so does hers.

This woman can't be Piero's wife, surely? She looks as though she's in her fifties. She has wild black hair streaked with grey. She's about nineteen stone and her face is like a large red cheese.

'*Mamma – mamma,*' Piero whines, excuses then flowing in Italian.

Suddenly I look over at Piero. I recall the lies he told me about his age. His giggly friends who followed us. His *sister* in the room below. My stunned eyes fall to his body, the flawless golden skin: an emblem of youth.

I know that Italian men are famous for living with their

mothers until they get married, and then turning their wives into their mothers, but still . . .

Oh shit, I think. He's probably no more than eighteen, nineteen. I've fulfilled Luke's prophecy – I've turned into a bloody cradle-snatcher and now I'm about to be beaten to death by his nutty mother.

I yank on the red dress sharpish, while she hurls a stream of abuse at me. His sister appears on the landing behind her, laughing and sneering. *Mamma* turns and gives her a light thwack.

'Sorry – sorry – *scusi*,' I say, trying to edge into the hallway.

I have to pass by his maternal bodyguard, so close I can smell her panting breath, anger mixed with oregano, passion with onions. I succeed in getting past and hurry down the stairs. But in the bottom hallway, his sister appears again, barring the way with spread arms and a mocking grin. I cry out. She just shrugs. I shove past her and she lets out a wail and *Mamma* roars. No doubt *she's* allowed to hit her kids but I am most certainly not allowed to touch them at all.

Before I leave, I take one last look back up. Piero is standing on the landing, looking sad and stupid. And his mother is coming after me.

O Dio.

Outside, his friends are huddled across the road. I start to run away. Piero's mother comes out on to the streets, hurling insults after my back: '*Prostituta! Sporca! Vai via!*

Vattene!' I'm a dirty prostitute who should go away. Shutters open; people poke their heads out; tourists turn and stare.

Seething with raw humiliation, I get lost several times on my way back to the hotel. On one occasion, I end up having to ask directions, and the man gives me a wide grin and says slyly, *'Ciao, bella.* I show you Venezia. You Americana? I show you good time!'

'Oh piss off,' I hear myself snap. *'Vai via* yourself and go jump in the canal. I just want to go home.'

6

Back in the *Pensione Calcina*. Back in my room. Oh, thank God. My heart still beating fast, I take a bottle of something alcoholic from the mini-bar and down it, gratefully feeling the burn. Safe now, I can see the funny side. I start to laugh, picture the cheese-faced woman yelling again and laugh even harder. And then, all of a sudden, the laughter turns into tears.

I didn't cry when I got made redundant; I haven't cried since. Now the crying just won't stop. I walk into the bathroom and watch the girl in the mirror with her puffy face, tears streaming into her mouth. Suddenly I feel appalled. *Get a grip*, I tell myself sharply. *It's just one guy. There are plenty more Italians in the sea, and on the land too.*

But my tears appear to have a life of their own.

The funny thing is, I'm not even worried about Piero any more. Yes, it was horrible and humiliating, but the main thing that keeps flashing into my mind is my last day at work. The way the secretaries were sniggering. I heard one of them muttering how relieved they were that I wasn't coming back. I remember my co-workers giving me looks of sympathy. I remember walking into my office in a state of complete fury. I wanted to throw my laptop across the room, stamp my in-tray into plastic shards, send my desk crashing through the window. I thought about how many evenings and weekends I had worked overtime without pay. I thought about the nights I'd gone to bed at 2 a.m. and got up at six. Bloody hell, I gave Charlton Cross the whole of my twenties. I gave them a whole decade of my life when all my friends were in normal jobs, were going out to bars and on holidays and having relationships. I even gave up Ciaran for them. And still they let me go.

My mobile phone buzzes. I see it's Reece. I let out a deep breath and pick up.

'Hi.' I just about manage to keep my voice steady.

'Hi!' She sounds so excited. 'So how did it go?'

'Oh Reece. I blew it.' My voice cracks and I put my hand over the phone, crying a bit more.

'What? What is it? What happened?'

'I . . . I just blew it. I got freaked out. I'm not quite sure why. I mean, he came over and chatted me up . . . and then I just ran off . . .'

'*You ran off?*' Reece laughs.

I feel my stomach tighten because I have a sneaky feeling Ciaran might be in the same room as her.

'His friends – they were following us in a pack,' I explain. 'They looked really dark and ominous, and I got scared they were going to attack me.' I find myself exaggerating with a flicker of shame.

'Oh my God,' Reece breathes. I hear her calling to Ciaran: 'Julia tried to sleep with an Italian but she nearly ended up getting gang-raped!'

Oh shit. I wait for Ciaran to say something mean, but to my surprise, I hear him say, 'My God – is she OK?'

'Are you OK?' Reece asks. 'Don't you think you should call the police?'

'No, I'm fine. I just ... Oh Reece,' I sigh. 'I think I should come home and start to apply for a new job. It was really nice of you to help me come up with this list, but I just need to face reality. This adventure thing – it's not *me*. I belong in an office.'

'Julia, you're just out of your comfort zone, that's all,' Reece insists. 'Look. You booked a return flight for Friday. You have five more days to grab an Italian. Now go on. Just Do It!'

Reece is always reading books like *Feel the Fear and Do It Anyway*. It's all very well for her to quote the theory, but I'm the one doing the practice.

'I need to apply for some jobs ...' I repeat.

Reece goes quiet. Then: 'But you looked for jobs before you left, and there aren't any. You know that. You said yourself that in the City, jobs are now an endangered species.'

I fall silent. The truth is cruel.

'Well, in that case I think I'm going to move on to number two on the list. I'm just not a one-night stand type of girl.'

'So are you finally going to give me a few hints as to what's on this secret list of yours?' Reece complains. 'I still can't believe that I haven't seen it. What is number two, anyway?'

'Scuba-diving,' I confess. 'After we did those classes, I felt I should put them to use. I want to see the under-water beauty of the world.' I feel uplifted at the thought. 'Yeah – I think I'll go right away. I can fly over to Sicily, just book it online—'

'*No!*' Reece nearly screams. 'You can't, you can't, you can't. You have to stay there and find a bloke and finish off the week.'

'What? Why?' I ask suspiciously. Is it that Reece doesn't feel scuba-diving is zany enough to be on my list? Maybe she feels I ought to be bungee-jumping off the top of Everest. 'I happen to think scuba-diving will be an amazing experience.'

'It's not that – I think it's a *great* idea. But seriously, you have to stay there. For the rest of the week. We've got a surprise for you.'

'Eh? What d'you mean by that?'

'It'll spoil the surprise if I tell you. No. You stay there and finish the job you came to do,' Reece commands sternly.

After we've chatted a little longer and hung up, I wonder what the hell this surprise could be. It sounds ominous. Maybe they want me to stay here because they're organising some sort of Coming Home party. I picture myself returning to the flat and finding paperchains hanging everywhere and a glitzy sign declaring CONGRATULATIONS ON SLEEPING WITH AN ITALIAN – WE ALL KNEW YOU COULD DO IT! I smile painfully at the thought. The trouble with Reece is that you never really know.

At least I've stopped crying. That's the lovely thing about Reece; after I've confided in her, nothing seems quite so bad.

I take off my red dress. Clothes carry memories in their hems and folds; I know that every time I wear it from now on, I'll remember this crappy night. I realise I only splashed out on it as a way of flicking a 'V' sign at the bastards who fired me at Charlton Cross. Now I feel stupid, because of course, they're all sitting in their offices right now, making millions, completely unaware of the dress's existence.

I go into the bathroom and scrub my underwear in the sink using a small bar of soap, then hang them up to dry.

I go to bed naked and stare into the dark. For a few scary moments I wonder if I'll ever get a job again. Then I console myself with a nicer worry: how I'm going to spend the next few days waiting for Reece's surprise.

7

The next morning, I wake up before five, jump out of bed, hurry into the bathroom in a panic – and then realise that I don't need to go to work. I'm unemployed. This is my new life, my new reality.

I feel too zinged up to go to sleep. Time always used to be a scarce commodity. Now there's too much of it; it sprawls out everywhere, threatening loneliness and boredom. I decide to go for a walk. Then, when I pass reception, something fabulous happens. Luigi waves and calls out that my suitcase has been returned! I'm so excited that I go back to my room, unlock it and fling it open. I press my clothes against my cheek, kiss my iPod and run my hands over my beloved copy of *The Lost Princess*.

Then I check the back lining, looking for the photograph tucked inside. I pull it out and stare at it. It's a faded picture of a young man with chestnut hair, wearing a blue stripy T-shirt, his eyes screwed up from the glare of the sun. I frown and push it back.

I pull open the curtains. A glorious dawn tints the rooftops, sighs over the Giudecca Canal and paints orange hats on the canal wavelets. I watch a distant *vaporetto* collecting passengers, the glints of black sunglasses. But I feel distant from the beauty, as if my sadness has formed another wall of glass between me and the view.

It's time to make a decision.

One of my favourite love/hate songs is 'Should I Stay or Should I Go?' I feel it start to dance through my head now and get a sudden sense of the present cleaving open into two paths. I could linger in Venice. I've yet to explore the Doge's Palace and see the prison where Casanova was locked up. Or I could do what I really want to do and visit those parts of Italy I've always longed to see ...

Three hours later, I'm sitting on the train, watching the scenery flit past. Hoping I've made the right decision.

Now I have another decision tugging at me: *should I contact Luke or leave him alone?* Finally, I take the plunge. I call up his number. As it rings, the mobile becomes clammy in my palm. What if he picks up and asks, 'Who the fuck are you? The woman from the plane? Oh, the *older* one, the one who's thirty-two? Was I really mad enough to give you my number?'

Instead, he answers with: 'Hey, you. Julia.' His voice is sexy and conspiratorial, as though we're lovers. 'Nice to see your number flashing up on my screen. I was wondering when you'd call.'

'Oh well, I just ...' I bite back a smile, happiness bubbling up inside.

'Where are you?'

'On a train. I'm – well, this sounds a bit mad, I know, but I've always wanted to visit Assisi so I thought, Why not just jump on a train and go? You know, when I was a kid I went to a Catholic school and I always loved that story of Saint Francis feeding the birds so that they flocked to him and sat on his palm.'

'Oh, I can do that, it's easy,' Luke boasts. 'Maybe I could come and visit you there. I'm really bored with Venice. It sucks.'

'Er, that'd be great,' I say, slightly taken aback but liking the way Luke takes everything in his stride. I suppose he is a seasoned traveller.

Then he goes on, 'Look, I'm kinda broke. I was wondering if I could crash on your hotel floor tonight. I swear it'll only be for one night – I'll be heading off tomorrow and I'm not an axe murderer. I mean, you saw my rucksack, didn't you? There wasn't room for an axe in it!'

I laugh and try to push away my doubts.

'That'd be fine,' I say, my heart skipping a few beats.

Luke says that he's going to jump on to the next train to Perugia. We arrange to meet later that afternoon at the hotel I've booked – the Hotel San Francesco. I switch off my phone. That went well. Almost too well. Let's hope the axe-murderer joke wasn't a double-bluff. But I too am glad to be leaving Venice. I suddenly realise why I hated the idea of a sinking city; it reminds me of the banks during the credit crunch, everything looking fine on the outside whilst we all slowly, slowly, slipped under-water.

8

'So – did you sleep with an Italian guy then?' is the first thing Luke says to me as we greet each other outside the Hotel San Francesco.

'Hey, Luke. I'm glad to see that you're as tactful as ever.'

'Life's too short to bother with small-talk bullshit,' Luke says brightly.

'Anyway,' I go on, studying my guidebook, 'I want to check out Saint Francis's tomb before it shuts.'

'Oh, just avoid the question.'

I look up at him in exasperation and gently hit him on the head with my guidebook. Luke yelps and laughs, pinching my waist. I giggle and dance away from him. I'm so glad I took the risk and called him. This must be what it's like to have a baby brother.

'D'you want to go in and ask the desk to look after your luggage? We can take it up later.' I don't mention that I still feel a little weird about being alone with him in a hotel room.

'I'm not that keen on churches,' Luke says wheedlingly. 'I believe in Fate but hell, I'm an atheist. What about you? Surely all bankers are atheists who see the world as just a load of numbers?'

'I'm . . . agnostic.'

'Indecisive,' he sighs, picking up his backpack and heading for the entrance and the check-in desk.

'Open-minded,' I retort after him.

As we walk to the famous church, I notice how deliciously tanned Luke is. It's only been a few days but he seems to have thoroughly avoided the 'pink' stage and moved straight to coffee. How come all I have are red cheeks, a scarlet band at the back of my neck and a few freckles?

'Wait,' he says, seeing the SILENZIA signs outside. 'Before we go in, tell me what did happen with your Italian guy. Come on. You can tell Luke. Trust me.'

I consider making an excuse, but the sensitivity in his eyes sways me. I end up telling him the whole sorry story.

'You see,' I blurt out in a moment of naked confession, 'I'm hopeless at adventure, Luke. I'm just not cut out for it.'

'It's not that you're not cut out for it,' Luke reassures me, stroking my arm. 'To me, that sounds like an awesome adventure! I mean, come on.' Seeing my face, he rattles on: 'You just haven't had much practice at it. You know, when I was eighteen I read a book that completely changed my life. It's called *The Dice Man* by another Luke – Luke Rhinehart. D'you know it?' When I shake my head, he carries on and explains: 'It's about a guy who decides to dictate all his decisions, based on the throw of a dice. He ends up on a pretty wild journey, as you can imagine. I don't think I've ever read anything since that's made such a strong impression on me.' Then he grins. 'Don't you worry, I swear by the end of your trip we'll have sorted out your Italian.'

We enter the cool, dark church – the astounding Basilica di San Francesco. I catch my breath; I'm close to tears. The hushed atmosphere is serene and it suits my mood. Opening up to Luke has enabled me to stop agonising and view my failed 'romance' with a fresh perspective. Maybe he is right; maybe I just need to get used to letting go. After all, this entire trip is completely out of character for me. I'd never considered before that adventure might be a skill one needs to learn; Luke seems to have turned it into an art form.

The church is mesmerising. I think even Luke senses the sweetness of the silence. We stand and gape up at the huge arches of the ceiling. Down in the crypt, I feel a sense of wonder as I think about St Francis. As a youth, he knew absolutely that he didn't want to follow in his father's footsteps and become a merchant; instead, he was overwhelmed by his passion to devote his life to serving God.

People are always saying that if prophets and saints were alive today, they'd be locked up. That those guys in the Old Testament who heard 'divine' voices were really suffering from schizophrenia. It's a cruel line of reasoning and not one I share. There is a genuine well of peace here, and over hundreds of years people have come to drink from it and take a little back home with them. No madman could have created this atmosphere. A sense of wonder fills me: I wonder if this might be an ember of faith rekindling, if I might start believing in God again.

We leave the crypt and climb the steps back into the main church.

'Hey!' someone calls out.

Luke spins around. A guy with a red bandanna and stubble waves over at us. At first, Luke looks bewildered, then his face lights up. He gives the guy a big hug, crying 'Lee!' A guard frowns at us and points to the SILENZIA signs, so we hurry outside.

Lee also has an American accent. The pair of them chatter away for a few minutes about what an amazing coincidence it is to have met and how many years it's been. Luke keeps smiling at me, as though he means to introduce me but is so excited by their chat he can't quite break off.

I drift away, wanting to give them some space, when I hear Lee remark: 'So you didn't bring Jodie out here with you?'

My ears prick up. I drift a little closer.

'Hey, no, man – we broke up.'

'Really? Shit, I thought you guys were getting married and all.'

'It didn't work out.' Luke flicks me a look and says hastily, 'You should meet Julia. Julia – this is Lee. He's come over for the wedding of some Italian friends ... er, what did you say their names were again?'

'Lucia and Giacobbe,' Lee says. 'You guys should come. I give you permission to gatecrash – you can be with me.'

Immediately, I feel doubtful. I groan inwardly when I hear Luke agreeing.

'I'm only here for one more night – I'm flying out tomorrow,' he says, 'but so long as I don't have a real bad hangover, I should be able to get up early, take the train to the airport and catch my flight. Yeah, we can make it.'

Tomorrow? I feel my heart sink. So this is our first – and last – night together. And now we're going to a wedding. Why do I feel so disappointed when, in theory, an Italian wedding should be lovely? I realise that I don't want to share Luke; I like the idea of us spending his last night alone.

'You don't look too sure about the wedding,' Luke muses after Lee has gone. 'I tell you what. We'll toss a coin.' He takes a silver one from his pocket. I reach to examine it, but he hangs on to it possessively. 'Hey, this is my lucky dollar – my dad gave it to me when I was a kid. When I'm travelling, I always rely on it.'

'Seriously?'

'Yep. It's a good way of travelling. You let Fate decide everything.'

'I don't believe in Fate.'

'Bullshit. I may be an atheist but Fate, I do believe in. Fate governs everything.' He holds up the coin. 'Everything is already pre-determined in the stars,' he says, pointing to the horizon, where the first few stars are spangling in the twilight sky. 'So the coin will just tell us so. Whatever way it lands, we'll meet the people we're meant to meet; we'll do whatever we were meant to do. So let's say heads we don't go, tails we do.'

'OK,' I say reluctantly. I've read somewhere that you can influence the fall of a coin if you put your attention on to it, so I fix my eyes on it like a laser. *Please let it be heads, let it be heads*, I pray.

The coin spins, deciding our destiny. Luke holds out his palm, a big grin on his face, and with a theatrical flourish, he reveals it.

Tails.

9

On the way back to the hotel, Luke tells me how his lucky coin has saved his life – heads told him to avoid getting on to a bus in Kolkata in India that promptly crashed; organised fantastic sex – tails advised that he look at the *Mona Lisa* in Paris, where he started chatting to the beautiful Dominique; and dared him to bungee jump – which he said was one of the most exhilarating experiences of his life.

I listen, enjoying the colourful romance of his stories, but I can't help feeling a bit cynical. I'm the opposite of Luke: I might believe in God, but I don't believe in Fate. I believe that we all make our own luck. It's not really a very uplifting philosophy. For example, I think that when I lost my job it was my fault. When I recall that terrible mistake I made just before ... I cringe, pushing it away.

'I think it's easier to say things are Meant To Be,' I

argue with Luke. 'Because that way, you avoid taking responsibility.'

'Well, you know what?' Luke says, as we enter the hotel room with his luggage. 'Since I'm heading back tomorrow and this is our last night, I think we should try a little experiment and let the coin dictate the future *all night*. And I promise that, by the end, you'll see the magic of my coin. It'll bring you something amazing, and you'll be forced to believe in Fate and admit you're totally wrong, wrong, wrong.'

I smile at him. He speaks with such passion, his brown eyes sparkling. How can I resist?

'OK,' I agree.

It's time to get ready for the wedding. Luke is so easy-going that even though we're still relative strangers, he lounges about as though we're been backpacking together for years. I feel a little self-conscious, though, so I insist that he goes and gets changed in the bathroom. I wish I had a coin to tell me what to wear. I finally decide on the red dress, despite the bad memories attached. Maybe tonight I can rewrite them.

I hear Luke in the shower, singing out of tune and I smile. I don't think I've ever laughed so much in ages; he is such fun to be with.

I can't help noticing that his passport and plane ticket are lying on a chair by his rucksack. He pulled them out of his pockets saying, 'Don't let me lose these!'

I find that I just happen to wander over to them and

my eyes oh-so-accidentally fall on them. I can't help taking a peek at his passport photo. Ha! Despite his good looks, he can't transcend the curse of a wooden expression and bad hair. So Luke was born in 1979. He's a Gemini.

Hang on! Hang on!

'Hey,' Luke says casually, walking into the bedroom, 'are you gonna steal my passport and do a runner?'

'No.' I jump violently. Luke is wearing a small towel around his waist; droplets sparkle like gems on his chest. I watch as he shakes a shirt out of his rucksack, then winks at me and goes back into the bathroom.

The door remains slightly ajar. I catch a glimpse of his muscly chest again as he pulls on the shirt. My cheeks warm. Then I call out, 'By the way, I thought there was a *seven-year* age gap between us. According to your passport, you're thirty.'

'Oh yeah.' Luke emerges in battered blue jeans, buttoning up his clean but crumpled shirt. 'Oops. Sorry, I lied.'

'You lied!' I cry, feeling my humiliation flood back. 'And you made me feel really old and weathered and spinsterly and terrible.'

'Whoa.' Luke looks amazed. 'That's a bit paranoid. Do you really want to know why I lied? I thought you looked young, maybe late twenties, so I just, I don't know, lied so we'd be a similar age. I liked the look of you, I wanted to get to know you . . .'

I feel absurdly pleased. And a little stupid. As Luke said, maybe I have been a tad paranoid.

'Say Julia,' he adds casually, fiddling with a cuff link, 'that dress looks real good on you.'

'Thanks,' I reply shyly.

As we proceed to the wedding, however, I can't help wondering if Luke has told any more lies. The word 'Jodie' floats across my mind, but I decide not to probe. After all, he's only here for a night and I'll never see him again, so why start a row? And besides, I realise glumly, remembering that I told him I still had a job at Charlton Cross – I lied to him too.

Something is up with Luke. When we entered the church, he looked seriously under-dressed next to all the chic Italian men in smart suits, yet he still attracted numerous admiring glances from females. Now we're standing in the pew, the ceremony is in full flow. Lee stands on one side of me and on my other, Luke is fidgeting with his order of service sheet, twisting it into a complex origami monster. I give him a look, half-reprimanding, half-teasing; he's behaving like a three year old.

'*Vorrei ora pronunciare voi l'uomo e la moglie,*' the Italian priest announces.

The groom's fingers flutter on the bride's cheek. She breaks into a goofy smile. He grins back as though he can't wait to kiss her.

A crack must have appeared in the cynical shell around

my heart, for I find myself smiling. I turn to see if Luke is equally moved, but he's now busy shredding his origami creation.

'*Benedizione*,' the priest's voice echoes up to the rafters.

Luke suddenly jumps up, squeezes his way down the pew and thunders down the aisle. I flush in embarrassed horror. The priest breaks off and the guests stir, pointing and muttering. Then he's gone and the service resumes.

I want to check that Luke's OK but I can't do a repeat performance and ruin the wedding. Then the ceremony sucks me in again and I forget him. The priest waves his hands. The groom embraces his new wife. Their eyes lock. Their smiles mirror sweet devotion. They savour the moment before kissing in ecstasy. I feel my heart thump with painful joy. I've always thought marriage was a noose around your neck. Now I feel converted – if only for an evening.

Outside, I find Luke sitting by a gravestone. His face is green.

'Are you all right?' I ask, putting a hand on his shoulder.

'Uh – yeah. Yeah . . .' But he seems a bit dazed. 'I just felt really . . . I don't know. It was so hot, I thought I was going to faint.'

He looks so distraught that I feel seriously worried about him, so it's a relief when he jokes, 'Don't suppose you have any smelling salts?'

'Would you like lavender or rosemary?'

'I actually just need to get really, *really* wasted.'

'Is that a good idea if you feel sick?' I ask.

'Yes, Mommy, it's an excellent idea,' Luke teases me.

But Luke's just the same when we walk down to the reception, which is being held at the bride's father's house. His sweeping gardens are filled with stooping olive trees and in the distance the sun is setting over Mount Subasio. We sit down at some trestle tables spread with lacy cloth and enjoy a delicious mushroom risotto with Sagrantino wine. I love listening to the bride's father's speech, even though I don't understand a word of it, for his Italian is so beautiful it sounds like classical music. Once again, Luke starts pursuing his origami.

'Do you have a vendetta against napkins?' I whisper in his ear. He grins and shrugs. I glance at him again, wondering. There's more to Luke's breezy backpacker persona than meets the eye. Jodie ... fibs about his age ... and now this bizarre allergy to weddings. This is my last night and I'll never find out who he really is; his memory will always be haloed with mystery. I find the idea romantic but frustrating.

Luke leaves his napkin and downs his wine. Then he starts on mine, so that when it's time for the toasts we both have to raise empty glasses.

'Phew, thank God that's over,' Luke says as the music starts up for dancing.

I see him delving into his pocket for his coin and say hastily, 'Hey, why don't we dance?'

'I have a better idea,' says Luke. 'You see that Italian

over there? He's hot, right? I think we should throw the coin on whether you should ask him to dance. Come on, don't look like that – it's what you came here for! Let's make it happen.'

'Oh, Luke, you're *so* embarrassing.'

'OK, I'll sweeten it. We'll toss the coin and *I'll* go ask him.'

Before I can protest, Luke has thrown it. He reveals the outcome with a smile. I wince, my heart fluttering. I watch Luke approach the Italian with a mixture of disappointment and excitement. Luke can't really fancy me if he's trying to set me up with someone else, can he? At the same time, I'm convinced there is a spark between us – so is the Italian just part of some game we're playing?

I watch Luke pointing me out and I put on a weak smile, fluttering my fingers in a mortified wave. Then the Italian strolls up, smiling. He's everything I dreamed of: tall, dark and handsome.

'I am Gian-Paulo. May I have this dance, *Signorina* Giulia?'

'Uh – yes.' I think my cheeks are so hot I could sit in the dictionary as a definition of the word 'scarlet'.

Gian-Paulo pulls me in close. Over his manly shoulder, I watch Luke watching us. He starts on a new glass of wine and keeps grinning over at me.

Why does life always do this? If we could only get things when we desire them, all would be well. But too often we yearn and yearn and yearn and nothing happens.

And then, just when you don't want it any more, life says, 'Here we are – just what you ordered. Sorry if it's a little late, sorry if it's gone cold and past its sell-by-date. You did *ask* for it.' I'm convinced that the gap between desire and fulfilment causes most of the pain in the world.

If this had happened yesterday, I'd be over the moon. But today I want to dance with Luke.

As the dance ends, I pull away from the Italian, smiling apologetically. He shrugs and gives me a charming smile. I walk back over to Luke.

He's chatting with Lee. They break off, flashing me Cheshire Cat grins. I have a feeling Lee's in on the joke – and that the joke, as usual, is on me. Suddenly I feel cross. I grab the coin, which Luke is threading between his fingers.

'Right,' I announce. 'I think it's time *you* did a dare, Luke. Now, what should it be?' I wink at Lee.

'Hey, I'm game for anything,' Luke shrugs, staring at me in amusement, his eyes daring me.

'OK, I think you should . . . I think you should . . .'

'The suspense is killing me,' Luke drawls.

'Heads you have to go up to the bride, pretend you've been hired as the stripper for the evening, then take off some clothes and provide us all with some entertainment. Tails you stay here with us.'

Luke chokes on his wine while Lee yelps with joy and does a high-five, telling Luke he's dug his own grave.

I toss the coin. Luke and I stare at each other, our eyes declaring war. I unveil my palm. Heads.

10

I can't believe Luke is really going to go through with this dare.

I watch him sashaying around the bride. She blinks in wonder. He starts to unbutton his shirt. Embarrassment flushes her cheeks. Her bridesmaids gather round, giggling. Now that Luke has an audience, he gains confidence. He yanks off his shirt, waves it in the air, then chucks it at them. They fight as though it's the wedding bouquet. Luke spins around, then begins to unbutton his jeans.

'Oh my God!' I exclaim out loud. Next to me, Lee is nearly wetting himself with laughter.

Several of the guests turn, point, stare. Luke really is enjoying himself now. He slides off his jeans slowly, bumping and grinding as he does so. He's wearing Calvin Klein underwear. He could model it for an ad. Giggles and exclamations pierce the air.

The question is: just how far is Luke prepared to go?

Surely he doesn't think the coin has dictated that he take *everything* off?

I'm so busy admiring Luke's body that I don't spot the danger. Lee does. He cries: 'Luke! Oh shit! *Luke!*'

Oh. Oh dear, oh dear. The bride's father is staring at Luke with the kind of expression you see in *The Godfather*, when people are about to be assassinated.

He releases a torrent of angry Italian.

Lee runs forward and I follow him. He grabs Luke's jeans; I grab his shirt.

Luke is oblivious. He is flirting with the hem of his boxers. The bride is bright red and half-covering her eyes, but unable to resist peeking. The bridesmaids are in hysterics.

Then he registers her father.

'Hey, sir, I'm sorry,' he blusters. 'I was just – just – ah—'

'Let's just get out of here,' Lee cries, lunging at one of Luke's arms and stuffing it into a shirt-sleeve.

The bride's father bunches up his fists.

'OK, OK, I'm going!' Luke can't resist teasing; he seizes the bride and gives her a cheeky kiss on the lips. The groom strides over; her father snarls, apoplectic. We run and run, pounding over the grass, then into the street, our ribcages splitting with laughter and nerves.

Luke and Lee stop in the street and say their goodbyes. Lee says he's never going to invite Luke to a wedding again, but there's a big grin on his face as he hugs him. Then we head back to my hotel. We're both pretty drunk and keep banging against each other; Luke puts his arm around my waist and my heart flips.

'So you see,' he says cheerfully, 'that's how you follow the coin and really experience adventure.'

'OK, I admit I'm very nearly converted,' I say as we enter the hotel lobby.

In the lift, Luke keeps his arm around my waist. I lean in a little closer and he gives me an affectionate squeeze.

In my room, the lamp creates a golden pool of light in which we stand opposite each other; our shadows twining in the darkness. I can feel my heart beating very fast.

Luke draws his coin out of his pocket and whispers, 'Tails I kiss you, heads I don't.'

My breath catches in my throat as the coin twirls. I have acquired faith in Luke's lucky dollar. I know it will come down tails.

The coin spins off his palm and rolls on to the floor. We both crouch down, squinting with drunk blurry vision. Then, at the same time, we spot it.

'Heads,' Luke says in alarm.

We stand up. I try not to stare at his beautiful, full lips with too much yearning.

Then Luke grabs me in his arms.

'Fuck the coin,' he says, and presses his mouth to mine.

We lie down on the bed together. Luke cups my face in his palms.

'I can't believe I'm going tomorrow. I've gotta be in Hong Kong, though – I'm meeting up with an old buddy and I swore I'd go. I'm gonna miss you like mad.'

I think about suggesting I come along to Hong Kong too, but something inside me holds back. I fear I might sound too intense. And I'm afraid that if I spend any more time with him, he's going to unlock feelings I've never experienced before . . .

'What about you – what will you do now? Are you much of a traveller?' Luke asks.

'I'm just going to hang around Italy for a bit – I have actually got a sabbatical off work,' I lie, feeling slightly sheepish. Then I think about the third wish on my list. 'In about two or three weeks' time I'm going to be in Tokyo. I've got this plan to visit the tallest building in the city.'

'I could meet you there! Two weeks' time would be fine.'

I see the anxiety in his face. Now he's the one who's worried that he's making heavy suggestions.

'I'd love to,' I say shyly. Luke lets out a whoop and plants a big kiss on my mouth. He whispers that I have finally managed to sleep with my Italian – for he's an Italian-American on his mother's side. We both laugh and kiss again; soft, sweet kisses that deepen and become raw.

When I sprawl my palms over his chest, he breaks off and tells me, 'I don't think we should . . . tonight. I think we should save it, for something to look forward to.'

I tell him he's a gentleman and he smiles and hugs me tight and I bury my face in his chest. We lie together whilst the night fades into dawn. Floating in a bubble of hazy bliss, we brush kisses, we whisper, we giggle, we confide, he tells me I'm beautiful and I tell him he's gorgeous. And then all of a sudden the light is slipping into the room and we realise the new day has come and Luke has to go.

We say goodbye three times. Every time he heads for the door, he chucks down his guitar and rucksack, comes bounding back to me and pulls me in for another kiss.

'I'm going to miss you, Career Girl,' he says.

He's gone now. I sit on the bed, full of wonder at this new emotion. My heart feels as though it's been twisted into a tight bud for many years and suddenly a few petals have unfurled. I want to laugh and cry. I'm conscious of everything in the room; the echo of his body in the bed, the flecks of earth left by his trainers, the beauty of the light falling on the carpet where we stood together. I've never felt so alive.

I go to the window and open the curtains. I watch a bird skim across the hills, catching pink on its feathers. I follow it as it curves up to the pale blue clouds and then soars up into a beautiful nowhere.

A few tears of joy leak from my eyes.

'Thank you, thank you, thank you,' I whisper, not sure if I'm thanking God, Luke or his lucky coin.

I realise that for the first time in years, I haven't woken up with a hollow feeling inside, yearning for Ciaran.

I pick up my mobile, checking for a text from Luke, only to see that Reece tried to call me three times last night. She's left a message, so I pick it up.

'Oh Julia! I tried to call you – what the hell are you up to? I hope you've found a nice yummy Italian' (giggles). 'Anyway, I have some great news. Ciaran and I are going to help you out with number two on your list! He's got two weeks off work and we're going to come scuba-diving with you. We saw this really cheap deal in Sicily so we're going to book tonight, but please call to say you want to come – in fact, you *have* to come! Bye, darling. Kisses and lots of love.'

I let out a wail. I've finally cured myself of Ciaran and now I'm going to spend a fortnight scuba-diving with him. If I see him again now, I know I'll only catch the love-disease again. No, no, *no*.

I have to find a way to get out of this.

2. Go scuba-diving

and

3. Stand on the top of a volcano

1

Of course, I can't get out of seeing Reece and Ciaran. I'm not ruthless enough to make extravagant excuses about life-threatening illnesses, et cetera to my best friend when she's just splashed out on a fortnight's holiday. So I fly over from Perugia, the nearest airport, to Palermo, Sicily, carrying Luke's scent on me like a second film of skin.

Reece has booked a villa in Taormina, on the northeast coast of Sicily, renowned for being one of its most beautiful towns. It's the perfect setting for scuba-diving. The website I check promises dives in caves and dives at night, when the corals light up like neon. I get to the villa, to find the others are not there yet, and I silently thank Reece for making such a good choice. We're perched on the top of the cliffs, overlooking a beautiful sweep of crystal-clear blue Ionian Sea. Golden flowers quiver on the hillside, reflecting the last of the afternoon sunlight. Sicily is a heavenly dream.

I bag the small bedroom, leaving the bigger one for Reece and Ciaran. Then I lie down for a nap, only to get a text from Reece – she and Ciaran are in a rental car and will be here in ten minutes.

I jump up, my heart beating wildly. Oh God, this is terrible. Every time I'm about to meet Ciaran, a volcano erupts in my heart. But then I quickly yank Luke back into my memory; I savour yesterday's morning-after euphoria. I was going to play elusive, hard to get, but now I decide to send him a quick text: *Hey Luke how's it all going? I am in Sicily now about to explore the ocean. How is Hong Kong? Jx.* I smile as I press *send*. My heart is calm again. Luke is the perfect medicine, like a paracetamol for my Ciaran migraines.

Then I hear the car pulling up outside. I hurry to the door.

'Julia!' Reece explodes into the hallway. She gives me a huge hug, chattering about their lovely flight and isn't it so great to be here and have I noticed that Sicily seems to be full of cats and isn't it wonderfully hot and she's heard the sea is so warm it's like a Jacuzzi.

I've been so overshadowed by my worry about meeting Ciaran that I've forgotten just how lovely it is to be with Reece. My wonderful friend; my surrogate sister.

She comes tumbling into the villa, enthusing about the light, the balcony, the bedrooms, the view, the smell of the sea in the air. Through the front door, I can see Ciaran opening up the boot of the car, his muscles rippling as he unloads cases. I suddenly remember how it felt, the day that I first met Ciaran.

I'd gone on a speed-dating night for professionals, during which I'd met an insipid banker, a solicitor who wanted to swing and a Professor at LSE who wanted a woman to 'look after him'. Five minutes with each of them was too long.

And then Ciaran sat down opposite me. I thought that he looked handsome in a preppy sort of way. Other women were glancing over and giving me jealous looks, as though they were keen to have their five minutes with him.

He was wearing a black suit with a blue and white striped shirt. His dark hair was shorn, which isn't a style I usually admire in men, but it suited him. His eyes were blue, with very long lashes. He possessed an air of grav-itas, as though smiling was a rarity. His eye-whites were laced with red and yellow; he had purple bags beneath them. Definitely a City worker.

'So your CV says you work in a bank?' he asked me.

'Yes. Charlton Cross.'

'Do you have any hobbies, anything you enjoy outside work?'

'Not really.'

'Right.' He stared into my eyes. 'Would you consider yourself to be a great conversationalist?'

I blinked. How bloody rude, I thought. Then I laughed, shrugging. I might as well be honest.

'OK, I realise I'm not making much of an effort to sell myself. My friend, Reece, persuaded me to do this. She wants me to have a love life but to be honest, I'm really far too busy. I'm a workaholic, and proud of it.'

Finally, he smiled. It was a crooked one, that curved up the left side of his face and crinkled his eyes.

'I'm afraid my reason for coming is even worse.' He lowered his voice and leaned in. 'My mum booked me this night as a present for my thirtieth birthday – can you imagine!'

I gazed at the small scar visible beneath his left eye. It gave his rugged face a vulnerability; I felt a sudden ache to reach out and touch it, to know the story behind it.

But our five minutes were up.

At the end of the evening, he was the only guy whose details I kept. Later, when he said the same about me, I was astonished. I couldn't quite believe that I deserved him.

Now, for the last eighteen months, he's been in a steady relationship with Reece. Who knows? They may end up marrying. I'll be Maid of Honour. Maybe I'll even become a godmother. Oh well. *C'est la vie.*

Ciaran comes walking up to the villa. He looks odd in his T-shirt and shorts, perhaps because his skin is so pale.

This is it. I feel like an alcoholic being presented with a bottle of wine. He walks up and his lips brush my cheek. I breathe in, taste his skin, remember past kisses with an ache. He walks into the villa. Reece loops her arm through his, leans her head against his shoulder. I breathe out.

Not too bad. Not as bad as usual. Luke is helping cure me. If I'm on a ten-step plan, then Luke is definitely step one.

I turn back to smile at Reece. I sometimes wonder if she can tell, whether she ever guesses . . . but I've learned to smooth out my face, and steady my voice. Sometimes I have nightmares and wake up drenched in icy sweat, hearing Reece screaming accusations at me. But in real life, it never happens. I suppose, given the history of what took place between me and Ciaran, it would be odd for her to even suspect.

I help her to wheel her case into the bedroom she and Ciaran are sharing; I'm next door.

And then the next case. And then the next.

And the next.

'Reece,' I say. 'I think you've brought enough for a three-month stay.'

Reece opens one case, shoves a handful of underwear into a drawer, then looks bored. She tests the bed by jumping up and down on it; her blond plait curls up and down, thwacking against her back.

'Looks like a nice firm mattress,' says Ciaran, and he gives her a sexy *we'll test it later* sort of look. I feel a faint burn of jealousy but I fight it. *Luke, Luke, Luke*, I repeat like a mantra.

'It's not just *my* clothes,' Reece insists, yanking open

Ciaran's case, eager to show him up. The elegant smell of bergamot wafts through the air. 'Look – he's brought along *three* boxes of Earl Grey.'

Ciaran is, as you might have guessed, a bit of a tea addict.

'So, what shall we do tonight?' I ask when we've calmed down. 'If you're both a bit knackered, I could cook. I bought in some pasta and tomatoes and a bottle of wine.'

'Oh, no, let's go and have some fun!' Reece cries.

'Yeah, we have no wish to run the risk of enduring your cooking,' Ciaran says. 'For one thing, I didn't have time to get travel insurance before I left.'

'Why would you need that?' Reece asks, puzzled.

'Well, I'm thinking of the hospital bills,' Ciaran says, grinning as Reece's mouth becomes an 'O'.

'You know, the only reason I allowed you to come scuba-diving was because I hoped you might drown,' I retort.

'You two . . .' Reece takes each of our hands and tugs us, sighing.

For this is the way that Ciaran and I have resolved the tension of our past. We're constantly rude to each other. We compete for the best insult; it becomes a battle of wits. Reece always plays the peacemaker. It sounds harsh, but it actually helps to keep things light between the three of us, to deal with our shared history . . .

'Come on, be nice to each other now we're on holiday,' Reece cajoles us.

'It's not possible,' Ciaran asserts, and I glare in agreement.

Ciaran drives us to the restaurant in the car he and Reece hired at the airport. He keeps grinding gears and muttering to himself, *'They drive on the right, they drive on the right.'* The traffic makes London look tame. Everyone hoots and the lanes seem to be a crazy free-for-all. At the same time, there's no sense of road rage and the horn-honking feels impatiently jolly.

Reece and I sit in the back. Reece rolls down her window and every so often she yells out: 'HEY! I'M REECE! I LOVE SICILY! I LOVE YOU ALL!'

Naturally, people stop and stare. There's no restraining this sort of Reece-style madness – she's bursting with so much energy it has to be expelled. But then they see Reece's fair hair and beautiful smile and they wave back.

Reece is just the same in the restaurant. She flirts like mad with the waiter and unravels half his life story from him before we get a chance to order.

I watch Ciaran with the faint curiosity that always itches me when I'm with them. I wonder if Reece ever gets on his nerves, but he seems patient with her. I also wonder if her flirting makes him jealous, but I never see any sign of it. The trouble with Ciaran is that he's something of a modern-day Mr Darcy. He keeps his emotions under wraps, beneath a deadpan, cynical exterior; his face is that of a male Mona Lisa. Even though Reece confides in me a lot, their relationship is always a fascinating mystery to me. An intimacy I've never experienced with a man, and wonder if I ever will ...

'This is *so* lovely,' Reece sighs. 'And don't you look great, Julia. I can tell you're in love. You look all sunny and relaxed – doesn't she, Ciaran?'

I feel pleasantly flattered. But Ciaran just snorts, for he's tapping away at his BlackBerry. I can't help but feel a twinge of jealousy. I miss my constant stream of work calls. Oh, to have my job back ...

'I just hope Cameron and Ashton are OK,' Reece muses. 'I got our neighbour Henry to agree to feed them but I bet they're missing me *so* much.'

'I expect they're sobbing like mad,' Ciaran remarks dryly, not looking up from his BlackBerry. Reece rolls her eyes at him.

Reece loves animals nearly as much as she likes chocolate. Fortunately, there is a 'No Pets' rule in our block of flats so the worst thing she ever brought home was a tank of fish. Reece, being Reece, managed to get odd ones: a goldfish that had a green streak on it and its dodgy-finned friend. She was convinced they were both neurotic and used to impose her own homemade brand of 'fish counselling' on them. Sometimes Ciaran and I would be in fits as we heard her speaking into the tank, asking them if they felt like 'freaks', whilst they blew back enigmatic bubbles in reply.

Then Reece asks me about Venice and I tell her all about the wedding in Assisi and Luke's striptease. Her eyes moon.

'Wicked!' She bursts into laughter so raucous that heads turn and eyes blink. 'He sounds so funny. Oh wow, oh wow – this guy Luke sounds just wonderful!'

'He stripped off at a wedding?' Ciaran asks, shaking his head. 'Sorry, but he sounds like a bit of a wanker to me.'

'*Ciaran!*' Reece yelps. 'He sounds *fun*. And you'd better be some fun on this holiday too, so turn off that bloody BlackBerry, or I will throw it in the sea, I swear.'

Ciaran wearily places it in his pocket. Then he looks at me, and says in a voice that sounds very earnest, 'Just so long as you're happy, Julia.'

I look into his eyes. They're unreadable.

2

That's when I decide to get seriously pissed. In fact, we *all* do. It's as though we make a silent, collective decision to ease the rising tension between us by ordering one bottle of wine, and then another, and then another.

'There is *no way* you're going to be able to drive home,' Reece warns Ciaran. 'We'll have to take a taxi, or hitch a lift with a sexy Sicilian. Hey, can we order desserts now?'

Reece has a very sweet tooth; she's the only person I know who eats bars of Green & Black's for breakfast.

It turns out that the Sicilians have a fetish for *gelato*: we order sundaes of pistachio, of toffee and coffee, of creamy chocolate, of Brazil nut crunch and walnut dream, scoops slithering with chocolate sauce, elegant chocolate sticks protruding from them lasciviously.

Reece and I look at each other. She pulls one from the dish and bites into it. We both start to giggle.

'Why do you girls always find Flakes so hilarious?' Ciaran demands.

'It's a private joke.' Reece gives him a kiss on the cheek, staining his skin with syrup. 'Sorry – I'm dying to tell you but Julia has always sworn me to secrecy.'

'Don't tell me,' Ciaran says. 'When you were a teenager, you muddled up a Flake with a tampon?'

Reece and I groan and tell him off for being so gross. But the sad fact is that the truth is possibly even more gross – and humiliating. Yes, I did just laugh along with Reece but I also felt a Pavlovian squirm of shame in the pit of my stomach. It reminded me of an incident I'd frankly rather forget.

I always associate Flakes with the year 1993. I was fifteen and Reece was about to turn sixteen. We both wore friendship bracelets we'd made for each other. The one I made was neat; hers was messy and multi-coloured, but though it frayed on my wrist I never, ever took it off.

We were both lucky/unlucky enough to go to a girls' secondary school in South London, on the fringes of Surrey. It meant that we spent our lessons focusing on our GCSEs without being distracted by boys. But without boys, life was bland. We would read out sex scenes from Judy Blume's *Forever* in awed voices. The newspapers regularly ran horror stories about teen pregnancies, but all we could think about was how lucky we'd be if someone snogged us, let alone forget to put on a condom.

It was Reece's birthday and she was having a sleepover. Sleepovers at Reece's were always the best. Her mum was very cool; Reece even addressed her by her first name, Zoe-Star. She borrowed designer clothes from her and they were often mistaken for sisters.

Reece was an only child, so she had the run of a huge sprawling detached house in Cheam. Sometimes I even saw a Mercedes in the drive. It belonged to her dad, who was never around because he worked in the City.

It was nine o'clock and we were all enjoying the sleepover. *Dirty Dancing* was playing in the background and Reece's mum had made us all Coke floats. I'd never had them before and I loved the way the ice cream sparkled in the fizz; I also tasted an underlace of vodka. At my sleepover, my mum had been nervous about just giving us Coke, fretting, 'I'm worried the caffeine might make you all hyperactive.' *And* Reece's mum had bought her three simply amazing birthday presents:

1. A gold puffball skirt from Top Shop.
2. A copy of *Women on Top* by Nancy Friday.
3. A box of condoms.

Which we were now playing with. We'd borrowed a cucumber from the fridge and were taking it in turns to practise pulling a condom on and off. I wasn't focusing all that well. *Dirty Dancing* was making me swoon. I was a secret romantic; at night I dreamed that someone like

Patrick Swayze would give me dancing lessons and defend me from being put in a corner.

'If you're giving a guy a blow job, you should put a condom on. You might get AIDS.'

This wisdom came from the mouth of Tracey, a confident girl who was very *mature*. She'd practically started her periods at the age of six and had permed hair and an imposing presence.

Tracey was sitting behind Reece, plaiting her hair. Everyone loved to plait or play with Reece's hair, for it was so long and blond. Even hurricane winds couldn't blow it out of shape; it always fell beautifully, persistently, as straight as a ruler. I couldn't help feeling a bit jealous of Tracey. Reece was *my* best friend.

'Blow jobs,' Tracey went on, 'are a practised art. Here, pass me that Flake and I'll show you all how it's done.'

We all stared at her with wide eyes. Slowly, she began to lick it, giggling nervously as flakes of chocolate flickered on to her tongue, staining her chin. Then, when she began to suck it, Reece covered her red face behind a cushion, nudging me violently. I laughed and watched, transfixed, as Tracey, now swept away and completely unself-conscious, reached her grand finale: *snap*, she bit off the end of the Flake. I jumped in surprise, then clapped as Tracey cried, 'Ta-*dar!*' We all agreed that Tracey was such an expert, she ought to give us all lessons.

* * *

'Hey, you,' Reece waves her spoon, interrupting my reverie.

We leave the restaurant and Ciaran's about to hail a cab, when Reece suggests that we should go for a walk. She skips between the two of us, looping her arms into ours as we stroll through the balmy evening, the cobbles clipping beneath our feet. We follow the winding medieval streets, which are bustling with tourists; we peer into shop windows selling ceramics, mosaics, puppets and porcelain dolls. The town softens into lush countryside, dotted with villas. Now that it's dark, the island's beauty is more mysterious. Olive trees glint silvery in the moonlight like wizened old men; they seem to me to possess an air of wisdom, as though they've silently witnessed centuries of life's tragedies and comedies being played out on the same stage. We pass a little house where a woman opens her door and puts out some food on a plate. Immediately a volley of cats appear, miaowing gratefully. The woman glances over at us and waves.

'Can you imagine anyone doing that in England?' Ciaran muses. 'She'd be mugged on the spot – or else the PC police would get her for putting food out and causing a health and safety issue on the streets.'

I laugh in agreement. It's strange how far away England seems. I've lived there thirty-two years and yet London has already faded in my mind. I picture my flat and the tube stations and the spire of St Paul's Cathedral piercing the sky, but I can't quite remember how it *feels* to be there, caught in its energy and the collective consciousness of its people. I have noticed one thing about Sicily though: the air is different. In Central London, whenever I blew my nose, my snot was always dirty. Here the air is delicate, perfumed with flowers and happiness and the easy pace of life.

We've walked quite a way now, left the town behind. The area seems more countrified, with fields of olive and lemon trees emitting a tangy scent. We're passing a farm when Reece announces that she needs to have a pee.

'I'll go by the trees.' She points. 'You stay here and keep guard.' She gives Ciaran a drunken kiss on the cheek.

'Come on, Jools.' She grabs my hand. When I pull back uncertainly, she insists: 'Come on, just duck under the fence – they won't mind. Our pee will irrigate their olives.'

'Charming,' I say, giggling too, for the walk hasn't entirely sobered me.

Arm-in-arm, we hurry across the fields. The farmhouse is a humped silhouette, tiles glinting in the moonlight. Reece finds a suitable olive tree to hide behind while I head for some bushes and pull my knickers down, squatting unsteadily.

'Oh wow,' Reece cries, distracted. 'Look – there's a chicken enclosure. Oh, look at the way they sleep with their heads tucked into their wings – how sweet!'

'Hmm,' I murmur, concentrating on trying not to wee on my knickers.

'Hey, chickens,' she cries drunkenly, 'I'm Reece. Are you feeling bored, cooped up like that?'

'Reece!' I cry, for I'm still pulling up my knickers.

But my friend is already dancing away, giggling. Suddenly a light flashes on, spilling on to the leaves of the bush I'm sheltering behind, staining the leaves bright green. I swing round, overbalance and fall, feeling wet earth on my thighs. 'Urgh!' I mutter, gazing up at the moon, which blurs into a triptych. Then I burst out laughing. I can still hear the chickens squawking – possibly they are attempting to converse with Reece, or possibly she has accidentally peed on one of them, I can't be sure.

It makes me laugh louder.

This is *fun*.

And then suddenly we hear a man's voice shouting. A throaty, Sicilian voice.

Adrenalin fires through me. I get up, pulling on my jeans and knickers, my thighs still icky and damp. The one voice has become several angry voices. I can hear Reece giggling, and the chickens squawking shrilly. The noises all spin in a dizzy cacophony. Then I see Reece running towards me. She is clutching a chicken and it's going mental.

Behind her is a man in a T-shirt carrying a gun. 'This way,' Reece chuckles breathlessly.

'Oh my God. Reece!' I cry. 'You can't steal the chicken!'

'But I want a memento to take home,' Reece says drunkenly, hurrying on past me, completely unperturbed that we're both about to get shot for being chicken thieves. 'Come on, Julia.'

'*Ladre! Andate via, intruse! Pazze!*' Go away, you crazy thieves and intruders, the farmer barks, pointing his gun right at us.

'Reece, I don't think he's joking!' I cry, my heart jattering all over the place. The farmer is young, in his early twenties, with a shock of dark hair and a stocky build. But he also looks very angry, and I'm afraid that his youth might cause him to act without wisdom.

'Sorry,' I appeal to him. 'Reece is completely mad. *Scusi*. Pardon.' Oh God, I do wish I'd learned more Italian.

'*Non toccare ai miei polli!*' Don't you dare touch my chickens!

'Oh, all right, then.' Reece gives the chicken a kiss, puts it down and it runs away, squawking with post-traumatic stress. She blows a kiss after it, then collapses into laughter again. 'Can we go now, or were you planning to eat us for breakfast?' she asks the farmer.

He barks something that doesn't sound too agreeable, but the word *polizia* stands out. And he carries on pointing the gun at us.

'I gave him back,' Reece argues in a small voice. She edges over to me, in crablike moves, and the farmer jerks the gun. She freezes, putting her hands up. 'Tell him I gave the chicken back, Julia.'

'Well, Reece,' I snap, sarcastic in my nerves. 'I know I've been planning to become a translator for some time now, but I just can't quite decipher his particular dialect.'

We both start to giggle with nerves. The farmer's eyes narrow; his expression darkens. He thinks we're laughing at him.

'Reece!' we hear Ciaran calling from a distance. 'Julia! Where are you? What's going on?'

The farmer's head whips round, then we hear the scream of sirens. Lights slice into the darkness, painting the olive trees with a surreal blue halo.

'Oh shit,' Reece cries.

I don't believe this. I'm still in a state of numb denial when the car pulls up and two men in uniform get out. Ciaran tries to stop them, asking them what's wrong, but they brush him off and come marching up to us. The farmer lowers his gun, launches into a stream of words, then points at us. I am now fully sober, my mind awake and sharp with horror. I thought Sicilians were meant to be laidback. When they weren't being the Mafia, that is. I mean, surely, surely we're not seriously going to be *arrested?*

3

I can't believe this is happening. An hour ago, I was sitting in the restaurant, my mouth creamy with *gelato*, being pleasantly buffeted by a sea breeze. Now I'm sitting on a wooden bench in a small cell that stinks of piss. Reece is slumped beside me. She's in a state of shock; and alternates between drunken whimpers and singing quietly to herself. When we were taken to the station, she tried to sweeten the officers with jokes and chatter. But for the first time in history, Reece's charm offensive failed miserably. The fact that they spoke no English didn't aid our cause, and I think the stern officer felt we were taking everything too lightly.

I caress the white band of skin on my wrist, which feels sticky and naked without my watch. My watch now sits in a box, along with my handbag, some loose euros and my passport. Oh, why did I have to be so stupidly sensible and carry that in my handbag at all times?

'Oh Julia,' Reece bursts out, 'what if we end up like those Brits who had sex on a beach somewhere – I can't remember if it was Dubai or Greece or somewhere – and were hung, drawn and quartered.'

She's trying to joke but I can hear the fear in her voice as she adds, 'I mean, they might report us in the papers or something . . .'

For a moment I share her dread. The papers could definitely seize on this. We could be portrayed as two drunken foul-mouthed chicken-hating disrespectful British slags. I picture my ex-colleagues thumbing through the papers and gossiping, 'God – first Julia got fired and now she's so desperate she's ended up stealing chickens,' with sorry shakes of their heads.

'I'm sure we'll be fine. I mean, this is Sicily and everyone seems very friendly here. We were trespassing, true, and we really did upset that poor farmer guy, but we'll make them see we didn't mean any harm.' I stroke her hair gently and Reece sighs, resting her head against my shoulder.

'I hope Ciaran saves us,' she says mournfully.

Ciaran did kick up quite a fuss when they hustled us into the police car. Then, when one of the uniformed men gestured angrily at him, he backed off and yelled that he'd get a cab and follow on. The last memory I have of him is seeing his lone figure on the kerb as the police car pulled away, the siren light flashing blue panic in his eyes.

When we arrived at the station, they had no translator,

so it was all the farmer's word against ours. They said they'd bring in a translator in the morning and for now we'd have to stay in the cell. The men were kind but firm, even when Reece switched from joking to crying.

'We should just get some sleep,' I say, though I can't imagine sleeping a wink with this hard wall pressing against my back and these slates digging into my bottom.

'This is all my fault,' Reece says. 'All you did was pee behind a bush. I was drunk and stupid and I'm sorry.'

'Forget it, it's fine. It was funny. You didn't mean any harm.'

'I always go too far. You told me to put the chicken down, and I should have. I'm sorry.'

We fall silent. I feel tiredness swim through my head despite the discomfort, tipping my neck forward. The past swirls, dilutes into the first colours of dream: the wedding in Italy, Luke stripping, Luke kissing me, the dinner, the ice creams, Ciaran's smile ... and then reality suddenly slices through like a machete – *we've been arrested* – and I snap awake. I try to imagine myself telling Luke all about this when we're free and it cheers me up a bit.

One day I will see the funny side of all this.

'Julia,' Reece says in a small voice. 'You have forgiven me, haven't you?'

'I have,' I say, 'though I'm not sure if the chicken ever will.'

Reece manages a giggle, then becomes sober.

'No.' She holds my hand tightly and stares into my

eyes. 'Not just for the chicken thing – for what happened with the chocolate Flakes. At dinner, when we had the ice creams, it brought it all back.'

'Reece, that was a long, long time ago. We were fifteen years old, for God's sake. No, wait – you were just sixteen.'

'I know, I know – but I always feel really bad about it.'

Another silence. I squeeze her hand. Reece always mentions that incident whenever she's feeling guilty. And I wish she hadn't, for there's too much space in the cell to think, to remember, and now memories are filling my mind ...

There were two of them.

The teen boys stood under the flashing lights. They weren't bothering to dance to George Michael like everyone else. Their arms were folded, as though they were far too mature to hang out at a high-school disco between St Mary's Girls and Surrey Boys School.

Then they started looking over at me and Reece.

We were dancing together, pretending we didn't care about boys, surreptitiously watching Tracey. She was dancing with a six-foot-tall rugby player. He had acne but his charisma was magnetic – and his lips were ferociously clamped on to hers. 'Look,' Reece whispered into my ear with a giggle, 'his hand's on her breast!'

We spun round and round together.

'Are the guys looking at us?' Reece asked.

'Yes.'

We both fell into hysterical giggles and danced some more.

I kept staring at the one on the left. I'd recently fallen for Tom Cruise after seeing him in *Cocktail*; this guy reminded me of him. I saw a gentle dreaminess in his eyes, a poetry in his full lips. He could have stepped out of the pages of the romance novels I read; I was convinced he had a sensitive name like Tristan or Simon.

'Oh God,' Reece whispered. 'They're coming up.'

They stood before us. Mr Perfect and his friend. I stared into Mr Perfect's eyes, but he was staring at Reece. He drank her in, as though downing one of Tom Cruise's cocktails in one swift gulp. Reece stared back at him, wide-eyed and quivering. He gave me a brief once-over, then looked back at Reece.

'Hey, my name's Justin. Would you like to dance?' he asked her.

That look. It felt like my Judgement Day. As though God Himself had swept His eyes over me, sighed to His angels and said, 'Well, Julia isn't bad, is she, but let's face it – I didn't put her on this earth to distract the opposite sex.'

It felt as if Reece and I were parting company. A door had opened for her; a door had been slammed in my face. Suddenly we were in the same place, but separate rooms; she was in a party of glamour, beauty and fun, whilst I was at a disco of disappointment.

Reece smiled at me and I just about managed one in return. She and Justin looked so fantastic together, her blond hair cascading down her back, his dark eyes reflecting her beauty. I realised that I would never have looked right opposite him. It would have been like putting an ugly weed next to an exquisite rose.

'D'you want to dance, then?' his friend asked.

I said yes, but took an instant dislike to him. He was brown-haired, buck-toothed. He was mediocre. He was like me.

Then I looked into his eyes and saw the worry behind his bravado. I thought that I should just make the best of it.

Twenty minutes later, the four of us found ourselves outside, at the back of the school, behind the big wheelie bins. The two boys were laughing and shoving each other and daring each other in hisses, 'I'll snog my one if you will – you go first!' Finally, Justin and Reece started kissing. My one – Guy – stared at me and despite myself, I felt a desire, not for him, perhaps, but for experience itself.

He leaned in . . .

I closed my eyes . . .

I knew just what a first kiss ought to be like. My romance novels had defined it: soft, tender lips brushing before deepening into something souful.

Guy shoved his mouth against mine and his tongue inside. It spun round vehemently. I felt as though I was a washing machine and his tongue was a dirty shirt. I felt sick. I wanted to slow down the cycle but he was dictating a top-speed spin.

I opened my eyes and stared at him. But his eyes remained closed, as though he was thoroughly enjoying himself.

I felt his hand slip down my arm, and tensed. His fingers froze with uncertainty. Then I broke off, wiping my soaking mouth with the back of my hand, and saw that *Reece and Justin had disappeared.*

I suppose that's why I did the very silly thing that I did next. I imagined that Reece and Justin were making beautiful, blissful love together. I saw ahead to the next morning and imagined us comparing notes on our men. I felt *competitive.*

I reached for Guy's trouser-zip. Was that too forward? He did look startled. Then he gave me a big grin of encouragement. How had Tracey advised us again? Lick slowly . . . oh God, it tasted vile, like uncooked meat . . . could I really do this? He was groaning and looking satisfied; his pleasure, keeping him happy, was all that seemed to matter. What had Tracey advised next? I shut my eyes and pictured her with the Flake bar, the way her demonstration had climaxed with her sinking her teeth in deep . . .

He screamed quite loudly.

I stumbled to my feet, appalled by my mistake. Out of the darkness, Reece and Justin appeared, buttons undone, hems flapping.

'Are you OK?'

Guy looked white. He shook his head and addressed Reece: 'Your friend's a fucking vampire!'

The next day, when my mum interrupted my maths homework to tell me that Tracey was on the phone, I felt dread curdling my stomach. She must just be calling to show off about her man, I thought. Because Reece and I had made a pact: we wouldn't tell anyone at all about my highly embarrassing *faux pas*.

'Hi,' said Tracey, 'I have *so* much gossip for you!'

She went on and on about her date. I felt relieved. Then there was a silence, and a snigger. 'So I kind of heard that Guy is decorating his locker with garlic and wearing a cross all the time . . .'

A sense of betrayal flooded through me, hot and shocked. How could Reece do this to me, how could she?

Back in my bedroom, I burst into tears. When Mum found me, she put her arm around me and gave me some stern life philosophy.

'Don't cry about men,' she said fiercely. 'I never want to see you wasting tears over a man. For God's sake, toughen up.' Then she sighed with a touch of poignancy. 'At my school disco, they all wanted to dance with me. I ended up with the most handsome man there – your dad – and look what happened. He went and left me to raise you and Alex on my own. Never trust a handsome man. Men are very bad at resisting temptation; they're much more selfish than we are. Their happiness comes first. I can tell you this now, if she hangs on to that Justin, Reece will have trouble later in life. It's much better to have a nice man whose looks are average at most.'

I felt shocked by this new revelation. My romance novels had always suggested that inner and outer were intertwined, that the most handsome men were the most goodhearted. My mother's logic seemed subversive but I sensed a truth in it. Later that evening I would pack away all my romance novels into a box and shove them under my bed. I felt tears welling up again and practised forcing them down. And thus an ugly seed was planted. I became a little too good at suffocating tears during my adolescence, for during my twenties I found that during funerals and tragedies, despite an urge for release, my eyes remained obstinately dry.

Back at school, Reece and I sat next to each other in class as usual, but I did my best to ignore her.

'I'm sorry,' she persisted. 'I shouldn't have told Tracey. I just – I just blurted it out and I made her *swear* not to tell anyone, and then she did . . . and . . .' Her voice trailed off into silence.

'Who cares?' My voice sounded strange and cold to me. 'As long as you and Justin are happy.'

'D'you think I care about Justin?' Reece cried. 'I just want to make up with you.'

We shut up when our English teacher, Ms Yates, came

into the classroom. She handed out our essays. When she laid mine down, I did a double-take. Reece gaped too, and then cried, 'Oh wow – Julia got an A plus!'

I frowned, convinced that the plus sign was really a bogey, or that Ms Yates had just had a religious awakening and couldn't stop drawing crosses. But she confirmed, in front of the whole class, that I had received the first A plus she had given in all her seventeen years of teaching.

I was so amazed I forgot to be mad at Reece. Besides, my vampire teasing immediately ceased. From then on, I became known in class as 'Julia the Square'.

From that day onwards my life changed forever. I plunged deep into my work. A grades became the norm for me. I realised that, unlike boys, schoolwork was something I was good at. It was logical, something I could control – something that brought rewards. I stopped bothering with my appearance, whilst Reece and everyone around me were obsessed with trying out the latest mascara and eye-shadow. When the school held a disco the following year, I didn't attend; I was too busy revising for a chemistry test.

And my decision paid dividends. I got good grades at A-level, a first-class degree, and a top job.

This has been our history: Reece got the men, I got the grades.

This is my point, you see. I'm a good girl. I obey laws, I play by the rules. I never drive an inch over the speed-limit; I always throw my litter into bins; I once offended a guy at Holborn tube station who was dying to give me his Travelcard which he'd finished using for the day – but no, I insisted on buying my own new ticket.

I'm just not cut out for jail. This isn't *me*.

Panic rears up inside me again and once more, I push it back down. I find myself praying, then feeling guilty. I'm agnostic, but my faith seems to suddenly coalesce into firm belief whenever I'm in trouble.

Next to me, Reece has fallen asleep. A dawn light is creeping into the cell, highlighting the dirty, scratchy walls. It paints scarlet streaks into her golden hair. She looks like a princess, waiting for her prince to save her with a kiss. When we were teenagers, I always used to think that Reece was like a creature out of a fairytale.

Even though I invested my identity in my academic achievements, I couldn't help secretly feeling that I had been cast as the Ugly Sister to her Cinderella. Even after all these years, I still feel a love for her, a desire to protect, coupled with – yes, if I'm honest – a pinch of jealousy. Reece with her looks, her money, and Ciaran. Reece who made a list of *Ten Things To Do Before I Die* for fun, not because she needs to find herself.

I let out a sigh, and pray once more that we will be released. Soon.

4

'We weren't stealing chickens because we wanted to have mad chicken sex with them or anything dodgy like that,' Reece says earnestly.

The Italian-Sicilian translator starts to speak, when I interrupt: 'Reece! Let me do the talking, OK?' I turn to the translator. 'We are ardent chicken lovers. Reece thought that the chicken coop looked as though it was broken and she was scared the chickens might escape and get eaten by all the cats or foxes. So we picked up the chicken, hoping to save its life.'

A hedge-fund manager has to do a certain amount of bullshitting to swing deals. Now all of my past experience is paying off.

We're sitting in a small room in the jail. The translator is beside us, conveying our story. The officer on duty today is different from the hardnut we had last night. He's plump, with dimpled cheeks and eyes the colour of the

Mediterranean. I see a brief smile flicker over his lips when he hears my explanation. Then there's a pensive pause. My heart beats like mad and I worry my story is ridiculous and I've gone too far. I open my mouth to try to rewrite it, when he suddenly slams his palms down on the table.

Reece and I jump and look at each other in alarm. What now? Oh God, please don't let him throw us back into the cell or—

'You can go,' the translator says. 'It's OK. But while you stay here, we would be grateful if you could respect our laws, stay away from farmers, and most of all, from chickens. Is that understood?'

Reece is so overjoyed that she flings her arms around the officer. He smiles and shoos her away. Outside in the station foyer, Ciaran is waiting for us. His face becomes radiant with relief. Is it my imagination or do the officers smirk as they hand us back our passports and money? As we leave, we hear a clucking noise behind us. When we turn, however, the officers look at us with perfectly straight faces.

Maybe it's because I'm so exhausted and stunned and weakened by jail, but things actually seem to get worse when we return to the villa.

Worse because I feel that I'm falling again. My eyes on Ciaran's hair, his lips; a consciousness of his scent; a shivery feeling at the sound of his voice. I'd thought that the rosy glow Luke had evoked in Venice had created an invincible shield around my heart. But we get back to the villa in Taormina and Ciaran is just so *gentle*. He gives Reece a tight hug and buries his cheek in her hair. For all the humour of the officers, the night has still left its mark on us. She sobs like a baby and he shushes her. And I feel dirty and tired and I just want someone – well, *him* – to hold me like that.

'Can you put the kettle on?' Ciaran mouths at me.

I nod dumbly. I find some bags of Earl Grey that he brought along in his case. Ciaran sits down on a chair and pulls Reece on to his lap. Her tears don't last long. Soon she's smiling and they rub noses in an Eskimo kiss.

And I feel as though a crack has opened up in the shield around my heart. Pain leaks in. Jealousy. Longing.

'I think I'm going to go to bed,' I say.

'Well, just for a few hours,' Ciaran says with a wink. 'We've got to go scuba-diving, remember?'

'After all this?' I cry.

'Well, it'll cheer us up,' Reece says eagerly.

I shrug and go into my bedroom. I slump on to my bed, suddenly feeling utterly drained.

Then I sit up. *Luke*. I sent him a text – he must have got it by now. I grab my mobile, needing his reply like a stiff drink. But when I scroll down, there's nothing.

Maybe he didn't get it. Or maybe he's jetlagged. I just know that he'd find the chicken story hilarious. So I send him another text: *Just got out of a Sicilian jail – arrested for chicken-stealing!* X I picture the shocked grin on his face when he reads it, the surprise that boring old Julia would do something so crazy. I smile, then hear Reece and Ciaran going into the bedroom next door. I quickly shove in some earplugs and slip into the deep sleep of relief.

'My name is Michele,' says the hunky Sicilian guy, 'and I'm going to be your scuba instructor for the next week.'

Yes, here I am. On a boat, about to plunge into the beautiful blue depths of the Ionian Sea. I realised that it was stupid to waste even a day of my holiday in bed. And besides, I didn't have much choice about whether I wanted to wake or sleep, since Reece banged on my door and bellowed, 'So are you coming then? Are you a woman or a mouse?'

And look at Reece now. She's in her wetsuit. You'd never know she'd skipped a night's sleep – her eyes are sparkling and her skin glows. People sometimes think Reece is weak because she's ditzy and cries easily. But in many ways I think she's much stronger than I am. Her jail stress has been wept away with her tears. She's bounced back, moved on, left the past behind.

Me, I take a long time to process things. I think I over-analyse. And here I am now, over-analysing about over-analysing . . .

Michele seems like he's going to be a good teacher. He's tall and stocky and quite handsome, in a rugged sort of way. There's a tattoo of a mermaid creeping out from his wetsuit, swirling her way around his neck, and he has several earrings in one ear.

'I also hear,' Michele says, 'that we have a couple of hardened criminals on this boat, taking my course.'

There's about ten of us on the boat and everyone turns and looks at each other nervously. Michele looks pensive. Then a smile flickers on his lips.

'Apparently there are some chicken-thieves about ...' He looks over at Reece and winks at her. She bursts into laughter.

'Oh, that was me.' She puts her hand up in delight. Everyone laughs, looking relieved that they're not in danger of being murdered underwater, after all. 'But don't worry, I'll try not to steal your boat. If it disappears, it has nothing to do with me.'

'I would be most flattered if you tried to steal any of my possessions – maybe you can steal my heart,' Michele says, looking Reece up and down. He couldn't be more corny, but he carries it off because he speaks with a certain ironic charm. '*Megghiu oj l'ovu chi dumani la gaddina!*'

We're not sure what the line means but he delivers it with a naughty twinkle in his eye. Reece giggles and Ciaran looks a bit cross and puts his arm around her.

Here goes. I stare down at the glittering water, my body humming with fear and excitement. *This is something I've always wanted to do ...*

I've only ever scuba-dived in a swimming pool before. Earlier this year, Reece pestered me to do a class with her. I said no, I was too busy – I had too much work. Then I heard that Ciaran was going to join us and I found myself saying yes.

After many Saturday-afternoon dives, we got our diving certificates. But a pool is hardly glam. You can't really swim dreamily through waves of chlorine or sigh over the white plastic walls.

So this really does feel like one of life's special moments. I plunge into the water. Down, down, down through layers of deepening, darkening blue. It feels beautiful down here. As though time itself has slowed. I seem to have left my cares, my worries about finding a job, my ache for Ciaran, my confusion about Luke back up there on the distant surface of the water. I flit over thousands of shrimps and colourful eels and corals. We swim after Michele into the *Grotta Azzurra*, the Blue Cave. I feel a weirdly enjoyable thrill of claustrophobia as we enter a small tunnel that leads us into the first set of caves. The floor is sandy and shafts of light dazzle down through its roof. In here, we discover more Encrusting Sponges, a Moray eel and some more corals coloured a spectacular scarlet. According to science, their colour comes from manganese salts, but I prefer the mythical explanation given by the Greeks, who believed that when the gorgon Medusa was beheaded, the blood that fell from her neck soaked a seaweed bright red and it was turned into coral.

After an hour or so, we split into two groups. One group decides to head back. I'm too enchanted to leave just yet, but Reece drapes her arms around Ciaran and tells him she needs to go to bed.

I tread water, watching her and Ciaran climb on to the boat, their wetsuits sticking as they kiss greedily.

I dive back down into the ocean, desperate to find oblivion in the deep blue. But my pain chases me down with the waves. Fish swirl about me; memories roar in my ears. The times that Ciaran and I made love. I keep trying to block them out, for savouring them feels like a betrayal. But oh God, I want them to happen again; I want to be back in that bedroom with him, feeling his mouth hot on mine, feeling him deep inside me. Why was I so boring when I dated Ciaran? So frigid? Why did I mess up?

When I get back on to the boat, Michele notices my pale, glum face.

'So, even though you are the accomplice to a chicken-thief, I am going to take a beeg risk and ask if you would like to come back to my villa for some Anisette. It is a very nice Sicilian liqueur,' he assures me in his thick accent. 'You will be happy, yes? You will not kill my chickens. Or me?'

I smile doubtfully. My first instinct is to say, 'No,' for I'm not entirely sure if going back to a stranger's villa is a good idea, especially after my experiences in Venice before I met Luke. Then I remind myself that Michele is our instructor and probably takes tourists off for a sociable drink all the time. He's just being kind – and anyway, the thought of going back to the villa and watching Reece and Ciaran mooch over each other is too depressing for words.

'OK,' I smile at him, nodding. 'Thank you – I'll come. But I won't have the liqueur, *grazie*. I'm not really a big drinker.' Best to stay sober, just in case.

Michele nods and claps his hands together.

'Come!' he cries. '*Quannu gatta nun c'è li surci abballanu!*'

5

I take a small sip of Anisette, rolling it around my mouth like a marble. Michele flashes me a big smile. I gulp it down. It tastes like liquorice. It's so strong that I think my eyes will pop out. But at least it's stopped me from shivering.

It's very hard to resist Michele's powers of persuasion, but even if I am about to get pissed against my will, I am enjoying his company – and his villa is lovely. It's homely and beautiful, with knick-knacks scattered everywhere and paintings of the sea hanging on the walls. Plus, there are numerous framed photos of his wife Violetta, who he proudly tells me is a 'beautiful woman', and about seventy odd children, cousins, grandchildren and other relatives. He explains that Violetta is out at the market, shopping for his favourite fish for supper, which makes me feel a little more comfortable.

'This is really quite nice,' I say, holding up my small

glass and swirling up the last dregs of the dark liqueur. Then, to my surprise, Michele scrapes his wooden chair closer to the sofa. He touches my pale cheek.

'You're a sad girl.' He pours another glass for him, then one for me. 'You love the Ciaran, don't you?'

I splutter in shock. 'Is it that obvious?' I ask in alarm.

'No.' He roars with laughter, slapping his sunburned knee. Then he points a finger at me. 'You scared, yes?' He touches the corner of his eye. 'I see what other people don't see.'

'I – yes, I like him,' I admit. I trace my finger around the rim of my glass. Michele watches me and I'm scared I can detect glints of lust in his eyes. Despite the fact that he has a beautiful wife who is out buying his beloved fish for him, does he still have an ulterior motive? Yet, though he makes me nervous, I also feel warm towards him. His eyes shine with his big-hearted affection and I find myself spilling out a confession: 'We used to be together. Years ago. And then it all went wrong.'

'Aaahhh,' he lets out a long sigh. 'The Reece – she is very beautiful, yes?' His hands curve the air as though tracing her shape.

'*No, actually!*' I sit up indignantly. 'She didn't steal him off me, you know.'

'*Scusi!*' He puts up his hands.

'No – *I'm* sorry,' I sigh. 'It's just that, when we broke up, *everyone* assumed that Reece had simply stolen him off me. I mean, I got into the lift once with this bloody bitch Melissa – my rival at work – who'd always had a bit of a thing for Ciaran. She used to make sarcastic remarks about how we made *such* a lovely couple. This time, she looked very happy to see me, and told me I ought to kick Reece out of the flat because it was going to happen every time I brought a boyfriend home. She didn't believe me when I told her the real story.'

'But he was tempted, yes?' Michele winks at me.

'No!' I protest. 'But it is strange. When we first started dating, I was terrified of taking him home to meet Reece. I was convinced he was going to fancy her. I tried to keep them apart as best I could. And then one day I was at work and he left a message saying he had gone to my flat and was waiting there for me. Michele, I literally *ran* out of the office. I jumped on the tube and I was in a nervous sweat' (here I do an impression for Michele of a woman on the verge of a nervous breakdown). 'I just knew I'd lost him. I thought I'd walk into the kitchen and find them on the floor.'

Michele sighs as though it's a lovely idea. I give him a dirty look and he grins, gestures for me to keep going. Which I do. It's so wonderful to be able to confide in someone after all these years.

'I just prayed and prayed all the way home – *Oh God, please don't let him fancy her, please God*. But even as I walked down the hallway, I knew that from now on, my relationship with Ciaran was ruined. I knew he would remark on how "lovely" my friend was. Then every time we were supposed to meet, he would choose to come to the flat, just to catch a sight of her. But when I opened the door ...' I shake my head in wonder, remembering that delicious moment '... Ciaran gave me this huge embrace and a kiss. I thought he must be feeling disloyal and guilty, so I said I wanted to get a glass of water from the kitchen, to test him.

'Reece was sitting there, wearing her *Hello Kitty* night-shirt, on her sleep-all-day, party-all-night routine. She smiled and flashed eyes at me,' – I give Michele a demonstration – 'to confirm she thought he was hot. I saw Ciaran look at her. I analysed him for the usual signs: lingering looks, an erection – there were just a few of the give-aways –'

Michele guffaws and I laugh too. Then I stare down at my glass and say quietly, 'But there were none. Down in the car, I asked him what he thought of her. I said, "She's really pretty, isn't she?" and he said, "Not as pretty as you."'

'He loved you,' Michele says softly.

I look up at him, touched by the tender expression on his face.

'I think he did,' I say sadly. 'But I just ... you know ...' I bite my lip, exasperated with myself, hating to admit my stupidity. 'I felt almost *disappointed*. I couldn't help feeling that if Ciaran preferred me to Reece, he must have poor taste. It reminded me of the old Groucho Marx joke: "I don't care to belong to any club that will have me as a member." If he liked me, then he couldn't be good enough for me . . .' I take a swig of my Anisette. 'And it went on like that. He was getting more and more romantic with me. It surprised me, Michele, as Ciaran seemed such a cynic when we met, but I've come to learn that cynics have hard shells because their hearts are soft. They put up a front to protect themselves, I think. Underneath, Ciaran turned out to be this real gentle soul. And yet it turned me off him.'

'Ah, love is like a seesaw,' Michele muses, 'one falls in love more, it is always the way, then it tips and tips until it is too late. And then, you came to love the Ciaran, did you? And then he wave you away?'

'As a matter of fact, *I* dumped *him*,' I splutter.

'Really?'

I feel mildly insulted by the doubt on Michele's face. But he doesn't realise just how complicated my story is.

'So, did he cheat on you?' Michele asks.

'No! Ciaran would never do that. He's very loyal. I just didn't have time for a relationship – I was busy working for my promotion.' I feel a glow of satisfaction, remembering how it felt to achieve it, followed by that familiar tinge of sadness, knowing what I'd sacrificed to get it.

'You see, originally, Ciaran and I got on really well because we both worked in the City, the financial district of London. So we were sympathetic about short lunches and long working days. But then the seesaw began to tip. He was definitely a little bit more in love with me than

I was with him. Every time we met, he brought me a present. My office was like a flower shop.' I wave my arms in the air, gulp down the rest of my drink. 'He phoned all the time and I began to tell my secretary to make excuses. I remember sitting in my office on Valentine's Day, knowing I'd have to leave early to meet him for dinner and not wanting to. *What's wrong with me*, I asked myself, *that I have a gorgeous guy waiting for me but I'd rather stay late in the office and work on my promotion?*'

Michele gives me a pitying look as though he wonders what's wrong with me indeed. He hastily unscrews the bottle and sloshes some more liqueur into my glass, gesturing that I should drink up quick.

'The thing is, before Ciaran came into my life, everything was under control. Now I had too much do, to keep it all going. I had no energy for late-night lovemaking or sleepy morning sex.' I blush a bit here. 'And with the loss of sleep I found myself yawning in important business meetings. For the last three years, I'd been waiting, hoping for and dreaming of my promotion. This was *my one chance*.' I appeal to Michele as though he's my romantic jury, pressing my hand against my heart. 'I knew I had to give it one hundred per cent. And deep down, I couldn't quite believe that Ciaran really loved me. I was convinced that one morning he'd wake up and realise, *Julia really isn't all that special – why the hell am I bothering?* And then he'd dump me and I would have missed out on my promotion for nothing.'

I let out a long, sad breath and swallow, ready to get to the end of my story. Michele really is the most fantastic listener. I haven't opened up to anyone like this before. 'It all came to a head on Valentine's Day 2007. We were meant to be going out and I knew he was planning a special surprise. I got my secretary to call him up and tell him I had a high temperature and couldn't make it. It's a really crap way to dump someone: treating them badly, ignoring texts or not returning calls in the hope that they will get the message. Before long, Ciaran did. And then he got together with Reece.'

'But if you say goodbye to Ciaran, why you love now?' Michele asks, puzzled. 'Because Reece has him? You want what you do not have, yes?'

'No!' I cry defensively, though I'm scared there may be a sliver of truth in what he says. 'I . . . I . . .' I clutch my glass. The story of how I came to fall back in love with Ciaran is such a painful and unexpected one. And I already feel exhausted from the dive and my confession. Suddenly I feel so drained the words seem to die, sad and grey, in my throat. I shake my head softly: *I can't speak any more.*

'You say enough,' Michele says, patting my hand. 'You go now – yes? I take you home?'

'Thank you,' I say gratefully. 'Thank you for everything.'

We get into his car, a battered blue Fiesta, and he drives me back to the villa. His driving cheers me up and makes me laugh – he shouts out insults and beeps his horn at every instance. I'm sure I've never heard so many Sicilian swearwords in one day, and he regularly invites me to spit contempt on his fellow drivers. 'Look at him – he drives such a beeg car because he has such a small cock, and the way he drive, he has no self-control to know what to do weeth it!' he cries.

Outside our villa, I turn to him awkwardly and say, 'Is it OK – is it OK if you don't tell Reece and Ciaran about . . .'

'Of course,' Michele agrees. 'Ciaran eez a lawyer – I don't tell them nothing. You should not love a lawyer,' he concludes.

I smile gratefully and lean over to give him a ginger kiss on the cheek.

Back in the villa, I find a note from Ciaran and Reece to say they've gone to pick up shopping and will be back soon. Reece has added a *PS: Do you fancy going up Mount Etna tomorrow? We'll find out the details in town.*

I take a shower, then check my mobile. Despite my confused feelings, I still crave a text from Luke. Surely he must have replied by now after my hilarious chicken-stealing text? Surely he would at least have been a bit concerned about the fact that I might have been slung in a Sicilian jail for life?

But no. There are no new texts.

I lie back on my bed and for the first time since leaving him I feel a cold fear in my heart. Could history be repeating itself? It's as though I'm back on that disco-floor again, watching everyone around me pair up. I imagine myself watching Luke with a woman he's met in Hong Kong, dancing close with her, leaving the disco together, laughing, kissing, off to have some fun in a hotel room together . . .

Even though I'm full of ache for Ciaran, it's the *humiliation* that gets to me. Being rejected all over again.

Then I shake myself. Maybe I'm just being too clingy. I need to chill out, be patient, and try not to check my mobile every five seconds. I busy myself with putting out some food for the stray cats, feeling a rush of pleasure as they run up, purring, tails flicking with delight . . . but still I can't quite shift the unease inside me.

6

I hate Mount Etna. I hate the stupid Jeep we're being driven in. Ciaran and Reece are sitting in the front beside our guide and I hate their idle chit-chat. I hate the way the sun slips away as we travel higher and higher up the mountain, winding through tiers of cloud. I hate the lava streams that we pass on the way, warnings of the damage that Etna has wreaked in recent years from its fiery and unpredictable eruptions. I hate the fact that when we get off at the bar-restaurant-hotel called *Rifugio Sapienza*, my legs feel cramped from the journey and my stomach churns with travel sickness.

The guide tells us that Mount Etna is the highest volcano in Europe. It's also one of the most 'lively' – which isn't good news for Sicilians.

The ancients used to believe that it was the site of Vulcan's forge. Its eruptions have taken many victims, Fate ploughing mercilessly over towns and farms, carpeting

121

them in fire and smouldering ash, burning people, animals and homes to cinders. Once it drowned the entire city of Catania; more recently, in 2001–3, it destroyed the entire ski resort of Piano Provenzano.

As we reach about 1800 metres high, civilisation falls away. We pass a furl of black rock from which peeks the white sloping roof of a deserted house. I try to imagine what it must feel like, to wake up one morning in your home and feel the threatening tremor, to gather up all your belongings into a bag, to run outside your home and see black funnels pluming into the air as though the earth is vomiting up anger, to smell blackened skin in the wind, to run and run knowing your life depends upon it . . .

I conclude that I also hate volcanoes.

Yes, I'm in a bad mood. Luke still hasn't texted me, and worst of all, I've completely blown it. I did something very stupid last night.

My talk with Michele had soothed me, but it also stirred me up. Later that evening, we went out for dinner and several couples started dancing on the balcony. I sat at our table, watching Ciaran and Reece swaying together, a beautiful silhouette against the smoky blue twilight sky, and realised for the hundredth time that I can never have him. That I have to accept he's not mine. I reminded myself that there was still hope for something special with Luke. After all, wasn't our last night in Venice pretty amazing? Then I checked my mobile and there was still no text from him. It had only been six days, but it still felt like too long.

I sent him a text at 8.34 p.m.: *Hey Luke hope you got my text how are you? J x*

Then at nine I just snapped: *If you don't want me to text you any more, then fine. Just tell me and I'll delete your number.*

Then at nine-thirty I felt mortified and texted: *Sorry, didn't mean to sound like a stroppy cow. Just let me know, though. J x*

Then at ten I thought, Well, I've totally blown this now and I'm feeling pretty drunk so I may as well just spew it all out: *Luke, I'm sad that you clearly have no interest in me anymore. I'll have to go to Tokyo by myself. So long. J*

Then at one in the morning I woke up feeling mortified again and texted: *Please ignore all my texts! I was v v drunk. J x*

There is *no way* he is ever going to text back now.

I've blown it.

We pull up at the gondola station. We're 2000 metres up the mountain, but we still have a long way to go. It's very cold: a shock after spending our last few days luxuriating in the sticky warm Sicilian air. Reece and I hire jackets from the station and Reece swaps her heels for some climbing boots.

The gondola isn't as I expected. I'd imagined some

fancy sort of mountain lift with plush seats and baroque swirls. But this is basically a simple lift, the sort you see on skiing slopes. We climb in. Black rocks pass beneath us, laced with streaks of gold and rust. I cross my arms and sulk.

Opposite me, Ciaran and Reece stare out of the window in excitement. And for the hundredth time, that sad shock reverberates through me. I let Ciaran go; I lost him to Reece. *I* did it. I threw away the best thing that's ever happened to me.

And now I've messed up with Luke. I know deep down that it's not just me – Luke didn't bother to text either. But in my current masochistic mood everything feels as though it's my fault.

No: it's clear that I'm just not destined to find love.

We're here. We all climb out of the gondola and on to the volcano. Feeling hot tears of frustration in my eyes, I blink hard and hide my face by bending down, pretending to stare out at the coloured volcano rocks.

All the books and movies assume that love is a God-given right. Everyone, they tell us, deserves someone special. But why should love be democratic? After all, when we watch talent shows, we cringe at the hundreds of people who turn up with horrific vocals and shuffling dance steps, harbouring an insane delusion that they're destined to be the next Mariah Carey or Michael Jackson. We all know that to be born with a gift is a rare thing. Maybe some people, like Reece, have a gift for love. And others, like me, are tone deaf and hit all the wrong romantic notes.

'Are you OK, Julia?' Reece suddenly asks. 'You seem a bit quiet.'

'You know, Julia,' Ciaran says in a joking tone, 'there was a famous Greek philosopher called Empedocles who wanted to prove he was a god so he threw himself into a crater here. He never resurfaced, funnily enough. Maybe you could prove you're a goddess.'

Even though I know he's just playing our usual game, I feel too fragile to join in. His words enter my heart like a knife. He glances over, waiting for a smart reply, but I turn my back on him.

'Look, isn't this gorgeous?' Reece picks up a rock coloured with a greeny hue, cradling it. 'Wow, it's still warm.' She pockets it as a souvenir.

Suddenly the guide comes hurrying down the mountain, yelling and waving his arms. I hear a noise in the distance, like sharp thunder.

'Shit!' Ciaran cries, watching other tourists running down and clambering back into the gondolas. 'I think it's an eruption!'

We all squeeze back into the gondola. As it jerks down the mountain, it has never felt so flimsy. I crane my head back to try and see what's happening. Reece starts to sob that she's too young to die, whilst I fall silent with shock. Ciaran, who is sitting in the middle between us, takes hold of each of our hands and squeezes them tight. I squeeze back, our enmity forgotten.

The gondola reaches its destination, and we are ushered into Jeeps that drive us away from the volcano at breakneck speed. Then, suddenly, we come to a halt. The guide points upwards, his face lit up with joy. Ciaran curls his arm around Reece and I keep holding her hand. We realise that the guide is showing us something special: we're far enough away for the eruption to have shifted from a thing of danger to a thing of wonder.

Scarlet rain spurts up from the crater, radiant against the darkening sky. It's like watching a magnificent firework display. I observe the lava, pure gold, glinting orange, ooze voluptuously down the slope. With my awe comes a sense of wisdom. All the worries which have overshadowed the day drop away. They seemed so huge this morning; now they are petty and trivial. The Force of Nature is so almighty that I am suddenly conscious of how big the world is, and how insignificant my problems are. I feel as though I don't want to waste another second of my life being sorrowful over disappointing loves, or regrets, or my lost job. I just want to live and enjoy love for as long as it lasts, to grow and evolve and see all the amazing things the world has to offer me.

'Come, come,' says the guide, who has been snapping photos. He looks nervous but exhilarated. 'We go now.'

Back in the Jeep, we're all still shaken. I must treasure

this moment always, I think. I must hold on to this wisdom and never forget it.

Ciaran reaches across and clutches my hand again. I turn to him and see the same joyful thrill in his eyes. We share a moment of pure happiness. I don't analyse it or worry about it. I just let it fill up my heart.

It takes us forty-five minutes to drive back to Taormina. Back in the villa, Ciaran and Reece keep pacing around and exclaiming about how wonderful it all is. Ciaran teases her for worrying that she was going to die and Reece punches him, grinning.

I'm scared that they're going to start making love; there's nothing more romantic than a scrape with death. So I pick up two of the boxes of Earl Grey and head for the door. The experience on the mountain has pushed my boundaries back and I want to act on this impulse before they close in on me again.

'Where are you going with those?' Ciaran asks, frowning. 'Are you off to make a cup of tea for the strays?'

'Never you mind,' I say.

I walk into town, searching for the police station where we were arrested. When I enter, I'm relieved to see that the nice policeman is on guard – the one who let us off. I pass over the boxes of Earl Grey, indicating that he should keep one for a gift and give one to the farmer too. He looks confused at first and then calls me *mafiosetta* in a teasing voice.

'It's to say sorry,' I explain, laughing shyly. 'To say not all English tourists steal chickens. To say I feel very privileged to be on this beautiful island.'

A smile beams on his face and he nods.

'*Grazzii.*'

I walk back slowly, wanting to give Ciaran and Reece space. The salty wind whips my hair. I feel happy-sad about Luke now: resigned but nostalgic. I wonder if he went back to that girl, Jodie. I feel calm enough now to hope that he's happy and has found the right person to be with, calm enough to accept that what we had in Venice was worth treasuring even if it was so short and sweet.

The only trouble is – I sigh as the villa comes in sight – it's so hard not to fall back in love with Ciaran. I've not spent this much time in his company since we were dating. But I just have to be strong. I just have to be really, really strong.

7

'I don't fancy going on the night dive tonight, I'm just too knackered. I think you guys should go on your own,' Reece says.

'Uh, well . . .' Three days have passed since Mount Etna, and every day feels like a delicious torture. Luke still hasn't texted and I've given up on him entirely now; my memory of him is fading from my mind. Which has created a vacuum for Ciaran to rush into. Being in his presence, hearing his laughter, watching the way he fingers his stubble when he's thinking, bickering with him, is just about manageable, but I don't know if I can handle being alone with him. I'm terrified that I might just blurt out how I feel.

'Can't you come out too?' Ciaran wheedles. I see his obvious reluctance to be alone with me too and I feel indignant. And then hurt. Does he really dislike me that much?

'Sorry.' Reece pulls a kittenish face. 'I'm utterly cream-crackered. You guys go.'

And so Ciaran and I end up driving over to the beach together. We remain silent all the way.

Oh, this is so beautiful! I forget Ciaran, I forget my yearning, I forget my troubles – it was worth coming out for this. Once again, just like the splendour of Mount Etna's eruption, I feel lifted above my cares.

Michele drove a group of us out in his motor-boat to the Ionian Sea, the waves inky and silver in the moonlight, the lights of the island twinkling in the distance. We've just plunged into the ocean and it's unbelievable! I spot a jellyfish with a pale pink centre, spotted with black dots; and fat, metallic-coloured squidgy eels, and an octopus of a deep yellow colour so that he can chamelionise with the seaweed. Some of the corals here change colour at night and the darkness has unveiled their magic. They glow like precious gems. I wish I knew what they were called; I find myself making up affectionate names for them. That red one there I shall name a Scarlet Jewel. Those blue ones, which remind me of a certain someone's eyes, will be Ciaran's Smile.

A diver drifts close to me; I realise it's Ciaran. Even though he's wearing a mask, I can feel his excitement, sense that the experience has softened him too. He points and I see a sparkle in the distance, like a mystery treasure chest – another coral reef. Then he beckons me to follow him. I feel a flash of pleasure and surprise – so Ciaran's not finding my company *quite* so hard-going. I dive after him, plunging deep, deep into the ocean . . .

How did I come to fall in love with Ciaran after I was the one to dump him? Well, it was a curious twist and turn of events . . .

First of all, before I learned to love him, I lost him.

I remember the night I found Ciaran and Reece together. I was late home from work, walked into the kitchen and found Ciaran standing there in his boxers.

He'd been stalking me for the last few weeks, begging for us to get back together. Turning up at my flat. Bombarding me with texts. Now irritation and pity flared up inside me. He's turning into a male Glenn Close, I thought. How the hell am I going to handle this?

'Look,' I said, putting my bag down on the side, 'Ciaran, I just don't want to be with you any more—' I broke off as Reece came running into the kitchen in her underwear. Then she saw me and giggled and asked if we could have 'a private chat'.

As Ciaran walked past me, heading back to Reece's bedroom, I saw the longing in his eyes, his regret and confusion – and I turned away from him, tears in my eyes.

'So?' I spat at Reece. 'How long have you been having an affair? How many months?'

'Julia!' Reece put down the tub of Belgian Chocolate

Häagen-Dazs she'd just yanked from the freezer. 'You've broken up! Nothing has ever happened between us until tonight – and to be honest, I kind of did it to cheer him up, only now I really do actually quite fancy him. And I thought you'd be *glad* – I thought I was doing you a favour, getting him off your back. I mean, all you ever do is moan about him.'

I was mollified. How could I argue with that?

And so at first I was happy for them. It *did* get Ciaran off my back and I was happy that Reece was having fun. For that's all I thought it was: fun. A fling. Reece tended to get involved with two types of men. Bad boys and nice guys. Funnily enough, the bad boys always liked her; her blonde sweetness beguiled them and made her the exception to their womanising ways. But Reece was never that interested in them. Perversely, she liked the straitlaced, serious, upright types. I think she wanted them to calm her down, but in the end they tended to find her wild ways too much, declare she was nuts and dump her. I suppose I should have realised that Ciaran fitted into the latter category, that he was the exact shape of Reece's fantasies.

Three months down the line, I lay awake one night hearing Reece and Ciaran next door. They'd left their door open; their giggles indicated that they were drunk. Ciaran was asking, 'Are you ticklish here? What about here?' And Reece was spluttering, 'No – yes ... no ...' and Ciaran asked, '*Here?*' which prompted rude hysterics.

I felt my cheeks burn in the darkness. I thought about getting up and closing their door but felt too embarrassed. Soon their giggles became groans and gasps. I suddenly felt a raw desire flash through me, imagining him inside her. The next morning I dismissed it. I told myself that I was sex-starved. And that I needed to buy some ear-plugs.

Did I change, or did Ciaran change me?

I got the promotion that I had shoved him out of the way to work for. My salary was huge. I was finally in the position that I'd wanted to be in for months. But when you fulfil a desire, after the glow of satisfaction fades, there's a curious sense of nothingness. Of, *so what next?* My obsession with my promotion had ballooned into every waking thought. Now it had burst. Now I felt empty.

One night I sat at home alone watching a rerun of *Dirty Dancing* and instead of sneering I was amazed to find something wet prickling at my eyes. Me, Julia, a cynic, a hardened career woman, reduced to a teenager again! I'd thought crying was something I had grown out of, but now, all of a sudden I had caught it like a virus. I kept shaking myself and wondering if I needed to see a doctor. Then I concluded I was getting sentimental in my old age.

I would sit at breakfast and watch Ciaran and Reece performing little acts of love for each other – making toast if one of them had a hangover, cajoling him or her out of a bad mood. I realised, in horror, that love is all about timing. You can meet Mr Right – but if your heart isn't ready, if it's brittle around the edges, then you won't recognise him. And all of a sudden I could feel my heart blossoming with the maturing of my thirties and there was nobody there. And the whole time Reece kept telling me how gorgeous, wonderful and intelligent and considerate Ciaran was. Torturing me as I realised just what I'd thrown away.

Until one morning I woke up and knew I was in love with Ciaran and felt a sense of complete despair.

There's a dreamlike intensity to being underwater. We swirl and drift together, sharing a sense of awe at the rapturous beauty of corals. Down here, I feel as if Ciaran and I can communicate with a silent connection, from heart to heart. I wish I could stay down here forever with him, in this beautiful blue dreamworld.

Ciaran suddenly points upwards and kicks up, up, up. I follow him slowly.

We burst up out of the ocean.

He pulls aside his mouthpiece. 'Shit – we're lost.'

We gaze across the ocean. Our boat has completely disappeared. We can see twinkling lights, which is reassuring; the trouble is, the lights glimmer in three directions, which could signify three different shores.

'Fuck,' I whisper.

Ciaran glances left, right, left, right, then concludes decisively: 'It's that way.'

'OK,' I agree, for I really have no idea.

'It's quite a swim. If you get tired, then tell me.'

'Hey, I'm not a wimp,' I retort. Immediately I regret it. I don't want to start bickering again. 'I expect they'll be looking for us – we'll probably meet them halfway.'

'Exactly.'

Ciaran starts to cut across the waves. I follow. Neither of us speaks, in order to conserve our energy. Even though I know I ought to be worrying, I can't help enjoying our crazy mistake. The sky is so beautiful, with the stars bright above and dangerous volcano steam wisping across the moon. I feel utterly alive.

After a while, however, my arms start to get tired. Waves lap against my face and seep behind my wetsuit; salt stings my skin and tongue. I can't see the boat at all. Did they just pull in and desert us? Maybe we went left and they went right. Maybe they're already frantic and have sent out a search-party. I feel panic stirring.

In London, living amidst the traffic, I often used to crave the countryside, feel hungry for greenery, for the colours of summer flowers and autumn leaves. I regarded Nature as benign and beautiful. But now that I've left the city for the wilder world, now that I've seen a volcano erupt, my perspective has become more Darwinian. Nature is both beautiful *and* brutal. And there is no doubt that it doesn't compromise: if you decide to climb a mountain unprepared, or foolishly lose track of time and drift away from your party in the middle of an ocean, Nature rarely shows pity. You get punished.

We could die out here.

I see Ciaran glancing back to see if I'm OK. I give him a little wave and put on a brave face even though I'm petrified.

And then we see the shore rushing up and I feel relief pound in my heart. My arms are truly aching, my mouth sour from too much salt.

Finally the water becomes shallow and we wade on to a powdery white beach. We collapse simultaneously, panting like mad. I pull off my headpiece, shaking my hair free, rubbing my face. Ciaran does the same.

'Fuck, that was some swim,' he gasps.

'I'm not sure if I can get up again now,' I tell him.

'Don't,' says Ciaran gently. 'Let me go. You just wait and I'll see if I can find the team.'

When I protest, he becomes insistent. 'Really – it's my way of making it up to you. I'm the one who led us astray.'

I sit on the beach, shivering slightly, as Ciaran pads off. I feel vulnerable on my own and I glance around nervously. I hear a ribbon of laughter in the distance, then wonder if I imagined it.

Then, finally, I'm aware of someone crossing the sand again. It's Ciaran, and his face looks stricken.

'I had a bit of trouble finding anyone – but then I spoke to this girl. She didn't really understand English, but in the end she said that if we go back to her in the morning, we can get a ride in her dad's fishing boat.'

'Well, can't we just walk back to the villa now?' I ask.

Ciaran slumps down on the sand. 'We're both really tired. I think we should just have a kip now,' he says.

'But – but – how far away are we?'

'Well ... we're meant to be on the Tyrrhenian shore and we're quite close to Palermo.'

'*We're at a different town?*' I shriek.

'They're very close together!'

I'm so inflamed, I grab a handful of sand and fling it at him.

'Oh, shit. I've got some in my eye!' Ciaran yelps.

'Oh no, I'm really sorry,' I say, leaning in guiltily. He stares up, blinking it out, rubbing his eye.

'Sorry,' I repeat.

'No, it's fine. I deserve it.'

'Oh God. Reece will be going mad. They'll all be looking for us.' I giggle, half-hysterically. 'I mean, can't we just go and call someone? Can't that girl help us?'

'I did try, but then she looked nervous – she clearly thought I was a nutter at first and I didn't want to push it. I was worried she'd withdraw her offer of her dad's help. I mean, if we go back in the morning, her father will be there so she'll feel safe, then we can call.'

'We can't exactly go to a callbox – we've got no money.'

It seems as though we have no choice but to sit it out.

'Are you cold?' Ciaran asks. 'It's actually warmer in the water.' He slithers down the sand and lies with his feet in the lap of the waves. I copy him and he's right: the delicious heat of the waves caresses my feet and radiates warmth through my body. We stare up at the moon and the stars. A silence rises between us. I think about saying something rude and sarky about him getting us lost, but it doesn't feel quite right to argue any more.

'I'm sorry to hear about your job,' Ciaran says finally.

Shit. Now he's being *nice* to me. We're having a serious conversation. We haven't done this for quite a long time. This feels a bit odd.

'It's fine, I wanted a break,' I reply lightly. I wish he hadn't brought it up. I was starting to feel as if this holiday had created a mist between the present and the past, and my terrible exit from Charlton Cross. I open my mouth to ask if—

Then I close it.

It's better not to know, I remind myself. *Just move on. Don't pick at a scab.*

But I can't help myself.

'So is there any gossip going round about me?'

Ciaran swivels his cheek to the sand, his eyes on me. 'Oh no.'

Ciaran was always very bad at lying.

'Don't worry,' he says, rubbing my shoulder. I feel the warmth from his palm shimmer through my body. I stare hard at the waves. Then, thank goodness, he takes his hand away. I try to fight the fantasies stirring inside me. The longing to feel him slowly smooth that palm down the length of my naked arm, to curl it around my cheek and pull me in for a tender, salty kiss . . .

'Do you . . . has . . .' Ciaran swallows. 'Has Reece said anything about me, er, recently?' He's trying to sound casual but his voice sounds like a string tightening on an instrument.

I rack my brains, sifting through things I can say, things I can't. 'To be honest, she hasn't really said much. I thought everything was going well with you guys?'

'Oh yeah, it's all great,' Ciaran says. Then: 'Actually, it's not really going *that* well. We're having some problems – one serious problem, in particular.'

I can feel my heart starting to pound violently. Oh God. This is horrendous. This is the sort of fantasy I used to have when they first got together. It would always conclude with me giving myself a mental slap. Knowing that my happiness would be Reece's unhappiness.

'We're just . . . it's just . . .'

I can tell that Ciaran wants me to coax it out of him but I just can't do it. I can't bear to listen to this; I'll *enjoy* it and it will just make me feel stinky and mean.

'Look, I think this has to be between you and Reece,' I say in a shaky voice. 'It's better if you don't discuss it with me.'

Ciaran opens his mouth to speak, then bites his lip. Then he starts again.

'The thing is, Julia – you know me. You're the only one I can really talk to about this.'

I feel his eyes on me. A sudden joy fills me. So Ciaran *does* still feel there's some kind of intimacy between us.

I turn and gaze at him. He stares at me, his eyes intense. I look away again. And as I do so, I see it. The boat. Someone on board is waving. I scrabble to my feet and windmill my arms wildly.

'They're back!' I cry to Ciaran. 'They did come looking for us – thank God!'

He half-smiles, half-grimaces and slowly gets to his feet.

We wade into the shallows, then swim over to the boat, and clamber up on board. After giving us hugs of relief, Michele's wife tells us off for leaving the party, saying we had them worried sick.

'Where's Michele?' I ask, dreading that he's spent the night tearing his hair out with fury over us.

'He went to make Reece OK,' she says. 'Your friend went crazy. She think you lost . . . he make her feel OK, say I will find you. And look – I find you.'

'We're really sorry,' Ciaran says again. 'It was all my fault.'

'Ciaran, thanks, that's really sweet of you, but—' I begin.

'No,' Ciaran insists. 'I'll take all the blame. And if I get thrown off the scuba course as a result, well, then, sod it.' He breathes out heavily and motions that I should sit down. Then he collapses next to me. He doesn't seem aware that his shoulder is hard against mine, his warmth infusing my skin. I'm acutely, painfully conscious of it.

As the boat cuts away through the waves, I stare back at the rim of beach where we lay together, alone in our beautiful bubble, and want to store it in my memory forever. It's ridiculous: I hardly care that they found us and that we're safe. The only thing filling my head is Ciaran's words. What did he mean? Now I'm beginning to wish I had just let him talk. Are he and Reece really about to break up?

8

Back home, Reece flings her arms around me and Ciaran at the same time, pulling us into a big group hug.

'Thank God you're safe!' she cries.

'Is Michele going crazy?' I ask.

'Oh, he was pretty worried, yeah . . . but he's gone back to his villa now. I should call him, let him know you're back.'

'*I'll* call him,' says Ciaran.

I can't help noticing the smell that is lingering in the villa. Is it *pot*? I know Reece likes to smoke it regularly, but what would she and Michele be doing, sharing a joint when we're lost in the depths of the ocean?

Seeing me wrinkle my nose, she opens the window and yawns.

'It's stuffy in here. I've been up all night worrying,' she sighs.

I say sorry again and we hug and I go into my bedroom.

I feel utterly exhausted but my body is gritty with salt and sand. I badly need a shower, even after being immersed in water for most of the night. As I drag myself into the bathroom, Ciaran's words keep echoing through my mind, over and over: *We're having some problems – one serious problem, in particular* ... I can't help thinking about the suspicious smoke, either. I know this sounds fanciful, but you could almost smell the intimacy in that smoke, as though the memory of it had coiled in the tendrils. And not just the smoke – the way Reece was behaving seemed a bit strange – almost as though she was *acting* concerned. And what about Michele coming over to the villa to *comfort* her – a euphemism if ever I've heard one. But no, surely she wouldn't do that ...

I climb out of the shower and rub my body dry. The little pink bottle of shampoo is empty, so I fling it into the bin.

And then I see it.

Reece has tried to hide it. She's wrapped toilet tissue around it, but the stick still pokes out.

I pull it out in shock.

A pregnancy test.

I peer at the thin blue line. For one shocked moment I think Reece is about to become a mum. Then I breathe out. It's negative. Phew.

I raise my eyes and look at my reflection. Guilt floods through me, painting my face crimson. Reece most certainly isn't having an affair; in my shame I conjured up a story. Maybe the smoke too was just a product of my horrible, warped imagination. No doubt she spent the night pacing, fretting, wondering if she dare take the test, wondering if Ciaran had drowned and she was about to become a single mother. Reece has always seesawed between cooing over friends' children and then moaning that kids would be too much hassle. But what if she and Ciaran are planning a family? Reece hasn't confided that to me, but all couples have their secrets. I can't expect her to tell me everything.

Then I put two and two together. Maybe *that's* why Ciaran is suddenly feeling edgy about their relationship. Now our conversation makes sense. He probably agreed to kids, humoured Reece when she suggested baby names (after all, look what she called her goldfish!). But inside he's panicking. He doesn't feel ready.

One part of me can't help feeling a little disappointed in Ciaran. He didn't seem the type to react like that. He always seemed mature, responsible. And now he's just being a typical scaredy boy. The other part of me sympathises; I'm definitely not ready for kids either. So I can understand him suffering a certain amount of panic.

I quickly shove the stick deep into the bin, so that it's buried deep beneath a nest of tissues.

Then I look into the mirror and make a resolution.

I love Reece very, very much. She's my best friend and I don't want her to ever feel bad.

I will forget Ciaran. I'll *never* flirt with him again. And if he ever starts to moan again, I'll tell him firmly to shut up.

Back in my room, I collapse into bed, utterly shattered by the night's dramatic events, revelations and emotional shell-shocks. I'm just about to sink into sleep when I hear my mobile beep. I groan and reach for it, screwing up my tired sore eyes to read the message. Then I see it's from Luke. I jump up, startled.

Luke.

He's actually texted me, after all those cringe-making painful drunken texts I've bombarded him with. I scroll down and think, Oh God. There are three texts from him. No doubt they are retaliatory replies – three ways of telling me to fuck off and never contact him again.

The first one says: *Sorry babe I lost my mobile! Am I an idiot or what! Sorry I didn't text how are you? X*

The second one says: *Can't believe u got arrested for stealing chickens! What's that all about? Also sorry you seem to be upset with me, but seriously I did lose my mobile.*

The third one says: *I hope we're still speaking. And still on for Japan. I've booked my flight! Have you fixed up a hotel yet? Text me all the details. Lxxxx*

A big smile of amazement breaks open across my face. Luke still cares for me. He still wants to go to Japan.

This must surely be Fate, I think, reassuring me that he's the one I'm meant to be with.

9

Now Reece and Ciaran have gone and I'm standing here in the empty villa. There's a sense of sweet sadness in the air even though I've not left yet; the floors already look bare without our mess; you can already hear the laughter and voices of the tourists who will replace us. Our holiday seemed to pass so quickly and I know I'll treasure it always.

I sit down on a wicker chair, leaving the door open so that the sea breezes whirl in, and take a mental snapshot of the view: the curve of the cliff, the pretty white church sitting in the grass, the sweep of the ocean beyond, so blue it looks as though it's a mirror reflecting the flawless sky.

I've ticked off numbers two and three on my list. I've scuba-dived and seen the beauty of the ocean; I've climbed a volcano and seen a glorious eruption. Plus, I've managed to nearly get arrested for stealing chickens as an unwelcome bonus! But somehow these are the least significant things about this holiday.

I've learned that I am still in love with Ciaran; perhaps a part of me always will be. But my romance with Luke has given me perspective. I've become conscious of how many years I have wasted, going through cycles of hoping and repression, of guilt and yearning. Like a snake with its tail in its mouth, my hopeless, useless love has been never-ending. And this trip has brought me back to the same conclusion once again: *Ciaran belongs with Reece.*

I think that love comes to us when our hearts are ready to receive it. I've been so busy obsessing over Ciaran that I've blocked out all possibilities. I've moaned to myself that there are no men out there, but the truth is I was never open to them. I never went back to dating agencies or surfed the net for introduction sites. I never sat down on a train next to a stranger and smiled at him, hoping we might strike up conversation; if he had done, I would probably have buried my nose in my BlackBerry. I was stuck in an emotional, Ciaran-shaped rut.

Not any more. I'm ready for somebody new. And, more importantly, I'm ready for love. In my twenties, I was married to my job. And though I'm still prickly about my redundancy, I feel grateful, truly grateful, that Reece pushed me off on this trip. I want to be with Luke and fulfil number four on my list. But I also hope it's the beginning of something special. Luke is the right guy for me. I'm fraught and he's laidback. I'm serious and he's fun.

The fact that he was so easy-going about all those crazy texts I sent him feels like a confirmation.

I stand up as a sudden gust of wind blows into the villa, caressing my hair. I suddenly remember how I felt, that morning when Luke left me in Venice, his kisses still a taste in my mouth, my heart fluttering with sweet happiness. I want to feel that again and again and again.

I can see my taxi in the distance. As I pick up my case and lock the villa door, I experience a faint sense of trepidation. As though I'm diving into new waters and don't know how deep I will go . . .

4. Go to the top of the tallest building in Tokyo

1

In twenty minutes' time, I'm going to meet Luke at the airport. If he turns up, that is.

I'm running a little late myself. I nearly trip as I hurry down the steps into Ginza subway, silently cursing. As I jog into the station, I experience one of my first tastes of Japanese culture.

In the etiquette of passing through the ticket machines, I do something fundamentally wrong, though I'm not quite sure what. I shove my ticket into the machine, then attempt to shoot through the barriers. They lock. The guard is brutal with me. He grabs me from behind, yanks me back into place. He shoves the ticket into the machine. He yells something in Japanese, then ushers me through. Going through a subway machine has never been so frightening; I feel as though I'm on an induction course for the army. But when I finally pass through, the guard flips from Hyde to Jekyll. He bows politely and gives me a

151

beaming, obsequious smile. I smile back, feeling as though he's pinned a medal on my chest – though I still don't know what any of it was about.

I check my watch. 'Oh Luke,' I whisper, as though I wish I could psychically vibe my plea into his mind, 'please, please don't disappear. Please wait for me.'

The subway is efficient and clean. After several changes, I get off at Narita Airport and then pound down towards exit three.

He's not there. After all my worrying, I'm only five minutes late. I keep checking my watch. Every minute feels like an hour. Will he come, or will I be stuck in Tokyo all by myself? The trouble is, Luke *is* erratic – after all, he did lose his mobile and maybe I've got the wrong exit and God, now I'll have to go back through the subway with the guard again all on my own and oh shit—

Just as I turn to go, I feel a breath on the back of my neck and a voice in my ear: 'Hey, you!'

I turn. He's right behind me. So close my nose nearly bumps his chest. He's wearing his Bob Marley T-shirt again. I'd forgotten how tall he is; how cute his sideburns are; how his conker-brown eyes sparkle.

'Hey,' I say shyly, blushing.

Then, as he turns his head, I notice the bruise on the side of his cheek and I wince.

'Long story,' he shrugs. 'I had an argument with a door-frame.'

'Ouch.' I wince in sympathy.

We head back to the subway and this time I manage to make peace with the turnstile. I tell Luke all about my experience with the guard and he laughs.

'Yeah, the Japanese are a mysterious mixture of different elements. I mean, on the one hand, they're incredibly well-mannered and if you just buy something from a shop, they'll do that cute bowing thing. But they've got a brutal side too – we saw it in the last world war. To my mind, it's an S and M culture, man!'

I laugh, wondering if his assessment is right. I know that you can't generalise about nations because individuals will always defy clichés. But when you're travelling, and you first enter a country, the sense of disorientation creates an urge to define, to summarise, to create mental signposts about how to behave ...

We get back on to the train. Everything feels slightly surreal. Ever since I started my *Ten Things* adventure a month back, the same sensation has come over me: an acute consciousness of the present, a slight disbelief that all this is actually happening, a sense that my mind and heart haven't quite caught up with it all. Experiences are layering on top of experiences. Already Sicily is becoming a distant dream – and yet I haven't even had time to digest it yet.

Then I look up at Luke and feel certain of one thing. I'm really glad we hooked up again.

We chat about the little customs of polite decorum on which Japanese society thrives. On the subway trains, for example, you're not meant to talk on your mobile or put on make-up. Then Luke adds that you're not meant to eat whilst walking on the streets, as it's considered uncouth. Here I am, generalising again, but it seems to me that Japan is a country of efficiency, cleanliness and order. You've got to admire it: its economy is thriving and crime rates are ridiculously low, perhaps due to high literacy and a society infused with traditional family and religious values. According to my guidebook, Tokyo is one of the few capital cities in the world where you can walk around safely at night.

'You know,' Luke whispers in my ear, 'I really want to kiss you but the guidebook also says the Japanese are prudish about public displays of affection.'

Of course, guidebooks can get things wrong. But the fact that it's forbidden makes it all the more sexy. I spend the rest of the subway journey chatting with him but my eyes keep slipping to his lips. I can hardly wait to get back to the hotel room.

'Wow, this is a hot hotel!' Luke cries as we enter the elegant lobby. Our hotel is in Ginza, one of the most stylish districts in Tokyo. Luke is so unreliable that I had to organise the booking.

'Oh, cool, I'm glad you like it. It's only three-star, but it seems like four, doesn't it? I got it for a bargain on the net.'

We get into the lift and Luke dumps his guitar case

with a sigh, rubbing his shoulder. I love the way he seems immediately at ease in the country, as though the world belongs to him and he's just wandering around his own grounds ...

'So are we gonna go out on the town tonight?' Luke asks. 'I've still got my lucky dollar.'

'You're not jetlagged?' I ask.

'Hell, yeah. But I wanna have fun. I wanna have the adventure of a lifetime.'

I smile at him; his exuberance is irresistible.

'Well, I did have this wish,' I tell him, 'to visit the Park Hyatt Hotel and go right to the top floor – I think it's on the fifty-second floor. I've heard it's the best view in Tokyo, and you can look down and see the scene where they shot *Blade Runner*.'

'Well, that sounds fucking brilliant,' Luke cries, ruffling my hair. 'Good plan, Julia.'

In our hotel room, he drops his case and bag and pulls me into his arms. He smells of tiredness and travelling; his T-shirt is a little sticky with jetlag sweat. And yet he's so wondrously sexy. I feel disappointed when he pulls away again, declaring that he needs a shower. If it was up to me, I'd let him ravish me right now. I remind myself that it's sweet that Luke is being such a gentleman: the waiting will make it all the more delicious.

He *is* being a gentleman, isn't he? As Luke disappears into the shower, I sit down on the bed with a feeling of slight insecurity. My sex life has been pretty lame for a number of years now. If I'm honest, the last really passionate experience I had was on a one-night stand with a guy from Charlton Cross a few months into my job. That was ten years ago. After that, increasingly I tended to ignore male flirting, passed up on opportunities for dates and flings. Until Ciaran. And ... well, let's just say that for all my aching for Ciaran, we didn't have a spectacular time in the sack. *Then* I had that awful experience with the Italian, Piero, in Venice. When you haven't had sex for a long time, you start to wonder if you're doomed never to have it again. I just hope that Luke wants me, that I can please him, that we can come together, so to speak.

Then I tell myself to lighten up. Sex is meant to be enjoyable, after all, and anticipation is part of the pleasure. Luke's here, we're in Japan, and we're going to have a wonderful adventure.

I feel glad that I saw Ciaran and Reece. If I hadn't discovered the pregnancy test, if I hadn't realised how serious their relationship had become, I might have arrived in Tokyo not fully able to enjoy the present. A little part of me would have been hankering after Ciaran, playing the *what-if* game. Now I know that I can close a door on Ciaran forever, that Luke is my only way forward.

Luke's mobile starts to play jazz. As it vibrates, it looks as though it's about to fall off the cabinet, so I quickly grab it and set it straight. I can't help looking at the caller display even though a stern voice inside tells me it's terribly rude and really none of my business to look at someone else's messages. Then my heart stops.

Jodie?

I also can't help noticing that Jodie has called *three* times today so far. Shit.

I remember that her name came up at the wedding. What did Luke's friend, Lee, say about her back in Venice? *I thought you guys were getting married and all.* And what did Luke reply? Something about it all being over. So who is she? An ex who's chasing back after Luke?

Luke comes out of the shower and I quickly step away. He asks if I'm OK and I smile, shrugging. I want to confront him, but something stops me. We've only been together for an hour. It's a little soon to be bringing up exes and making accusations. I'll just seem like a madwoman.

Then I experience a flicker of fear. I can feel myself opening up to Luke and it's scary. I've already been hurt once with Ciaran, and I want to protect myself. I need to be sure that Luke isn't playing me. I can't ignore this. At some point tonight – maybe when we've had a few drinks – I shall bring up the subject of Jodie and get to the bottom of it, once and for all.

2

'OK – it's time for Fate to give us a little guidance,' Luke says.

'You've got your lucky coin?' I ask teasingly. We've eaten noodles and we're meant to be heading for Shinjuku and the Park Hyatt, but Luke has organised a quick diversion on the way. The issue of Jodie lingers in my mind but I'm still excited to be with Luke. He's just so wonderfully unpredictable ...

'Nope, not the lucky coin this time,' he says. 'Since we're in Japan, we're going to explore Fate the Japanese way.'

He leads me down a street filled with shops and souvenir stands selling colourful knick-knacks, snacks and rice crackers, and we arrive at the Asakusa Kannon, the oldest and most popular temple in Japan. It was built in AD628 for Kannon, the Buddhist Goddess of Mercy and Happiness who can release all humans from suffering.

Luke tells me that Japan is a predominantly Buddhist country. They don't tend to separate material and spiritual values; their religion is quite goal-orientated and offerings are made in the hope of receiving blessings, money, success and love. While it makes me smile to imagine a high-flying Sony employee sitting in the temple, begging for a promotion, I do muse that it's honest and natural, to pray for the fulfilment of our desires.

Outside the red temple are large incense burners and we have to wash our hands to purify ourselves before entering.

'Look,' Luke says, 'I read about this on the net. We have to drop a hundred yen into here,' he points to a silver box with a slot, 'then, silently asking a secret question, we pick up one of these bamboo sticks. You see there is a number written on it? OK ... so then we have to find the drawer with our number on it,' he points this time to rows and rows of wooden drawers, 'then we pull out a slip of paper and it tells us our fortune. Oh, and if it's crap, we can just tie it to one of these metal stands, 'cos they say the wind will blow the bad luck away.'

My question is simple: *Is Luke The One?*

I go to the drawer and uncurl the paper, my fingers trembling with excitement. The answer isn't very inspiring. *The wish that you are making will not come to fruition; trouble may lie ahead.* I quickly screw it into a ball.

'Was yours good?' I ask, noticing Luke's sober expression.

'Nope.'

'Me neither.'

We both shrug it off and tease each other, but as we leave the temple I can't help feeling under a shadow. I remind myself that I shouldn't get too swept up in Luke's beliefs. After all, I believe we shape our own lives. Only my heart can tell me if Luke *is* The One, not a silly piece of paper.

I realise Luke is looking hard at me and ask him, 'What's up?'

'I'm just thinking that you've changed since I saw you in Italy.' He falls silent, and naturally I take the bait.

'How so?'

'You were pretty tense when I first met you. And now you seem a lot more chilled, a bit happier, more free. Something like that.'

His words make me glow inside. I *do* feel happier, there's no doubt about it.

As we head towards the subway, however, I muse that if I'm different, then Luke is probably the cause. Isn't it funny how everyone you meet brings out a new colour in your personality? We can be entirely different people at work or with a lover, and two close friends can sometimes view us with clashing perspectives. Reece always brings out the sensible mother in me; Ciaran makes me feel desperate and melancholy; Luke, meanwhile, makes me feel a bit like a naughty schoolgirl. He makes me want to throw caution to the wind, break my boundaries, do things I've never done before . . .

Which makes me feel that I could fall in love with Luke.

We get off the subway and walk into Shinjuku and I'm absolutely overwhelmed.

I've seen many pictures of Tokyo skyscrapers in magazines, and have turned the glossy page without emotion. But seeing them in reality is so very different. I'm simply stunned by them. Twenty-foot tall walls of neon in pink and blue and green and orange fireworking against the deepest black of the night. The adverts for Sony and Nokia and Nova flash so that the colours appear to be alive, breathing and jumping from building to building.

I feel as though the colours pour into me until my heart is one big swirling rainbow. I've never been interested in art, have rarely visited a gallery. Tonight, I'm a converted woman. I'm conscious that the moment is not dissimilar to the one I experienced on Mount Etna, despite the fact that this is manmade beauty. I feel drunk on visual pleasure.

Beauty makes the heart tender. I blink, tears in my eyes. In the end, I can't walk any more. I just have to stop and stare. I look up at Luke and see he's sharing the same experience. We stand there like zombies, the crowds gently pulsing around us.

Then he reaches out and takes my hand. Just as Ciaran did on Etna. But this feels much sweeter. Because Luke is mine.

We wander about for a while, still feeling as though

we're on another planet. The crowds grow thicker. About 80 per cent of them are Japanese businessmen who have spilled from their offices to enjoy the night. They all wear black suits. Luke and I play a game to see if we can spot someone wearing brown or navy – but there's not a single one. Clearly there is an unwritten rule in Japan that colour must be saved for skyscrapers.

We stumble down a back street and discover where many of the businessmen are heading. There are small, rowdy karaoke bars and brothels with large picture boards outside. The girls they advertise have dyed straight hair, innocent eyes and appear to be dressed for men with a schoolgirl fetish. Somehow, though, none of this feels as sleazy as London's red-light districts, and though the men are drunk, there's no fighting or swearing, just an atmosphere of debauched jollity.

'Hey, look at that.' Luke points. I look up and see a plate-glass window. Oh my God. A couple of businessmen seem to be fondling *a lifesize plastic doll.*

'Bizarre!' I giggle. Then I cry with a burst of passion: 'Oh Luke, this is all wonderful. I'm really glad I'm here tonight with you.'

'So am I,' he says.

He leans down and kisses me, and we look at each other and stand very still in the swirl of crowds.

'Let's go find the best view in Tokyo,' Luke whispers.

3

We get lost a few times before we find the Park Hyatt Hotel. It's very plush and has a slightly decadent air about it. We get into the lift and zoom up to the top. There, we stand by the plate-glass window and stare out over Shinjuku. I can see now why it made the perfect setting for *Blade Runner*. The neon pulses and dances in the darkness; it really does look like another planet.

And then a shadow falls over my mind. *Jodie* – the image of her name flashing up on Luke's mobile. I open my mouth to ask him about her, then close it. This is such an amazing moment and I don't want anything to spoil it.

Luke turns and glances into the bar. Various tourists and businessmen are milling about, drinking and looking suave. I'm not sure we can afford it, but Luke tugs me in and we order two mineral waters, the cheapest thing on the menu.

163

Now, I'm sure if I'd turned up at the bar on my own, I wouldn't have dared speak to anyone. I stand there, feeling a little bit self-conscious and out of place, but Luke radiates his special brand of charisma. Before we know it, we've struck up conversation with a couple from Hawaii who have flown over for a business trip. Even better, they offer to buy us drinks; Luke has a beer and I get a glass of white wine.

'I'm Betty,' the woman introduces herself. She smiles stiffly and I get the feeling she's a fan of Botox. 'And this is my husband and business partner, Doug.'

Doug has grey hair, a booming voice and a charming smile. He shakes our hands vigorously. I'm about to open my mouth to introduce myself when Luke cuts in.

'I'm Michelangelo, and this is my wife . . .' He looks at me with a sparkle in his eye and I realise that this is a game he's daring me to play.

'I'm – er – Jeanette,' I say quickly, smiling up at him with mock wifely devotion.

We all sit down in comfy leather chairs, a lamp pooling golden light on to us. The waiter brings us our drinks. Then, as a fresh group of people enter the bar, I do a double-take. There's a flash of blond hair; a dark, pin-striped suit; high heels supporting long, long legs. The group disappears, led by a waiter to a table round the other side of the bar.

I shake myself. I must have been mistaken – that couldn't possibly be who I thought it was.

Sensing my anxiety, Luke reaches over and pats my arm gently. 'Is my wife OK?' he whispers, and I repress the urge to giggle.

'So what brings you to Tokyo?' Luke asks our newfound friends, narrowing his eyes. He's being very cool but I can sense a tangible bristle of excitement at the game he's initiated. I realise that in some peculiar way he's turned on by all this – and the weird thing is, I feel a bit turned on too. We're sharing a secret, weaving a web of lies together.

'We're here on business, but we love having fun too. How about you guys?'

'We came,' Luke says grandly, with a twinkle in his eye, 'to visit the tallest building in Tokyo and look down at the fine view from the top floor. So here we are, fulfilling a dream together.' He smiles at me.

Doug, who has been watching Luke over the rim of his glass, gives him a slightly patronising look.

'I think you'll find that the tallest building here would be the Metropolitan Goverment Building, forty-fifth floor,' he says, with a touch of glee.

'Well, it's the view I wanted to enjoy,' I point out, feeling a touch irritated. 'I wanted an amazing view, and I've got one.'

Betty gives Doug a look as if to say *be nice!* Looking a tad embarrassed, she enthuses, 'We love the Kabuki theatre here. We went last night.'

'Oh, we love the Kabuki theatre too,' Luke says. 'We

took our kids last time – and they just adored the bit where they chop off the samurai's head with a sword and the fake head goes bouncing across the stage.'

Kids! I nearly choke on my drink but manage a maternal smile when Betty asks me their ages.

'Um, they're six and nine,' I say. I try to sound casual but there's a breathy nervousness in my voice and I'm aware of my heartbeat.

'Oh, what are their names?' she coos.

'There's Laurie ... and ah – Michelangelo, after his father,' I improvise.

'Michelangelo the second,' Luke says, nodding. 'But she had Laurie from her last marriage.' He smiles at me. 'I'm actually husband number four, aren't I, honey?'

'Um, yes.' I suffer a burst of indignation coupled with a wild desire to laugh. I can feel Betty looking at me and musing, *Gosh, she must have either started young or got through them quickly*, before she quickly covers it up with a polite smile.

'At our wedding, you should have heard her father's speech,' Luke says. 'He said that Jeanie was competing with Liz Taylor for the world record for collecting husbands!'

'Oh well, you have to follow your heart,' Betty sympathises, whilst Doug merely frowns.

'Well,' I intercede, determined to beat Luke at this game, 'I really wanted to marry Mikey a good deal sooner, but obviously I had to wait for the results of his sex-change op.' I rub his arm softly. 'I mean, I loved you when you were Linda and now I still love you as Michelangelo.'

As soon as the words are out of my mouth, I think, Fuck, this time I've gone way too far, I really don't know how to play this game. But Luke gleams with delight. Betty and Doug, on the other hand, exchange surreptitious looks as if to say, *Um, we'll just make this the last drink.*

'So, d'you have kids?' Luke addresses Betty.

'Ah . . .' I caught her checking out Luke earlier and now she looks confused, as though she's trying not to fancy a man who once had breasts. 'I . . . yes, well – I'm not sure if I want kids, to be honest. I'm not entirely sure if I'm ready. But hell, I am nearly forty so I guess I've left it a little late.'

I give her a pitying smile, as if to warn her that motherhood is a gift she shouldn't miss out on.

'We're pretty busy with our exporting business,' says Doug. 'That's the main reason why we're in Japan.'

Then Doug downs his drink and thumps his glass on the table. I know he's about to make excuses to leave, but Luke doesn't want the game to end. He hails the waiter, crying, 'Another round – it's on us!' I have no idea how we're going to afford these drinks. Since Luke is a penniless backpacker, perhaps I should rephrase that: I have no idea how *I'm* going to pay for these drinks. I just hope we split the bill.

But a game is a game, and neither of us can stop.

The next round of drinks loosens up the atmosphere between us. Luke and I manage to get into the swing of schooltalk; we discuss the difficulties of home-schooling our children and how he won't allow Laurie to have a My Little Pony because he feels they're sexist. Betty's obviously not a big drinker, because her face softens and her eyes lose their focus. She suddenly leans forward with an earnest face and asks: 'So did you find you could still have kids even with Michelangelo's – you know – *change*?'

'Betty!' her husband barks. 'You can't ask that!'

'Oh sorry,' she flushes, 'I just—'

'Ma'am,' says Luke, looking just as earnest, 'I can assure you that my cock may be the result of an operation, but it's extremely large and I'm still able to give my wife much pleasure –'

'You sure do,' I sigh.

' – as well as impregnate her.'

Doug splutters out his drink but Betty laughs, enchanted. Then she looks at me and asks, 'And you enjoy being a full-time mom and letting Michelangelo play the man?'

'Oh, she won't ever need to work again,' Luke says.

Luke's words are spoken lightly, but they feel like a knife in my heart.

'Well, actually, honey,' I say, unable to keep the barb out of my voice, 'I would like to go back to work, you know. Once upon a time, I was a high flyer.' Suddenly I don't need to act any more. 'I gave up work, but I'd really like to feel there's a door still open for me back in the City.'

Luke puts his drink down on the table.

'Honey, we've discussed this. You know the kids need you.'

He glares at me and I glare back. He's opened a wound, a very raw wound, and I feel so cross I could slap him.

'The truth is,' says Luke, 'that neither of us work. We don't want to get caught up in the rat-race right now. It's like Lily Tomlin said – even if you win at the rat-race, you're still a rat. Let's consider what the rat-race produced – *greed*. And as a result of that greed, that striving to fucking spin faster in your wheel than the wheel next door, we ended up with crazy bankers and a recession that's the worst in decades.' He speaks with such a venom at this point that I think he's entirely forgotten that I used to work in the City. 'And worst of all are these reality TV shows. I mean, it's kinda funny, watching these delusional wannabes get up and croak on stage, but it's all really very sad, all these thousands of people who are driven not because they feel they have a gift, or anything to give to society, but because they just want to be rich and famous, when in fact there can only be one winner, who after climbing their big mountain of riches-and-fame dreams will release a shit single and be forgotten about in a year's time anyhow. It means we've got this whole generation who are chasing the mirages of fame and fortune and feeling suicidal that they can't get on to the cover of *Entertainment Weekly* instead of enjoying life or doing something useful or travelling.'

169

My anger cools. Luke speaks with real passion; I sense he's being sincere. This is his life manifesto, his motivation for travelling. At least, I think it is. Maybe he is still acting and I just can't see it. It strikes me then how little I actually know about him.

'So you live off a Trust Fund?' Doug asks. When Luke shakes his head, he puts on a paternal, condescending voice and says, 'You know, I'm gonna have to disagree with you, Michelangelo, on this point. God spent six days making this world before He took a break, and He made man in His own image. Clearly, He put us on this earth to work.'

'God created Eden,' Luke protests vehemently. 'Adam and Eve were in idle bliss. When they got thrown out and had to work, it was their *punishment*.'

'And I presume that when your kids grow up you're gonna shove this – this – slacker ethic down their throats?' Doug taunts him.

'My kids?' Luke cries. 'My kids are gonna grow up happy. They're gonna grow up *free*.' He breaks off, his eyes blazing, and when I touch him on the arm, he jumps. I give him a look and a little smile to remind him that we're just playing, but his whole expression is one of raging anguish. I pull away, frowning, utterly confused. Luke hit my weak spot and now his has just been exposed. He has skeletons in his closet. Maybe Jodie is one of them; maybe there are plenty more ...

And then I see her. The girl I spotted when we first sat down in the bar – the girl who I thought looked dangerously familiar. I blink in disbelief: of all the people to see, in all the places ...

I attempt to lean back into the conversation. Luke is now animatedly talking about how Italians understand the value of a siesta, the balance of play and work. But it's too late. She's already recognised me.

I see her whisper to a colleague by her side. He's tall and dark, clad in a suit that clearly cost him thousands. I don't recognise him; maybe he's my replacement at Charlton Cross. Melissa glances over again, and smirks. I feel my heart sinking. In the space of few seconds, my Luke-tinted bubble of bliss has burst and now the ugly past comes rushing in. I pray: *Please don't let her come over. Please ...*

She's coming over.

Just seeing that sneer triggers memories. I relive the pain of that day, the day I left the offices of Charlton Cross for good, and I feel a childish flare of anger. I wanted to leave all that behind me. I find myself thinking, If Fate does exist, then it can't like me very much. The omen in the temple shivers in my memory. I was happy; why did it have to do this to me? Don't I deserve happiness?

This isn't going to be fun.

Her blond hair swings as she walks; her toned legs ripple. She stands on the edge of our group. I try my best to ignore her, but Luke looks up brightly and says, 'Hi, there.'

'Hey.' She smiles and cocks her head to one side. 'Julia. Good to see you. So how *are* you doing? I don't think I was around the day you left. I mean, one day you were

171

there – and the next, your office was empty. You didn't even leave so much as a paperclip behind.'

She stares at me and I can see she's willing me to ask about Charlton Cross, to drink in my hurt. So I toss back my hair, beam a smile at her and say, 'I'm having a great time, thanks – really enjoying taking a break.'

I hear my voice ring out clear and confident. But inside, my heart is beating like mad and my stomach is twisting into knots. I feel as if I'm back at school again face to face with the nasty bully.

'Why don't you join us for a drink,' Luke begins, then breaks off as I give him a ferocious look.

'Oh, I'd *love* to,' Melissa coos. She grins at our American friends, 'I'm Melissa Crow – Julia and I used to work together.' She emphasised the *used*.

'*Julia?*' Betty looks deeply confused. 'So did you change your name to Jeanette?'

Luke and I glance at each other, aware that we've been rumbled. Suddenly he jumps to his feet, crying, 'I've just had a text from the nanny – Laurie's got a temperature. We're gonna have to head back.'

We get up, saying hasty goodbyes, Luke tugging me away sharply, me tugging back and nearly tripping over his sneakers as I throw some yen on to the table for the drinks – and then we flee. Waving weakly, I turn back one last time – to see Melissa staring after us, looking cheated of her prey. As we get into the lift, Luke starts to laugh and I go into a state of shock.

4

On the subway, Luke and I sit in silence. Then, unable to bear it any longer, I burst out: 'I lost my job.'

'*What?*'

'When I first met you, I told you I was a hedge-fund manager. I lied. I'm sorry, Luke. I did work for a firm called Charlton Cross in the City – you know, the financial district, like your Wall Street – but I don't any more. That's why I'm travelling. They fired me because I made a stupid mistake. I was just so tired – I'd been working non-stop, seven days a week and I was supposed to buy some shares for a client. I forgot to email the broker to buy them and in the meantime the stock went up fifty per cent . . . and well, with the recession, that was that. My career was over. And nobody could have been more delighted than fucking Melissa. Great.' I lean over and bury my face in my hands. I feel a sudden gush of nausea and for a terrified moment I fear I really will puke, here and now, on the subway. I hear Luke calling my name, feel him rubbing my shoulder. But I need to stay in this cocoon, find my breath, my heartbeat again. I replay the moment they told me I'd been let go: as though someone had punched me in the chest. Oh God, I think, oh God.

Luke doesn't say anything for the rest of our journey. He just keeps his hand resting on the flat of my back, a firm and comforting pressure, whilst I keep my face in my hands and suffer my mini-breakdown.

'Here we are.' Luke helps me off the train and guides me gently towards the exit.

We walk in silence to the hotel. I peek at Luke, wondering if I'm freaking him out, but he just looks anxious and then, catching my eye, smiles at me.

'Nearly there.'

He speaks with such kindness that I feel as though I just want to hug him. But I can't, because I know that if I do, I will release gallons and gallons of tears and flood the streets of Tokyo. I battle my tears ferociously, keep them coiled up in my eyes.

We pass by a group of homeless men. In Japan, even the homeless are neat and clean; their boxes sit in the subway with folded clothes and umbrellas for shelter. I try to find perspective; I tell myself how much worse my existence could be, how lucky I am not to be on the streets, but nothing can ease this pain.

Up in the hotel room, Luke sits me down on the bed

and asks, 'So, my dear Jeanette, d'you want to talk about it?'

I do, but I can't: the knot in my heart is too tight and I can't bear to unpick it. So I just shake my head numbly.

Luke strokes my cheek with the back of his hand. Then he leans in and kisses the corner of my lips. I'm slightly taken aback. I'm upset – can't he see this is inappropriate? I turn to tell him that I'm not really in the mood for this, but he silences me with a strong kiss. I find myself responding to him, reaching up and running my fingers through his thick, wavy hair. He pulls me in tighter, crushing my breasts against his chest, his long fingers tugging up my skirt. His kisses taste beautiful, flavoured with the spices of dinner, the vodka in our drinks, the colours of our adventure. He runs his finger over my knickers, teasing, his lips silent against mine, smiling when he hears my breath become ragged, his eyes glazing with passion. And I realise that although sex is the last thing I need, it is also the thing I most need. My desire is like a pill that drowns out my pain. I gasp as he pushes himself inside me, suffering a shiver of pleasure and a whimper of pain as I hear Melissa's voice cut through me once again. Luke stares down at me, his eyes cloudy, his lips bright. Then he loses control. As he rocks me to a fierce and frenzied climax, I close my eyes, losing myself in orgasm, in the relief of dark forgetting . . .

*   *   *

'So Jeanette ... how are you feeling?' Luke asks me. It's 6 a.m. We've woken early, partly from our jetlagged body clocks being confused and partly because we had more interesting things to do than sleep.

He smiles down at me, stroking back a strand of hair from my face and I smile back up at him.

'I'm feeling good – and bad,' I admit. 'I mean, it was wonderful, but I'm still a bit raw. I don't know if I'm ever going to get over losing my job.'

'But come on, Jeanette,' Luke says, 'now you can be free to have some fun!'

This time my smile is slightly pinched. I don't want to joke about this; I want him to take my pain seriously.

'Well, I'm still pretty upset,' I say at last.

'But it's not really such a big deal, is it?' And there's something in his voice that I don't like; I feel as though he's deliberately needling me.

'I happen to think it *is* a big deal,' I say. 'I mean, I invested my identity in my career, I gave so much to it. And now it's gone and eventually my money will run out and I don't know if I'll ever be able to work in the City again.'

'So?'

'*So?*' I'm flabbergasted. I was expecting him to sympathise. To agree how terrible my story was, to console me with a kiss.

'I think that you getting fired was maybe the best thing that's ever happened to you,' he says instead, with a shrug.

'What! Why? Why would you say that? So I can – I don't know – stay at home like some housewife and have kids?' I cry. Then I catch myself, realising I'm echoing elements of our fake couple conversation from last night. I realise I'm testing him: I want to know how many words Luke spoke in jest.

'No,' Luke says. 'Hey, no need to get feminist with me – I'm not the type who would ever dictate how a girl should live her life. I mean, that must be obvious by now.' He sounds slightly injured and in my selfish state of grief I can't help silently objecting, *Hey*, I'm *the one who's upset*.

'I think it's great because you've escaped the rat-race,' he goes on. 'It diminishes life – it turns it into a survival of the fittest, which means that whatever you gain, someone else loses out.' He speaks earnestly. 'Getting caught in the rat-race leads to a dull existence. I think it screws up your heart because you're constantly looking out to see who's coming up behind you. And let's face it, there's always someone better than you, so you're always going to be that little bit jealous, that little bit unsatisfied. It's just a capitalist noose around your neck. Fuck – you have been released from all that bullshit, Julia. You're free. That's Fate.'

'It's not Fate,' I cry savagely, more tears spilling from my eyes. 'It's all my fault. I wasn't good enough, I got tired, I made mistakes . . .'

'And yet here you are now,' says Luke. 'You're not in

an office. You escaped and came to Italy and Sicily and Tokyo.'

'Because my friend Reece talked me into it. Because of the fucking credit crunch. Sorry, I shouldn't be swearing at you. But believe you me, if forty per cent of the world's wealth hadn't been wiped out, I would gladly be back in a bank right now.'

'Rather than here with me?'

I'm so inflamed that I hear myself snapping: 'Yes!'

Luke throws back the covers and cold air bites me. He gets up and yanks on a T-shirt and jeans.

'Where are you going?' I cry.

'I just wanna go take a stroll round the fish-market. They open real early. It was something I always wanted to do if I came to Tokyo.'

Then he tugs on his trainers and leaves.

Now I really do start to cry. I've got a feeling Luke and I just rowed. Our first row. And it seems so utterly *unfair*. I was confiding in Luke. I was pouring out my soul and he got angry just because I can't agree with his hippie philosophy. I mean, if we all lived like Luke, I carry on arguing in my head, how would the world survive? They'd be no industry; nobody making the guitars he plays; nobody cooking the noodles we've eaten; nobody driving the subway trains; running hotels. No fish-market. Competition drives people forward. It triggers progress, and progress is evolution. If we all stepped out of the workplace, we'd all just starve and die. Only a very few, a privileged few, are lucky enough to have the luxury of free choices. Maybe Luke is rich; maybe he does have a Trust Fund and that's why he can nurture these impractical ideals.

But as I lie in bed and sob, I hear a voice inside me admitting that Luke's not entirely wrong and I'm not entirely right. I recall bad memories from my working life. When I got so exhausted from overwork that I couldn't sleep any more, and I would lie awake in bed with a brain like a wind-up toy that just kept going round and round. When I used to see my grey face in the bathroom mirror, exhaustion sagging into my skin. When the office called me at two in the morning and told me they needed me to come in. It wasn't all perfect.

When Luke returns, I sit up, looking to see if he's still cross. But he seems chippy. In fact, it's as though we never rowed. He sits down on the bed and enthuses about how amazing the fish-market was. Then he puts his hand on the small of my back and says: 'So, are you feeling better?'

'Yeah. Yes.' I smile and lean in, resting my head against his shoulder.

There is a silence and neither of us is quite sure what to say. So, out of nervousness, I change the subject. I rather randomly tell Luke about how when we first met and he pretended to be twenty-five, I thought he thought I was terribly old. I tell him it nearly became a complex;

that I was convinced I was past it. He starts laughing, saying, 'Hey, Julia, you told me you got freaked but I didn't realise it was *that* bad.' And then he pulls me towards him and gives me a kiss, teasing: 'You kiss real good for an old lady.'

I punch him and he grabs me, laughing, and kisses me again.

And then takes off his T-shirt.

I guess we're not going to continue our discussion, which is probably a good thing. I feel hollowed out with tears. I feel ready to forget again ...

This time our lovemaking is much slower and more sensuous. Luke guides me into all sorts of positions. I feel wave after wave of pleasure lapping over me. In between breathless kisses, the thought shivers across my mind: Wow, do Ciaran and Reece do this? And: Wow, this is just so heavenly, why did I stay celibate for all those years? And: It should have been this way with Ciaran but now I'm glad I'm experiencing this with Luke. And: He really is the most fantastic lover. And: This is bliss. Bliss. Bliss ...

At one point, when he's deep inside me and my head is thrown back, throat arched, Luke narrows his eyes and demands: 'So right now, would you rather be here with me or back in the office?'

When I beg him to continue, he smiles triumphantly, as though he's scored a victory for anti-capitalists everywhere.

5

The following evening, Luke and I go to the Kabuki theatre in Ginza. The building is over a century old, a novelty in a city of post-high-tech glass and neon. We pay for headphones to hear a crisp English accent translating the Japanese being barked out on stage. They perform a traditional Japanese play called *Na Mo Takashi Homare No Ishikiri*, which translates as *Stone-cutting Kajiwara*. It's about a Taira General who is asked to test the sharpness of a sword by cutting two human beings in half; he deliberately makes it fail in order to keep it from falling into the hands of his clan.

The actors' costumes are extraordinary, rich colours in sculpted silk; their faces are white and painted with thick, clownish make-up. Luke keeps making me laugh by lifting up my headphones and mimicking the actor's hoarse, emphatic barks under his breath.

Eventually, however, the play soars to a profound ending

and we both sit in electrified silence as the General finally demonstrates the true power of the sword by cutting a large stone basin in two.

That evening, Luke's lucky coin comes into play again. We end up in the back room of a bar, playing poker with some dubious-looking guys. It turns out they're from Vietnam, over here on a trip themselves – though they don't specify the business they're involved in. They offer us a glass of snake blood each.

'Julia's not gonna wanna do that,' Luke laughs.

'Hey,' I cry, feeling zinged up. 'I'll do it.'

I regret it, of course. The drinks come in small glasses that look as though they ought to hold sherry; the liquid gleams a violent red, as though the snake's soul still winds through it. I take one sip and gag. The Vietnamese laugh and clap. I try another sip and spit it out, to their great amusement.

'So we'll buy three bottles and take them home with us, right?' Luke laughs.

We lose at poker, but thankfully we escape before Luke is cleaned out of the little money he has.

Back at the hotel, we make love in the shower, the steam curling around us, the water splashing joyfully on to our skin, into the 'O' of my mouth as I shake with pleasure. Luke nuzzles his nose against mine and whispers that this is one of the most special moments he's ever experienced.

We don't want to go to sleep – we've so much to talk

about. We've also got the munchies. Bundling coats over our bare bodies we hurry down to the local store for some midnight-feast ammunition. We end up with some bizarre snacks; back in our room we share a pot of Häagen-Dazs Sencha grade Green Tea ice cream, which is as bright as grass and tastes strangely addictive. We discuss films, and politics, and women's rights; we share childhood memories, stories behind scars, thoughts on life, the universe and everything.

'I don't believe in this reincarnation thing,' says Luke at one point. 'I think we have one life and that's it.'

'Well, I heard that reincarnation was once in the Bible, then they took it out, because they felt we'd all just sit back and do sod all and wait for our next life.'

'Well, that's not something you'd ever have a problem with, is it?' Luke teases me. 'I mean, I just hope I can cure you of your workaholism.'

'I think I'm doing pretty well.' I grin. 'But I believe reincarnation could happen. I mean, life goes through cycles. The seasons change; summer's beauty dies into winter.'

'*Nature's first green is gold, her hardest hue to hold,*' Luke quotes.

'Oh wow – that is one of my favourite poems. Do you like Robert Frost too?'

'I love him.'

We smile at each other with the thrilled recognition of compatibility. It feels like we've been doing this all day: finding patterns. We've both had the same recurring dream.

We both adore the song 'Glory Box' by Portishead and the film *Dangerous Liaisons*, and we both think Ang Lee is the greatest director alive. We're so different, but we're so alike.

Luke opens another tub of ice cream: English Milk Tea. He offers me a spoon and I lick it; I see his eyes flash to my tongue.

'I wish we had these flavours back home,' I say. Then, carefully: 'So what about exes?' I hesitate. 'Any significant ones there?'

'I guess Jodie was the closest to a real relationship,' Luke muses, looking gloomy. 'She still wants me back. But ... it just wouldn't work.'

Jodie. We've been having so much fun I'd actually forgotten about her. Now I feel a rush of insecurity.

'Because you don't want to settle down?' I ask.

'Maybe I would settle down, if I found the right one.' Luke drizzles some ice cream on my shoulder, then licks it off. 'Yummy. You know,' he says with a grin, 'it tastes so much better on you. Your skin is like the salty sauce.'

'Sweet and sour?' I giggle as he pushes me back on to the bed.

'Uh huh ...'

The next morning we go to the fish-market together. Then we share noodles and walk through the beautiful gardens of the Emperor's Palace in the centre of Tokyo.

In the evenings we economise by buying a salad and

sharing. We walk up the hills at Shibuya, gazing at the famous love hotels, where you can book a room for an hour at a time.

Then we go clubbing and end up chatting to a bunch of middle-aged Brits who work in Japan and we all dance to Kylie under blue neon. We finally leave at 3 a.m., joining the taxi queue. Luke catches my arm and says, 'I wish we could do this always – just me and you, going from country to country.'

'We'd run out of money pretty quick,' I say. The moment the words are out of my mouth, I wince. There's me being Ms Practical again. Ms Boring. And I realise that I had to come out with it, because I can't quite get used to this new me who drinks snake blood and sashays to Kylie at some random club in Roppongi. The Puritan in me keeps looking on in bemusement, asking, 'What happened to you, Julia?'

In the back of the taxi, I reach for Luke's hand and squeeze it.

'It would be amazing,' I agree.

We smile at each other and I see the driver watching us in his mirror, a wistful look on his face.

The next morning, when Luke is out at the fish-market again (I need a lie-in – he has so much energy!) I drag myself up and call up Reece. I rave proudly about how wonderful Luke is and she tells me he sounds so amazing she feels jealous! I am tempted to ask her about the pregnancy test, but bite my lip. Reece will tell me when she's good and ready, though I feel a tiny bit hurt that she hasn't brought it up. We are best friends and normally we share everything.

Still, it's wonderful to talk to her and we gossip and laugh and I say goodbye full of love for my dear friend.

Then I call Mum in the US. I go on and on about Luke. She sounds very taken aback; we don't speak that often and I rarely mention men. Then, in a burst of excitement, I tell her I want her to meet him. I haven't asked Luke yet, but I want him to follow me on to America to help me fulfil number five in my list of *Ten Things*. Of course, I haven't even told him there is a list, but I know he'll love the idea.

When Luke comes back in, he finds me staring at the picture I keep tucked into my suitcase: a man with chestnut hair, squinting in the sun, his mouth curved into a crooked smile.

'Is he my rival?' Luke asks, seeing my pensive face.

'He's my father,' I tell him. He blinks and I shrug. 'I don't really know him, to be honest. I haven't seen him since I was little.'

'Would you like to see him again?'

'Yes. But, well ... I'm still close to my mum. I mean, she brought me up ... she's in the US now, as a matter of fact – in New York. She married this dashing American banker and moved out there.' I bite my lip, suddenly feeling nervous.

I was so jazzed up on the phone I forgot to worry about what Luke would think if I ask him to meet my mother. Will he think I am a bit pushy? He seems to really like me, but this is all so new to me, and I'm not quite sure of the rules of relationships. I can't help feeling a little afraid that I've got something so good I might just blow it.

'What about you?' I ask. 'How are your parents?'

'Uh, they're . . .' To my surprise, Luke shudders. 'Let's not go there,' he says, his face darkening. Then he makes an effort to lighten up. 'You know, I have a *great* plan for an adventure. Let's just take off today and hit Mount Fuji. I was talking to someone about it at the fish-market and they said it's awesome. Plus, they have these famous hot springs there that'll cure all illnesses.'

'Um . . .' For a moment I'm flummoxed. I want to dig my heels in and insist that I wanted to do more things in Tokyo. Then I realise I'm just being boring and control-freaky. I need to just let go and surrender to Luke's glorious whim. So I look up at him and grin, and tell him it sounds like a great idea.

And then, on the way to Mount Fuji, everything changes.

We're both a tiny bit fraught from having packed so quickly and dashed for the train in order to get the bus in time, after having made a last-minute reservation over the phone. Luke's mobile has kept shrilling and he's kept ignoring it. Now, finally, he pulls it out of his pocket. And I see Jodie flashing up on his screen.

'I've, ah, gotta take this,' Luke says. He clicks open his phone and says, 'Hi.' And I swear I've never heard someone load so much guilt into one syllable. He presses his lips together, fingering the fading bruise on his cheek.

I stare out of the window, pretending not to listen. The weird thing is, I can actually *hear* Jodie and she's *screaming*. It sounds as though she's having hysterics. I feel disturbed for Luke and sorry for her.

Luke just says, 'Yeah,' and 'I'm sorry,' a lot in a low voice. Finally, he cuts in and says, 'Look, now is a pretty bad time, I'll call you later.'

He clicks off his phone, swallowing.

I sit in nervous tension. Is Luke a modern-day Mr Rochester? Does he have some madwoman hiding away in his attic back home?

We stay silent for the rest of the journey. I stare out of the window as the sharp lines of the city soften into rugged countryside. At Mount Fuji, we're thankfully distracted from our problems with a hunt for the guest-house. Finally, we obtain directions from a local shop and follow a leafy path round to a small, wooden lodge.

Indoors, signs advise us to place our shoes in wooden slots and pull on some slippers. We're given a key and taken through a communal lounge up to our bedroom. It's really rather like a homely youth hostel, with futons on the floor and a wardrobe of cosy blankets, and a sink in the hallway that everyone shares.

Luke drops his guitar and rucksack and gives a feline

stretch. I sit down on the bed. He sits down beside me and opens his mouth to speak . . . when his mobile rings.

We sit and wait as the rings echo round the room.

Silence. The song of an unknown Japanese bird.

Then Luke gets up abruptly. 'I'm gonna take a shower.' He departs, carrying his towels *and his mobile.*

I remain on the bed, feeling numb. It's so quiet here, except for the sweet birdsong and the buzzing of cicadas; I long for the distraction of city noise, the cacophony of traffic. Trying to ignore the leaden feeling inside me, I unpack, putting my clothes into the wooden slots in the wardrobe. It's then that I notice Luke's passport.

He's left it out again. Luke mentioned that he's lost his passport several times in his whirlwind of adventure, so the first thing he always does in a new hotel is to take it out and put it on the top of the nearest cabinet.

I pick it up and stare at his photo as though I wish it could speak and tell me who he really is. Then I flip back through the pages, decorated red and green with stamp after stamp. I reach the latest stamp for Japan and flip back, frowning. Hang on – there's no stamp here for Hong Kong. In fact, according to this passport, on 9 June – the day Luke left Venice – he entered the United Kingdom.

Oh my God.

Part of it makes sense. Luke is such an enthusiastic traveller – if he'd really been to Hong Kong, he would have been spilling over with anecdotes. In fact, he's hardly even mentioned the place.

So what the hell was he doing in England? And why did he lie about it to me?

We go out to get some dinner and the atmosphere worsens. We talk in terse sentences about the weather, make plans to travel up Fuji early tomorrow morning. A culinary novelty distracts us: black eggs. They're cooked in sulphurous water so that the shells are stained black, but the eggs are white inside and taste delicious. But I'm too anxious to digest a thing. My stomach churns as though I've eaten rocks. Just like the old days in the City, when my nutritionist told me I was suffering from too much acid. I thought my relaxing travels had sorted this stomach problem, but now it seems to be back with a vengeance.

As we walk back to the guest-house, the pain tears away at me. I feel too ashamed to tell Luke he's given me a stomach-ache, so I pretend I have a stitch. We pause in a garden where there are Shinto statues decorated with little amulets and bells. The men look other-worldly; I gaze into their weathered stone faces and pray silently for knowledge, for understanding.

'They say in Shinto-ism that there are no absolutes,' Luke says softly. 'There's no absolute right or wrong, nobody's perfect. Humans are fundamentally good, it's just that they can be misguided by evil spirits . . .'

I catch a glimpse of Luke's face, shadowed green in the glade, and his expression is one of tortured sadness. My heart twists. *Just what is wrong with him?*

6

Back at the guest-house, I decide I can't wait any longer. I have to confront Luke.

'Why don't we go to the hot springs bath?' I ask.

'I don't know, I'm kinda tired,' Luke says with an uncharacteristic lack of enthusiasm.

'Come on, it'll be relaxing.' I rub his shoulder but he flinches and I recoil in hurt shock.

Seeing this, he says hastily, 'Hey, sure, let's go for it,' and picks up his towel.

Downstairs, we slide open the wooden door to the hot springs and put up the Occupied sign so that we can have complete privacy. *Caution*, the signs warn us. *If you experience any dizziness during the bath, then please exit immediately*. We strip our clothes off, leaving them in the wooden basket, and tiptoe forward. I suddenly feel strange being so naked with him in such a matter-of-fact way, without the romance of sheets and darkness.

The hot springs have been harnessed into a small marble bath, its steps decorated with elegant bamboo shoots and flowers. Clouds of steam float about us, ethereal and dreamy. We sit on the edge of the bath, dipping our legs in.

'God, it's actually pretty hot,' Luke says.

'Luke,' I say gently. 'Tell me about Jodie. Tell me everything.'

Luke falls silent. I stare into the steam and pray desperately, *Oh God, if You are out there and You are listening to me, please make him tell me the truth.* When I look up, I see that Luke's shoulders are shaking. For one utterly indignant moment, I think he's laughing at me. Then I realise with a jolt of shock that he's *crying*.

'Luke, are you OK?' I put my arm around him.

'Sorry.' He smudges his fingers against his nose, collecting tears. 'I'm sorry,' he hiccups, draws in a breath. 'It's just ... Jodie – I miss her. I don't want to upset you, but I do miss her.'

I feel sick. As though a vat of green acidic jealousy has just been tipped into my stomach. At the same time, I feel compassion towards him. I ruffle my fingers through the 'v' of hair at the nape of his neck and say softly, 'Tell me about her.'

'I let her down. I let her down real bad.' Luke claps his hands over his face, bends forward, and lets out a groan. I wait, trembling but patient. He turns to face me, his eyes bloodshot, his face softened and saddened with tears. 'We were meant to get married.'

I let out a sharp breath. 'So what happened?'

'I just couldn't go through with it. The thing is,' Luke is gushing now, as though he's been longing to release these words for days, 'I always felt I was never cut out for the marriage/kids thing. I just want to be free. After I left college, it became a cycle – I'd get a job in a bar, go travelling, meet a girl, enjoy a holiday fling . . . and then they'd want more. They'd want me to take them home with them. But I couldn't, so I'd leave early one morning without saying goodbye. In fact, it got to the point where I was so nervy that I'd pre-empt them, leave before they had a chance to get heavy, just steal off and leave them not knowing who I really was, where I'd gone. It became a habit. A bad habit.'

My mind is whirling, trying to comprehend this new reality. Is Luke pre-empting himself now – forewarning me that I'll wake up tomorrow morning and find that his rucksack has vanished? I frantically analyse the last week, wondering if I've put pressure on him, been too possessive, made assumptions. But all I can remember is Luke's words as we got into a taxi: *I wish we could do this always – just me and you, going from country to country.* That came from *him*, not me.

And what about this girl he was meant to marry?

'Look,' I say, 'I haven't tried to be that way with you, have I?'

'Hey.' Luke puts a damp hand on mine. Through the whorls of steam, I see his brown eyes widen. 'I'm not about to walk out on you, you're great.'

'So . . .' I frown. Is Luke just trying to appease me? What happened?'

'Jodie was a girl I met in Belgium. In the main square in Brussels – the Gran'Place – late at night. Everyone was hanging out, chatting, laughing, drinking.' A fond look mists over his eyes. 'She told me she was from England, from a place called Essex. She wore white jeans and had pretty blond hair and pink lipstick and a totally nutty laugh. She was really down to earth and we hit it off right away. She was a traveller like me, only she'd come to Belgium on a hen night. She was just looking for some fun. We shared one night of passion, and somewhere along the way the condom got lost in the sheets, but we were too pissed to really register that. And after the hen night and her friend's wedding, she came travelling with me to Singapore. We were gonna travel the world . . . and then I found out that she was pregnant.'

'Pregnant?' Another volcanic lurch of shock inside me. *Pregnant?*

'Yes. So I headed with her to England. I figured it was Fate. I had tossed the coin just before I met her and it'd told me to go to the square. And hell, it was the only time in my life I'd ever had sex without a condom, so it had to be predestined. I thought I had to learn some kinda lesson, that Fate was telling me it was time I grew up, settled down. And so I thought I should marry her.'

'Oh right,' I say, unable to keep the anger out of my

voice. 'And don't tell me, before you proposed, you tossed your lucky coin in order to decide?'

Luke looks awkward.

'How stupid can you be, basing your life on a coin!' I cry. 'You know, Luke – this is all because you don't want to take responsibility. You don't want to face the consequences of your actions, so you let a coin do it. But you're the one who creates the options and who tosses it. You probably influence the result. It's not Fate – it's *you.*'

'You're wrong, Julia.' Luke defends himself. 'You speak of responsibility – that's exactly why I stayed with her. I felt I was doing the right thing. I moved in with her and I got a job. In order for me to stay in the UK and help look after our kid, we would actually have to get married anyway. But every night – every night I would wake up with a silent screaming inside of me. I kept seeing her putting that ring on my finger, and it felt as though she was going to lock me in chains forever. The wedding day loomed closer and closer ... and closer. Her family kept visiting – she had so many fucking Essex cousins, you wouldn't believe it – about seventy of them! And I just couldn't back out.'

My heart is beating very fast. My mouth is dry. I'm terrified that Luke is about to reveal that he tossed his coin and it told them that she ought to have an abortion. And I know that if those words come out of his mouth, I'm going to fall out of love with him in that instant.

'So ... did you end your engagement?' I ask, hearing my voice become small and trembling.

'No – no, I couldn't.' Luke sighs. 'I mean, she was waking up every morning with morning sickness – I had to clean up her puke. She was such a lovely girl – so straightforward, and simple, and so sweet. I just couldn't do that to her. I knew she'd never understand.'

'Go on.'

'Well, I kept on trying to delay the wedding, making excuses which made it all the worse. We ended up with a date the month before she was due to give birth. The night before our wedding was supposed to be my stag night. But I couldn't face it. I told Jodie I was meeting with some old buddies from the US, but I spent the night on my own in some bar in London. Later on, I wandered through the graveyard at Highgate, and found the grave of Karl Marx, all beautifully lit up in the moonlight. Visiting that place was something I'd always wanted to tick off on my travels. And I felt that all the other places I'd planned to see were lost to me. It felt as though my life was over.

'I woke up on the morning of our wedding fully sober. But a wisdom had come to me during the night. I knew that sooner or later, I would end up leaving Jodie, whether it'd be next month or next year. Marrying her would only make things worse, 'cos then we'd have to divorce. So I left the house in my suit, with my rucksack all packed, and my guitar, and my passport – and I got a taxi to Stansted Airport. In the bathroom, I changed outta my suit and pulled on my good old jeans – and I felt I wanted to cry with relief. I left my suit there in the cubicle, all crumpled up and spread over the seat, 'cos even though it had cost me a fucking thousand pounds I never wanted to see it again. And then I got on to a random plane. A plane to Venice.'

'And then you ended up sitting next to me!' I cry in horror. 'And you made up all that crap about leaving England because an eleven year old had mugged you.'

'No, that bit was true,' Luke protests. He laughs nervously, then stops when he sees my face.

Suddenly it all makes sense. All those jigsaw pieces of warning that were there all along – only I refused to let them form a puzzle.

Luke's strange discomfort at the Italian wedding.

That tender but sheepish look on his face when we shared our first kiss in Venice, when he said we shouldn't rush into sleeping together. At the time, I thought he was being a gentleman; now I realise that the ghost of Jodie was there in the bed with us.

Those impassioned words he spoke when we played a game with the Texan couple in the Park Hyatt Hotel bar, about the sins of the rat-race.

And the game itself – as though it flowered from his guilt, as though he was testing out what it might feel like to be in a couple, playing his role with nervous regret, knowing what he'd lost.

And lastly, that big bruise on his face. Clearly Jodie, or one of her family, got mad at him. And who could blame them?

'So . . .' Luke's hand folds over mine. 'Have you forgiven me? Are we OK?'

Are we OK?

It's such a ludicrous question that I want to laugh. But then the situation is so overwhelming, neither of us are sure what to say – or do – next.

Finally, I manage to look Luke in the eye. 'So what now?' I ask shakily. 'Jodie calls you sixty times a day and you just ignore her? I mean, have you even *seen* your baby? Do you know its sex, its name?'

'Of course I do!' Luke cries defensively. 'After Venice, I went back and faced the music. It turned out that our honeymoon would never have happened anyway, 'cos a few hours after I fled, she went into labour, about three weeks early.'

I try to imagine how it must have been for Jodie, to have experienced that dizzying mixture of grief and euphoria: suffering the urge to curl up and die just as new life springs from your body. And despite my own pain, I feel deep compassion for Jodie. If she were here now, I'd give her a hug and tell her how bad I feel for being involved in this mess.

'I saw the baby,' Luke goes on, his voice ragged with emotion. 'My son. When I got back, I found that Jodie hadn't named him. She said she couldn't do that without me and she'd been praying I'd come back. So I chose Winston, after my favourite book, *1984*.'

'She still loves you,' I reply.

'I know she loves me,' Luke cries, 'and I love her! And I love Winston. I mean, when I saw him, I thought . . . I thought I was gonna feel a revulsion, knowing he was the cause of all my problems . . . but I just felt this amazing feeling of wonder.' His voice softens. 'He has exactly the same colour eyes as me.'

'Go back to her,' I insist. 'Go back and be with them.'

Luke drops his eyes and shakes his head sadly. 'I can't. I just can't.'

'And when you went back to Jodie, how did she feel when you said you were leaving again – coming out to Tokyo to meet me?' My voice is barbed; I already know that Luke hasn't said a thing about me to Jodie. I'm not surprised when he hangs his head, though my disgust only increases.

'She told me to go,' he says, sounding more and more desperate. 'She said she wanted me to be happy and free, and that if I needed to go and travel, I should do it. As long as I came back to her.'

'She's too good for you.'

'I know.' Luke emits a bitter laugh and fingers the circle on his cheek, where his bruise is now a ghostly crescent, a memory of pain. 'She was OK about me going, but her dad wasn't.'

'Well, I think you deserved that.'

'Yes.'

'So . . .' I blow out my breath. My chest is simply bursting with questions: *So what do you feel about me? Was I just an indulgence? Did you see Jodie in your mind when you made love to me?* But there's no point in asking them because the answers will only stab my heart. 'Look, I've booked a flight to the US. I'll be heading there in a few days' time. So you can be rid of me then and go back to Jodie.'

Luke's expression is tormented.

'I don't know if I want to go back,' he bursts out. 'I like you!'

I try to pull my hand away from Luke's but he clings on, his palm caressing mine warmly, and I feel a shivery weakness inside. I remember our lovemaking. Sharing ice cream. Dancing together. Whispering our dreams to each other. Colluding as we pretended to be Jeanette and Michelangelo. Luke breathed life into romantic fantasies that I've nurtured since I was a teenager ...

In a moment of weakness, I say, 'You could come to New York with me. My mum says she'd like to meet you.'

I see panic flit across Luke's eyes, although he conceals it quickly. And I see the future. Due to Luke's selfish insistence on living in the present, I would end up like Jodie. Maybe not pregnant, but a fool. I'd end up yearning for what we had, clinging on in the hope that we can create it. But we can't. Tonight we've both stepped out of Eden. There's no going back to that sweet innocence.

I pull my hand away from his and pad out quickly, grabbing my clothes.

Later, Luke comes into the dark bedroom. I've been lying in bed for the last few hours, fully dressed and hunched up in a foetal ball; God knows where he has been. I hear the covers lift up. I cringe and yearn for him simultaneously. I feel him caress the back of my neck gently, say my name, but I pretend to be asleep. The pretence lasts all night.

The next morning, when Luke leaves for the shower, I grab my bag, dump a spray of notes on the bed and run away from the hostel. At the bus-stop I stand and watch the dawn rising behind Mount Fuji. Trees, skeletal, beautiful, flame into scarlet silhouettes. My hands shake; I'm scared Luke will come chasing after me. The bus judders up and I feel a wrench as I get on; a voice inside me screams to go back, go back, kiss him, make up, but I force it away and push myself down on to a seat.

As the bus pulls away, I see him in his T-shirt and shorts, laces tangling, running up. His eyes scour the bus but they miss me. The bus accelerates and he never sees me, never sees the tears in my eyes, my trembling wave: *goodbye forever*.

7

It's then that I make a massive mistake. I go back to Tokyo, to the same hotel we first stayed at in Ginza. I'm too fraught to go travelling or hotel-hunting; without really thinking about it, I just head there on autopilot.

But, of course, the moment I pass over my credit card to check in, I feel like clawing it back. I can still hear the echo of his laughter in the lobby. In the lift, when I look into the mirror I find it has preserved a memory of his smile.

In my hotel room I call up the airline and arrange to change my flight. They advise me that if I want to bring it forward to tomorrow morning I'll have to fly to Chicago and change to NYC. I tell them it's not a problem.

Then I sit on my bed for five still minutes. They feel like five hours.

My loneliness fills the room. Everything seems to droop and weep as though infused with my emotion; I swear if

202

I turned the TV on I would hear crying. I sit on my bed and listen to the sounds of the five hundred odd guests in the hotel, small pinballs of noise that ricochet down rooms and corridors: footsteps, doors slamming, showers hissing, people discussing dinner, people arguing, a child screaming, an orgasm peaking, an illicit cigarette being smoked from a window. It sounds as though everyone in this hotel has someone – lover, friend, partner, father, child – except for me. I get up, pick up my handbag, slam the door and head down the corridor.

Outside, I wander through the streets feeling afraid. I remind myself that Japan has one of the lowest crime rates in the world. On the flipside, I don't know any Japanese; with Luke, we were united in our linguistic ignorance, we shared our confusion of street signs and maps, constantly looking out for each other.

But Luke belongs to someone else . . . someone else . . . someone else . . .

I force myself on to the subway. When I was with Luke, I would have got into any carriage but now I'm careful to pick the pink, Women Only one. I'm about to send Reece a text on my mobile when I remember Luke mentioning that mobiles aren't allowed on trains. Does this apply to texts too? I shove my mobile in my bag, folding my arms uncomfortably.

I get off the subway at Akihabara. This was somewhere I wanted to tick off before I headed to the US to see Mum. But my footsteps drag on the pavements. In my hotel room, I was desperate to get out. Now I'm out I just want to be back there, crying my eyes out.

Akihabara is the electronics shopping capital of the world. I walk through streets flashing neon and techno screens. Shop windows are packed with manga comics; signs and stands sprawl on to the pavement. My head and heart are still pounding to make sense of what's happened. Something inside me wants to assign blame. I flip from declaring that Luke is a total lying bastard to feeling that I was simply naïve, idealistic, stupid.

I tell myself that it's not enough to just observe Akihabara. I want to breathe in this place and feel it beat in my heart. I want to feel I can be an adventurer without Luke, that my newfound spirit wasn't just an illusion created by his dazzle. I go into a shop that looks as though it's selling costumes. Immediately, I feel like backing out. It's full of tiny black skirts and white blouses – what is this Japanese obsession with schoolgirls? I pick up a manga comic and flick through it. I follow a narrative for a few pages about a sexy schoolgirl who ends up getting raped. Feeling appalled, I make a swift exit.

As I stand on the street, I can feel the energy of the city thrumming through me. I want to curl into a ball and sob. I want Reece here to give me a hug. I want Ciaran to make his trusty cup of Earl Grey. I even want my mum with me, even though I know she'll just tell me that I was an idiot and all men are crap.

I walk on in a zombie daze and find myself in another

shop. It's full of trinkets, dozens of key-rings, *Hello Kitty* paraphernalia. Then I do a double-take when I see a row of small cages containing giant beetles. I stare at them with a curious mixture of attraction and revulsion. I wonder if they're a delicacy to be eaten with noodles.

'I hear that teen boys like keeping these guys as pets,' a voice with a New Zealand accent informs me.

I turn and see a guy grinning at me. He's in his forties, with thinning dark hair and an ugly, simian face. He's wearing jeans and his wooden beads hang over a purple and green tie-dye T-shirt. His smile is wry and his eyes look kind.

'I suppose they're less high maintenance than a dog,' I say.

I end up chatting to the guy, who introduces himself to me as Dave. He says he's on the backpacker trail; he's made friends with a bunch of other tourists and they're all planning to do karaoke tonight so would I like to come?

It's only when we've caught the subway to Asakusa and I'm climbing the stairs to his flat that I feel dread twisting my stomach. I realise I said 'yes' to stick up two fingers at Luke and show I could have crazy fun without him.

But now I'm scared. I have no idea who the hell this guy is. He knocks on the door, telling me he's left his bloody key inside but his flatmate has already got a little party going. I hear footsteps, a slam. He grins at me and

I become convinced it's a leer. My hands are clenched at my sides, my palms oozing sweat. Every part of me is poised to run if the door opens to reveal a gang of knife-wielding rapists ...

And then the door opens and I enter a room of laughing, happy people. Dave is clearly popular, for he's greeted with smiles, hugs and kisses. Everyone accepts me immediately, as though it's normal for a stranger to become part of their gang. Their warmth feels like a shawl around my body, a relief from my painful loneliness.

Dave's apartment is a curious mixture of East and West; he's superimposed his colourful personality over the minimalism of his cool metal and black leather furniture, big bright tie-dye scarves draped everywhere like exploding flowers.

I'm introduced to Freda, a German girl with pink hair, to Alberto, an Italian boy, to Oz, a handsome Turk. I end up chatting to Markus, a German in his late twenties with glasses and spots on his high, sculpted cheekbones, about the lack of crime in Japan compared with the West. It's a random, drunken conversation and he argues vehemently.

'Of course, let's not forget the *yakuza* – the Japanese have organised crime here as you get anywhere. But even so, there is a striking lack of street crime, and I put it down to a mixture of things – their religion, their literacy, their inherent self-control, the way they channel their death drive into manga and leave it there. So you can't really argue that art and film and video games cause crime as we do in the West . . .'

For a few brief minutes I argue back and Luke is forgotten. And then I remember, and the pain hits me all over again.

It's becoming hot in the apartment, breaths mingling with the sweet thickness of weed smoke, so it's a relief when we all troop out. The six of us share a cab and head for Shinjuku – the place where Luke and I wandered through the streets together, drunk on romance.

I have spent the last ten years avoiding karaoke at my office Christmas parties. I was so po-faced and serious that nobody dared to drag me up on stage. They'd be shocked if they could see me now, standing in a bar, Freda's arm slung affectionately around me, singing a Take That song.

The room blurs before me. People drinking, laughing, talking. I hear myself singing but it's as though I'm floating above it all, looking down on myself. My mind is still in the past, analysing every scene I shared with Luke, holding memories up to the light as though searching for water-marks of hurt or betrayal.

In the shower: did he really mean it when he told me I was so sexy?

In the back of the taxi: why did he say he wanted to travel the world with me when he knew he was with someone else? Was it just a line? Or did he mean it?

And that bloody lucky coin. Well, back in Venice, it

did tell me not to kiss him. I really should have listened to it.

Tears stream down my face. Freda seems to feel it's all part of the experience of singing 'Unchained Melody', for she smiles, pats me on the back and we carry on.

I step down from the stage and go to the bar, avoiding the group, needing a moment to myself. I get a drink and take out my mobile. I can't help it; I find myself scrolling back through the pictures stored on my phone. Here's my favourite. Luke is standing outside the temple, holding up his fingers in a 'peace' sign, a big goofy smile on his face. He looks so boyish and innocent; you could never have guessed, from looking at him, that he'd be capable of inflicting such lethal heartbreak.

Suddenly I become conscious that Dave is peering over my shoulder. When I start, he grins at me, waving his bottle of beer, his eyes bloodshot.

'I know that guy,' he says. 'Luke DeAntiquis. He's a great bloke, isn't he? A real dude.'

'It can't be the same Luke,' I say, feeling spooked.

'It's gotta be – I'd recognise that Bob Marley T-shirt any day! He loved it so much in India, he used to wear it until he stank and I was arm-wrestling him to go wash it.'

'But that can't be possible.'

'Hey, the backpacking circuit is quite small, so even though we're making our way across the world we tend to end up in the same places, the same clichéd tourist spots. So over a period of a year, you'll definitely bump into the same people twice – the first time that happened to me, I was amazed at the kismet of it – but now it just seems logical, commonplace. I met Luke in Bali, playing his guitar on a beach. A very interesting guy.'

I tell myself that I don't need or want to know anything more about Luke. The spooked voice inside me is even trying to persuade me that it's all a set-up, that Luke has somehow sent this guy over to act as an amorous defence lawyer for him. But that's impossible. The irony of my situation strikes me: I run halfway across Japan with the intention of forgetting Luke for ever, then the one random guy I bump into ends up talking about him.

I suppose Luke would call this moment Fate.

Then I tune into what Dave is saying, realising that it's something significant: '. . . I mean, his dad is one of the richest oil barons in America.'

'*What!*'

'I know – he keeps it really quiet, doesn't he? And he walks around with his ripped jeans and his bashed-up guitar. His dad wanted to give Luke his fortune, pass over the business to him. So Luke grows up this only child, this well-behaved boy who gets all A grades – and then all of a sudden in his early twenties he just flips out, gets on a plane, leaves it all behind him and goes AWOL. He's been bumming around and courting trouble ever since.'

I stare into my drink, digesting Dave's revelation. He mistakes my silence for disinterest and, changing the subject, starts chatting about the amazing Buddhist wedding he saw yesterday. I suddenly lean over and give Dave an almighty hug. He tenses in surprise, then hugs me back. As we pull apart, I wish I could find the words to explain that I've found redemption in his story, a glimmer of insight into my heartbreak. Since Fuji, I've been busy imagining Luke as some sort of women-hating demon. Now I realise this is the mistake I made from the very start. Back then I thought Luke was an Angel of Adventure, with wings strung from guitar strings, his lucky coin kissed by Divine Providence. In fact, he's neither of the two. I've superimposed extremes on to him. He's just human. Charming, sweet, lovable. Irresponsible, boyish, troubled. Fucked up by his parents and fucking up other people in turn, though well-intentioned all the while. Perhaps not so very different from a lot of men.

'Maybe you should sing again,' Dave advises, stroking his cheeks to mimic the tears I released.

I smile, feeling tempted. Then I see my mobile buzzing. As I pull it out, a pink neon strobe light spins over my Nokia screen, highlighting his name. I put the mobile back into my bag and pick up the mike. It's agony not taking his call, but I have to be strong. I can't speak to him ever again. Tomorrow I'll be en route for the US, travelling far, far away from him; tonight all I can do is sing away my pain . . .

5. Meet my favourite childhood author, Herbie French

1

My trip to the US does not begin well when I nearly get arrested for being a terrorist.

My flight from Tokyo to New York via Chicago leaves at eleven in the morning. My journey seems to be ill-fated from the very start – it's just one problem after another. I slump in the taxi, feeling hungover with alcohol and grief, saying goodbye to Tokyo. I know that my memories, once neon with bliss, will now always be darkened with Luke's betrayal. Then at Narita Airport I find I'm much too early, so I have to hang around for hours, drinking hot chocolate. It tastes much as it does in England, frothy but slightly insipid compared to the glorious hot chocolate drinks in Italy, which simply ooze calories, and are so thick you can hardly stir them.

In between hot chocolates, I seriously consider jumping up, going back to the check-in desk and asking if I can change my flight to go back to England. I'm meant to be seeking out my favourite childhood author. Herbie French is a famous recluse with a mysterious past so I thought he'd make an interesting challenge. At the time, it seemed like a good idea to put him on my list. But now I'm in such a foul mood I feel that I can hardly be bothered.

Anyway, I can't get out of visiting America, because my mum is expecting me. It's been over *two years* since I last saw her. I was always too busy with work. Besides, we've never got on that well. But two years is too long. If I cancelled now, she'd never speak to me again.

My mobile shrills and Reece's name flashes up on the screen. I can't bear to take her call. I feel so stupid and embarrassed that I raved about Luke to her. I can just picture her reporting the news back to Ciaran – '*Julia can only attract the worst type of bastards . . .*' And then they'll kiss smugly and carry on with their baby-making. Maybe Reece is even calling to tell me she is finally pregnant.

I feel petty and silly but I just can't face anyone else's good news right now.

I stand up wearily as my flight's called. Then I get into trouble because I don't have a clear plastic bag to put my toiletries into. I ask around but it turns out they don't supply free ones like they do in English airports.

Now time is ticking past – why the hell did I waste it all drinking hot chocolates? Feeling panicked, I rush over to a touristy shop. A-ha! I spot an ornament which comes housed in a box wrapped in a plastic bag. I can kill two birds with one stone and give the ornament to Mum as a present.

I stick my Vaseline and toothpaste into the bag. But the official at security, a pretty girl with a stony face, is not impressed.

'You should have a clear plastic bag with a Ziploc,' she says.

'Well, there weren't any, and in England we get them for free ... and that *is* a plastic bag!'

'You should have a clear plastic bag with a Ziploc,' she repeats, and I sense I'm on dangerous ground. Her eyes narrow fiercely. 'OK for now,' she says, 'but next time – *be careful*.'

Be careful! I feel as though I'm in a play at the Kabuki and she's about to draw out a samurai sword and chop off my head at any moment.

Then she looks at my feet and I see a slight distaste flit through her eyes, but she's too polite to voice it.

I feel a flush on my face. This morning when I was packing in a rush, I realised that one of my tights had a hole in it and a blister was forming, so I yanked a random sock on to one foot. I pulled my boots over the top and didn't stop to think that I'd have to take them off at the airport and walk through security looking like an idiot.

Urgh, I think blackly, this is all your fault, Luke. We should have been at this airport together, hugging and kissing goodbyes.

* * *

On the plane, the choice of romantic comedies playing out on my small TV screen makes me wince. I go to the tiny toilet at the back of the plane, only to find that my period has started. I've no paracetamol, which means hours of agony ahead. I slump in my seat, spirals of pain tightening in my groin. But it almost feels like a relief, a release, a physical manifestation of my emotional anguish. I feel like a jaded old woman with grey hairs in her heart: I feel as though I will never love again.

In Chicago, I need to take an internal flight to NY. I discover that this means I have to go through security all over again. The thought makes my head throb with exhaustion. I just want to jump through the hoops of time and materialise, like a beamed-up character from *Star Trek*, on my mother's doorstep.

I wearily dump my handbag into a plastic tray. Then I add my coat. Then I take off my boots and thunk them in too.

The security guard on the other side of the gates is short and ginger, with a wiry moustache. He beckons me forward. Then his eyes fall to my feet. His expression is momentarily, perversely joyful before the horror shadows it, as though to say – *I've been so bored all day and now I've finally got ONE!*

'YOU!' he yells. 'THIS WOMAN'S ONLY WEARING ONE SOCK! SECURITY ALERT! SECURITY ALERT!'

I gape, utterly disorientated. 'Me?' a voice inside me cries in bewilderment. 'Me, a nice middle-class white girl

from England who fits none of your tedious stereotypes
– you think I'm a *terrorist*?'

I'm so shocked that I actually start to laugh, hoping
he'll also see how ludicrous this is.

'Look, I got up early this morning and I—'

'DON'T MOVE!' he screams. 'SECURITY ALERT! I
NEED BACK-UP!'

Back-up? Is he joking? Is a squad team about to pin
me to the floor?

I stare down at my sock. Does it look *that* suspicious?
Aside from the knobble of my ankle and the fact that it's
a hideous shade of brown, it's pretty obvious that there's
nothing more in it than my foot. I look up: everyone is
staring at me. People are pointing. Eyes are mooning. I
just can't believe this is happening to me.

Then back-up appears: a large female security guard
who comes waddling through the gates and leads me to
a booth, where she asks me to explain Why I Am Only
Wearing One Sock.

'I have a blister,' I say, an edge coming into my voice
now. 'Look.' I take off my sock and waggle my toes at
her. I can just imagine her filing a report later, earnestly
noting *I checked to see whether the suspect had Athlete's
Foot but found no evidence – even so, I recommend we
detain her whilst further investigations take place.*

To my surprise, my aggressive manner seems to work.
Maybe Americans prefer a forthright attitude. As I become
indignant, the seesaw tips; she becomes gracious. Even so,

I am told to sit tight and wait whilst she picks up my sock in a pair of black tongs and takes it away to be – analysed? Interrogated? Maybe its M&S label will be filed on an international database.

My mobile is still on silent, and in my bag, it dances urgently for my attention. It's a call from Luke. I feel so nervous I nearly accept it. What if I'm about to be put away for thirty years and Luke is my last lifeline? Then I see the official returning, carrying my sock.

'It's OK, you're free to go,' she says, proffering it like some kind of olive branch. I take it with an ungracious scowl, yank it back on and get out of Chicago Airport as fast as I can. On my way out, however, I hear an announcement crackle over the tannoy: 'Our security alert warning system has now gone from orange to red.'

Despite myself, I grin, shaking my head in wonder.

I get a yellow cab to Mum and Anthony's place in upstate Manhattan. Mum has never learned to drive, since her father died in a road accident when he was in his early twenties. She refused to pay for my driving lessons when I was a teenager and so I ended up learning when I started work.

New York, New York. It's great to be back in the city that never sleeps, to feel its heartbeat of thrumming energy. However, I am feeling a bit angsty at the thought of seeing Mum again, and it coalesces with my tiredness into irritation. There are numerous reasons why we don't get on.

She has a tendency to worry, and be incredibly fussy. When I was a teenager she'd go on and on about not drinking, not smoking, why vegetarianism would leave me with brittle bones in old age, how I should never sleep with a boy until I was at least thirty-four and then making sure I used at least three condoms but not the pill as that came with side-effects, et cetera. I'd be a good girl and listen until it all got too much and I'd snap and tell her where to go. Then she'd look upset and tell me it was only because she cared. Anyhow, the stuff you have to suffer from your parents as a teenager generally doesn't stop when you grow up – probably because in their eyes you never do grow up. When I saw her two years ago, I was a high-flyer on a six-figure salary with huge responsibility and yet she still criticised my choice of shoes, toothpaste, hair and demanded to know why I wasn't married.

I pay the driver, my head swimming with exhaustion, wearily drag my suitcase up the steps of her townhouse . . .

The moment I see her, my annoyances feel petty. The smile on her face is radiant and I feel a spontaneous flow of love. We hug tightly. I tell her she's looking well: her hair is so glossy you can't tell it's been dyed to hide the grey, and her outfit is modern compared to the stuff she wore in England, when she used to dress as if femininity was a sin.

Then I turn to Anthony. In theory he's my stepfather,

but in my heart he is simply Mum's new husband. She married him after I'd already left home to work in the City. Before Anthony came along, Mum lived a bleak life of scrimping and saving, her only pleasure the soaps on TV when she got home from work. Now she lives a life of luxury and does charity work for a hobby; Anthony truly has been her knight in shining Armani. Ciaran met him once and joked that he looked like a debonair devil. He's tall, with a patrician sweep of grey hair and as he shakes my hand, he smiles his charming smile.

We go into the kitchen, where Mum offers me a cup of tea.

'What's all this?' I ask, spotting trays covered with cheese and pineapple on sticks, and stalks of celery and little iced fairy cakes.

And then I notice the faint burble of voices coming from the closed door of the living room.

'We invited some friends over to say hi,' Mum says brightly.

'But, Mum, I've been travelling for *hours*.' I'm conscious that I sound like a six year old, but being with your mother involves an automatic regression to kidulthood. 'I'm *tired*.'

I see her face tighten.

'Well, I just thought that Luke would enjoy a special little welcome to New York. Where is he, by the way?'

Shit. I'd completely forgotten that I'd told Mum he was coming over with me. I feel my stomach churn. When I lost my job, naturally I told Mum that I'd 'left it because I needed a break', although I think she suspected. Aside from my joy at the thought of bringing Luke over and showing him off to everyone, I'd also hoped he would distract her from the icky job subject.

'Luke ... we broke up, so ...' I take a stick of celery and bite into it hard. I hate the look of disappointment on her face. I feel like a teenager coming home with a B- for my homework. Only this is far worse, because I've failed in the Test of Life. No man, no job – just my suitcase and a dodgy, criminal sock.

'It's just a shame you're going to miss Alexander.' Mum sighs. 'He's in Hawaii with Samantha – his first holiday in three years.' My brother is an even worse workaholic than I used to be. But perhaps it's just as well he's not here. There's always been a spark of sibling rivalry between us; his success will only highlight my failure.

I'm propelled into the party. Faces spin before me. I pump a thousand handshakes. I smile so that my cheeks feel as though they're on a gym workout. My brain is so tired it's beyond tiredness. A high-pitched ringing pinballs in my ears. Everyone seems twice my age, except for a little kid called Isabella who runs around looking cute.

I start telling one person about the sock comedy and then I find everyone suddenly falls silent to listen. I brighten up, excited by a captive audience, adding little flourishes like 'My sock is due to stand trial next week – it's currently on probation.' Everyone bursts into laughter and I even take my boot off and show them the cotton offender.

Mum just stands and watches me in bemusement. Then, when she offers me a bagel, I have to remind her that I'm trying to avoid wheat.

As usual, she ignores me, fussing, 'You really ought to eat up.'

Oh God, I'm so tired. I thought Mum and I were going to get along but already we're rubbing each other up the wrong way. If Luke was here now, he'd be standing with his arm around me, distracting her, charming her, telling her how wonderful I am.

Then I remind myself that it would all just be Luke's special brand of bullshit.

Suddenly I hear a female voice enquire: 'Hey, can I meet the famous Julia?'

2

'This is Lucy,' Mum says, introducing her. She gives me an agitated glance which I can't quite fathom.

'Hi, Lucy.' I hold out my hand and the girl glides forward and shakes it warmly. I see a wary look in Mum's eyes, and light dawns. Poor Mum – I think she's scared homosexuality is a disease that I might catch.

Lucy's handshake is firm and sure. I feel a faint tingling shiver up my arm and I blush. Because Lucy really is very attractive.

She's tall, with dark curly hair, much of which is heaped on her head in some complicated arrangement involving sparkly combs and clips. She's dressed entirely in black but she doesn't look like a Goth; her pencil skirt shows off an enviably willowy figure, whilst her tight-fitting top emphasises the swan arch of her neck and the shape of her breasts. Her nails are scarlet; bangles slither on her wrists. Her skin is flawless and so is her make-up; neat lines of kohl rim her pretty green eyes. She exudes an air of elegance and self-possession, which might have been intimidating were it not for her smile, which is as friendly and open as they come.

Mum would faint on the spot if she knew that number seven on my list was *Kiss a girl and see if I like it*. It's not that I'm bisexual – at least, I don't think I am. But I've recently become 'curious' in the Katy Perry sense of the word. It seemed like a fun, slightly crazy thing to add, to balance out the more serious wishes on my list.

'Lucy's an artist,' my mum says. 'She painted this amazing portrait of me and Anthony and she has exhibitions all the time – she's really quite famous.' She smiles at Lucy, who beams back. And then the question mark of a 'what do you do' look comes over her face.

'Julia's currently travelling,' Mum says, with disapproval.

I'm used to being able to stand at parties and answer this question with pride. Now I suddenly realise how unfair the question is – just an excuse to put someone in a box. No doubt Lucy thinks I'm some kind of hippie bum who's never achieved anything. I suddenly feel a flare of guilt for all the times I've asked that question and made a snap judgement.

'I used to work as a hedge-fund manager at a big firm in London – but now I'm having a break,' I tell Lucy. Then I hastily change the subject. 'You know, I'm here to see my mum but I'm also on a mission. When I was a kid, my favourite book was *The Lost Princess* and I know the author, Herbie French, lives in New Y—'

'Herbie French!' pipes up little Isabella, who's been eavesdropping.

I smile down at her. I'm not normally very good with children but with Isabella I feel instantly at ease. 'You like him?'

'He's her favourite too,' Lucy says. 'I have read that story to her at least twenty times. Isabella's my niece, by the way.'

'Aunt Lucy made me these,' Isabella says, showing off her earrings: delicate twists of gold that glitter against her fair hair.

'I actually have a kind of plan.' I swallow, wondering if I dare confide in Lucy when I've only just met her. But there's something honest and friendly in her green eyes. I trust her. 'I know this sounds like a cliché, but I'm on a trip where I'm doing all the things I've always wanted to do – *Ten Things To Do Before I Die* type of thing. I know Herbie French is quite old now but one of my wishes is to meet him and get his autograph before he . . .'

'You wanna go and meet *Herbie French*?' Lucy looks doubtful. 'I think that might be a little bit hard. You see, he's been a recluse for a long, long time. He lives in upstate New York, out in the sticks. I passed by there once and his grounds were surrounded by barbed wire. He doesn't even come out to get his mail – this guy in a suit collects it. Herbie's a ghost. He hasn't seen anyone in *two decades*.'

'This sounds like a very silly idea to me, Julia,' my mother interjects and I jump, realising that she's been listening. 'Why on earth would you want to see *him*?'

Of course, this only makes me more determined.

'Well, in that case,' I announce, 'I'll just have to be the first person in two decades who has succeeded in meeting Herbie French!'

Lucy stares at me hard.

'Well, I do admire your get up and go,' she says, 'but this is not gonna be easy. I mean, I can try to help you – I have a few contacts in publishing. Come to think of it, I even know his agent.'

'Can I come?' Isabella asks excitedly.

'Why not,' I say, rubbing a burning eye with the heel of my fist. 'That'd be great!' Suddenly I feel exhausted by small talk when my heart is so black and blue.

Lucy gives me a tender look and puts her hand on my wrist. Mum glances over nervously and I swear I see a naughty glint in Lucy's eye as she increases the pressure.

'Julia looks really tired,' she says gently. 'She's been up for hours – I think she needs her sleep.'

I'm grateful to Lucy because a few others chime their agreement and I get to say my goodbyes and collapse in my bedroom.

It's a nice room. The walls are duck-egg blue and though it's clean, it's cluttered with knick-knacks which create a homely feel. A simple wooden cross hangs on the wall.

And on my bed is my quilt – the one I used to have on my bed back in Surrey when I was a teenager. It's got a gorgeous apple-and-cherry-orchard print on it, though now the trees are threadbare, the cherries faded to palest pink, and the fields have a few holes in.

As I crawl up under the quilt, I feel as though my tiredness has become a monster, hammering multiple fists behind my eyes, exhaling a fog of black smoke. I see my mobile vibrate again. *Luke.* I reach out, longing to hear his voice, but then I pull back and close my eyes. I want to sleep, not just for the physical relief, but because I need to dive deep, deep into oblivion.

I sleep . . . and sleep
  and sleep . . . and sleep
  . . . and sleep . . .

Now and again I rise up close to the surface, aware of the light, of tossing on to my back, of sheets tangling around my feet, of Mum opening the door and looking in. Once I stumble to the bathroom, semi-conscious. But I always curl up and dive under again, like a creature in hibernation. I want to shut the world out, shut out the harsh winter of my heartbreak and just hide in the dark and quiet.

3

I wake up feeling muzzy and confused. *Where am I?* I see the cross on the wall – so I'm with Mum. In the US. The clock says 9 a.m. So I've slept for . . . a whole day and a half! I can smell delicious scents wafting from the kitchen – eggs and bacon and fried bread. Mum did always like cooked breakfasts. My stomach leaps with hunger but I stay curled up under the covers a little longer.

And then I start crying again. I find myself thinking, Whoa, I've only been awake for five minutes – isn't this a bit quick? But I've been holding back this dam since my brief release during karaoke, on the plane, during the taxi-ride, throughout the party. The tears pour out and all my fears come rushing up with them. I've lost Luke; I've lost Ciaran; he and Reece are going to have babies and forget me; I've lost my job; nobody's ever going to love me; I'm using up all my money travelling; when this trip ends I'll have no savings, no job, no love, nothing. I cry rivers, until a new fear wells up: *Am I having some kind of breakdown?* All of which makes me feel worse because now I can add a new worry to my list – *I'm going to end up in a strait-jacket.*

Finally, finally, my tears stop. And then, after the raging of the storm, I feel a sweet sense of peace. I hug my pillow, aware of myself in the present, in this room, the past forgotten, the, future tingling with hope. The depressed voice in my head says, *Just stay in bed all day and sleep.* The optimist says, *Go and chase up Herbie French. It'll be an adventure, it'll cheer you up, and every step you take along these journeys will give you answers to all the questions about love and destiny that are churning inside you.* The depressed voice replies drearily that, *There's no point. If you meet someone new, it'll just be another failed love affair. This trip is pointless; in real life there are no happy endings.*

And then I remember Lucy's words from last night: *Herbie French hasn't seen anyone in* two decades.

That stirs something inside me – the part of me that loves a challenge. I drag myself out of bed and into the kitchen.

Mum beams at me and asks if I enjoyed my long sleep. She fusses around me, sits me down on a chair, and places a big plate of fried delights under my nose. I bite into the eggs and a yellow deliciousness fills my mouth. Yummy, I think, and then ponder how curious life is. Just a few minutes ago, I felt that my existence was unbearable and now I'm enjoying an egg.

'So what are you doing today?' Mum asks after I've finished eating and am drinking my third cup of tea.

'I'm going to go and chat to Herbie French,' I say, crossing my arms and giving her a challenging look.

Mum rolls her eyes and takes away my plate.

'You do have strange ideas, Julia. I mean, you could just go and enjoy the shops, but you prefer to go chasing after some mad recluse.'

I realise she's right. The trouble is, now I've lost my job, I've got no goals to get my teeth into. I suddenly become conscious of the perimeters of our personalities, how hard it is to change, how we always circle back to the same habits.

I watch Mum doing the washing-up. Now that I'm fresh and awake, I can see she's changed from two years back. She looks more happy and relaxed now that she's retired early. I think Anthony's love has had a profound influence on her; she has healed after the terrible pain she had to suffer years back. It's too early to ask her about Dad, though. It'll have to wait for another day.

Back in my room, I remember Lucy with a flutter of excitement. She offered to help with Herbie. I have her mobile number, but if I call her, will she take it as some kind of come-on? I know I sound prejudiced and naïve, but I'm not sure how it all works, how lesbians manage their female friends, whether it's important to make it clear that's all you're looking for. I have a feeling, though, that the only way to play it is to be as natural as possible. I press the green call button, hearing my breath quicken a little as her phone starts to ring.

4

'Well – here we are,' Lucy says, switching off the engine.

Lucy very kindly offered to drive me over to Herbie French's home. Her car is a Cadillac, the colour of a canary, shiny and cool as hell. With Lucy at the wheel, it naturally draws attention from every passer-by.

We've driven out to the Hudson Valley; we just passed by the famous Lyndhurst Castle, a Gothic Revival mansion of astounding beauty. I get out of the car. It's a stunning day, a few lazy clouds dreaming across a cornflower-blue sky. Lucy said it would be like an oven in New York City, but here the sun sprawls down gently, warming the fields of green and gold. Birds soar and butterflies dance. This is a heavenly place to live.

'You OK, honey?' Lucy helps Isabella out of the car.

The girl looks decidedly pale. She goes to the side of the road and promptly throws up over some wild flowers.

A few seconds later, however, as we make our way down

the road to Herbie French's property, Isabella is running around chasing butterflies. I smile; her joy is contagious. How quickly children's moods change; they can throw off sadness like an old toy. As adults, we tend to hang on to things more; misery can become a bad addiction we get into a habit of indulging. I wish I could heal more quickly after Luke. But my heart still feels sore from the bruising.

As we get closer, however, my stomach starts to imitate the butterflies flapping around us. I'm about to meet my childhood hero – this is *so* exciting! On the drive over, Lucy asked me why *The Lost Princess* has such a hold on me. I explained that this is a long story in itself, and I promised to tell her later. In truth, there is a history behind it, but I'm not entirely sure I can understand its mysterious hold myself.

Then, through the trees, I catch a distant glimpse of Herbie French's house. I hear myself gasp. It's just like something out of a fairytale – beautiful, magical and ever so slightly sinister. The house is large, made of ancient stone, with lattice windows that glint in the sunlight. I can hear the splash of a fountain. On the lawn, there are hedges cut into the shape of a peacock and I see the dark, mysterious opening to a maze.

Then we circle the corner and I stop short.

'Oh no!'

The grounds of the house are surrounded by barbed wire. In fact, the yellow Danger signs warn us that if we touch it, we'll probably sizzle.

'Fuck,' I mutter. Lucy winces.

'Like I said, this isn't going to be easy.' Then she glances over at Isabella. 'Hey, what have you got there, honey?'

I'm too busy staring in dismay. I walk a little further and discover a set of large gates and a security booth, in which I see the impassive silhouette of a guard.

Lucy joins me, eyeing up the guard thoughtfully. I see determination in her eyes and feel a flash of hope. I suspect that Lucy has special skills of persuasion.

'Hey there,' she calls.

The guard sits still, staring straight ahead, ignoring us.

'It's a nice day, isn't it? Hey, we're actually here with my niece – she's only eight years old, and she has a nature project for school.' Lucy beckons Isabella to join in on the act.

Isabella hurries up, her palms cupped together, holding a secret treasure.

'And part of her project is to take samples of the Golden Hedge Hyssop flower.' Lucy points. 'So I was wondering if you could just let us through these gates so we can do the project. We won't disturb anyone. We promise we don't mean any harm.'

The guard stares at Lucy.

'It's private property,' he grunts.

'What if I gave you a present?' Isabella cajoles him. She goes up to him, holding out her locked palms and his face softens. I suddenly worry she's holding a frog or a giant spider. Then I hear a sound emanating from her palms, as though she's carrying a heartbeat. She spreads them open and a butterfly flies out.

The guard starts, but his surprise doesn't translate into delight. He just scowls.

'No,' he says.

Lucy sighs.

Isabella, realising that we're not going to make it through the gates, starts to throw a tantrum.

'I want to see Herbie French,' she wails. The guard scowls even more. Now we've been completely rumbled.

'Maybe they'll have a nicer guard next week,' Lucy whispers to me.

We start to head back towards the car, when I stop and turn and stare through the trees. The fields around the house are overgrown but a thin, rough path has been trampled through the long grass. The wind blows the grasses apart and I swear that for one moment I see a figure standing there, dressed in a white suit. But when I look again, the grasses reveal nothing but green. I feel like *Alice in Wonderland*, when she's looking through the tiny door that leads into a wonderful garden.

'Ah – Mr French!' I hear a voice behind us.

We turn to see a group of Japanese tourists who have come up to the front of the house and are snapping photos. The guard grimaces but endures them.

I nudge Lucy and we hurry away. I feel mortified; reality hasn't just burst my bubble but jolly well trampled all over it. When I was a kid, Herbie was famous but I didn't realise that his reclusiveness has turned him into a global myth. I thought we were being entrepreneurial and clever to find his house, but now it turns out we're just ants in a trail of tourists who pass by his grounds every day, hoping for crumbs of his celebrity.

Lucy's right: this mission may be impossible.

But as I get into the car and we drive off, I take one last look back at the house. And I think, We can't just give up, not now. We just can't.

5

It's early evening. New York is zinging – you can feel the fizz in the air. Taxis honk. I hear snatches of chatter and laughter from the streets below, ribbons of music from bars and clubs. I'm inside. I watched TV for a while with Mum and Anthony, mostly to keep them company and be polite. Even though Mum's very traditional, she's got hooked on Celebrity Gossip TV reports – although she savours them with disapproval rather than admiration. 'When she dyed her hair blond, I knew she was heading for trouble,' was her verdict on Lindsay Lohan. 'I think Kristen Stewart and Robert Pattinson ought to just come out and admit they're in love,' she said with a sigh.

Now I'm in my room. I'm feeling fraught. Not because of Herbie, though that was disappointing. But there's still hope. At the end of our trip, Lucy squeezed my hand and said we'd try again tomorrow.

No, it's because I'm holding my phone and I can see

Luke is calling me once again. Where is he right now? What time-zone? Is he sitting up awake at night, thinking of me, or in some café in Tokyo?

This is call number 19. I hadn't expected him to be this persistent.

The call stops. Then a text informs me I have a voice-mail.

'Hey ... it's Luke. I have no idea where you are, Julia. Maybe you're still in Japan. Maybe you're just a few feet away from me. I went to the hotel in Ginza and they said you'd checked out. Well, I just – I just want to talk. You ran away and it wasn't fair, you have to give me another chance to explain. Please just call me. We don't even have to meet – we can just chat. Well, bye now.' He gives a forced laugh. His voice drips sadness.

I'm scared my resolve is going to slip, that my hard-line position will soften. Maybe I should call him ...

And then a voice of warning whispers, *What, and end up like Jodie, pining for him whilst he gets bored and goes gallivanting off looking for new victims?*

I realise that I need some advice.

I need Reece.

I pick up the phone. What time is it in England? They're six hours ahead so it must be ... around 11, I think. Which means I can call her!

I suddenly feel incredibly relieved. I've been avoiding Reece for the past few days. She's sent me jolly texts asking what Mum thinks of Luke and I've sent vague replies. I just felt too embarrassed to admit it had all gone horribly wrong. I kept picturing her and Ciaran buying bags of nappies to put into storage, sharing baths while they discussed baby names. Now I realise that my pride has been so foolish. I know that a part of me has been wondering, if Reece is meant to be the ditzy one, how come I'm turning out to be such a fuck-up? But Reece is my best friend. She's the one person with whom I can be vulnerable.

I pick up the phone and dial the flat, bursting with my news.

'Hey,' a male voice replies and my heart sinks. It's Ciaran.

'Uh – is Reece there?' I ask.

'No, she's out right now. I don't really know when or what time she'll be back.' Pause. Then he adds in a slightly bitter tone: 'I expect she'll roll in around three a.m., pissed out of her skull.'

'Well, she can't be drinking too much, can she?' I say, feeling very awkward, as though I'm being disloyal to Reece by even discussing all this. 'I mean, not with you guys trying for a baby. I know Reece is a bit mad but I think she'll surprise everyone and be a great mother.'

There's a long silence. And then Ciaran says, '*What!*'

'You know – you guys ...' My voice shrinks. 'Trying for a ... baby.'

'What? What is— Reece – is she pregnant?'

'Um – no. No. I know she did a test and it came out negative and I thought ... I just ...' Suddenly I realise that my imagination has taken a few random incidents and painted them into a picture – one that I've got so used to looking at, I've been convinced that it's reality. Reece has never actually *said* that she wants a family.

'Has Reece told you that she wants to have a kid with me?' Ciaran asks, incredulous.

'Sorry,' I say. 'I think that maybe I'm just muddling you up with this other couple I know who used to work at Charlton Cross – you know, Hector and April. They're trying for a baby and I'm pretty jetlagged and everything . . .'

'What's going on?' Ciaran demands. 'I just can't believe that Reece would want a baby. I mean, we're not even sleeping in the same room right now, so it would be extremely hard. In fact, the last time we slept together was long before Sicily . . .' He breaks off, his voice trembling with pain and anger, as though he's said much more than he intended.

I fall silent. This is getting curiouser and curiouser. Maybe Reece feared she was pregnant and that put her off having sex with him. I feel oddly relieved. I couldn't really see Reece as a mum. She'd probably accidentally set her baby down in the fish tank and forget about him.

But I'm not sure what to say to Ciaran now. I've made quite a *faux pas*.

'By the way,' Ciaran says, calming down a little, 'Reece says you're going to Vegas in a few weeks' time.'

'She did?' Reece wormed that out of me when we spoke

on the phone in Tokyo and I was in too good a mood to resist her. It's next on my list of things to do. Number six. She was supposed to keep it secret.

'So we're just thinking about booking flights. It'd be cool if we all met up again, right?'

There's charm in his voice, and sweetness too. But I immediately fly into a jumpy panic. Sicily was bad enough, waking up each day filled with ache for him. And for all Ciaran's moaning, I don't believe he and Reece are moving apart. Last year, they fell out spectacularly on 12 February about him spending too much time at the office. But by St Valentine's Day they were all pink hearts and love again.

And I've realised recently that I really need to do this trip. I need to work my way through my *Ten Things* and return home with some kind of sanity, some kind of life plan, some perspective.

I'm conscious that I've created a long silence on the phone and this time Ciaran's voice is filled with caution.

'I mean, are you happy for us to gatecrash?'

'Well, I'm not even sure if I'm going,' I say quickly.

'We'll just head out there anyway. I need to let rip, so does Reece. I'm actually going to plunder my ISA. Fuck it, it'll be fun.'

'Well, actually, I *am* going to go,' I blurt out, 'and I'd really rather be on my own. I mean, no offence. I just . . . I . . .'

There's another long silence.

'None taken,' says Ciaran. 'Bye then.' And he hangs up.

Shit. What a completely disastrous phone call. I've not only told Ciaran that Reece did a pregnancy test but I've also managed to completely offend him. I hug myself, full of dismay. I heard the hurt in his voice and it cut me. I can't bear to inflict the slightest pain on him.

I go back into the living room for a while. Mum is watching *Celebrity Gossip* again. When I get back to my room, I discover that Luke's call tally has reached twenty-two.

6

'You know, if we head into the *K* Bar with that kite, we're gonna get some seriously weird looks,' Lucy says.

'Oh, right.' We've just picked it up at Big City Kites, a store which has recently reopened in the city. It's bright yellow – nearly as yellow as Lucy's splendid Cadillac. I can hardly wait for Isabella to see it.

'Let's drop it in my car.'

So we leave it in her boot and exit the parking-lot. Lucy checks her watch – it's three o'clock. In an hour's time we're due to pick up Isabella from school, giving her Latino Nanny a break.

I'm feeling better this morning. My depression has lifted. Being with Lucy helps, as she has such a gutsy, get-up-and-go personality. Plus, she's always murmuring sarcastic witticisms that make me laugh.

Today is the day when I'm finally going to meet Herbie

French. We've come up with a first-class plan, which involves a kite.

It has to work.

Lucy suggests that we go get a drink. It's obvious that she hangs out in all the most stylish bars in New York. The *K* Bar doesn't even have a name on the outside, but its black and white décor simply screams elegance and money. As we enter, the doorman greets her by name with a slight blush.

I shoot Lucy an admiring sideways glance. I get the feeling she's used to commanding respect. Oh God, am I developing what Reece would call a *girl crush*?

Not of the lesbian kind, of course.

But I can't help but think that Lucy is just so impressive: so pretty, so charismatic, so charming, so together . . .

And our relationship feels so simple. After all the complications of Luke and Ciaran, it's nice just hanging out with a girlfriend. It reminds me of how it used to be between me and Reece in the days before Ciaran came along. I feel a pinch, suddenly aware of the shadow he's cast over our friendship.

'So d'you think this Herbie thing is going to work?' I ask Lucy as we sit down by the bar.

'Oh sure,' says Lucy, sipping on her tomato juice. Her eyes sparkle. 'Everything I do is always a success.' She says the words without arrogance, just stating a fact.

I look down, remembering that I used to be like that. So sure of myself. But it's easy to feel that way when life is going well; it's more of a challenge to maintain your self-belief when things are going badly.

'So what's your secret?' I ask her.

Lucy looks me straight in the eye, her expression thoughtful. 'You've gotta go after what *you* want. Either you make things happen by yourself, *con*structively, or life makes it happen to you, *de*structively.'

'What d'you mean by that?' I ask. I'm intrigued. Since the start of my travels, I've become more and more open to other people's philosophies. Everyone's got one: the creed that governs their life, their moral decisions, their love, their work. And Lucy is such a fascinating person that I do want to hear her creed.

'Well, I just think that you can't stand still in life. My ex was a very successful businesswoman and she used to say that a business never sits in stasis. It's either evolving and expanding, or it's going backwards. And it's struck me that as individuals, we're the same. And – well, this is just a kind of life philosophy of my own that I've developed – but I think that you've always gotta keep moving ahead. I see what happens sometimes with friends. They get stuck in a rut. They end up in a bad job or a lousy marriage and they don't do anything about it – they want to, but they don't quite get it together enough to make it happen. And the longer the situation goes on, the harder it is to change it. So.'

She takes a sip of her tomato juice. 'That situation is always a dangerous one. Because I think life listens to our thoughts, happy or sad, and if we don't change the things that are wrong, then life surely will. People get fired from the job they hate, or their partner leaves them. And it's always far worse if you wait for life to sort it out for you, because by then you're hurt, you're battered, you're bruised, you're going to take a while to heal. My feeling is that if a job or a love affair is going wrong, get out early. Don't let things turn to shit.'

Her words electrify me. Of course, I can't help immediately applying them to my situation.

Luke – well, things hardly dragged on there. Our love affair was over before it had barely begun.

But when it comes to my job, I think she's right. There were times when I sat on the tube on the way to work and had fantasies about being made redundant, so that I could spend a few months on an island in the sun. And then I'd quickly bury them, reminding myself of how lucky I was to have my job and wondering how I'd survive without my salary and ordering myself to see the best in what I had. I got used to persuading myself to settle for second best. And yes, I was afraid of change. If I hadn't been fired, I would have stayed in that job until I retired. I would probably have had a heart attack at the age of fifty-five and about three people would have turned up at my funeral. Including my boss, who would have been staring down at my gravestone saying, 'So, Julia, before you breathed your last breath, did you manage to get those figures for the Hampton account?'

'It's scary,' I say quietly. 'I mean walking away from things. You can fantasise about it, but in reality it is frightening.'

'Sure it is,' Lucy agrees, 'but it's also exciting.' She narrows her eyes at me. 'I've talked for ages, now it's your turn. So you're a high-flyer, huh?'

'I *was* a high-flyer,' I say wryly. 'Until I lost my job.' There. I'm getting a bit better at saying it these days. I don't see the point in using the 'I resigned' euphemism.

'Well, you're still a high-flyer,' Lucy says generously. 'I mean, it's not the job that makes you, it's you who makes the job. You're still you.'

'Thanks.' I feel cheered.

'And what about Herbie? You say you've got this list of things you wanna do – well, if he's made your top ten, he must be pretty important. Why's that? What's this all about?'

'I . . .' I stare down at the a watery circle on the bar left by my glass and make squiggly patterns with my forefinger.

'It's secret?'

'Kind of.' I clear my throat. 'It's a childhood thing. I liked his book and . . . it's complicated.'

Lucy holds my gaze, smiling. 'You're a very mysterious woman, Julia.'

I smile back, finding a blush creeping over my cheeks. The way she said that – it sounded almost as if she was flirting with me. I quite like the idea, though I also feel strange because it's not something that's ever happened to me before.

'I will tell you,' I promise. 'I really will – but I think I'd just like to meet him first.'

'Hey, look at the clock!' She slaps the bar. 'Now we're gonna go and get Herbie. Come on, let's get going.'

We pick Isabella up. She's wearing the mauve uniform of her private school and her fair hair is tied into a pretty plait, knotted with a dark purple ribbon. Then we head over to Herbie French's place.

The countryside is as beautiful as ever. We pull up a little further down the road this time. As Lucy switches off the engine, she turns and looks at me. Even though she's grinning, I can see that my fearless friend is actually a little *nervous*. I whisper that my stomach feels like a washing machine and we both chuckle, united by our nerves.

We get the kite out of the boot and Isabella goes crazy.

'Oh wow, oh wow, I want Mom to get me one just like it!'

'Sssh,' Lucy laughs. 'We have to go *quietly*. Now, are you gonna pin the note on to it?'

It all feels rather ceremonial. I take the note, which I folded into a snug square this morning and tucked into a small pink envelope. It's a letter to Herbie and it's so personal that I haven't even shown it to Lucy. But, as Isabella helps me to pin it to the corner of the kite, I feel that I've done the right thing. This letter is *raw*; it's the real thing. The fact that I spilled my soul is going to make it different from the thousands of sycophantic fan letters that Herbie must get every day of the week.

First of all, we need to get the kite up and going. We've had to cancel this excursion for the past few days because the wind wasn't strong enough. Today, however, it's whipping fiercely and Lucy, holding the kite, only has to unwind the string for the wind to take hold of the kite and whisk it upwards.

'Can I have a go, can I have a go!' Isabella cries.

'Sure you can, but I'm gonna keep my hand on yours, darling. We've gotta be careful it doesn't tangle with this electric fence,' says Lucy.

I watch the kite billow upwards. It zigzags over the fence, flirting with the breeze, roaming a few feet into Herbie's grounds. If only I was a kite or a bird, it would make this whole project so much easier . . .

We approach the fence slowly. Isabella soon tires of the kite and Lucy takes hold of it, focusing hard on keeping it under control.

'Look, here's a hole,' the little girl says, exploring the bank. 'We could climb through under here.'

'Hey, we're not tunnelling under the house,' Lucy laughs.

Isabella looks disappointed but she takes Lucy's hand obediently. As we approach the gates, we fall silent, looking to see if it's the same moody guard from last time. To my relief, this one is different. And he looks a lot nicer. He's tall and slender, with hair as fair and thick as honey. He's young, too; perhaps he's new to the job, which will make it easier to charm him.

'Hi,' Lucy calls out. 'Great weather for kite-flying, isn't it? Such a fresh breeze . . .'

He immediately perks up at the sight of Lucy. But his smile is cautious; he runs his eyes over us, as though trying to work out whether we should be labelled as green, orange or red in the security stakes.

'If you wanna get some proper flying, you should go to Governor's Island,' he recommends.

'Really?' Lucy asks. 'Now that sounds a good idea. Can you give us directions?' She nods and pretends to look fascinated as he explains where we ought to go.

And then my heart jumps as I see a figure walking down past the yellowed lawn from the house. *Shit.* It's the guard we saw a few days back. I hope and pray that he won't recognise us – but Lucy isn't the sort of woman you'd forget easily. His eyes immediately flash with recognition.

The blond guard breaks off and gives his colleague a friendly grin. 'I was just helping these fine ladies with a few tips on kite-flying.'

'Oh. You guys. You're back again,' he says. His voice is mild, almost resigned.

We all freeze up. The fair-haired guard frowns. Then Lucy smiles.

'Yep, we just thought it'd be nice. Here, Julia, you hold

the kite.' She passes it over to me, giving me a meaningful look: *it's time now*.

'Wait,' the younger guard snaps, his face darkening. 'You were here *before*?'

'Just a few days ago,' the other one says.

Our friendly guard completely flips. He starts raving about dangerous repetition of contact, about how we might be potential stalkers. I even hear the word 'conspiracy'. Lucy gives me a sharp nudge in the elbow. We'd better see this through before we get told to leave. Surreptitiously taking my nail scissors out of my bag, I snip the string. The kite is free. It sings with the wind for a few feet, then starts to slip down, down, swirling and twirling before it's caught by a bed of grass.

Damn. It's not gone quite as I expected. I'd hoped that it would land close to Herbie's house. I had visions of him looking out of the window and ordering his butler to go and get it.

'*What the fuck is that?*' the blond guard yells, gazing over at the kite.

'Excuse me, there's a kid here—' Lucy begins indignantly, cuddling Isabella close to her. The little girl is looking frightened.

'You shoulda thought of that,' he cries. 'This is a conspiracy! You guys are up to something. What the hell is attached to that kite? Is it some kind of explosive?'

'Oh, please,' Lucy says sarcastically. 'Do we really look like extremists from the Anti-Children's Writers Front?'

'In our job, you can't be too careful,' the darker guard says more gently. 'You wouldn't believe the lengths some people go to, to try to communicate with Herbie. We get people putting messages into bottles and throwing them over . . .' He lifts up his fringe to show a nasty scar zigzaging into his hairline.

'It's our job to guard this place,' the blond guard grits out, 'and I'm gonna go get that kite and then you're all coming down to the cops to explain just what game you're playing.'

My heart stops. Oh God, this is getting really nasty. I stare at the house, silently pleading for Hebie to appear, to pick up the kite and call off his guards like dogs.

'We're going,' Lucy says hotly. 'But I'm not impressed by your paranoid and ridiculous behaviour. You have no business speaking to us like that.'

'*You're* not impressed!' The guard is puce now. 'If you so much as dare to return within a hundred foot of this property, we're gonna have you arrested *on the spot*! We've got your faces now. You're on CCTV.'

Isabella bursts into tears. Lucy's face is white with fury. I feel like jolly well socking the guard. But that would only make things worse. We lead Isabella away and head back to the car. I give my kite one last glance. Then my heart crumples. The wind has caught hold of my note. It teases it away from the kite, blowing it somewhere into the thick of the grass. Now there's no way Herbie will ever find it.

Back at the car, Lucy and I both cheer Isabella up with a big hug.

'Our kite – he'll catch it and kill it,' Isabella sobs.

'No, the wind will blow the kite away, it'll be fine,' Lucy improvises.

In the car, though, we all sit silent and sober. I'm beginning to realise that my fairytale fantasy really was rather foolish. I picture the guard grabbing hold of the kite, then coming across my note. I cringe at the thought of him reading it.

When I wrote the note last night, I'd only intended to put a few polite lines about how nice it would be to meet him. But I was in a confused and emotional state after speaking to Ciaran and Luke's succession of calls. I found myself pouring out everything in a frenzy, until I'd covered three pages: a confession as much as a fan letter. Perhaps it felt easier to confide in him simply because he was a stranger, someone who didn't know me and therefore wouldn't judge me. I told him everything: how much *The Lost Princess* meant to me, and the magical effect it had on my life. In the morning, when I read it through, I worried it might be too sentimental. Then I hoped that it might touch him. I had a naïve vision of him being brought the note and tears trembling in his eyes as he read it. I had a fantasy that Herbie hadn't spoken for months and all of a sudden he'd say, 'I have to meet this girl,' and his butler would nearly faint with the shock.

But what if Herbie isn't the lovely old man I think he is? I mean, children's writers aren't necessarily the kindest of souls, are they? Didn't Enid Blyton neglect her children – and wasn't Roald Dahl a grumpy old sod despite being a genius? What kind of man hires guards like those? I suddenly have a horrible image of the guards sitting in their booth, sharing a beer and reading out snatches of my letter in between hoots of laughter. And I want to drum my fists on the dashboard of Lucy's car and just scream.

Frustration overwhelms me. Why did I construct this stupid list? Why can't I just travel like normal people do? I gaze out at New York as we enter Manhattan, at the spectacular skyline. And then I realise it's not enough just to go from country to country collecting pictures and postcards. For I know this Herbie thing isn't really about him. It's about me – my childhood. It's about things I've been trying to bury for a long time.

When Lucy drops me off home, she gives me a bright smile. I can see she's already shaken off our failure. It's happened, her expression says, now it's time to move on. But though I smile too, it's forced. The strangest thing about this pain is that it feels so very personal, as though in some way I've been rejected by my father. It doesn't even make sense. And yet I can't shake off the feeling.

I'm just entering the hallway when Mum calls out, 'You're just in time – Reece is on the phone.'

Shit! I've just suffered a threat of harassment and now I have to explain to Reece why I told her boyfriend about her supposedly wanting his baby when in fact she hasn't slept with him for months?

'Um ... tell her I have to dash out,' I say quickly, to my mum's bemusement, and hurry off to my bedroom. I sit there for some time, holding a copy of *The Lost Princess* in my hands and looking out of the window at the birds soaring about the city, circling into the clouds.

7

5. *Meet my favourite childhood author, Herbie French.*

I'm sitting on my bed, staring at my list. I can't quite bring myself to score my pen through number five even though I know it's hopeless and time to give up. So I just put a little 'x' by it.

I can't help feeling sad. 'Forget about Herbie,' Lucy insisted. Over the last few days, she's been very kind and has looked after me. She took me on a guided tour of New York: the Empire State building, Times Square, Central Park, Chinatown, the Metropolitan Museum of Art. I've spent half my life on London Transport but I've never overheard conversations like, 'He's a sensitive guitar-playing pussy-ass bitch,' or, 'One of the Ten Commandments is "Thou shalt not sleep with the wife of the man you shake hands with". I didn't shake his hand so that's OK.' New Yorkers are just so funky and cool.

We also visited her gallery, where I marvelled at her paintings. They shocked me. They were so utterly unexpected! Six-foot-square canvases, slashed with greys and browns, the silhouettes of guns and tanks and soldiers veiled by brush-strokes of camouflage murk. She told me she'd spent weeks interviewing US troops who had returned from Iraq and Afghanistan, then played their recordings as she'd painted, channelling their pain, their wounds, their fear, their rage, through her brush.

Seeing this other side to Lucy, a side that shows she cares about the world and loathes the war, only made me like her even more. We spent the afternoon in Classy Coffee, in a part of New York called Huntington, talking about politics and putting the world to rights. Then, this morning we'd gone to the other extreme, when Lucy had dragged me over to her stylist for a makeover.

I'm very happy with the haircut he gave me. My dark hair has grown since Venice, and it was straggly with split ends. When he twirled me in front of the mirror and I saw the stylish layers he'd cut into it, my heart danced.

I'm just not sure about the Botox injections.

'A year ago everyone was saying Botox was embarrassing,' Lucy confided, 'but now everyone has it. Fuck it, nobody wants to look old, do they, and no matter what they say, no skin cream is going to keep you looking twenty. I have them every month, so do all my friends.'

And so I lost my Botox virginity. I can't help staring at my reflection and trying very hard to frown. But no matter how hard I attempt to pull it together, my forehead remains an obstinate blank.

I let out a giggle and think about how much I want to call up Reece and tell her about my latest adventure – but I'm still dreading speaking to her.

I'm conscious of a weight on me. If I'm going to give up on Herbie, I also have to acknowledge the other reason I made this trip. I need to talk to Mum about Dad. Which is scary.

With a sudden flash of inspiration, I head for the kitchen. I decide to try to sweeten her by cooking her and Anthony a meal.

I've not done any cooking for years. In London, I live on Marks & Spencer prepared meals, bought on the way to work, stuffed into the office fridge, then thrown into the microwave back home. Ciaran is a great cook. He would often cook for Reece and they'd let me join them with a plate of lovely roast chicken and veg. I could taste his love in the food, all the energy he'd invested in it to win her appreciation, so every mouthful was one of tainted bliss.

Now I flick through the multitude of cookbooks on Mum's spotless kitchen shelf. Salmon pie. That looks interesting and pleasantly ambitious. Mum's kitchen is crammed as though she's preparing for the 2012 apocalypse. There are bags of oats, pasta and rice; a hundred tins of beans; a museum of spices. Every food item has an understudy.

I'm just getting going when Mum appears.

'I'm cooking dinner for you and Anthony tonight,' I tell her.

'Oh great! But that pastry looks a bit lumpy – are you sure you softened the butter prop—' She breaks off when she sees my face. 'OK. It's your treat, Julia. I won't interfere.'

As I gather together all my ingredients, I ponder possibilities. Then I decide it's best to just come out and say it.

I turn to Mum, who's watching me intently and looks as though she's about to burst with choked-back advice, and say awkwardly, 'Mum – have you heard from Dad recently?'

Mum jumps so violently that a wooden spoon smacks to the floor. She busies herself with picking it up.

'No,' she says finally. 'You know we're not in touch.'

'Yes, but it has been two years since I saw you, so . . .' I ignore her angry expression and press on. 'I'd really like to get in contact with him. I know you're not happy about it and I've respected that for a long time. But things have changed.'

Mum looks shocked. My father left when I was too young to even hold his face in my memory. He remained a presence in my mind, a collage of traits which never formed a complete picture: a wave of dark hair, penetrating blue eyes, eyes that smiled even when his lips never did, big hands with square fingers and dirty, broken fingernails, a deep, husky voice. Throughout primary school, I often used to ask Mum where Dad had gone. She'd be sad and vague. When I became a teenager, I began to ask the question with more authority. She stopped giving me neutral answers and told me how horrible and hateful he was. Soon she had persuaded me that it would be better never to meet him – not that he had ever shown any interest in seeing me, either. During my twenties, I barely ever brought the subject up. Something has simmered inside me for nearly a decade – and I sense that if I don't speak about it now, it will one day reach boiling-point.

But I can understand Mum's shock. She thinks the story of Dad is a closed book, End of Story. She can't understand why I'm suddenly flipping through the pages again.

'I haven't heard from him in over a decade,' she says sharply. Her whole body is now bristling with tension.

'I know he hasn't been in touch, but I just thought that if you could give me his details, I could track him down. I mean, I could hire an agency to find him. It might not be that hard.'

Mum falls silent.

'You know what he did to me,' she says. 'I don't understand why you want to meet him.'

'But—'

'I thought you came here to see *me*. And now it turns out you're just after *him*.'

'It's not like that!' I cry. 'Of course I came here to see

you. I just – look, it's not a question of whether he's good or bad. I know he's not a very nice man ...'

'Oh, that's an understatement!' Her face is scarlet; she's on the verge of an explosion.

'I'm really sorry to upset you, Mum,' I plead. 'I just want to have one meeting. And that'll be it.'

I look over at her and she stares at the pastry I've half-rolled.

'Now look what you've done,' she says. 'It's all lumpy.'

She comes over, yanks the rolling-pin right out of my hand and gives the pastry a good going-over. I stand there, trembling, wondering if I dare push her any more, or if I should just drop it. I seriously underestimated how badly she was going to react to this.

'He's probably in jail now anyway,' she says.

'What! Why would you say that? He left you and I know that was really unkind, but that's not a criminal offence, is it?' I say gently, trying to laugh, to lighten the terrible atmosphere.

She continues with her remake of my pie, smoothing the pastry into the Perspex dish, opening the tin of salmon and forking it into the middle.

'He was arrested for armed robbery when you were two – and it wasn't his first spell in jail.'

I stare at her in disbelief. My first instinct is that she's just making this up. Mum has integrity and she's not the type to lie, but I know how desperate she is to keep me away from him.

261

'Well, why didn't you tell me this before?' I ask her, hearing the suspicious edge in my voice.

'I *told* you he was a bad man – I told you all the time. I just didn't want to upset you with the details because you were young.'

'But you ... I mean, did you find this out before he proposed?'

'Yes, I knew then. The point is,' she snaps, 'I didn't care then, or now, about his shady past. It was what he did to *me* that I cared about.' She smooths the pastry over the salmon. She's so stressed out that she's forgotten to pour the eggy mixture in first and the pastry is an uncharacteristic mess, all lumpy and lopsided. 'The thing is,' she attempts to correct it, causing the middle bit to tear, barely noticing, 'I was very young and silly. I thought he was a rebel – I thought he was glamorous. When in fact he wasn't even a very good criminal. He botched his first job and ended up in prison, and he only got dragged into crime in the first place because he had an addiction to gambling. He told me he was going to *church* – it turned out he was spending all his spare time in a casino or the bookies. I was pregnant with you just before he went to prison and I waited and waited for two years for him to come out – and when he did he just went straight off on a "job" in France. He hadn't the slightest interest in being a proper father, and by the time you were five he was gone altogether. I was stupid, Julia – and now you're being equally stupid.'

She turns to me, then looks away quickly. We've both got tears in our eyes but we're not very open about emotions in our family, so we take a minute to compose ourselves.

'The thing is,' she insists, 'even if you *do* get back in touch with him, he won't want to hear from you. He'll hurt you, and – well, I don't see what the point of it would be, how any good can come of it at all.'

'But it's been so many years – he really could be different by now,' I say.

Mum gives me a look in which I read: *How can you be so naïve?*

But, 'OK, fine,' she says, shrugging. 'You go and meet him then – and find out for yourself.'

And then she marches out of the kitchen.

'Mum . . .' I call after her. Then I realise it's probably best to end the discussion there.

I turn back to the pie. For a moment frustration bubbles up inside me and I nearly smash the whole stupid thing to the floor. Then I remove the ruined top layer of pastry, pour in the eggy mixture over the salmon, watching it swish and bubble. Then I smooth out the remaining pastry with a rolling-pin, and the rhythm of the act, the comfort of turning disorder into something neat and controlled, soothes me. I wish I could explain everything to her. All the time when I was a kid, Mum drummed into me that Dad was evil, evil, evil without going into the specifics. She saw him as an 'other', someone she had cut off completely. For me, it was different. Once at school, a teacher asked us all to draw a picture of ourselves, with arrows pointing to the parts of us that we'd inherited from our mums or dads. Reece drew an arrow pointing to her coat, indicating that her love of luxurious clothes came from her mum, whilst the arrow linked to her eyes demonstrated that she had inherited her father's blue ones. My whole picture was covered in arrows linking me and my mother. I drew a picture of a piggy bank and scrawled *Mum says you should always save money*. I attributed my dark hair to her; my large feet; my love of books.

But I could only think of one arrow that linked me and my father. I drew a wobbly red line from my heart and scrawled *Sometimes I do bad things like my dad does*.

I grew up thinking that there was something dark lurking inside me, woven deep into my DNA, impossible to scrub out. I think that was another reason why I worked twice as hard at school. It wasn't just the fact that boys weren't interested in me. I felt I had to obey the rules, be a square instead of a rebel, in order to make up for my father. To right his wrongs by being good.

Now I know better. I realise that I don't know my father at all. I hate what he did to my mother, but I also sense that her perspective is tainted by bitterness. Yes, she's right, I was naïve – naïve to think she'd be happy to help me track him down. I thought that after all these years she would have healed, but her wounds are still raw and perhaps always will be. The trouble is, there's this drifting feeling inside me that isn't just a symptom of my rootless existence right now. It's been there for a while and I was so busy with work I could ignore it, force it into the background. It's as though my sense of self is a jigsaw and pieces are missing, as though I've got a jagged edge to my heart and a hole in my soul.

And I wish I could explain all this to Mum but I'd need to find the words and I just know she'd refuse to hear them.

Mum reappears forty minutes later, just as I'm pulling the pie out of the oven. Her eyes look very red but her expression is much softer. She puts her arm around me, leaning her head against my shoulder, giving me a sideways cuddle. I smile and her eyes sparkle and I know we've made up.

And yet. I know now not to bring the subject up again, but I can't deny this longing in me, this desire for knowledge . . .

In the dining room, all three of us sit down to eat. Anthony sighs over the pie. 'Wow, this is absolutely delicious.'

'Well, Mum was the one who sorted it all out really,' I say, and she beams.

We all fall silent. Under my lids, I watch Mum and Anthony together.

'So how much longer are you going to be staying with us, Julia?' Anthony asks.

'I'm heading for Vegas next week,' I tell him.

'So you didn't get to see Herbie French then?' he goes on.

When I look down, Mum squeezes my wrist and tells me it was a lovely idea even if it didn't come to anything.

After dinner I go into the hall and pick up the phone. I intend to speak to Reece but at the last digit I tell myself that after an afternoon of such intense emotions, it will be too much to face her too. Yes, I know: I'm a chicken. But at least I'm not a chicken-thief.

8

'Why don't we go and visit Herbie?' Isabella asks in a bored voice.

'I'm really sorry, pet, but we just can't. If we do, we might get thrown in jail.'

'I might meet a nice boyfriend if I go to jail,' the little girl reasons. 'And I've heard you're allowed to watch TV there all day every day.'

I bite back a smile. 'I'm really sorry about Herbie. But there's nothing we can do.'

I'm looking after the child for the afternoon. Lucy called me up about an hour ago, saying that she'd agreed to take Isabella shopping at Barneys and had completely forgotten that she was meant to be meeting with a movie star who wants Lucy to paint her portrait. I happily volunteered to take care of Isabella and Lucy dropped her off with a grateful smile, promising to come to my little 'goodbye gathering' later. Yes, today is the last day I'm spending in New York. Tomorrow I'm booked on a flight to Las Vegas, where I will gamble amongst the glitz and hopefully not watch all of my money being sucked away by a roulette table.

I pick up my mobile, checking the caller display. Luke's calls fizzled out a few days ago, and yesterday they stopped altogether. Even though I never wanted to take any of them, somehow I feel rather sad that he's stopped calling.

Isabella sighs and sets about drawing a moustache on her Barbie.

'Why can't you just walk through the fence?' she asks, sketching in a beard now.

'I'm not Superman – or Superwoman. I can't just walk through fences.'

'No, but there was a hole in the fence,' Isabella says impatiently, pulling off poor Barbie's head with a flourish. 'I saw it when we went before. By the trees.' She gives Barbie's beheaded face a kiss, as though to apologise.

'I . . .' I'm lost for words. I feel as though my soul has been dry and cracked for the last few days and Isabella has just offered me a glass of water. An extraordinary thirst rises up inside me, overwhelming reason. 'OK,' I say. 'But only if you agree to put Barbie's head back on. And if you swear to wait for me outside Herbie's fence, OK?'

'OK – great!' Isabella cries, her eyes sparkling. 'I'll be good, I swear, I swear.'

As we get ready to leave, I pick up my handbag and wonder whether I am really going to go through with something this insane. And then, as we sneak outside, something stronger than me takes over.

The taxi pulls up alongside the country lane.

'Stop here, please,' I say.

'You don't want me to take you up to the gates?' the driver asks.

'No, no,' I laugh weakly. 'We're fine.' And then I'm so nervous that I miscalculate the tip and give her loads. The trip was expensive enough as it is. She grins and says thanks about five times. At least I've made someone's day.

As the taxi pulls away, I watch it go with the knowledge that we're now stranded. If that evil guard comes after us again, we'll have no car we can leap into to escape. We'll be stuck out there; if he comes chasing after us, we'll have to climb a tree or something.

'Hey – let's hide!' Isabella is getting into full spy mode.

We cross the road, and Isabella shows me the hole she had noticed last time. It's been created by an oak tree, whose gnarled roots dominate the bank. One of the roots has been chopped back, and a ragged hole has been created in the fence as a result. The guards must have missed it because grass and wild flowers have sprung up, concealing it well. Only an observant child could have spotted it.

'Wait!' I stop Isabella before she dives forward like an eager rabbit. 'I'm worried it might be electric. I want you to wait for me here. You can hide behind the tree.'

Isabella looks a bit scared. I tear up a stalk of grass

and stretch it out, hoping the bolt won't zigzag through it into me. As soon as it touches the metal, it's seared into black smoke.

'It's electric,' I confirm, shaking.

Isabella puts on a brave face. 'We're like Frodo and Sam in *Lord of the Rings*, aren't we, Julia?'

I'm not sure who those characters are, but I certainly don't want to be equated with a beardy hobbit. Before I go any further, I tell her to keep low and stay by the trunk so that the guards can't see her. I promise to come back for her in a few minutes.

I pull out my nail scissors, snipping at the grass and flowers to clear the way. Isabella thinks this is hilarious, but it's all right for her, she's half my size.

Here goes. Trying to squeeze my body into as slim a shape as possible, I slither through the hole. I can't help thinking of my father – did he ever do this when he was breaking into properties or escaping from jail? Like father, like daughter. The thought makes me want to laugh and cry at the same time.

It all seems to be going well, until I feel my neck suddenly snap back. Isabella gasps, her eyes widening in horror. I hear a sizzling sound, reach up and feel that my hair's got caught.

'Oh God!' I cry. I feel it come loose as I slither through, and turn to see a clump of dark hair billowing from the fence. I touch my scalp. I can smell burned hair – urgh. 'How do I look?' My poor new hairdo is probably ruined.

'Er, OK,' Isabella says, cocking her head to one side.

Then I see the house, standing there like a magical place at the end of the swaying yellow grass, and my heart flutters with happiness. I've made it past the first hurdle. So I've sacrificed a bit of hair – but it's worth it. I'm in his grounds! I've beaten the nasty guards!

Now for the next part of the challenge. I need to sneak across the open space from the tree to the long grass. Then I need to tunnel through that. After which, I shall walk straight into the open and knock on the door of the house. And just hope the guards don't notice me at any point along the way.

I crouch down and peer out at the guard's box; it's quite some way away as we're on the left side of the grounds. Then the sunlight glints on a flash of blond hair.

Which means the most unfriendly guard is on duty – great.

The sun dazzles my eyes. I can't tell if he's looking over. I glance over at Isabella who is taking some chocolate out of my handbag, and hurry into the long grass. I calculate that I'll be in the open for just ten seconds – and I pray he doesn't glance over during that time.

'OK,' I whisper to Isabella again, my voice hoarse with nerves. 'See you soon. Be a good girl and wait for me, OK?'

'OK. May I have all the chocolate?' she asks.

'Yes.' I grimace. 'OK. Wish me luck!'

I run. I plunge into a sea of thick grass. I crouch

down, veiled by the wilderness, panting. Dreading shouts, threats.

Silence. The wind shushes through the grass, as though reassuring me that I'm protected. I glance back. Isabella looks happy enough, shielded from view by the trusty oak tree. I tunnel through the grass on my hands and knees. My jeans are going to be covered in green stains, but who cares?

Too soon, I reach the end of the grass square. In order to get to Herbie, I have no choice now but to stand up and walk out into the open and knock on the door of that house. I stare down at the guard's box, waiting, waiting. Time passes, the sun slides behind the clouds and I feel sweat crawl across my forehead like insects; I pray for the moment to come.

Then I see them: tourists. They walk up to the gates and start distracting the guard.

'*Now!*' I tell myself, then jump up and run for it.

I reach the front door and knock frantically upon it. There's no reply. My heart is beating like crazy. I'm so hot from sun and excitement, I feel I might faint.

I'm about to reach up and knock again.

And then . . .

. . . the wind blows. The sun beats down. The birds sing.

A voice in the distance. An angry voice. The guard has spotted me. He's stepping out of the box.

I hammer desperately upon the door. And then I turn and see him . . .

My God.

I draw in my breath sharply. A man is standing, looking at us. He's terribly old and his back is painfully stooped and he's clutching his walking stick as though he'd topple without it. He's wearing a white suit, the ebullient collar of a pink shirt folding over the top. His face is wizened like an old brown apple and his beard is stringy and white. One eye is blurred with the pinkish mollusc of cataracts; the other is bright and sharp and sparkling.

I open my mouth to speak to him, but I'm too choked up. I'm amazed at the strength of the emotion churning up inside me. He just seems so familiar, like a magical figure from a dream, like someone I've known all my life. And yet, and yet – how can that be, when I've only just met him?

9

'*You!*' the guard calls out. 'How the hell did you get in?' Then he stops as he realises that he's seen me before. His eyes bulge and an ugly look comes over his face. 'I told you that if you dared to come back I would report you to the cops. Well, now I will.'

He turns to Herbie French. 'I'm real sorry, sir. I have no idea how this woman got in here. I just—'

'Oh, do shut up,' says Herbie French. His voice – aristocratic, English, fragile – shakes me. Up until now, he has still seemed like a mirage, and hearing him speak makes him into flesh and blood, rounded and real. He turns back to me, reaching inside his jacket pocket for something. It doesn't appear to yield what he's looking for, so he tries another pocket, then another.

The guard hovers, panting, still giving me vicious looks as though he's certain that, any minute now, his employer will come to his senses and order my execution.

'Ah, here we are.' Herbie pulls a letter out of his inner pocket with a trembling flourish. 'Are you Miss Julia Rothwell – the author of this letter that I found a few days ago when I was walking?'

I feel my heart stop. *He found my letter*.

'I – I – yes,' I say.

'We found the kite too. It will be taken in for chemical analysis,' the guard adds threateningly.

'Your letter was so very charming,' says Herbie softly, ignoring him. 'Now. Where is Gerard? I want to take tea with this lady in the maze.' He turns to the guard and suddenly his sweetness vanishes in a flash of Rumpelstiltskin temper. 'Where is Gerard, I said! Get hold of him immediately, Dibbs! What do I pay you for – to sloth about doing nothing?'

'I'm s-sorry,' the guard stammers. 'I'll radio him right away.'

'Miss Rothwell, do follow me,' says Herbie. 'I'm sure you'd like to see my maze, wouldn't you?'

'Please, call me Julia,' I say, holding out my hand. But he stares down at it with an anxious frown, as though I've performed an act of great indelicacy. I quickly remove it.

'Julia,' calls Isabella from the oak tree. 'Where are you?'

'May I bring a child with me?' I ask. 'She's eight years old, is called Isabella, and she loves *The Lost Princess* as much as I do.'

Herbie nods. 'Very well. You may fetch her. Dibbs – instruct Gerard to bring three cups!'

Terrified that he might change his mind, I scurry back to the entrance and call Isabella to me.

As Herbie guides us into the maze, I turn back and give the guard a triumphant glance. He looks as though he wants to throttle me.

We follow Herbie through the twists and turns of the maze. As green shadows darken over us, Isabella grips my hand tightly. I must admit that irrational fears start to creep up on me too ...

When I reach the centre of the maze, however, a smile of delight beams on my face. It's already laid out: a white table with a cloth and a pretty, old-fashioned brown teapot that looks destined to dribble becomingly. A few copies of *The Lost Princess* are piled up beside it. The table has swan legs and is surrounded by three ornate, wrought-iron chairs also painted white. Near to the table is a sparkling fountain.

A man – who appears to be some sort of butler – strolls forward, carrying a silver plate of biscuits. We sit down and he pours tea into each cup.

'Are you happy with tea, Isabella?' I ask. She nods, though I can tell she is pretending to be grown-up and feels intimidated by Herbie.

'This blasted table!' Herbie suddenly cries, making me jump. It wobbles, and the spilled tea blots the tablecloth. To my shock, he pulls off a cardboard cover from a copy of *The Lost Princess*, folds it into a tight square and shoves it under the offending table-leg. I recall my own precious copy – dog-eared but wrapped in tissue and Bubble Wrap.

'Well, er, I suppose you have loads of copies,' I say cheerfully.

'Hmpf,' Herbie says. 'I'd really just like to burn them all. As a matter of fact, I *hate* the dratted book.'

I swallow hard. I get the feeling that he's just being provocative for effect.

'Well, I *love* it,' I say passionately, and Isabella nods as she bites into an Oreo. 'I think it's an amazing book.'

'In your letter,' Herbie French's face softens, 'you said that when you were five years old, your father read my book to you every night. My father read to me too when I was that age – all the fairytales, with the evil stepmothers and poisoned apples and wicked sisters. Of course – *ppft!* – these days, they think children ought to read about fluffy bunnies in case a book about a witch gives them *psychological trauma*. Dear God! But, nope, my father made me a reader, and that turned me into a writer.'

'Well,' I confess, 'I . . . the thing is . . . I remember my dad reading to me, but I know that our memories can lie to us. If I'm honest, he can't have been there at all.'

'Was he a superhero?' Isabella asks earnestly.

I laugh and gently tug her ponytail. She squeals and laughs too.

'No. It's just – well, my father was a bit of a naughty man. He was a gambler and he got into trouble, and my mother threw him out of the house. I remember being cross with her at the time because I missed him. So I sneaked into her room one day, looking for things that would remind of him, when I came across a copy of *The Lost Princess*.'

'Ah ...' Herbie says. 'Now, I remember this story in your letter. She said to you, "I don't want you to read this – it's not a very nice book." Ha! The biggest compliment an author could receive.'

'Why couldn't you read it?' Isabella asks. 'There's nothing bad in it.'

'Well,' I go on, 'I realise now that she was biased. She hated it because it belonged to my dad. But the moment she tried to stop me reading it – well, I became obsessed with doing just that.'

'Exactly!' Herbie agrees. He thumps his knee. 'That's why I was so delighted with those ratty, narrow-minded, right-wing idiots who tried to have *The Lost Princess* banned from schools. The more they harped on, the more the children lapped it up. Those stupid censors sent my sales through the roof. You can't buy publicity like that.'

'Absolutely,' I say, grinning. 'But it is the strangest thing – I used to wake up in the night, and I swear that I could see someone sitting at the bottom of my bed, reading *The Lost Princess* to me. He looked like Dad, he sounded like Dad, and every word in that book resonated with his voice. But he can only have been a dream, or something I made up, to deal with him going. The book is very special to me in that respect. And also because the Princess is so feisty. She tells the Prince to go away and turn back into a frog because she doesn't want to flounce around in silly dresses; she wants to fight dragons, protect her kingdom and be in charge. I think that inspired me.'

'It inspired a lot of girls,' Herbie says glumly. 'They took it all the wrong way. They think being feisty means punching each other in the playground and feminism is about kicking boys in the balls. I inspired several generations of women who just ended up behaving like the worst of the male species.' And he glares at poor Isabella, who clearly hasn't punched anyone in her life. She shrinks rather nervously.

'I don't think *every* girl took that message from it,' I protest gently.

'Oh, they all got it wrong,' he sighs. 'Even I did. The happy ending where the Prince does turn back into a frog and she spurns her rich suitor from the neighbouring kingdom to marry nice Mr Froggie ...'

'I *love* that ending,' Isabella enthuses.

'But it's all *bullshit*!' Herbie cries, ignoring me when I clasp my hands over Isabella's ears. 'It feeds the idea in kids that love is redemption, that happy endings are a given, when in real life it's all just divorce and death. Divorce, death and taxes – there, Mark Twain's certainties have, in our age, become a trio.'

By now, I'm feeling distinctly uneasy. Emotions churn inside me – awe coupled with a jumpy fear. It was naïve of me to imagine that a famous recluse would be warm and socially graceful. The man who wrote *The Lost Princess* loved humanity and poured that love into his book. The man he's become is irascible, opinionated and unpredictable.

There's a silence. A breeze blows through the maze, rattling the china on the table. Our tea has gone cold and I'm wondering if, for Isabella's sake, we ought to be going.

'Maria,' Herbie says then. 'She was the one who inspired *The Lost Princess*.'

I know that Maria was Herbie's ex-wife. I read on Wikipedia that they were married for a decade, during which time she supported him whilst he wrote his children's classic. The book was published, they divorced and Maria moved back to Italy with a new husband and refused to explain or deny anything. Rumours flew round that success had gone to Herbie's head, that he had used Maria and then tossed her away like garbage. For a while he was hated in much the way Ted Hughes was blamed for bullying Sylvia Plath. But once it became clear that Herbie was no longer writing or remotely interested in the merry-go-round of fame, people left him alone and a cult of respect and mystery evolved around him.

All this I know, but I don't say a word. My heart is beating fast, for I know I'm about to hear Herbie's side of the story.

'Even when I courted Maria – I was a thirty-year-old post-graduate in Cambridge and she had come over from Rome to learn English – I knew she was in love with another man. But she was only seventeen and I thought it was just a silly crush she had on her teacher. I behaved like the Prince in my book. I courted her the old-fashioned way and I took my time and I never gave up. It took me three hundred and sixty-five days and three hundred and sixty-five bouquets to even get her to go on a date with me. And even then she went home early with a headache. Supposedly. But I thought I'd win her over slowly, and I seemed to succeed. I even persuaded her to move to the US with me. She became a good friend as well as a lover, and greatly encouraged my writing. But she could never hate me. I ought to have known there was something wrong there. If a woman isn't capable of hating you, then you shouldn't walk her up the aisle. But I did. I did . . . and I hoped that one day she would wake up and love me. That she would finally be mine. And yet that feeling of longing was what made her my poison, my slow drip of addiction.' His voice drips gloom; he seems to have forgotten we're even present.

And then suddenly he blinks and sits upright. 'You know why *The Lost Princess* took so long to write?' He sighs, then answers his own question. 'Cancer. Maria was diagnosed with it just as I was two-thirds of the way in. Well, I dropped the book and devoted every second of the day to making her feel better. I realised I'd been selfish, shutting myself away to write about a princess based on her, when she was right in front of me, needing me. I thought that if she died, I would die too. I truly believe that a broken heart is a real medical condition, one that can kill you. But she came through ...' He blinks hard, then hastily takes some tea.

I want to reach out and touch his gnarled hand but I don't think he could stand it. So I hold my breath and stare at him with gentle sympathy. Isabella fidgets uncomfortably, but manages to keep quiet.

'She conquered it. She was a fighter, just like my princess, and she slayed her dragons of illness. I carried her home from the hospital, over the threshold like a bride. Like a princess in a fairytale. I told myself that everything would be fine from now on, and I busied myself with the book. And on the surface it was – I got a publisher, the book sold in its hundreds then thousands ... Maria was always smiling. On the outside. But inside, something was wrong. I knew that *he* was always there, in the background.'

Now I understand why Herbie wrote about his rival, caricaturised as a rich king in the book, with such venom, why the story had such potency.

'And one day I came back from a book tour, having signed thousands of books, to find *her* signature on the bottom of a note on my kitchen table. She had gone, back to her family in Rome. That was when I bought this house, and came back to live here. I've been here ever since.'

Silence. I stare at Herbie, wanting so much to offer comfort and love. I'm just reaching the point where I feel I can't restrain myself any longer and I'm going to jump up and just hug him, when he collects himself, coughs and offers me the plate of biscuits.

'Are you going to write another book?' Isabella asks shyly.

Surely he would have written many more books by now, if he had wanted to.

'I've finished my new book,' Herbie says casually, though I can see he's delighted by the shock and awe on my face. 'But nobody will ever read it, because I won't allow it to be published.'

'Ohhh!' Isabella cries, jiggling up and down in her chair. 'Please may I read it?'

He pauses, and when I realise what he's considering, I nearly faint with excitement. He reaches for a briefcase sitting by the table and pulls out a sheaf of papers on which are scrawled his spidery handwriting. And then he sits there and in his quavering voice, he begins to read from *The Mermaid Who Hated Fish*.

I only hear a few words before he puts down his papers and I suddenly realise that we've tired him out. He's not used to visitors; we've probably given him more excitement than he's had all year.

'Please read some more!' Isabella cries. She looks sad when I put a firm hand on her arm.

'I think we need to show Mr French some consideration. We've had a wonderful afternoon, but it's time we ought to be getting back.'

10

I offer to phone for a taxi, but Herbie insists that we are taken home in his chauffeur-driven Mercedes. It's long and black and sleek, with tinted windows.

'I do go out sometimes,' Herbie says, with a smile, 'it's just that nobody knows. My driver takes me through New York, or Manhattan, or Harlem. And I sit and I watch. I watch the people.' He looks sad for a moment, as though aware that he will always be separate from the rest of the world. Then he says, with old-fashioned courtesy, 'Well, goodbye, Isabella. Goodbye, Julia.'

I offer my hand, tentatively. He frowns. I let it hang in the air. And suddenly he scoops it up and plants a kiss on it.

'It has been – so wonderful to meet you.' His voice cracks and for one moment I hear the loneliness in it, the loneliness of the little boy in this elderly man who wishes he had friends to play with.

'Perhaps we could come back and see you again one day?' I suggest.

'Oh no.' He shakes his head nervously, but I see a flash of light in his eyes. I want to push it but I don't dare.

'But you can write to me,' he suddenly volunteers, to my surprise. 'I can't guarantee a reply, which is selfish of me, I know. But I do like to receive letters. I read every one I get.'

'OK,' I say in excitement. 'I'll write to you often. And please, please publish *The Mermaid Who Hated Fish*.'

Herbie gives me a vague sort of smile that promises nothing. But I know that, the next time I come through New York, I'll definitely be looking him up.

Isabella and I are on such a high we can hardly focus. There's a bar in the back of the limo. We play about with the drinks and I pour her a sumptuous orange juice. She keeps making me high-five her palm and yelling, 'We did it! I met Herbie French! I can't wait to tell all my friends at school, they're gonna be so jealous!'

And we're so overwhelmed that we completely forget about how long we've been gone, or whether anyone might have been worried. Fortunately, we're only half an hour late at Lucy's. She goes wild when Isabella announces we've just seen Herbie. I leave aunt and niece together and say that I'll see them at my leaving party later.

The driver then takes me home. The Mercedes pulls up

by the house and I thank the driver and step out. Mum's face is pressed against the window. Immediately, I'm transported away from the magical afternoon and find myself slap bang up against reality.

Since Luke, I feel as though I've been living my life on two levels. Inside, my emotional weather has been constantly grey and cloudy, whilst on the outside, I've been supposedly full of sunshine. Now, finally, my happiness feels integrated, whole.

My leaving party is just a small affair: a few of Mum's friends, Lucy and one of her exes – a stunning Swedish woman who works as a film producer in LA – and Isabella, who sits obediently on the sofa, combing her Barbie's hair.

'Honestly,' Mum says of me, 'burrowing under fences and crawling through fields ... You were just the same when you were nine – such a tomboy!' She sounds disapproving but there's a proud look in her eyes.

I feel glad that Lucy didn't join me in the final Herbie excursion, as much as I love her, since Mum would inevitably have attributed all the success to her. It would have diluted my triumph. And Lucy doesn't need an ego boost. For the first time since I've lost my job, I feel glorious, I feel exhilarated, I feel – *yes!* – that I believe in myself, that I can do anything, achieve the impossible.

Or maybe the American sense of get up and go is taking me over!

I decide that number five on my list has been my best

experience so far. It's just a shame that I didn't manage to get my father's details on this trip as well. I don't think I can ask for them again before I leave tomorrow.

Mum catches my eye as though she knows just what I'm thinking. When the phone rings a minute later, she jumps on it, eager for a diversion.

'It's Reece,' she says. 'She's been trying to get you for days.'

'Oh, I ...' I break off awkwardly. 'Can't you say I'm out?'

'I've told her you're in,' Mum says. We're back in normal teenager verus mother mode again. 'Come on, Julia. Be polite and speak to your friend.'

I roll my eyes, mutter excuses to Lucy, who nods and grins, and take the phone out into the hall.

'Hi, Reece,' I say brightly, my voice singing with guilt.

'Hello, stranger,' Reece says in a testy voice, and I realise that she must be justifiably pissed off with me.

'Sorry,' I say quickly. 'When we were in Sicily, I saw your pregnancy test in the bin. I thought you and Ciaran were planning to start a family and I just accidentally mentioned it to him on the phone. I know it was very indiscreet.'

'Oh God, no worries!' Reece's voice lifts and she lets out a giggle, which confuses me. So just what *is* pissing her off? 'But it's hilarious that you could possibly think we'd ever have kids. I'm so fed up with him. We're practically on the verge of splitting up. That's why I've been bloody ringing you. What the hell have you been doing that you've had no time to speak to your best friend?' Her words are light but I hear the hurt in her voice.

'I'm sorry ... I've just ... I can't believe that you're about to split up,' I cry. 'You've been together for so long – I thought it was all fine between you.'

'Exactly. Fine is the word. Fine is boring boring boring. Thank God I'm *not* pregnant.'

Boring? How can anyone find Ciaran boring? It's like saying that David Bowie's *Life on Mars* is a cute pop song or that the Sistine Chapel has a few pretty scribbles on its ceiling.

'So what about Luke?' Reece goes on, as though my love life is far more interesting than hers.

I take a gulp of iced tea and stare at the wall. I've been waiting for this moment for so long. For Reece and Ciaran's relationship to come to a natural end. I ought to feel euphoric. Instead, I just feel blank. Luke has left my heart closed in a tight fist. All the love has drained away; I've got nothing left to feel.

'So come on,' Reece repeats. 'How is it that you broke up with Luke?'

'Well ...' My voice catches. 'It turns out that he was with a girl, and he got her pregnant, and because he's some kind of lame commitment-phobe, he left her and their baby son and just went travelling. He forgot to mention these small points when we first met.'

There's a long silence. I wait for Reece to commiserate.

'But why did you dump him? I mean, that makes him sound so *exciting*!'

'Oh, maybe if he'd fathered six more children with various women around the globe, then he would have been even more attractive,' I snap.

'Hey hey,' Reece bounces back at me. 'I suppose I'm so fed up with Ciaran that any other guy with a bit of spice in him sounds a lot more fascinating. But you know, Julia, he has left this girl, hasn't he, so what's the problem?'

'But – it shows he's unreliable and irresponsible and really not a very nice person.'

'I think it's brave of him,' Reece asserts. Maybe she's just in a mood to argue and whatever I say, she's going to disagree. 'I mean, look, some couples spend decades being unhappily married because neither has the guts to leave. At least Luke's being honest with you.'

I feel completely flummoxed. Does Reece really believe that? I feel as though she's taken hold of my judgement and turned it inside out. Was I too harsh on him? Surely not?

And then Reece says in a cajoling voice: 'Ciaran mentioned that you weren't happy about us coming to Las Vegas. Are you really going to wander about all those casinos by yourself, losing money?'

Now I feel mean and embarrassed, for I can't tell her the real reason I wanted to stop them from coming. 'I'd love you to come, Reece, you're my best friend – of course I want you there. But won't you and Ciaran just be miserable if you both come?'

'Well, I said that to him, but he wants to tag along anyway. He says it's one last chance to save our relationship.'

'Oh, so Ciaran wants to save it?' I ask quickly.

'Well, maybe,' Reece says. 'He's also burned out. He says he wants a break from the City.'

I feel a flash of sympathy for that.

'All right then,' I say at last. 'The more the merrier.'

'And you should ask Luke to come along too,' Reece tells me. 'He'd be fun! Seriously, if you get bored, *I'll* look after him.'

'Luke?' I say in disbelief. 'He has no money except his lucky dollar. No, Reece, there'll be plenty of rich Texans for you to leap on. And yes, I'd love to have you there . . . *both* of you.'

As I switch off the phone I pause, Reece's words ringing in my mind. Did I overreact when Luke told me about Jodie? Have I behaved like a bitch by not returning his calls? I remember the pleading tone of his messages and feel my stomach curl.

Since my argument with Mum, I've also become conscious of history repeating itself. My dad left her when we were kids, apparently went off to be a playboy and romp his way around the world. I always thought that psychology maxims about children rewriting their parents' histories were a cliché, but now I know they're real: when I dated Luke I was unconsciously seeking out a replica of my dad. All right, so Luke isn't a criminal, and he certainly isn't heading for jail, but he is utterly unreliable and impossible to pin down. And yet . . . Luke was wrong to lie to me, but perhaps my rage was out of proportion. Maybe I've never quite forgiven Dad for deserting us. Maybe that's why I've also been unable to forgive Luke; the two of them are blurring in my heart.

But it's too late now. Luke has stopped calling me. He's given up on me, has moved on. It's over. Isn't it?

I go back to the celebration party feeling somewhat more pensive.

'Well, it has been *so* amazing to meet you,' Lucy declares. 'You're just incredible – the first fan in twenty years to get to see Herbie French in the flesh. The next time you're in NY, you have to look me up. We'll do Salinger next, right? If he's still alive.'

I laugh with delight. We're up in my bedroom. My cases are packed and all my socks are firmly wedged into plastic bags this time round. The party has pretty much ended, but Lucy came up because she says she has a present for me. I can tell by the shape that it's a painting. I tear off the wrapping paper.

'Wow!' I cry, my heart thumping. 'It's *me*!'

Lucy smiles. 'You do love it, don't you? I just knew you'd love it. It'll be valuable one day.' And she winks at me.

Do I love it? To be honest, I'm not sure what to make of it. I like Lucy's style but this is definitely one of her more abstract pictures. I suppose that triangle is meant to represent my ear. And is that blue streak my eyes? But the point is, she did this picture for me, and she painted it with love; the luminosity of her affection is there in the thick brushstrokes.

I tell Lucy she's a brilliant painter and an even more wonderful friend. I tell her that she's one of the coolest people I've ever met and I hope we stay friends for years to come. Lucy gives me a tight hug and I hug her back just as tightly. My heart floods with warmth: I've never even felt this sort of emotion with Reece and I've known her practically for all my life. Then I feel Lucy's palms caressing my spine in soothing circles. I remember reading somewhere that there's a mystical snake that coils around our spine; desire pulls the energy down, divine love pulls the energy up. Suddenly I sense a tension between us. Lucy pulls back. Her green eyes glance at my lips. I feel desire flutter inside me – and then I panic. As she leans in, I turn my head. Her kiss lands on my cheek.

Lucy stares at me. I stare down at my lap.

She stands up and I look up – and I see something in her eyes that surprises me. A vulnerability. Lucy has always seemed so strong, but now she's raw with the pain of rejection.

'Well, I guess I'll see you around,' she says lightly, composing her face into a mask of polite interest.

I don't want us to part company like this. I *want* to kiss her. Sort of. Maybe I should just jump up and kiss her myself, right now. Maybe I should, but I don't quite have the nerve.

'Lucy, would you like to come to Las Vegas with me and my friends?' I blurt out, on the spur of the moment.

'To Vegas?' she asks in surprise.

'I'm going with a couple of friends – Reece and her boyfriend, Ciaran.'

'Well, I did want to get on with some new paintings for a show, but I could spare a couple of nights.' Lucy's face lights up in joy. 'Hey, why not? Sure.' She holds my gaze with her sexy, magnetic eyes. 'I'll come.'

6. Gamble in Las Vegas

and

7. Kiss a girl
and see if I like it

1

I press the green button on my phone then put it against my ear, the plastic slippery against my moist palm. With every ring, I want to hang up. I become conscious that I'm pressing my lips together tightly, which Ciaran used to say I do whenever I'm feeling nervous or upset.

I'm sitting on a bed in a plush bedroom in the Mandalay Bay Hotel, Las Vegas. It's cool in here but baking hot outside. Next to me, Reece gives me a sharp nudge in the ribs to say, *Go on, then.*

'I don't think he's going to pick up—' I break off as I hear Luke answer. Damn. 'Oh – hi.'

'Hi.' In that one syllable I can hear his suspicion.

It has been three weeks since we've spoken.

'Hi, how are you?' I ask awkwardly.

'I'm not so bad ... not so bad.'

Silence. Oh God, this is excruciating.

'It's kind of a surprise, hearing from you,' Luke says at

last. 'I mean, I was calling and calling, and you just ... and now – here you are.'

I'd forgotten how enticing his voice is. A light, sexy purr. Despite myself, I feel something tug at my heart.

'I'm actually in the US right now,' I say, laughing uneasily.

'Are you serious? So am I! What state?'

'Las Vegas. I'm here with my friend, Reece. We, er, wanted to ...'

'... lose all your money in the casinos and feel a high whilst you do it?'

'Something like that.' I smile at Reece, who is listening, fascinated.

'So,' Luke hesitates. 'Do you girls wanna helping hand with that?'

I hear the nerves in his voice. Wondering if he's gone too far, suggesting a reunion. I open my mouth, then close it.

'*Go on*,' Reece whispers.

Why am I doing this?

Because of Reece.

We both arrived in Vegas this morning on separate flights. When I told Reece that Lucy was going to join us in a few days' time, she got really excited and did a crazy little dance around my hotel room.

Then it turned out that we were at cross purposes. She thought I'd meant *Luke*. When I pointed out that I had no wish to exchange so much as a syllable with Luke ever again, she told me I was being utterly cruel and unfair, until I practically felt as though I was on trial for war crimes.

Then she pushed and pushed for me to call him.

'No,' I resisted, turning my back on her, hanging up my clothes briskly.

'A call means nothing. It can last all of five minutes.'

'Maybe.' I relented; I did have to admit that a part of me was still curious about him. The situation had been left so open-ended. Perhaps some closure would be a good thing.

'He's probably halfway across the world anyway,' Reece asserted. 'So call him, call him, call him.'

Except that Luke isn't halfway across the world. He's just a few states away, and he wants to come here – and suddenly it's all happening so fast. I stare over at Reece. Normally she is so lazy and carefree that when she does get determined about something, her stubbornness knows no bounds. If I don't agree to let him come, she'll probably bang on my hotel-room door all night until I call him back. For a moment I wonder why this means so much to her.

On the other end of the line, Luke waits, the silence blooming between us.

'All right, you can come,' I reply finally. Then I can't resist adding: 'You can bring Jodie if you like.'

Reece frowns in disapproval, but I swing away, ignoring her.

'Jodie's in England,' he says quietly.

'Well, then come by yourself,' I say at last.

A pause.

'No,' he says in a subdued tone. 'Maybe I just shouldn't come at all.'

'What?' Now I do feel mean and cruel. 'But it'll be great, you'll enjoy it.' Hang on. How come the tables have turned and now *I'm* the one begging him to come? He's playing his guilt game again – he does it so well.

'Well, cool – thanks!' Luke cries, his voice as bouncy as an excited puppy. 'I'm gonna book a flight and get over to you right away. I'll see you tomorrow then, Jeanette.'

I can't help but laugh as I remember the game we played with the American couple in Japan.

'I'll look forward to it, Michelangelo,' I reply. And then we say goodbye and I switch off my phone and pretend to murder Reece.

'There,' I snap at her. 'Are you happy now?'

'Yes! I only want *you* to be happy, Julia.' Reece gives me a big hug back. 'I just think you and Luke have something special. I feel it, here.' She touches her heart, looking earnest. 'You're meant to be together.' Then she swishes her hand through my hair. 'And your new haircut makes you look gorgeous. Luke will love it. I can see this *Ten Things* project has done you a power of good.'

'It's just a haircut,' I say nonchalantly, feeling quite touched by Reece's speech.

'It's more than that,' she cries indignantly. 'You've changed, Julia. You're not checking your BlackBerry every five minutes. You don't look like a vampire any more. You look years younger. And I take full credit,' she beams, laughing as I punch her gently. 'But seriously – you do look great. Ciaran commented on it.'

'Really?' I ask, surprised.

I saw Ciaran this morning, very briefly. He was looking worse for wear: jetlag had painted dark circles under his eyes, his Sicilian tan a ghost lingering on his pale skin. Did my heart jump when I saw him? Yes, the same as always. I can't ever seem to stop the physical effect he has on me. He only has to smile and my heart will dance to his tune. But now I feel a little more detached, a little more in control about the situation.

'So, are we all going out tonight?' I ask Reece.

'Oh, I don't know – Ciaran and I might just be too busy *making babies*,' Reece says sarcastically.

I grin sheepishly, knowing that she isn't going to let me forget my *faux pas* no matter how many times I apologise. I open my mouth to ask how things are going between them, then close it. Maybe it's better not to ask. After Reece goes, I sit down on the bed, feeling full of trepidation. Ciaran tonight; Luke tomorrow. Talk about an emotional hurricane. It's all a little bit too much for one trip.

2

So. *Gamble in Las Vegas* is number six on my list. I always thought that Las Vegas was one of those places you had to visit. Now I'm beginning to wonder if I should have chosen the Pyramids in Egypt. Or the Great Wall of China instead.

When we arrived this morning, I was fairly under-whelmed by Vegas. The sky was grey and cloudy. Everything seemed oversized and slightly tacky. The main roads were a gush of honking cabs spewing fumes, and under a grubby palm tree a random American pushed a card into my hand. It had a picture of a blonde 'Hot Babe' on it, with a number to call. I tossed it back at him in annoyance.

Then in the evening, my opinion starts to change.

Ciaran, Reece and I head out to get some dinner. The Mandalay Hotel is on The Strip, which is basically one long runway of hotel glitz. We catch the Monorail, a yellow train with a ticket machine that advertises *We're about to deal you the card you need*, which makes me smile. As we travel down The Strip, I see that Vegas is a place that needs to be appreciated after dark. The night waves a magic wand: dull becomes glitz, brashness becomes grandeur. It's a little like being in a cartoon version of Japan; neon screams brand-names Coca Cola, McDonald's, Walmart. We pass all the famous hotels: New York-New York; the MGM Grand; Planet Hollywood; the Bellagio; Caesar's Palace. Each soars into the sky, ferociously competing to be bigger and better, each a mini-continent in itself, boasting a sprawl of shopping malls, restaurants, casinos, live shows, spectaculars, bars, pools. At Treasure Island there are live shows where pirates clash with sirens; there's the infamous X-Scream extreme roller-coaster ride which lifts you 900 feet into the air and then freezes at a 30-degree angle; there's the Bonzana Gift Shop, the world's largest gift store, and the Interactive Star Trek Experience, considered to be a Mecca for Trekkie fans. There's so much to do, you could spend a year here and probably not see everything.

Lingering over all this debauchery like a spectre is the recession. There are hotels which began in the boom and now hang suspended in mid-build, their skeletal frames home to ghosts and the elements. Opulent houses which once contained happy families, had millions wiped off their value and now sit empty with forlorn *For Sale* signs wilting outside. On the plane over, I even read one article declaring that Vegas is in danger of completely going bust if business doesn't pick up, and every hotel is frantically offering deals for meals and accommodation and fun.

Well, Vegas might be losing money but it hasn't lost its sparkle. We sit on the Monorail, flipping through our guidebooks, exhausted and exhilarated by choice. All three of us are hot and sweaty. Though it was overcast when we arrived, the temperature seems to be rising.

'I think we should head for Paris Las Vegas,' says Ciaran. 'I want to see their mini-Eiffel Tower.'

'Well, I think we should have gone to the Rumjungle,' Reece says. 'I wanted to see the wall of fire around it.'

They both look at me and I realise that the triangle of love and friendship between us has shifted. Suddenly, it's no longer Ciaran and me being rude and Reece playing peacemaker.

Now I'm the peacemaker.

'OK,' I say briskly, feeling weirdly as though I'm dealing with two kids. 'We've already passed them a few stops back. So I think we should go to . . .' I stare at the map of The Strip above, seeing that we're heading towards the end. 'The Circus Circus Hotel. That sounds fun.'

Reece pouts. Ciaran nods but looks a bit sullen.

But neither of them can stay in a bad mood when we come to the spectacular place that is Circus Circus. Ciaran cheers up hugely when he realises that it featured as a malevolent playground in *Fear and Loathing in Las Vegas* by Hunter S. Thompson, one of his favourite writers. And Reece simply gapes at its gaudy beauty: the sweeping neon faux-circus stripes in blues and grey above electric orange that screamy CIRCUS CIRCUS.

Inside, we're not sure where to eat, so we head for the Garden Grill where Reece and I order pasta and Ciaran opts for a turkey steak.

'I hear your friend Lucy's going to join us in a few days' time,' Ciaran says 'What's she like?'

'She's wonderful – you'll love her. She's an artist and she's really glamorous. Here.' I proudly show them a pic of her on my mobile phone.

'Wow,' says Ciaran, then winces as Reece nudges him sharply.

'She's a lesbian,' Reece points out. Then she tosses back her hair and adds, 'By the way, Luke is coming too.' She gives a little smile, as though anticipating how annoyed Ciaran will be.

Sure enough ... 'What!' Ciaran cries. 'That tosser is coming here? I thought you and he were over, Julia? That guy has more skeletons in his closet than an MP!'

For one nano-second I wonder if Reece just wanted Luke to come to annoy Ciaran. So I hastily change the subject. I tell them all about New York and my adventure, breaking into the grounds to reach the house of Herbie French. Ciaran looks quite stunned when I tell him that I finally got to speak to him.

Reece just asks, 'Who's Herbie French?'

Ciaran chokes on his Coke. 'How can you not know who he is?'

Another argument starts to simmer. Reece points out hotly that French lives in America, so why should she know him? She hisses that when Madonna was asked who Enid Blyton was, she had no idea. I hastily ask for the bill.

When we get on to the Monorail this time, the others sit in hostile silence. Ciaran pulls out a handkerchief and mops the sweat off his brow. I feel so uncomfortable. Would it be better just to head back to our rooms, or try for one last attraction to cheer them up?

So, back at the Mandalay, I suggest we go to the famous Aureole Tower. We sit in the lounge close to a forty-two-foot wine tower. It's made of glass and we gape at the 9,500 odd bottles glimmering inside it, in all shades of scarlet and burgundy and deep gold.

'Wow.' Ciaran's eyes sparkle with excitement. He turns to Reece and his expression softens. I feel the yin and yang of emotion; I'm both touched and jealous. 'I'm going to buy you a bottle, darling. Would you like red or white?'

'Red, please,' Reece whispers.

A waiter takes his order. We watch in enthralled silence as a Wine Angel, donning rock-climbing gear, is hoisted up the tower via motorised cables. I can see her lips moving and I figure that she's chatting to staff on a cordless mike. The Angels, all dressed in black, flit through the tower, picking out bottles and delivering them to people below.

Finally, Reece's bottle arrives, presented with a flourish. Reece looks at it and folds her arms.

'I've changed my mind,' she says. 'I want white. Please send it back.'

Ciaran blinks hard. I touch Reece's arm but she shakes me off. We watch as our Wine Angel returns the bottle of red to its correct place, then goes hunting for a bottle of white. Then, when it finally arrives, Reece takes one sip and says she doesn't like it and wishes they'd got red after all.

Ciaran gets up without a word and walks out of the bar without looking back.

Back at the hotel, I go into my bathroom and look in the mirror. My reflection looks knackered. It's as though my jetlag is piling up. Part of me is still washing with the Venetian tides, another is still embracing the night in Sicily, another is waking up for a Tokyo dawn, and yet another is strolling downtown in daytime New York. But I've grown used to this feeling of disorientation now. I've even started to like it.

I just wish we hadn't had such a tense evening. Dear God, I hope we're not going to have to endure a whole week of this. I squeeze a splodge of Ayurvedic cleansing lotion into my palm, smoothing it over my face. My fingers tremble on my cheeks. I still feel shaken after seeing Reece and Ciaran fight. Somehow the ugliness of it all reminded me of when I was a kid, watching my parents bicker, realising they were fragile human beings like me.

I know this sounds paranoid, but somehow I feel as though I'm to blame for the breakdown of their relationship. I'm not particularly superstitious, but I've always believed that our thoughts are powerful things, not to be underestimated, and I'm suddenly scared that my secret yearning has worked some kind of voodoo.

Then I tell myself not to be so stupid. It's just a product of my ongoing guilt about secretly liking Ciaran. But what if they do break up? Then what? I thought my feelings for Ciaran had withered away, but ... will they blossom again?

In bed, I can't sleep. I'm so tired but I feel too anxious to relax. Picking up my notebook, I attempt a really tedious task in the hope it will send me off to sleep – working out how much money I have left. Seeing those skeletal, half-built hotels today disturbed me. I can't help feeling that I ought to be tightening my belt rather than throwing my precious money into slot machines.

Within five minutes, I'm more awake than ever. In fact, I'm practically having a bloody heart attack. Have I really spent *that* much? How? Where did it go?

Shit.

At the start of my trip, I made a sharp mental note of everything I spent. Over the last few weeks I've relaxed and forgotten to keep count. Now I'm not sure I even have enough to complete my *Ten Things* list. Maybe I can *just* about do it – if I economise.

Tokyo. That's where I slipped up. I didn't realise how expensive it would be. And I knew Luke was a backpacker so I felt sorry for him, picking up meals and treats along the way, when all the time he's seriously rich.

I feel angry with him – but then I remind myself that he didn't con me. I did it out of pure love and affection. It felt right at the time.

I still can't quite believe he's supposed to be here tomorrow. A part of me is convinced he won't turn up. For one thing, how will he get the money for his flight and hotel? But if he does come – well, then, I'll see how it goes. I just feel grateful to Reece for making me call him. I do need to resolve this; I do need to talk with him, to lighten this pain that is still heavy in my heart.

I put my notebook to one side. I'm definitely going to have to economise. One slot machine a night will have to be my maximum. I'm about to switch off the light, when there's a knock on my hotel door.

It's Reece. Her face is streaked with tears, her cheeks scarlet.

'What's up?' I ask.

'He dumped me,' she confesses in a choked voice. 'It's all over. Bloody Ciaran dumped me.'

3

I stare down at Reece. We're curled up in bed together. She's cried herself out and is now sleeping soundly. I myself am wide awake. I'm in a state of shock. I can't believe Ciaran could just dump her like that – and say those nasty things. He told Reece she was ditzy and stupid, and that he was sick of her. I'm sure he said all this in the heat of the moment – they were both in a very volatile mood this evening. And I have to admit that Reece was behaving like a six year old and being a complete pain over the wine. But still – it seems so harsh.

I feel as though a bubble has been burst. I've secretly ached for this moment to happen. But I always imagined that they'd split amicably, or that Ciaran would dump Reece in a gentlemanly fashion. I'd always believed that his cynical exterior hid a heart of gold – but maybe he's hardened over the last eighteen months. Reece said he even pulled her hair and she was scared that he'd be violent with her. I can't help wondering if I've been carrying a fantasy of Ciaran around with me. Perhaps I don't know him quite as well as I thought I did.

And I can't help thinking how difficult this trip is going to be now. I am grateful that Luke and Lucy will be joining us, or the tensions would be unbearable.

In the morning, Reece seems to have cheered up a little. I spoil her by ordering up breakfast and she munches on a roll whilst I take a shower.

When I come out of the bathroom, I catch Reece standing by my side of the bed. She's holding something and she quickly twists her hands behind her back. I put my hands on my hips, narrowing my eyes. I think I can guess what she's got hold of.

'Reece!' I cry. 'That *Ten Things* list is *private*.'

'I didn't read it,' she says immediately. 'I thought it was a shopping list.' Then she pauses, and a sparkle comes into her eyes. 'I can't believe we shared a bed together last night. I hope you didn't lie there fantasising about snogging me.'

'What!' Then I blush fiercely, remembering.

'Number six,' Reece reads aloud. 'Gamble in Las Vegas. Number seven, kiss a girl and see if I like it.'

'Oh Reece!' I cry. 'Look. I don't fancy you – OK? We're *friends*.'

'Why not?' Reece looks offended. 'Are you saying I'm a dog?'

I grin. 'Sorry, you're just not my type,' I snigger. 'I prefer brunettes.'

Reece pokes out her tongue, then collapses on the bed. I go over and ruffle her hair. It's meant to be affectionate, a gesture that says *Are you feeling all right after last night?* but she looks awkward.

'Oh Reece!' I practically shout. 'Don't be an idiot. For all I know, I may hate women. The whole list is meant to be about fun and adventure, right? So that's what I'm doing.'

'Cool.' Reece leans over and gives me a hug. 'I'm cool with that.' Then she draws back. 'But is that why you've invited this Lucy girl over to Vegas?'

I shrug, blushing slightly. 'Well, we are actually good friends.'

'Julia!' Reece pokes me in the ribcage. 'I didn't realise you were so debauched. Gambling and bisexual kisses – who would've thought it. You've definitely changed. You're becoming wild.' Then she peers at my list again. 'I don't see how you're going to do number eight. It sounds very abstract.'

'Well, I'm going to India after this,' I say. 'I felt it would be the best place to explore number eight.'

'Oh, right,' Reece says, still looking confused. Then: 'And what about number ten?'

Suddenly my heart judders in shock. Oh God. Did I actually write down *Tell Ciaran O'Hare I love him* on the list? Then, when I glance over and see a blank space,

I breathe out in shaky relief. Oh, thank God, thank God. Yes, I remember rewriting the list, leaving number ten open. Ciaran had been on my list. Then I felt it was inappropriate and took him off it. Now my final goal is flickering, uncertain.

'I just like the idea of doing these nine things,' I explain to Reece, 'and then I'll get to number ten and I'll know at that point if there's anything else I really need to do. I like the idea of a bit of mystery. It makes it all less predictable.'

I just hope that by the time I get to it, I might be able to replace it with something a little less painful than declaring unrequited love to Ciaran.

'Hmm,' Reece says. She screws up her face earnestly. 'Maybe it'll be *Have a lesbian marriage and buy a turkey baster . . .*' She squeals as I shove her.

'But seriously,' I ask, feeling slightly bemused by her high spirits, 'are you feeling OK?'

'Oh, fine,' Reece says breezily. 'I'm really looking forward to meeting this Lucy now. And Luke. I *so* cannot wait to meet *him*.'

I walk away, frowning, plugging in the hair-dryer. In a few hours' time Luke will be here and I feel as jittery as hell. Just how will it feel to come face to face with him again?

4

I'm waiting in the lobby of the Venice Hotel. I watch the
hordes of tourists queuing up by the check-in desk –
Americans, Chinese, Europeans, all looking haggard with
jetlag but bright with anticipation. How can Luke afford
this place, I wonder. I also wonder why he booked a
different hotel instead of staying in the Mandalay Bay
with us.

I'm not sure how I feel about meeting him. I alternate
between feeling fluttery with nerves, then detached, then
angry. On the Monorail over here, my emotions played
out a hundred different reunions. We kissed passionately;
I slapped him round the face; we argued; I walked off in
fury; he walked off in guilt. But when he steps out of the
lift and strolls over to me, there's no melodrama. It just
feels incredibly awkward.

He's looking as handsome as ever and his charisma is
sweet in his smile, cute in his brown eyes. He opens his

arms to give me a hug but something inside me balks. He drops his arms uneasily. Then I feel like a cow, so I step in just as he turns away. Finally, I offer him my hand. He gives it a quizzical look, then shakes it gently, smiling. His grip becomes a caress. I pull my hand away.

'You're still wearing your Bob Marley T-shirt,' I observe.

'Uh – yep.' He grins down at it. Then he looks me up and down in a way that I find both sexy and insulting. 'You're looking great.'

'Thanks.' I fold my arms. 'I think it would be good to talk, don't you?'

'Yeah. I actually thought it would be nice to take a gondola ride,' Luke says. 'I mean, we never got to do that in Venice, did we? Then we can … talk.'

When I first arrived in Las Vegas yesterday, the guide told us that it contained all of the world in one city. Many of the hotels along the Vegas Strip are European-themed. The Paris balloon, for example, boasts a small-scale Eiffel Tower. The Venice Hotel is supposed to resemble Italy's most beautiful city. Its most showy spectacle is a waterway based on Venice's canals, with gondolas and a shopping mall dressed up as a piazza. There is even a replica St Mark's Square.

Naturally, it takes us a while to walk over there; the hotels around here are so big I wished I'd remembered to bring my hiking equipment. Really, if Scott was alive today he wouldn't bother with the Antarctic, he'd just hike his way around here. When Luke casually mentions that he booked into the Venice Hotel so I wouldn't feel crowded being in the same hotel as him, I shoot him an ironic glance.

We walk in silence for most of the way, conscious that we're saving our words for the privacy of the gondola. I glance over at Luke and he glances back, and I can tell we share a slightly surreal sense of disbelief that we're here now, reunited in such unexpected surroundings. And I feel a moment of sadness, remembering the giddy way I danced down the steps of Narita Airport station in Tokyo, excited about meeting this great guy I'd kissed in Venice, in a state of blissful ignorance. Back then, I could never have imagined that I'd be here with Luke, having fled from him after discovering he was nearly married with a kid. I feel a flicker of cynicism, and wonder if all relationships walk down an inevitable path of romantic innocence to painful experience.

What will Luke and I be doing tonight? How will we feel about each other in a week, a month? Will we even be in touch in a year's time?

We slip into the gondola.

'Hey, this is quite impressive,' I say, glancing at the blue ribbons of water. 'I was a bit sceptical about trying to replicate Venice – but this isn't bad.'

'I think it's great!' Luke exclaims.

He slides a little closer, so that our shoulders are touching.

'I'm sorry,' he says. 'I've wanted to say that for weeks now.' He grabs my hands. 'I'm sorry, I'm sorry, I'm sorry.'

I pull my hands away.

'So have you been with her? With Jodie?'

'Look, Julia, I'm not with them, OK? I know I have a kid, and I love Winston, but it's never going to work with Jodie. I'll be friends with her for life, for Winston's sake, but that's all. I've actually been with my dad.'

'What's he like?' I ask softly.

'He's just some guy. A bit of a hippie. He lives in California . . .' He breaks off, seeing my face. 'What?'

'Do you have to lie about everything?' I cry hotly.

'*What?*'

'You! You – I know *for a fact* that your dad is a big oil baron, and he's loaded, and he wanted you to work in his company only you rebelled and went off and did your own thing.'

'How did you know that?' Luke goes pale.

'I called up Jodie,' I say. Then, just as he looks completely crazy, I shake my head. 'I'm kidding. When I was in Tokyo, after I came back from our thing on Mount Fuji, I went to a bar and I bumped into this guy, Dave. He said he knew you. He said you met on some beach in Bali.'

'What?' Luke's face lights up. 'Dave from Bali? Oh wow, but that's – wow! You say you just bumped into him?'

'Yes.'

'But don't you *see*?' Luke cries, seizing my hands again. 'That is Fate with a capital F. I mean, what are the odds

317

of you just *bumping* into him and him knowing me and you discussing me? How can you say it's not meant to be between us?'

I stare up at his brown eyes. His expression is so earnest, so ardent that I find myself softening. I have a sudden flashback: Luke and I in the shower together, kissing hungrily, Luke whispering that this was one of the most special experiences he'd ever had. He said the words with such conviction, with such sweet passion, I can still feel their echo shivering through me.

'So why did you lie about your father?' I ask quietly.

'I lie about him to everyone,' Luke admits. 'I just feel so embarrassed that my dad is this big evil right-wing oil baron. I can hardly believe we're even related. But I don't lie about anything else,' he says hastily.

I'm about to say, 'Oh sure,' when he carries on firing: 'Besides, you lied to me. You told me you were a hedge-fund manager when you'd got the sack.'

'That's different,' I say, blushing.

'Is it? We both felt ashamed of mistakes we've made. So we tried to hide the past because we felt it didn't belong to us.'

We both fall silent. Luke stares at me; I stare into the distance. The artifice of this place suddenly strikes me. Despite every effort to replicate Venice, it's just not the same. The light in Venice has a translucence that can't be imitated by artificial means. I suddenly want to get out of this boat and this fake river, but Luke leans down and plants a kiss on the edge of my lips. I turn, wanting to tell him to stop. But when his warm lips touch mine, I find myself responding. I close my eyes, feeling his hand move down my spine, pressing against the small of my back, pulling me closer.

Then my eyelids flutter open. His are closed; he's engrossed in the kiss. I want to drown too, but it feels as though the knot of tension in my heart is tighter than ever, and the kiss makes it throb like a wound. I pull away from him, pressing my hands against his chest.

'I'm sorry.'

Luke smiles at me, as though I'm just playing, and leans in again. I turn my head and he kisses my hair, lightly biting my ear.

'Stop it!' I cry, clamping my hand over my ear. 'Seriously, I just can't . . .' I knit my fingers together.

'Are you sorry I came?' Luke asks in a wounded voice.

God, why does he have such a knack for making *me* feel guilty? I open my mouth to have a go at him. Then his brown eyes melt me.

'Look, I'd like us to be friends,' I say. 'I'm glad you came – I do like you, very, very much. But it'll take time, you know. To trust you again.'

Luke sits in silence, brooding.

'This place just isn't Venice,' I remark, trying to lighten things up. 'It's just not the same. I mean, those Venetian houses have shopping malls behind them, selling Nike. It doesn't work for me.'

Luke gives me a wobbly smile, says, 'Maybe we can go back to Venice. Maybe we can spend time there after Vegas.'

'My friends are coming along tonight,' I say. 'It would be really nice to hang out together. Just see how everything goes.'

Luke nods. He looks beaten down. My guilt rears up again, but I fight it hard. *I'm doing the right thing*, I tell myself. *He has to earn my trust. If he really likes me, then he'll be patient.*

'Oh wow!' is the first thing Reece says when I introduce her to Luke. 'Julia never told me you were this gorgeous!'

Luke laughs, unabashed, as Reece gives him a huge hug. I roll my eyes at him to reassure him that she is always like this.

All the same, seeing Luke through Reece's vision reminds me of indeed how yummy he is. I see the chestnut glitter in his thick hair, the sweetness of his melted-chocolate eyes, appreciate his athletic build as though I'm seeing him for the first time.

'Hey, good to meet you,' Luke greets Ciaran, proffering a hand.

I get the feeling Ciaran has taken an instant dislike to Luke. He forces a smile and shakes his hand but I can see something snarling in his eyes.

'Hi,' he says politely. 'I hear you recently became a father. Congratulations.'

Luke's eyes widen. He quickly drops Ciaran's hand. Reece mutters, 'Oh God,' under her breath. Then we all stand there, simmering in the heat and one of the most embarrassing silences I've ever endured.

Then Reece breaks it by bursting out: 'So, did you propose to Julia on the gondola?'

Luke laughs, shooting me a bemused look.

'Reece has a colourful imagination,' I say, giving her a playful slap.

'The answer is no,' Luke says. 'I'd like Julia to be with me, but she's kinda put me on probation. So I guess you could just say that we're friends for now.' He stares into my eyes, his expression flirty. 'I'm hoping if I maintain good behaviour, I'll get a reward.'

We all laugh – well, all of us except for Ciaran. Suddenly I feel anger flare up inside me. I just don't know what's got into Ciaran; I've never seen him behave like this before. I feel like shaking him and crying, 'You're the one who dumped Reece. You're the one who behaved like a bastard. What the hell is going on with you?'

We head for the casinos. For once there's no indecision: we all agree that the Bellagio is our first choice. Outside the hotel are the famous glorious fountains, lit up gold so the frothing water looks like ambrosia. Pavarotti's arias fill the air; the light seems to dance in time with the music. Luke's spirit of fun has lightened the group. Reece, Luke and I keep joking and chatting, whilst Ciaran strolls behind us, arms folded, as stony as a Mafia gangster. By the fountains, we stop to take a few photos on our mobiles and Luke makes me and Reece laugh by threatening to do a striptease and jump into the water. Reece wolf-whistles and eggs him on, but Luke chickens out, saying he doesn't want to get arrested just before he's about to win a million dollars at Blackjack.

'What about you, Julia?' Luke asks teasingly. 'D'you think you might be a millionaire by the time the night's over?'

I grin, but my stomach churns, recalling the calculations I did and remembering just how little I have to play with. Anything I gamble will risk cutting short my trip, sending me back to England at the end of this Vegas holiday.

'And have you got anything to gamble *with*?' I ask. I mean to sound teasing too, but I'm conscious that there's a barb in my voice.

'Don't worry, I'm not gonna beg you for a loan, if that's what you're thinking,' Luke jokes.

'Oh no,' I say, though secretly I was wondering.

'I worked for my dad's company for the last few weeks – just shitty office work – but now I have some money of my own.'

'Cool.' Now I feel sheepish.

'Julia's just so tight and mean with money,' Reece asserts. 'I once bought her this little pot which is perfect for stashing joints in, but she just used it to keep all her spare pennies and tuppences and convert them into pound coins at the bank.'

'Well, I think Julia needs to let go and have an exciting time tonight,' Luke announces, putting his arm around my waist. Then, suddenly, without warning, he picks me up. I let out a squeal. People turn and look, pointing and laughing. Someone even snaps a photo on their phone. I see a spray of golden water shooting towards me. Luke stares down at me, his eyes dangerous. 'So, do you promise you'll go wild tonight or shall I throw you in the fountain?'

'LUKE!' I scream, beating my fists against his chest, hearing Reece's giggles in my ears. 'OK, yes, I'll gamble. Just put me down!'

As Luke puts me down, I straighten my skirt, laughing and fuming. Reece punches me gently on the shoulder, her eyes still streaming with tears of laughter. Luke leans in to give me an apologetic kiss, but instinctively I find myself turning my cheek, a shard of Jodie twisting in my heart. Like Lucy's, his kiss goes astray: it lands on my jaw. Ciaran is watching us and there's a sad smile on his face that makes me feel sorry for him.

And then we hit the casinos.

It's weird: this feels like Tokyo all over again. Luke brings out the reckless adventurer in me. I gamble my money with acid in my stomach but soon it's replaced by butterflies of happiness. I win at poker, roulette *and* on the slot machines. I gamble carefully, not risking too much, but end up a thousand dollars ahead. I now have enough money to complete my trip and enjoy a few treats along the way. I feel on such a high that as money comes clattering out of my James Dean slot machine, I turn and give Luke a massive hug and place a tiny flutter of a kiss on his lips.

That evening, Reece slips into my hotel room and asks me to plait her hair for her. She sits in my bathroom and raves about how wonderful Luke is.

'I mean, I know it was terrible of him to leave Jodie and his baby Winston, but he said he was going to send all his winnings home to them. I think that's sweet.'

'It's a gesture,' I concede begrudgingly.

'So, are you going to get back together?' she asks.

I pause, fingering her silky hair.

'No,' I say. 'Not just yet.' I catch her eyes in the mirror, staring at our reflections. She looks so pretty in the soft haloed light. You'd never know she'd just been cruelly dumped in a harrowing break-up. I wish I could be as relaxed and forgiving as her. But something inside me changed, the day Luke confessed his past to me; there's a shell around my heart that no one can chip away. My mistrust of the male sex has been exacerbated by Ciaran. I can't help wondering if all my years of being in love with him were based on an illusion; if I failed to see what a bastard he was. Has sacrificing my twenties to the workplace left me naïve? Are all men really nothing but selfishness and trouble? Then I remember how much fun Luke is. I mustn't become too cynical.

'I don't know,' I say at last. 'I'll just have to see.'

'OK,' Reece says, with a glint in her eye. 'But you should be careful. Men aren't as patient as women. Don't keep him waiting too long, or he might slip away . . .'

5

Where is everyone? I'm waiting in the lobby of the
Mandalay when I catch sight of myself in the mirror. I'm
dressed up tonight, in jeans and a black jacket over a
shiny gold top. I can't help picturing Luke walking up
and raising his eyebrows, commenting that I'm looking
good. It should be a nice evening – all four of us have
agreed to hit Vegas together, which should defuse any
Reece/Ciaran tensions. I'm also feeling quite buzzy about
hitting the tables again. I've brought along a bit more
money tonight – I'm feeling a lot more confident after
yesterday's win.

I stare at the enormous aquarium in the lobby, at the
fish shimmering amongst swirls of seaweed. It reminds
me of Sicily. Those deep ocean dives with Ciaran; the way
we marvelled at the blue world beneath the waves.
Although that was a different Ciaran – a man I thought
I knew well.

I turn and see him come out of the lift. He strolls over, smiling. I try to smile back at him but I can't inject any warmth into it. Ciaran's face falls. He frowns, shoves his hands in his pockets and looks edgy.

We stand there in silence for about five minutes, watching the merry-go-round of people checking in and out.

'So ... where's Reece?' he asks eventually.

'I'm not sure.' I wish she would just hurry up and save me from this painful atmosphere. 'I'll call her.'

But when I ring her, there's no reply. I stare down at it, frowning.

'You haven't . . .' I hesitate. 'You haven't upset her again, have you? She's not crying her eyes out upstairs, is she?'

'No!' Ciaran cries sharply, looking affronted. 'Why would *I* upset her? I doubt she's shedding many tears over me. Any tears at all, in fact.'

'Well, she was pretty upset last night,' I retort, then break off in bewilderment. I can't understand why Ciaran is being so cruel.

And where the hell is Luke? I crave his presence, his silly jokes and lightness. Then I could just pretend Ciaran wasn't here.

My mobile shrills. It's Reece. Oh, thank goodness.

'Hey, you.' Reece's voice is cheery. 'What's up? Are you gambling tonight?'

'What? Reece, Ciaran and I are in the lobby at the hotel. I thought we were meant to all be meeting down here?'

'Oh, yeah.' She gives a scatty laugh. 'The thing is, I bumped into Luke and we got some tickets for *Star Trek*. It turns out Luke *loves Star Trek* – it was his favourite show when he was a kid.'

'What? Well, we can come and find you, I suppose.'

'Look, I just can't face seeing Ciaran tonight. I just can't. He'll be rude and keep putting me down. Can you do me a massive favour and look after him tonight, and in return I'll look after Luke as I know you want to escape from him. We'll do each other a big girly favour.'

'Well, actually I sort of wanted to see L—'

'I just – you know – I've had such a horrible time so far and I'm here to have *fun*.'

'I – OK,' I say at last. 'Maybe we can all hook up a bit later for a drink.'

'Yeah – cool. I'll text you when the show's over. Oh, Luke's here and he says hi and that he's dying to see you and that he promises he'll keep me under control.'

'Oh, great,' I say. I manage a smile. 'OK, bye. See you soon.'

I switch off my phone, feeling rather shocked. Then I remind myself that Reece is just being her usual friendly self; she doesn't mean any harm. I look at Ciaran. I know he's going to take this all the wrong way. I suffer a please-don't-shoot-the-messenger moment and I consider just making up an excuse.

'Er, Reece and Luke are kind of – they both love *Star Trek*,' I lie, knowing Reece has always made vomiting noises whenever the show came up on the TV. 'And they've gone to the *Star Trek* convention, so we'll meet them later.'

Ciaran shrugs. He seems so blasé that I feel relieved in turn. This is fine, I reassure myself; in fact, it's really very sweet that Luke is bonding so well with my best friend.

This time when we enter the casinos, I feel eager to gamble. I want to win, win, win. I picture myself meeting Luke later and boasting about all the risks I took, and seeing the amused admiration in his eyes. As we exchange notes for chips, Ciaran must have noticed the excitement on my face, for he whispers teasingly, 'Look at you. You're becoming an addict.'

'No, I'm not,' I snap, refusing to return his smile.

We join a Blackjack table. Blackjack is rapidly becoming my favourite game. It's much simpler and quicker than poker, and yet the challenge of trying to get a count card as close to twenty-one as possible without going over requires skill, and evokes a delicious adrenalin rush when that final card is turned over ...

I win a few games, lose a few games. In the end, I'm ahead. Ciaran, however, seems to be suffering from a run of bad luck.

'I think I should quit while I'm not ahead,' he sighs. 'I still have six more days to lose the rest of my money.'

'Oh, OK,' I say, feeling slightly deflated. I bite my lip, wondering if it's rude to suggest that we split up. I'd quite like to have a go on that roulette wheel ...

'Could we – could we have a chat?' Ciaran asks, shoving his hands in his pockets. 'We could take a walk along the Shark Tank back at our hotel.'

'Why not,' I agree uncertainly. As he raises his hand to push back his dark hair, I notice how bitten-down his nails are.

For all my antagonism, I feel a flicker of sympathy for him. And I acknowledge what I've been trying to ignore all evening – just how handsome he's looking tonight. He has a different kind of appeal to Luke, who's tall and cute in a boyish, backpacker way with his ripped jeans and floppy brown hair. Ciaran's more conventionally attractive: smart and polished, with his high cheekbones and brilliant blue eyes.

But tonight I feel suspicious of his looks. Did I fail to see past them? To see the darker shades of his personality underneath?

A huge shark comes soaring out of the blue depths, heading straight for me. I let out a gasp despite myself. Ciaran chuckles. The blue of the tank glows on his face, the shark a flickering reflection in his pupils as it rears away.

The Shark Reef Aquarium at the Mandalay is pretty amazing. It has a walkway about a mile long. On all sides we can see sawfish, green sea turtles and giant rays. There's even a golden crocodile.

'So how are things with Luke?' Ciaran asks.

'We're just friends for the minute,' I reply, though I

have a feeling he doesn't really want to talk about Luke. He wants to talk about someone else.

'So what about Reece?' I ask, getting straight to the point.

An angry look darkens his face. I feel angry myself. If he starts to slag her off, I'll let rip at him.

'I'm feeling pretty gutted, if you want the truth,' he says, to my surprise. He stares at the tank; a little fish waves its fins at him. 'I mean, this is twice in a row that I've got dumped. First by you, then Reece. I might start getting a complex.' He laughs lightly, but the hurt on his face astonishes me.

Before I can say anything, a cackling voice screeches: 'Hello, hello, hello.'

I spin round to see a girl dressed in a perky cap and shorts. A parrot is sitting on her shoulder, its beady eyes curious. He's clearly here to entertain us – but his timing could not have been worse.

'Who's a pretty boy then?' the parrot squawks.

'Piss off,' Ciaran replies irritably.

The parrot blinks as though savouring this fascinating new phrase.

'Reece didn't break up with you, you broke up with her,' I blurt out.

Parrot Girl raises an eyebrow, sensing that now isn't a great time. The parrot seems to have become attached to Ciaran, for he calls out, 'Goodbye piss off goodbye piss off!' and the girl mutters, 'Oh Jesus, it's going to take weeks of training to undo this one.'

'OK – in theory I dumped her. But she pushed me into it,' Ciaran says.

'You're playing with words.'

'Because I feel like such a sucker,' Ciaran says, his voice like a whip. 'I take my girlfriend to Sicily to go diving and she gets off with the instructor whilst I'm stranded in the ocean, on the verge of drowning. You saw it. You were there too.'

I open my mouth a few times like one of the fish in the tank. *My God*. My memory goes on a frantic rewind. Yes, I remember that night. I remember my suspicions too, when we came back from our ocean detour. The smell of pot in the apartment and the self-conscious way Reece looked; it was obvious that she had been flirting with Michele, not to mention what a lustful character he was ...

'And then I find out he's not the only one. When I accused her, she said that we were obviously having an open relationship. But she might have told me earlier on. I suppose she forgot,' he says, his voice stinging with sarcasm.

'Reece didn't mention any of this to me,' I say slowly. 'Are you really telling the truth?'

He stares at me. I'm shocked to see a film of tears in his eyes, and I touch his arm.

'I'm sorry,' I murmur.

He suddenly pulls me into a deep, tight hug. I hug him back, feeling him bury his face in my collarbone. Anger reverberates through me: *I can't believe Reece would do this*. I reach up and stroke his hair. Ciaran is always so strong and sarcastic, so good at covering his emotions up that it's easy to forget how deeply he feels things. In the tank, a shoal of bright fish veer towards us and then change direction.

Ciaran pulls back, looking a little embarrassed.

'You know, I think I need a drink,' he says. 'How do you fancy the vodka bar?'

The Red Square Russian restaurant has a refrigerated walk-in showcase that stores over 150 types of vodka. It's rather like an alcoholic Narnia, glacial and beautiful, the bottles glittering in their display cases like Russian artefacts.

There's a long thick strip of ice on the bartop on which to put our glasses. I touch my fingers on it and then press them to my throbbing forehead. It helps to cool my shock.

Ciaran raises his glass, chinking it against mine.

'To you – to wonderful you. Thanks for hugging me, thanks for cheering me up.'

I chink my glass against his, feeling slightly overwhelmed.

'I don't think Reece meant to hurt you,' I say finally.

'A moral intention doesn't justify an immoral action. In fact, it makes it all the more fucking worse.'

I fall silent. I still feel shocked that Reece lied to me. I can see she might have felt embarrassed about admitting her affairs, but we tell each other everything. I also feel really bad for misjudging Ciaran.

'Maybe you're right in some ways about Reece not wanting to hurt me,' Ciaran adds thoughtfully, 'I think she's just off her head so much these days, it's starting to change her.'

'Are you saying Reece needs rehab?' I ask in alarm. I have a sudden vision of a terrible addiction that's snaked into Reece and that I've been too self-absorbed to notice.

Ciaran frowns. 'It's a bit of a Catch Twenty-two, I think. She's in her thirties now, she's getting bored with life, she lacks direction, so she's smoking more pot, and it doesn't bring out the best in her. She seems more emotionally vague these days, as though she's not really properly aware of the people around her and how they might feel.' Aware that he's getting het up, he quickly gains control of himself. 'I'm not being melodramatic. I'm not saying she's about to move on to heroin. I reckon it's just indicative of a deeper problem in her. I don't know . . .' He shrugs.

'What were you looking for with Reece? Marriage and kids?' I ask.

'I'm pretty nervous of both,' Ciaran says, 'but if I was going to do that with anyone, it would have been her.'

I nod, though I can't help but feel a cut in my heart. What Ciaran had had with Reece was obviously much more special than what we had shared.

'Oh well,' he says glumly, 'maybe I'll just go back to that speed-dating agency where I first met you.'

I colour, feeling slightly embarrassed. Ciaran and I

haven't talked about our past for a long, long time. I thought he'd forgotten he ever met me there.

'You can come too,' Ciaran says, nodding at the barman to give him another vodka. 'I'll find you a sexy rich toyboy and you can find me a woman who doesn't want to screw men up and tear them apart.'

I stare down at my lap. I've always wondered if Ciaran sensed that I still had feelings for him whilst he was with Reece. Clearly not. He's already set his sights on a rebound fling.

'Well, I think I might try to make a go of things with Luke,' I say quickly.

'You said earlier that you were just going to stay friends.'

'No – well, he wants more, but I'm seeing how things go.'

Ciaran stares at me with a look I can't quite fathom.

'You always see the good in people,' he says.

'Thanks,' I say, trying to work out the subtext: does he think I'm naïve?

'For God's sake, Julia!' Ciaran slams down his glass. 'What d'you think is happening right now, right this minute?'

'We're . . . drinking vodka,' I reply with a smile on my face, though I've twigged right away what he's implying with a sense of horror.

'I mean – it's so fucking rude! She's meant to be your best friend – and right under your nose, she just grabs Luke and goes off with him.' Ciaran rubs a hand through his hair. 'Reece wasn't like this when I first met her. She was spoiled then, but nicer.'

I stare into my ice-cold vodka. I have a vision of them entwined in a bed together, Luke's lips hot on hers, his hands roaming over her body. *No*, I tell myself, *no*. Ciaran's just jealous and bitter and angry right now. I lift the glass to my lips and gulp the contents down in full, feeling the fire blaze down my throat.

'Another?' Ciaran asks.

'I think I need to get back,' I say pleasantly. 'Luke and Reece are expecting us to join them for a drink. I'll send them a text, shall I, saying we're ready to hook up?'

'Please don't,' Ciaran protests.

I ignore him, fishing my mobile out of my bag. I'm about to text Reece, when I see a little yellow envelope sitting on my screen.

Sorry no drink on. Decided to go to bed early tonite.
Rxxx

I nearly drop my phone. Then I tell myself, fiercely, that there's no 'we' in the text. But ...

'I'm going to head back,' I mutter. 'I need to get some sleep.'

'I'm sorry if I hurt you, Julia,' Ciaran says, putting a hand on my arm.

I pull away.

'I think I'll just stay and drink here,' Ciaran says at last.

I grab my bag and hurry away, unable to bear another minute with him.

6

I hurry down the corridor to my hotel room. The vodka's hit me belatedly and my head is swimming. I'm about to open my door, when I turn and look across at Room 245. Reece's room. I press my ear against the door, keeping an eye out for any other guests, hardly able to believe I'm doing this. Did I just hear . . . a groan? Or was it just my paranoid imagination? I hammer on the door. Hard. When she doesn't respond, I hammer again. I keep knocking, tears spilling over: *If I open this door and see them together, I don't think I'll be able to bear it. Oh God, in many ways Ciaran's theory makes sense. How can I have been so naïve? Reece has made it so obvious she likes Luke, but surely she wouldn't do that to me, surely she wouldn't—*

'Hey.' Reece opens the door, looking sleepy, tousled in her pink nightshirt.

'Hi,' I say. I try to peer past her, to see if I can make

out a silhouette hiding down by the bed. 'I just – I really need to talk, if that's OK.'

Reece frowns, rubbing her eyes and steps back. Immediately I go to the windows and pretend to ruffle the curtains, checking to see if there's someone behind them. Then I tell her I need the loo and dash in. Empty. Then I turn to the shower curtain. There's a silhouette behind it: *got you!* But when I yank it back I see a life-size plastic doll sitting in the shower. I blink in surprise. It's just the sort of surreal thing Reece *would* have in her hotel room.

I stare at my reflection in my mirror. My cheeks are flushed, my pupils dilated. I feel slightly foolish but relieved. Ciaran was wrong, wrong, wrong.

I go out into the room. Reece is sitting cross-legged on the bed. Shopping bags are scattered on the floor; she reaches down and pulls out a box of Krispy Kreme dough-nuts and starts munching on one. I sit down on the edge of the bed and take one too.

'So, did you have a good evening?' I ask gingerly.

'You know, Luke just spent the whole evening going on and on about how much he likes you,' Reece says with a yawn.

'He did?' I ask, my heart leaping. 'What did he say?'

'That you were sexy. And intelligent. And gorgeous and funny and wonderful.' Reece smiles. 'He's mad about you. I tried to put him off you, but he's totally hooked.'

'Why did you do that?' I cry. 'Don't put him off me!'

'Sorry,' Reece says, stung. 'I thought you didn't like him.'

'I'm not sure,' I say. I frown and reach for another doughnut, then mumble through jam: 'Ciaran told me that you . . . you . . .'

'I what?' Reece asks, sounding defensive. 'That I'm some evil whore slut who slept with the whole of the world's male population just to upset him? Don't look at me like that. You should be on my side.' She grabs my hand, yanking my arm. Then she says sadly, 'You are on my side, aren't you?'

'Of course I'm on your side,' I say automatically. 'I just don't get why you didn't explain before.'

'Because I thought you'd tell me off,' Reece says in a girly voice. 'And OK, I was behaving like a bit of a slut. I just got bored. God, if I was a bloke, everyone would be slapping me on the back and saying "nice one". Why shouldn't we girls have our own fun if we want it? And the scuba-diving instructor asked me if I could help him see how long he could survive without breathing by going down on me.'

I giggle despite myself.

'Reece! You've really upset him, you know.' Then I cock my head to one side 'Was he good in bed?'

'Oh, amazing!' Reece says, and then proceeds to tell me in enormous detail just how skilfully they attempted a number of different positions that left her wishing she'd kept up her yoga classes.

We both laugh and fall silent. Reece chews on another doughnut.

'I got Luke to move hotel rooms as well,' she enthuses. 'He's just a few rooms down from us now. I mean, it was stupid, him being all the way out there at the Venice Hotel even though I *love* that place – those gondola rides are so cool.'

'Oh, you did a gondola ride?' I ask. Now I feel as though my special ride with him has been diluted.

'Before *Star Trek*,' Reece giggles. 'He tossed his lucky coin and it told us to give it a go. Him and that coin! He just cracks me up with his "If it's tails, we'll jump off a cliff, if it's heads, we'll fly to the moon" mentality.'

'Do you like Luke?' I ask her suddenly. The vodka has made my tongue bold. 'You can be honest. If you do, just tell me.'

'Well, if he wasn't yours then yes, I think he's gorgeous and dangerous and sexy and I think you'd be mad not to go for him,' Reece says. 'But he's yours – right?' She looks up at me from under her lashes and I feel an uneasy lurch in my stomach. For how can I really say he's 'mine' when I don't believe that we can ever own people. Plus, I'm still not sure whether I do want to get back together. But I nod firmly and Reece smiles, as though everything's sorted.

Back in my hotel room, insomnia bullies me again, tossing me from one side of the bed to the other, teasing me with sleep and then slapping me awake just when I think I'm cured. I sit up. Switch on the light. Grab my notebook.

On a whim, I decide to write another letter to Herbie French. I've been intending to do this since I last saw him. I tried to on my final night in New York, but I wasn't sure what to say and found myself scrawling a few lines on the weather. Herbie French isn't a man who would ever waste time on such trivialities; I pictured him reading it and remarking aloud in his dry, cackling voice, 'Julia's analysis of colossal clouds is really the most tedious thing I've ever had to endure.' The letter never got sent.

I start by telling him about how I'm beating the system at Vegas. I can imagine my boast making him smile. And then I find that I start to gush about Luke and Ciaran.

I tell him everything. How Luke wooed me and lied to me. How I've spent years yearning for Ciaran and I'm not sure if I'm wasting my time or holding out for something special. I tell him that I think Reece might be competition and that makes me want Luke more; and surely it is shallow, just to want him because I sense a threat from my best friend?

Who do you think I should choose? I ask him passionately. *I know you won't mince words. Tell me what you think Princess Lacertes would do.*

When I finish, I feel tired and emotionally drained. I read the letter through. I can detect the influence of vodka on my prose, but it's certainly written from the heart. Is it *too* personal? Perhaps, but then again, Herbie knows all about my father, so why stop there? I trust him.

I fold it up, pop it into an envelope, scrawl his address on it and take it down to reception, asking the man there to take care of posting it. He glances at the name and address with a raised eyebrow, then nods. I go to bed feeling a little better.

7

I'm glad that Lucy's here. I'm glad because she's defusing the tension in the group. Plus it's helping to take my mind off that deeply embarrassing letter I wrote to Herbie French.

I tried very hard to reason with the receptionist.

'Can't you just call up the post guy and get him to take it out of his van?' I begged.

'I'd lose my job, ma'am.'

I keep cringing at the thought of Herbie French opening the letter and saying, 'Writing to me about my book was one thing, but what's all this drivel about her love life? What the hell does this woman take me for – an agony aunt?' I might as well have written to him confiding how I once suffered from piles in my early twenties and just be done with it. Herbie and I shared a special moment; now I've tainted the memory. I'll probably appear in *The Mermaid Who Hated Fish* as a bottom-feeding sea-creature with goggle eyes.

Still. Lucy is fitting really well into the group. There's only one person who hasn't taken to her.

'I just don't like her,' Reece complains in a private aside.

I flinch in surprise. We glance over at Lucy, who is sitting at a bar table between Luke and Ciaran. They're all still chuckling about a discussion we started earlier about hand gestures meaning different things in different countries. Luke told how he'd learned from his mistakes by bitter experience: in the Philippines he once beckoned someone with a finger, which is so offensive that it's punishable by law. Lucy, meanwhile, starts telling them that the 'OK' symbol between thumb and forefinger doesn't go down very well in Greece, where it means ... er ... get lost. Luke and Ciaran seem particularly amused by this one.

The scene reminds me of just how great Lucy is. She has the ability to shine her personality on to people like a spotlight, softening them, opening them up. I can tell Reece is jealous because both guys are clearly a little bit in love with her. But there's no competition between them, given that neither of them can have her. And so, in her way, she's binding them together.

'She's so attention-seeking,' Reece moans.

'She's just extrovert,' I say in defence of her, surprised by the uncharacteristic venom in my friend's voice.

'Hmm ...' Reece lowers her eyes, fiddling with the label on her beer bottle. 'So how are you and Luke doing?' she says, changing the subject.

Me and Luke? Over the last few days he's been cooler with me. He's stopped tickling me or giving me surprise gifts or teasing me that he's just tossed his lucky coin and it's instructed him to kiss me. And, in keeping with the inevitable laws of attraction, his step backwards has made my feelings tango forwards.

I'm not sure if I dare admit this to Reece, but something inside me is starting to melt. If there's an iceberg in my heart, the peak has definitely gone, though it hasn't suffered full global warming yet. I know Luke is immature and he's selfish and scatty and screwed up – but he's also boyish and sweet and funny. I could see us getting back together by the end of Vegas. It's a definite possibility.

Then Reece puts her hand on my arm.

'I'm sorry. I really thought you were going to get back together. But friendship's good, isn't it? I mean, friendships often outlast marriages.'

'Uh . . .' I feel confused. Is Reece talking about the reservations I had a week ago when I first arrived?

'Luke was pretty depressed about it last night, though.'

'Really?' My stomach twists and my eyes flash. 'So did I come up in some sort of post-coital chat discussion?'

'Of course not!' Reece cries. 'Julia, you know I would never . . . I mean, I don't even fancy him – and he's still heartbroken over you.'

'So what happened?' I ask.

'Well, you know more than I do. I mean, Luke just

knocked on my door at around one in the morning saying he felt down. He sat on my bed,' Reece starts to giggle, 'and then he tossed his lucky coin to see if he ought to raid my mini-bar, and he had to toss it about five times before it said he should. He's just so funny; even when he's depressed, he cracks me up. And then he got really pissed and said he's learned to accept that he'll only ever be friends because you'll never be able to forgive him and he has to accept that.'

'Oh right,' I nod breezily, silently seething. *Well, it was nice of him to tell me.*

'I think he's devastated,' Reece sighs.

I stare over at Luke, who's now showing off to Lucy that he can juggle bar-mats. He manages to keep about five in the air at once; then they all come raining down, one of them landing in Ciaran's drink. Lucy shakes her head, smiling, and Luke laughs hysterically. The barmaid tuts but, like everyone, she can't stay mad at Luke; she gives him an indulgent, adoring smile as she mops up the mess.

Devastated, indeed.

Well, if Luke is going to be 'devastated', so am I. I'm going to show my devastation by going out tonight with the gang, by putting on my best clothes, by looking great, drinking loads and having the wildest, most wonderful time imaginable.

Mr Luke DeAntiquis, I can do devastation a million times better than you, I tell the mirror fiercely as I pencil kohl around my eyes. And I go back to my wardrobe and pull out my favourite red dress, the one I bought in Venice. Just to show I'm in mourning.

'Here's to Vegas!' Reece lifts her glass. I notice that Ciaran smiles at her as she does so, as though he's forgiven her. She doesn't smile back.

'To becoming millionaires!' Lucy cries.

'To going crazy!' Reece continues.

'To randomly marrying a stripper!' Luke cries. Then, when everyone gives him a collective look, he laughs and says, 'I'm just kidding.'

I down my drink, flicking a glance at Luke. I knew deep down that we were never going to get back together; Tokyo shattered everything. But I still feel humiliated and churned up. I thought he was cooling off to play hard-to-get, not because he was actually cooling off. A part of me can't help protesting, *Well, he didn't try very hard to get me back, did he? Am I not worth fighting for at all?*

'Whoa, Julia, you downed that Apple Martini pretty fast,' Ciaran notes.

'I think I'll have another,' I say.

'Here's to that one,' Luke agrees, nudging me. I grimace at him and he looks taken aback, then downs his drink and carries on cracking jokes, seemingly oblivious.

'You know,' Lucy says, reaching forwards to grab some peanuts from the bowl on the table, 'my room is next to yours, Luke, and I can hear you through the wall, singing in the shower at the top of your voice.'

'Ah, you're about to suggest I should be on *American Idol*, right?' Luke says, and we all laugh as Lucy raises her eyebrows.

'Of course, if we were in Pennsylvania, I'd be arrested,' Luke says casually.

'How so?' Ciaran wants to know.

'Well, the other day I was looking up all these dumb laws in US states.' Luke chuckles. 'Mostly they were written a hundred years back but nobody's gotten round to getting rid of them. And in Pennsylvania, it's illegal to sing in the bathtub. For real.'

'No,' Reece challenges him. 'You're just kidding us because we're naïve Brits.'

'I'm not,' Luke says. 'Seriously – they get madder and madder. Like in Alaska, it's an offence to push a live moose out of a moving plane, and you can shoot bears but you can't wake a sleeping bear to take a photo.'

'Bollocks,' Reece squeals, causing heads to turn.

'Bullshit,' Ciaran agrees more quietly.

'I'm serious.' Luke slams his palms down on his thighs. He turns to me, his eyes sparkling, and stares deep into my eyes. 'You believe me, don't you, Julia?' he says.

I've lost my voice. He's been pretty much ignoring me so far this evening and his sudden blast of charm undoes me.

'I . . .'

'You see?' Luke says triumphantly. 'Julia believes me.'

'He's actually right,' Lucy interjects. 'I remember reading about this a while back. Like in California, animals are banned from mating publicly within fifteen hundred feet of a school, or place of worship.'

'Well, we have laws like that in England,' Ciaran says. 'I mean, we have to, with all the mating elephants in the streets outside making such a racket.'

'Come on,' I say, glaring at Lucy and Luke. 'You Americans are just trying to wind us up but I'm afraid we Brits are too smart.'

'Oh, you wanna place a bet?' Lucy teases me. 'Because I can show you. And if we're right, then you Brits have to buy all the drinks tonight.'

Reece, Ciaran and I look at each other and nod in agreement.

'Done.'

'OK . . .' Lucy pulls her BlackBerry out of her handbag. Ciaran groans. Reece cries that she's cheating. Luke rubs his hands together and nudges me. I smile at him begrudgingly.

'See?' Lucy holds up a Googled web-page. 'There are loads of US websites poking fun at these laws.'

'Oh shit,' Ciaran says, glancing over, 'it looks as though the drinks are on us – right, Julia?'

'Oh my God.' Reece grabs hold of the BlackBerry. 'These are *so* funny. In Idaho, it's illegal for a man to give his sweetheart a box of candy weighing less than fifty pounds. Well, that sounds good to me. In Illinois, it's illegal to speak English, American is the official language.'

'Oh, that's the same throughout America,' Luke crows. 'You guys are gonna be in jail if you don't start saying *tomato* the right way.'

'In Iowa, kisses can last as much as but no more than five minutes,' Reece giggles.

Luke turns to me and says, 'Well, I don't know if we'd have a problem with that, would we, Julia?'

I blink hard, a blush rioting over my cheeks. Just what the fuck is going on? Is Luke some kind of schizo? How can a guy swivel from being hot, cold and lukewarm in the space of a few minutes? I manage a sort of twisted half-smile and turn away. Ciaran glances over at me; Lucy also gives me an *Are you OK?* look; Reece just frowns. Suddenly the table has gone very quiet.

'Well,' Luke smashes the tension. 'Let's all just get another round of drinks.'

This is *fun*. This is just the sort of night I should have been enjoying every Saturday in my twenties when I was too busy doing bloody calculations. I'm three drinks in now and I've even stopped caring about Luke. I'm not going to waste the evening playing games with him whilst he decides one hour that he wants us to be friends, the next that we're destined to be together, and the next that we should just be friends again. I'm having too much fun.

In fact, we're *all* having fun. Despite the rocky start, we're all having a good old giggle together.

We go gambling. We eat at Rumjungle. We have a night-swim in the pool. We get some more drinks in.

And then we end up in Lucy's hotel room, completely wasted, and start on her mini-bar. Reece goes into the bathroom to fix her hair.

'Reece was telling me that you've been acting out some kind of list – *Ten Things To Do Before You Die* type-thing,' Luke says slurrily, holding up his bottle of rum.

'Reece has got a big mouth,' I protest indignantly.

'So you really are acting out this list?' Ciaran asks, looking animated. 'What's on it?'

'Oh – just things. Like sleep with the Loch Ness Monster. Or have a sex change.' I smirk at their bemused faces. 'I'm just kidding. The list is *secret*. And Reece is not meant to be blabbing it around to the whole of Las Vegas.'

I wonder what Ciaran would think if he knew that number ten had once been *Tell Ciaran O'Hare that I love him.* Thank goodness I scrubbed it off.

'Presumably sleeping with an Italian was part of the list,' Ciaran muses. 'I mean, I've heard you and Reece having girly chats about that being a standard female fantasy ...'

'No,' I object hotly, but my flaming cheeks give me away. Lucy nudges me and I laugh, shrugging.

'That was me.' Luke gives an inebriated sigh. 'I'm Italian-American. I helped Julia fulfil that one in Venice. I'm just glad I helped you tick that box.' He grins but there's an unmistakable sting in his voice. I feel guilty, and then angry. I feel like retorting that the first desire on my list wasn't actually to *Sleep with an Italian-American and then find out that he's just deserted his fiancée and newborn baby*. But I keep my mouth shut.

'So what else is on it?' Ciaran badgers me. 'C'mon, Julia. Give us a clue.'

Just as he's finishing his sentence, Reece comes bouncing into the room. Ciaran's face blackens. Luke's lights up.

'I can tell you another one,' she giggles drunkenly. 'It's *Kiss a girl and see if I like it*.'

Luke's eyes bulge. Ciaran's face whips from me to Lucy and back again. I give Reece a fierce *shut up* look. She bites her lip and mouths an apology. Now I'm worried that I've seriously offended Lucy and she'll think she's just a novelty on my list. Even if nothing ever happened between us, I've adored every minute of our newfound friendship and I'd hate to lose it.

To my relief, Lucy just smiles and clears her throat.

'Anyway, Lukey,' Reece says, 'I just saw a shooting star on the balcony – you have to come out and see it with me.'

'But I want to know how come Julia's turned into a lesbian,' Luke says.

'Luke . . .' Reece cajoles.

He takes her outstretched hand and follows her out on

to the balcony, though he gives me one final, bemused glance as he goes.

The silence becomes deadly. My cheeks are on fire; I can feel a burn in the back of my throat.

'So – are you a lesbian?' Ciaran suddenly blurts out. 'I mean, I always wondered what went wrong between us – is that it?'

I squirm uneasily. 'No, no. It's just . . .'

'You're just bi-curious, right?' Lucy interjects smoothly.

'Exactly!' I cry. 'Something like that. Except it was my own private thing and I didn't really intend to share it with the rest of the world.'

'Right,' Ciaran says apologetically. Then: 'But I mean – wow. I mean – it was just . . . Yeah. Right.'

I suddenly feel Lucy reach over and squeeze my hand. I squeeze back, comforted by her support. She carries on holding it. Ciaran's eyes hover on our locked skin. His pupils dilate. I get the feeling he can't quite handle this; I also get the feeling that Lucy is enjoying teasing him. I remember her saying that after suffering a lifetime of prejudice, the best way to handle it is with humour.

'Haven't you ever felt *you* might be bi?' Lucy asks Ciaran. 'I mean, Luke said the other night that he's slept with a few men in his time. How about you?'

Ciaran actually spits out a small mouthful of beer.

'Fuck – no,' he says, looking revolted.

'Oh, 'cos Luke told me that he thought you were very

handsome,' Lucy says with an offended shrug. 'But then again, I believe that everyone is bi.'

'Uh – well, I mean, if that just applied to women, I'd be cool with it,' Ciaran mumbles, adding something that neither of us can catch. Then he jumps to his feet. 'I'm going to the bathroom.'

We listen to the sluice and gush of water. Lucy's palm becomes a caress on my knuckles. I bite my lip, my heart hammering. She leans over, her breath warm on my neck, dropping whispers into my ear like wishes in a well. *Just relax ... don't be scared ... I think you're beautiful ... I'd like to ...* I can't help feeling that this is a really bad idea; I'm drunk and still confused about Luke – and what if Lucy has serious feelings for me? But another part of me tells me not to be scared, I'm supposed to be having an adventure and breaking my boundaries and ...

I turn and stare into her beautiful green eyes.

And then we kiss.

To begin with, I can't enjoy it at all. Sex requires that we lose our self-consciousness. The paradox of intimacy is that we need to become strangers. I just keep thinking, I'm kissing a woman, I'm actually fulfilling number seven on my list and this is so weird, I'm kissing a woman ...

And then I close my eyes. This feels nice. It's different from kissing a man. There's an element of predatory aggression in a male kiss that I find exciting. But this is a different shade of pleasure: her kiss is sweeter, softer; I like the warmth that flows through her lips.

I curl my hand up and for a moment I'm not sure where to put it. Finally, I cradle her jaw in my palm. Again, there's a moment of double-take; I'm used to stubble and her skin is amazingly soft. Then I caress her hair, her curls light as blossom, and I forget myself and start to enjoy the embrace.

Lucy seems to be enjoying it too. Her touch is more confident; her palms caress my hair, my neck, my shoulders, moving downwards. I draw in my breath . . .

. . . and all of a sudden her hand is on my breast and I freeze up.

Her eyes flit open. She looks both tender and amused. Then her eyes close and we carry on kissing.

My eyes don't close. For, right behind her, I can see Ciaran. He's come out of the bathroom and he's hovering in the hallway, pretending to fiddle with the coffee-making set, but I can see his eyes are on us.

The naughty thing is, I feel oddly turned on, knowing he's watching us. I picture Ciaran's eyes on Lucy's hand on my breast and feel a shiver.

A sound from the balcony makes us start. Our bubble bursts. We remember where we are. Who we are.

Luke and Reece head back in, smelling of ciggie smoke and giggling intimately.

'What's up?' I ask in a high voice, the echo of shock still ringing in my head: *I just kissed a woman, I just kissed a woman*.

'We just . . .' Reece looks up at Luke and laughs throatily. 'Nothing. Private joke.'

I look at Ciaran. He is still goggle-eyed. I look at Lucy. Her green eyes are warm and sexy. Suddenly the room feels incredibly hot. What if Lucy expects me to go to bed with her now? I'm pissed. I'm half in love with Ciaran, half in love with Luke as it is without splitting myself into three. I don't want to ruin our friendship and wake up hungover with regrets. But by kissing her I feel as though I've lit a fuse and now she's expecting fireworks.

'Let's all play Strip Poker,' Reece cries. 'Let's play Truth or Dare! Let's stay up all night!'

'I have – I have to go to bed,' I cry, jumping dizzily to my feet.

'Oh, boring Julia,' Reece cries, and Luke sing-songs, 'Boring Julia ...'

I ignore them, say good night to Lucy and Ciaran, and stagger out into the hallway. Now that I have to walk, I realise just how drunk I am. It's as well I'm staying five rooms down. I manage to stagger to it whilst palming the wall. Then I sift about in my handbag for my room-key. I hear a door click and sense someone behind me. Maybe it's Lucy. I quickly flee into my room and slam the door behind me.

8

Is 4 p.m. too late for breakfast?

Having gone to bed at six, I've slept in and only just showered and dressed. If this was England, I'd probably only be able to find jam and scones at this time of day, but the cool thing about Vegas is that the buffets last all day long. I go out into the corridor and knock on Reece's door but there's no reply. She must still be sleeping. At this rate we'll all be turning into vampires.

'Hey,' I hear a voice behind me.

Oh.

Lucy.

For the first time ever, she's not looking 100 per cent polished; her hangover flashes in the whites of her eyes despite her carefully applied make-up, and her hair hangs about her shoulders in a tangle. I try not to look too awkward around her.

'Hi. How are you?' She looks me straight in the eye;

her stare has a steely, challenging gleam to it. 'Shall we get some brunch together?'

'I'd love to,' I say brightly, trying very hard not to stare at her lips or blush.

Normally, whenever Lucy and I are together we can't stop talking; we buzz with such shared enthusiasm and fascinating ideas. Now we walk down the hall in complete silence. As we get into the lift, I'm conscious of our jeans brushing together in a millimetre of contact and I jump violently. We stand in silence. Down in the Bayside buffet, we drift in a hungover haze through the buffets. This has to be one of the most elegant and understated buffets in Vegas, with its golden walls and speckled tables and exquisite view of the tropical water garden. But the array of seafood on offer makes me feel sick. Alaskan King crabs ... peel and eat shrimp ... spicy Szechuan chicken ... I feel my stomach turning and quickly opt for scrambled eggs, coffee and orange juice. Then, when we sit down: silence again.

Lucy and I reach for the salt at the same time. When her skin touches mine, I leap. The salt overturns and sprawls its white grit across the table.

'Julia!' Lucy cries. 'For God's sake! This is unacceptable. You're treating me as though I'm a leper. I know that last night was probably some drunken experiment, but I'd like to think we had fun, and that we can now still be friends. Right?'

'I'm sorry, I'm sorry,' I say meekly. Suddenly I realise

how appalling my behaviour is. I reach over and give her a warm hug.

'OK,' she says more softly. 'Eat your eggs now before they get cold. There's nothing more vile than cold scrambled eggs.'

'I just – I actually did like kissing you,' I blurt out. 'I'm just not sure . . . my love life is so complicated as it is. I did think I liked Luke, but there's someone else too. Well, there *was* someone else. He still casts a bit of a shadow over things.'

'Ciaran?'

'You know? Did he say anything?' *And are my feelings that obvious?* I add in silent panic.

'No. It's just the way you look at him sometimes.' Lucy looks sad for a moment, then quickly carries on eating her eggs. Then, out of the blue, she says, 'I think you should go for Luke.'

'Luke?' I ask in surprise. 'But he's all over the place. And besides, I think he's falling for Reece.'

'When they left last night, they went to their own rooms,' Lucy says. 'And Luke is only being indecisive because you're holding him at arm's length and I don't think he has a lot of self-confidence.'

'Really?' Sometimes it's easy to forget that we're all human.

'What about Ciaran?' I ask in a small voice.

Lucy frowns. 'I can see he likes you – but I worry that it's just a rebound thing. He's been in a serious relationship. By getting with you, it's just a way of feeling close to Reece. He's been hurt bad and he misses her.'

'Go on,' I say, even though a part of me is screaming at her to shut up. Lucy isn't mincing words but I do trust her judgement and intuition; I'm sure her detached viewpoint on events is far more perceptive than my blurred, emotional one.

'I also think you just want Ciaran because – well, you only told me a bit about your relationship in New York, but from what you said, when you had him, he didn't really do it for you. You only wanted him once he'd gone. But history has a habit of repeating itself. You might hunger after him now, but if you had him . . . well, I think you'd just lose interest.'

'Right,' I say, managing to keep my voice steady.

Lucy changes the subject then and starts talking about Vegas. I'm itching to keep discussing Ciaran. After all these years of not being able to gossip about him to Reece or a girlfriend, it feels like such a release. But I'm conscious that, given our history, Lucy has already been incredibly generous to give me any advice at all. I carry on chatting but I can't focus and I certainly can't eat another bite of my eggs. It's going to take me a while to digest her words, to work out whether she's right.

'. . . and so I've gotta head off myself,' Lucy says, dabbing her lips with a napkin.

'What?' I suddenly tune into her words. 'You're going?'

'Yeah, I just booked a flight a few hours ago. You know,

I have some business to do in New York, I've gotta gallery interested in my paintings.'

'Wow, that's just so brilliant.' I'm gushing a bit, but it's my way of apologising once again to Lucy.

'Well.' Lucy gives me a smile, then bites her lip. 'Look me up in New York if you're about.'

'Definitely,' I agree. And when she reaches out and gently touches my cheek with her fingertips, I feel a sob of regret inside. *It's actually a shame I'm not cut out to be a lesbian*, I muse, *since Lucy would be the ideal partner*. And then I smile and hug her, and tell her I hope this is the start of a lifelong friendship.

Back in my room, I call Reece on her mobile again. But there's still no reply.

I sit on the bed and flick on the TV. An episode of *Friends* flashes up and I stifle a yawn, aware that we've got another long night ahead of us. Reece will no doubt get in touch when she wakes up. A vision slithers into my mind, of Reece and Luke in the shower together, of Reece whispering, 'I bet Julia was never this much fun, was she? She's so *boring* that when you tried to have hot shower sex, she just made you scrub behind your ears.' Then I shake myself. I'm getting paranoid. And Lucy asserted that Luke and Reece went to separate rooms last night. I know Reece is a wild flirt and she does have something of a crush on Luke. But I know that she'd never cross that line ...

Except ... the only epithet Reece ever attaches to me these days is *boring*. She used to like me being the sensible one. She said I was like a big sister who looked out for her and kept her out of trouble. She respected me and when she teased me for being straight, there was always affection in her voice. These days her words have salt in them, and when she flings them at me, they sting. She seems so intent on impressing Luke that I think she has to make out I'm the greyest shade of grey in order to make herself look more colourful. I've half a mind to go out with them tonight and gamble away all my money, ride a rodeo, do a striptease, attend an orgy and marry a random stranger just to bloody prove her wrong.

I flick through the channels, surfing movies and shopping ads, aware that I'm talking myself into a bad mood. This is probably the first time since arriving in Vegas that I've had space to think; though since my conversation with Lucy, a self-awareness is coming over me. I miss the intimacy of my warm friendship with Reece; I think that's maybe why I kissed Lucy. Not because I desperately fancied her but I wanted to draw her closer to me because I'm lonely. A sadness comes over me and I hastily reassure myself that back in London, Reece and I will probably return to being great friends and flatmates again. After all, just as people bring out different shades of our personality, so do countries. Their culture, their values, seep into our consciousness, shaping our thoughts and actions. We are in Sin City, after all. It's bringing out the wild neon in Reece but back home she'll probably return to shades of normalcy. I hope so.

And what about Luke? Is Lucy right that I should go for him? Her words surprised me but I do respect her judgement so much. However, it does feel as though things have gone flat between him and me.

I flick on to a news channel. More reports of war, of shootings, of tragedy and sadness. I swallow, feel somewhat sobered and suddenly guilty about being here in such a pleasure-seeking city. Then, just as I'm about to change channels, I see a familiar face on the screen. Herbie French. I sit up.

'And finally, we've just heard that Herbie French, author of the famous children's classic story, *The Lost Princess*, died last night from a heart attack, at the age of seventy-six . . .'

9

It's about four in the morning, and I can't sleep. I get up and go out on the balcony. My tears have dried now, leaving sticky streaks on my cheeks. The cool temperature feels blissful; the sky is a soft blue and for once the heavy metal energy of Vegas has quietened to a softer tempo. I didn't go out last night. Reece called me up around eleven and I tried to explain to her about Herbie, but she was very drunk and cried, 'So what? You only met him once. Stop being boring, Julia, and just come out and get pissed!' After that, I switched off my phone. Around 2 a.m., there was some drunken giggly knocking at my door but I ignored it, staring at the TV screen, hugging my pillow tight, tears trickling down my face.

This room is becoming claustrophobic. I feel a hunger to be with someone. Someone who will give me a good hug. Would Reece mind if I woke her up? I suddenly feel nervous and upset that I was so angry with her yesterday.

I tiptoe out into the corridor and then stop short. Ciaran is standing outside his room, the door ajar, his arms folded. As though he's waiting for someone. I'm about to retreat back into my room, when he sees me.

I go over to him, still feeling flustered and shaky.

'Have you seen Reece?' he begins. Then he puts his hand on my arm. 'Are you OK, Julia? Why didn't you come out with us last night? Are you still suffering a hangover from hell?'

'Um, no. Someone I just met – Herbie French, the author – he's dead. I just heard it on the news.'

'Fuck.' Ciaran rubs my shoulder. 'I'm sorry.'

The news hits me again and I feel sorrow welling up in my throat. 'It seems stupid to feel this upset,' I say shakily. 'I only met the man once.'

'It doesn't really matter how long you've known someone though, does it?' Ciaran says earnestly. 'It's about the connection you have with them; it's about how special they are.'

I smile at him, touched by his sympathy. Then it strikes me that for all his kindness, he's looking quite agitated. For a moment I forget Herbie.

'Who are you waiting for?' I ask.

He takes a step backwards, inviting me into the room. His navy suitcase is wide open on the bed. Most of his shirts have been neatly folded and repacked, nestling alongside his emergency boxes of Earl Grey tea.

'What this?' I cry in dismay, forgetting the news report. 'What – you're going?'

Ciaran looks sheepish. 'I just felt . . .' He runs his hands through his hair. 'I just felt I should go. Because we were meant to meet and she's not coming – so I may as well go on alone.'

'But it's five in the morning, Ciaran! Reece is never up at this time. She probably only just went to bed.'

'I know that. But about five days ago I booked for us to go on a dawn helicopter ride over the Grand Canyon. This was before we broke up. My last-ditch attempt at sorting things out. It's meant to be the most wondrous experience. Don't get me wrong, I'm not looking for some big reunion. I just thought we could make up in some way, end things on a positive note.'

I can't help feeling surprised. Ciaran hasn't shown Reece much affection over the last few days. He's such a dark horse that it's almost impossible to know what's going on inside his heart. A lot more, it seems, than he lets on.

'Well, have you knocked on her door?'

'No reply. Maybe she's asleep. Maybe she's now banging some Elvis impersonator.' Ciaran suddenly engulfs me in a tight hug. 'Sorry,' he murmurs, his breath tingling warm on my shoulderblade, 'I shouldn't be taking it out on you. Not when you've just had bad news. Only I feel gutted . . . humiliated. I think my stupid male ego wants to feel reassured she felt *something* for me.'

'There's no need to feel like that,' I say, rubbing his back. 'After all, you're the one who ended it. I'm sure when you're back in London you can still stay friends. I'm sorry about your helicopter ride, though.'

Ciaran looks glum. Then something sparkles in his eyes and he looks at me. Even before he suggests it, I feel a thump in my heart. How can I refuse?

'OK,' I say. 'I'll come.' Then I frown, aware of Ciaran's eyes sliding over me. 'What? Oh.' I look down and realise I'm still in my pyjamas. 'Give me five minutes and I'm all yours.'

Back in my room, I flick on the TV again and watch it as I get dressed. More reports about Herbie. His wizened face appears on the screen, followed by footage of him as a younger man, when he first published *The Lost Princess*. He's sitting in a bookstore, his fair hair tousled, his face bright with excitement. A little girl asks him to sign her book. He does so, his manner kindly and sweet. Herbie was a different person then. Will we all end up like him – each year adding a new layer of hurt and cynicism like rings on a tree?

When a limo arrives and picks us up, Ciaran and I remain silent in the back as we ease through the streets, both of us preoccupied with our own worries and sorrows. So when we get to the helicopter, our chirpy guide, Chuck, says he hasn't seen such long faces in ages. Chuck is very tall and very thin, and quite hyper. He keeps making stupid jokes to cheer us up, but when neither of us respond, he mutters something about 'moody Brits' under his breath, which does actually make me smile.

Ciaran and I sit beside each other. The helicopter is all ours. Slowly, it rises into the sky.

'Are you feeling OK?' Ciaran asks me again and I nod, managing a smile.

'But there is something on my mind,' I say, needing to confess. 'As a matter of fact, a few days before Herbie died, I sent him a letter – a really embarrassing one.'

'How so?' Ciaran asks, his eyes flashing with interest at the word *embarrassing*.

'I – just – just some stuff about my emotional state.' I squirm uncomfortably. What on earth would Ciaran say if he knew that I had asked Herbie whether I should go for him or Luke? 'It makes me cringe to think that he probably read it just before he died.'

Ciaran ponders and then says in a deadpan voice: 'You're right. He probably read the letter and was so appalled it caused his heart attack. There's no doubt about it, Julia. You killed him.'

I laugh in outrage and slap him lightly. He laughs too and says in a more serious tone, 'He won't forget you. You gave him something special.'

I fall silent, hoping that Ciaran's words are true. In reality, I have no idea how Herbie remembered me. Maybe he forgot my visit the moment I left in his limo.

We stare out at the view.

'Isn't this just totally awesome?' Chuck enthuses, waving his long, bony fingers at the window.

'It's scrubland,' Ciaran replies in such a deadpan voice that I suddenly feel like bursting into giggles. I get the sense that Chuck now sees us as a challenge. As though he's determined that by the end of this trip, he'll have us singing the 'Stars and Stripes', waving flags and proclaiming that the Grand Canyon is the best of all the world's wonders.

'Just look at that *sky*!'

He's right. The sky is simply stunning, gold arrows of dawn firing through the blue. But neither of us are really interested.

'So d'you think that you kissing Lucy the other night might have got Luke going?' Ciaran suddenly asks in a loud voice. I can barely hear him over the sound of our helicopter.

I think Chuck overhears, for a look of mild horror passes over his face.

'I didn't do it to impress Luke,' I mouth in embarrassment. 'I did it because I just wanted to see what it was like.'

'And what was it like?'.

'It was very nice, thank you.' I blush. 'Besides, I don't think Luke and I are going to get back together,' I say in a resigned voice.

'I don't think Reece and I are going to get back together either,' Ciaran says in an equally flat tone.

'Just look at this *sky*!' Chuck whinnies. 'Check out this *dawn*, folks.'

It's the panorama that grips me – the endless breadth of view. I can see so far, I swear I can see the curve of land against the sky. Maybe this is why Americans are so free, so unbounded and open to new ideas; their geography reflects their character. But today I can't connect with the landscape. I can't seem to connect with anything.

'I'm not sure if I believe in love any more,' Ciaran shouts.

'Me neither,' I agree. And we sit there, gazing out at the beautiful, romantic scene, consoled and united in our misanthropy.

Suddenly we become aware that we've landed at the bottom without even noticing we were descending.

'So that was the Grand Canyon,' Chuck says in a woe-begone voice. 'One of the Seven Wonders of the World.'

'Fuck – really?' Ciaran asks. 'I didn't even notice it.'

Chuck looks as though he's about to burst into tears.

But when I climb out of the helicopter, my gasp of pleasure cheers him up. The vastness of the canyon is astonishing; it has a Biblical quality to it. Over the last two billion years, the dramatic rock formations have been shaped by the whims of the wind and the rain. We've landed on the banks of the Colorado River and hear the distant spray of the Navajo Falls.

'You booked a romantic champagne breakfast for two.' Chuck beams roguishly. There's a small table with a green shelter curving over it; on the table he lays out a chequered cloth and pulls out luxuries from a wooden basket decorated with hearts.

I sit down gingerly on a wooden bench. I can't help looking at this fabulous spread and feeling that it's all rather inappropriately intimate for us.

Ciaran raises his glass and says sourly, 'To the end of love! To hatred, misery and a quick death.'

'Absolutely.' I raise my glass, then down it quickly. The bubbles dance in my stomach and I can't help but enjoy a squiggle of happiness. Sitting here, it's hard to really believe that love doesn't exist; it feels as though a Creator, a divine intelligence, must have carved these very rocks with love.

'D'you think it's just us?' Ciaran asks. 'I mean – you dumped me. Did I smell? Do I have BO? Bad breath? Am I too rude?'

'No, no, no, no,' I protest. 'I think love is just about timing.' I shield my eyes as the sun squints into them. 'I know you will find someone special, one day soon.'

'Maybe I was just too good,' Ciaran says. 'After all, Julia, I treated you better than I've treated any woman and then you cruelly dumped me.'

'Oh, Ciaran . . .'

'No, it's fine. Perhaps you've simply confirmed my theory that you have to treat 'em mean to keep 'em keen.'

'Come on, don't head down that route,' I cry, suffering a horrible vision of him hardening into a bastard who sleeps with women and then leaves before they wake up, addicted to using and abusing.

'Well, you say that, Julia – but look what happened. I mean, for example, let's consider Valentine's Day 2007.'

'Valentine's Day 2007?' I suddenly realise that was before Reece. That was *our* Valentine's Day.

'Time to head back,' Chuck interrupts us cheerfully. 'I'm afraid we have to stick to our schedule but it's been a sheer delight to take you on this tour. You're one of the best couples I've ever shown around here.'

10

Back on the helicopter, an awkward silence sits between us. And then Ciaran finally dares to break it.

'Valentine's Day 2007.' He laughs lightly, staring down at his palms. 'Remember?'

I remember. Due to my lack of interest, my relationship with Ciaran was already beginning to splutter, and this was the day that really blew the flame out. But why bring this up now? I feel uneasy, seeing Ciaran like this. One of the things I've always loved about him is the silent strength he emanates. Now he seems so raw and vulnerable, as though he's determined to rake through every relationship he's had, label it a disaster and blame himself. And I want to tell him that *I* was the one to blame; *I* was the idiot who didn't see how amazing he was.

'I was planning to take you up in a hot-air balloon. You can book them, you know. You can fly from Surrey.' He stares out of the window as the helicopter rises, the dawn gilding the high planes of his cheekbones, then turns and gives me a bitter smile. 'It wouldn't have been quite the same as this, though.'

'I'm really sorry,' I say. 'I was ill that day.'

'Bullshit. You got your secretary to make an excuse. You wouldn't even take my call.'

I blush violently. Then I feel him nudge me in the ribs.

'In actual fact,' he says, his voice light, as though he's telling a jokey anecdote about someone else, 'I was going to suggest that we celebrate a postponed Valentine's Day.'

'A *what*?' I laugh, maintaining the light spirit even though my heart is throbbing. I'm not sure where this conversation is going. It's all very well talking about Luke and Reece, but now this is about *us*. At first I thought he was displacing his Reece angst on to me; now I'm bewildered and shaken.

'Well, I knew you were working like crazy for your promotion. So I figured we could have a belated Valentine's Day – on the twenty-first of February.'

Regret smarts through me. And there I was, standing in my office, superimposing my limitations on to Ciaran, convinced that he wouldn't understand about my workaholic ambition for my promotion. And all the way he was being incredibly considerate, working around me, being romantic, thoughtful *and* spontaneous in his gesture.

I want to say, 'I'm sorry I was so stupid. If you did that to me now, I'd leap at the chance.'

Do I dare, do I dare, do I dare?

I feel a momentum gathering inside. This is it. I'm going to tell him. I'm going to confess to him that I have loved him for eighteen months and only Luke has managed to distract me – albeit briefly. But when I open my mouth to speak, I just don't know how to begin. If this was a book or a film, I'd launch into a grand speech and he'd listen with dreamy eyes and make a grand speech back. But the helicopter is whirring and Chuck is nattering to the co-pilot and it suddenly feels so absurd to just come out with it.

Don't worry about anyone else, my courage argues back. *Just say it. This is the moment. Even if he knocks you back, at least it's finally out in the open.*

'I'm sorry,' Ciaran says abruptly. 'I'm really embarrassing you now. And fuck, I was just as bad with Reece. I neglected her, I wasn't there for her a lot.'

'I think you were wonderful to Reece,' I object, even though I recall Reece complaining about his long hours to me from time to time.

'The only time Reece and I were any good was in the bedroom,' Ciaran sighs. 'And that's not enough.' He straightens up and I see emotion pass across his face before it becomes blank again, as though everything has been packed neatly back into his heart and the key turned. He shoots me a wicked glance. 'I'm just sad our Valentine's Day failed because I never got to see you in those blue pyjamas.'

I can see Ciaran's trying to lighten the tone, possibly

even backtrack because he's embarrassed by the vulner-ability he's shown me. But I feel utterly mortified. How can I declare my feelings for him now when he's just taken the piss out of my nightwear?

'I saw you were still wearing them earlier. I never could persuade you to get rid of them. You're obviously very attached to them.'

My laughter fades into a smile. I think I know what Ciaran's getting at. He's comparing me and Reece in his head. He's obviously imagining all the times he had crazy hot sex with Reece in thirty-nine different positions, with her orgasms sopranoing to the ceiling. Then he's remem-bering a rather different experience with me. He's no doubt recalling the time, not long before the dreaded Valentine's Day, when we were walking past an underwear shop and he suddenly dragged me inside.

'Why are we going in here?' I snapped.

'I just think it might be nice if you wore something like this,' he said, fingering a pair of lacy scarlet knickers. To pay him out, I made a terse remark that it was chauvin-istic of him to expect me to dress like a page three model, then took a call on my mobile and discussed exchange rates of sterling against the yen. I remember leaning against a stand of Wonderbras, speaking on autopilot because my subconscious was beginning to whir. I realised that Ciaran was making a statement by bringing me into this shop: that he wasn't happy about the sex we were having. At the time, I thought he was over-sexed. Now I realise I was really rather frigid. No ... frigid is the wrong word. I was just knackered. Sex requires energy, and it's hard to feel in the mood when you feel so exhausted the moment you hit the pillow at night your eyelids cement themselves together. Standing in that sex shop, aware that I was failing to satisfy him, made me feel resentful towards Ciaran. I thought: He wants more than I give him. I'm under so much pressure, I've got so many demands at work – how the fuck does he expect me to take care of his stupid overly-demanding sex drive? I turned my mobile off and marched out of the shop. He followed, looking sheepish.

And then there was that one morning ...

I remember that.

I was getting ready for work. Dawn was arriving, the dark fading into a pale blue that filtered through the curtains. I'd left him in bed to have an extra sleep, but Ciaran seemed hungry for something else. He climbed out of bed, wearing his pyjama bottoms, his torso naked, and came up behind me, curling his arms around me, gazing at our reflections in the mirror, kissing my neck. He led me over to the bed, but I tugged away irritably. Telling him I was late for work. Telling him I didn't want to take another shower after sex. So he whispered in my ear, 'We don't have to have sex, then. Let me just touch you.'

I forced a smile, wishing he'd get on with it, hoping he'd be quick so that I could hurry out of the flat and go to work.

We lay down, and when he pushed up my skirt, I repressed an impatient sigh. Then, as he slid his palm up my thigh, slowly, millimetre by millimetre, I felt something inside me prickle; something waking up. I tried to dampen it down. He brushed the tips of his fingers over me, light as a feather. I felt his eyes on mine and I resented them; they almost felt like an intrusion into me. And yet. His touch was so light, so teasing, so delicious. A blush burned across my cheeks; I found myself arching against him. I closed my eyes and I heard my breathing escalate and he caressed me into a deep orgasm, pressing his lips hard against mine, swallowing my gasps.

Then I lay there, shaking, stunned by the shivers rippling over my body. He was breathing hard too, even though I hadn't touched him. I could tell that he was thrilled to have opened me up. And I felt so raw, so vulnerable, that something inside me snapped shut. He leaned over to kiss me again, but I scrambled off the bed, tugging down my skirt.

'Right. Work,' I said briskly.

I remember the look of hurt in his eyes. He lay back down on the bed and stared at the ceiling. And I left feeling terrible and strange and churned up inside.

That was our last encounter before Valentine's Day. The experience had scared me, made me feel I might really fall for him. And then I'd lose my focus and possibly my promotion. In the end, I was ruthlessly determined to dump him.

Now, as our helicopter swoops down over Vegas, I gaze at Ciaran, blushing at the intimacy of the memory. And he gazes back – and for one jumpy moment, I'm scared that he can look inside me, see my thoughts.

I quickly look away.

11

After our helicopter ride, we head back to our rooms to get some more sleep. In the hallway, we give each other a tender hug and Ciaran thanks me for cheering him up.

In my room, I lie down on the bed, feeling as though the trip has simultaneously stirred me up and warmed my heart. As I slide into unconsciousness, the positive emotion predominates: the way you feel when you're a child and your mother has tucked you up and kissed you and read you a story.

Vegas swirls its colours into my dreams. Ciaran and I are flying together, circling over The Strip, pointing at the Eiffel Tower, the Paris balloon. As we glide and soar, lights shimmer through our souls, streaming beauty across the sky like comets. Then the dream spins like a coin and lands in a new location. We're in a casino, tossing dice. Ciaran tells me that if I throw a three, my *Ten Things* trip will end happily, but if I throw a six, my trip will be doomed. James Dean, immortalised as a cardboard cut-out, comes to life and strolls over to the table. He folds his arms, frowns, and gravely wishes me good luck. Ciaran puts his arm tight around me and I feel the tension building. I rattle the die in my palms, watching it bounce and bound across the table ...

... and just before I see the score, I wake up.

It's one of those dreams which leaves a pleasant emotional aftertaste. I lie in bed for a few minutes, feeling sweet and rosy with happiness. I close my eyes again, reliving the moment where we flew together, our souls mingling colours like love. Then I remember the surreal bit in the casino and laugh out loud, wondering what Ciaran would say if I told him James Dean was wishing us luck.

I sit up in bed. The clock says it's now 3 p.m. – I've slept for hours. I feel much better now, though a little muzzy around the edges.

I brush my teeth and shower. Put on my jeans and my favourite Monsoon top. In the hallway, I wonder who's up. I head back to Ciaran's room and bang gently on the door.

No reply. Maybe I should just leave him alone. And yet ... something niggles inside me; he seemed so upset after our helicopter ride.

I reach into my handbag to get my mobile. Then I realise that I only have Ciaran's old Nokia mobile number. He got a BlackBerry when he started dating Reece and I don't have his new number; Reece has always been the connection between us.

I could call reception and ask them to put me through to his room, but maybe he's having a nap or something.

Back in my room, I pace around, switch on the TV. There are still reports about Herbie dying. Footage of kids bustling around to his gates, leaving bunches of flowers and letters and tributes and copies of *The Lost Princess*. The camera does a close-up of a little boy reading his book: it's sentimental but all the same, I feel tears in my eyes.

'Herbie French, the reclusive writer, aside from his lawyer and staff didn't see any member of the public for nearly two decades,' the reporter asserts.

'Hey,' I say to the screen, '*I* saw him.' But the world will never know about that.

I am keen to tell Ciaran about the news report, so I head over to his door and knock again.

No reply.

Downstairs, I eat another brunch afternoon tea at the Bayside buffet. My stomach seems to be in a bit of a bad mood about my erratic dietary routine, so this time I just stick to fruit and yoghurt. As I eat, I recall my dream with a tender smile. It would be so very easy for me to start falling for Ciaran again; he only has to rain a few words on my heart for it to start blossoming again. But Lucy's words echo uneasily in my mind: *You might hunger after him now, but if you had him ... well, I think you'd*

382

just lose interest. Maybe I should keep my heart in check and just spend our last days in Vegas trying to keep Ciaran happy and Luke and Reece under control. After all, Ciaran isn't himself either right now. I could go and get a stupid crush on him, and then, when he feels more together, he might tell me where to get off and I'll just end up humiliated . . .

'Julia!'

I turn and see Reece skipping through the tables, exuberantly waving a banana.

'Hey, girl, why didn't you come out with us last night?' She comes and plants a big bananary kiss on my cheek and I push her away, groaning. But I can't help grinning. It's hard to stay mad at Reece for long.

Then Luke appears, looking worse for wear, carrying a large toy shark under one arm. I flick a look between him and Reece as they sit down at my table, wondering how they spent their night. Their eyes look bloodshot enough to suggest they were taking a cocktail of various substances. Even though I know that Luke and I aren't destined to be together, I still feel a little bit jealous.

'So are you ready to party tonight?' Reece cries. 'Now Lesbo Lucy's done a bunk and Ciaran's gone too, there'll be nobody to hold us back.'

'What?' I put down my spoon. 'Ciaran's gone? I only saw him a few hours ago.'

'Yeah. He was in reception a little while back. He was pissed off with me over some helicopter ride and he said you'd stepped in and then he said he'd just decided to pack and go because some kind of work crisis came up.'

'Oh. Right.' Disappointment leaks through me like grey slush. It doesn't surprise me that he upped and left. But he didn't even say goodbye.

'Well, that's the official story Reece is putting out,' Luke says. 'I'm just glad the contract killer I hired did a good job.'

Reece screams with laughter. I give Luke a glare and he gently kicks me under the table, to assure me he was just kidding.

'Oh, I can't believe our flights are in two days' time,' Reece moans. 'I feel really at home here. I'll have to go back to scrubby old England, but you'll get to go back to New York.'

I feel surprised. Although I agreed with Mum that I'd spend a few more days with her before I leave, I'll be quite happy to be back in England, back in my flat with its home comforts.

'I wish I could just be employed to smoke pot all day,' Reece declares.

'Reece,' I chide her, noticing a few heads turn.

'You should find a cannabis farm and offer your services,' Luke suggests, and they both giggle rather wildly.

That evening we three head out to the casinos again.

I miss Lucy, but at least I know we'll stay in touch. Ciaran is a different matter. Even as we sit on the Monorail, joking and laughing, I feel despair that I may never see him again. His relationship with Reece has ended on such an ugly note that I can't see them staying friends. I'm sure his work crisis was an excuse. Ciaran left because he wanted to run away and lick his wounds. The flat will be a different landscape. A white space where his mug used to sit; an empty hook where his jacket used to hang. And then what? I have no good reason to stay in touch with him.

The thought of not seeing him again makes me feel frantic.

I'm still addicted to Ciaran. I'm not even sure how to define my feelings for him any more, they dance so rapidly through the rainbow of emotions. There have been times when I've lusted after him, times when I've ached with love, times when I've even hated him. But now I just feel full of deep, warm affection. I want his friendship. I want to look out for him. I want to cheer him up. And even though it will be painful to do it, I want to reassure him that he can find love again, that he deserves a good woman who'll treat him right. I want to see him happy.

I can get hold of his email, I reassure myself – make some excuse to get in touch. But I still feel scared I've lost him forever.

So I'm in a pretty reckless mood when I enter the MGM Casino tonight. Normally I try to stay relatively sober whilst I'm gambling, then get drunk when I've got winnings to celebrate. Tonight, I just don't care.

'Yesterday we had a wild night,' Luke says, lifting his glass at the bar. 'Let's have an even wilder one tonight.'

'Let's paint the town pink,' Reece cries, laughing wildly.

And it strikes me as I watch Luke's face just before he downs his drink – that his 'party animal' persona, his boyish lust for smashing boundaries – is a jazzy wrapping-paper that hides something fragile underneath.

Later, much later . . . there are lights, beautiful sparkling lights. Casinos look a bit like heaven, I tell Reece, and she laughs and says, 'Disguised as hell.' Poker table. Cards look all blurry. Can't count my chips. Reece helps me. Her giggle is wet in my ear. And then the dealer says, 'Well done, lady, it must be your lucky night,' and, 'Yees!' I raise my arms in the air. 'I've won, I've WON!' And now at the roulette table Luke asks me what my lucky number is and I say 'Twenty-one,' and he asks why and I lie and say, 'It just is,' when actually it's the date I first met Ciaran and it spins round and round and I've lost . . . oh well, time for another drink.

And then we're out in the sharp fresh air God it's so hard to walk straight we all link arms do a monkey walk making loads of noise people are laughing at us and then we go to the salon and Luke asks if he can get some Botox in his dick and I think that must be the funniest thing I've ever heard and I think blue would be a really really nice colour and Reece says 'I want pink' and God I wish I could sober up can they hear me slurring my words this is *so* embarrassing. And Luke says, 'Let's get another round at that bar,' and I tell him if I have one more I'll passssss out and he says, 'Chill,' and I watch an Elvis on stage blur into three Elvises no make that four and Luke has his arm around me and around Reece and we're all smiling and laughing and then a stranger comes up to Reece and says, 'Hi, gorgeous,' and Luke says, 'These two woman are my wives we believe in polly – polly – polygamy,' and we all laugh and pretend we spend our lives waiting on Luke which is so funny and the church lights are so bright and now I'm feeling really good really free only my body seems to be spinning away I'm losing control can hear voices saying, 'Watch out, Julia,' and the floor is coming up towards me fast fast hard.

12

I'm awake. I lick my dry lips; my tongue is swollen with thirst. I fumble for a glass of water. As I move, a pain which has been crouching behind my eyes jumps up, banging its fists against my lids. I hear a thud as the glass hits the floor, spraying water into my shoes.

I groan.

My eyelids are glued with gunky sleep. I open them a centimetre. So I'm in my hotel room. And there's nobody else in this bed with me. Good. That's a start. I desperately need to go into the bathroom for more water. But it seems so, so far away. So I burrow down under the covers. I want to sleep, but something is wrong. Something to do with last night . . .

I press my fingers to my throbbing temples, massaging them gently. Flashes of the night before come back to me. Drinking – yes, there were loads of Apple Martinis. The green curve of a roulette table . . . Luke laughing wildly at something . . . Yet I can't quite work out what happened that's causing this black feeling in my chest.

Money. It has to be money. I must have blown hundreds of dollars. I should get up, call my bank, hear the awful truth—

A knock at my door. I don't want my room cleaned. *Just go away!* I yell silently at the door. *Just leave me alone with the world's worst hangover.*

The knocks get louder.

'Julia!' I hear a voice calling.

'OK,' I whisper. 'OK.'

I get out of bed. Standing up proves a little too much for me, so I crawl to the door on my hands and knees.

I reach up and yank the handle open. It's Reece. She looks appalling. Her blond hair is a messy nest and streaked . . . *pink*. She stares down at me and laughs at the state of me. Then her face falls.

'Oh Julia,' she says. In just two words she manages to convey the news that last night was very bad.

She staggers in and collapses on to my bed.

Being with Reece sobers me up somewhat. I automatically start becoming Ms Sensible. I take possession of my pain and struggle to the bathroom. The taste in my mouth is horrible, so I scrub my teeth with delicious minty toothpaste, then glug back a lovely cleansing glass of water. For a moment I have a strange sensation that there's something wrong with my hands, but I'm too bleary to quite register what. I shrug, fill another glass up, then go to

Reece's side and pass it to her. She takes a doleful sip.

'Tell me then,' I say in trepidation. 'How much money did we lose? And why is your hair pink?'

'That – that was at the salon,' Reece says. 'That's when you had your nails done. We were pretty drunk at that point.'

I do a double-take and stare down at my nails.

'Ah! Blue!' I gape at the plastic talons, the colour of blue Smarties.

'I think I lost loads of money,' Reece goes on. 'But you weren't so bad – you were on a winning streak again.'

'I was?' I suddenly notice a pile of chips dumped on the other bed in my room. Some have rolled on to the pillow and the floor. I go over and grab them, enjoying their reassuring trickle through my palms. 'Oh, cool. I think I've made a few hundred at least. Oh, thank God for that.'

Already my hangover feels lighter as sunshine fills my mind. I'm not about to go bankrupt or have to sell my flat and move into a squat.

'Well, I'm glad *you* had a good night,' Reece says in a broken voice.

'Reece – I'm sorry,' I say, going back to her side. 'Here.' I pour some chips into her lap. 'We'll share them, right? You can have half.'

'Thank you,' she whispers, but she doesn't look very consoled.

Then she lets out the longest sigh I've ever heard and

stares down, twisting her fingers, playing with a blue plastic ring. It's then I twig.

The ring is on the third finger of her left hand.

'Shit!' I cry. 'Oh, Reece.'

Reece starts to laugh. I try to join in but I can't.

'Who ... what ... oh God,' I groan. 'Oh dear. Oh dear. Oh God.' I'm so shocked I can't speak in sentences involving more than one syllable.

Reece is still laughing hysterically. 'What if he asks for custody of the goldfish? Cameron and Ashton will be traumatised – he won't understand that they need fish counselling.'

'I think you're going to need a first-class lawyer,' I say queasily. Fish aside, Reece does have money. And assets – courtesy of her father. I picture some American guy barging into our apartment, grabbing our TV and Reece's pair of pink fluffy slippers. I open my mouth to bring this point up, then close it, fearing I might be sick. My head begins to throb again with even greater intensity.

My mobile rings. I pick it up – it's Mum. She calls so rarely, so I know this has to be something serious. But then I see the look on Reece's face. This is an emergency. I let it go to voicemail.

'So who is he? Can you even remember?' I ask.

'He has ... brown hair,' Reece giggles.

'*Brown hair?* Well, that's a strong start. Like Cinderella, we can tour round Las Vegas looking for brown-haired men and you can kiss them and see if it triggers any memories,' I say, with a touch of sarcasm. I can't believe Reece can't remember the guy. How could she be so stupid?

'Oh God, Julia.' She suddenly stops laughing and clutches her head. 'What am I going to *do*?'

Silence. Then my mobile shrills again. Mum. I have a feeling this is important.

'Sorry,' I say to Reece. 'Just let me check Mum's OK.'

'Hello, love.' Her voice is merry but strained. 'How's Las Vegas?'

'It's – fine. Very good,' I manage.

'You sound funny. You haven't spent all your money, have you?'

I can't believe this. She's called up to lecture me about money? Next she'll be suggesting I invest in a piggy bank.

'Mum, this really isn't a good time. I'm sorry but—'

'I've got something important to tell you,' she says in a rush.

I sit upright. Suddenly Reece is irrelevant. My heartbeat starts to quicken.

'I . . . should have told you earlier,' she goes on, defending herself in advance, 'but I thought you were happy. It wasn't until we had that – chat – that I realised you weren't. Well. A few months ago, I heard from a man called John Ruston.'

'Who's John Ruston? What did he say?' I ask.

There's a sudden bang on the hotel door and in walks Luke. His hair is standing up on end, there are flowers of lipstick on his cheek, one sleeve torn off his shirt.

'Good morning, Great-Mother-of-Goldfish,' he declares,

and Reece giggles wildly. Great. Last night is a blur but I should imagine that he encouraged her to marry this random stranger. He was probably the Maid of Honour and donned lipstick for a laugh. I can't help thinking that Luke is a very bad influence on Reece. But maybe I just sound like a schoolmarm.

I go back to my phone.

'Mum,' I say quickly. 'Don't hang up. I just need to go somewhere quieter.'

I make for the balcony. As I leave the cool air-conditioned room, the baking sun slaps its rays on to me and within seconds I'm drenched in sweat. Plus, this might be private but the reception out here isn't so good. When Mum speaks, it's as though someone has turned the volume down. I try pressing the volume up on my phone, but she still sounds as though she's at the other end of a tunnel.

'Mum, can you speak up?' I ask. 'Reception's tricky.'

'Is this better?'

'Just about. Well, maybe a bit louder?'

'YOU WANT ME TO SHOUT?'

'YES!'

'JOHN RUSTON CALLED AND SAID HE WAS A FRIEND OF YOUR FATHER!'

'What? But where is Dad, why—'

'YOUR DAD IS WORKING IN INDIA, IN TAMIL—' She breaks off. 'Do I have to keep shouting?'

I press my phone so hard against my ear that it hurts, straining to hear.

'What's he doing in India?' I ask, dreading the answer.

'I don't know. Look, pet, Anthony and I are about to go out for dinner – it's a charity fundraiser,' she goes on, her voice so distant it sounds ghostly.

Oh, great. No doubt she chose this moment to call up so she had an excuse to escape quickly.

Then I remind myself of just how hard it must have been for her to make this call at all. I ought to be angry at her for not telling me this back in New York, but I still remember how hurt she was, and I appreciate the fact that she's obviously mulled it all over and decided to do the right thing.

'I'll give you this John Ruston's phone number, but before I do, promise you won't do something silly, like flying halfway across the world and trying to meet up with him? Promise just to talk to your dad on the phone? I really don't think it would be safe for you to meet, not out there.'

'But why didn't he just call himself? Who is this John? Why did he phone you?'

'Well, your father's a coward, he'd never have the guts to call himself,' she says in disgusted voice.

It's clear that my mother's anger has obscured her sense of logic.

'But that's weird. I think maybe he's ill or something. I mean, what did this John person say on his behalf?'

There's an awkward silence before Mum goes on: 'Well, he – he wanted to know how you and Alexander were. What you were doing. It was frankly just ridiculous, after him not being interested all these years,' she says, and her voice fades and then disappears.

'Mum? *Mum?*' I cry.

'I have to go,' she says, very slowly and loudly. 'That's all I ever want to say about this. Now – do you have a pen so you can take down the phone number?'

I scramble about through my pockets, yanking out an I LOVE VEGAS pen which I must have picked up some-time last night. I scrawl John Ruston's number on the back of my hand.

Then we say goodbye.

I stand on the sweltering balcony for a minute. After all this time, just when I thought I had to give up, I have a chance of meeting my dad. God, that was so brilliant of Mum. I wish she was here now – I'd give her a huge hug.

I hurry back into the room, bubbling with excitement. But when I make my announcement to Luke and Reece, they hardly seem to hear me. They just exchange nervous glances. My smile fades. That black, nervous feeling I woke up with this morning comes flooding back.

'Uh,' Luke begins. He runs his fingers through his hair, leaves it sticking up on end. 'There's something we gotta tell you. Kind of. Yeah.'

My eyes fall to his left hand. He's wearing a pink plastic ring on his wedding finger.

He gives me a terrified look, then turns to Reece and says in a trembling voice, 'Er – hello, wife.'

13

Bang bang! It's been a long time since I've really hated anyone. At work, my evil nemesis Melissa was always giving me backhanded compliments like, 'You're really efficient at getting your paperwork done – you'd make a great secretary.' I used to moan all the time to Reece and Ciaran how I hated her guts, but I didn't mean it. I worked in a cut-throat industry, after all. So it comes as an ugly surprise to learn how it feels to really hate someone. It's far worse for you than the object of your fury.

Bang bang! I'm sitting in my hotel room and I swear I can't even look at a piece of furniture without wanting to tear it up and toss it out of the window. I want to break things and yell at the sky and ask God just what His problem is.

Bang bang!

'WILL YOU STOP KNOCKING ON MY DOOR – I'M NOT GOING TO COME OUT!' I yell hoarsely.

The banging stops.

I sit on the bed and I feel so hot with fury that it becomes unbearable. So I go into the bathroom and tear off all my clothes. I sit in the bath and swivel on the shower. The icy water hits me like hailstones. I keep replaying all the times Reece has told me over the past few days that she doesn't fancy Luke. But now I wonder if the roots extend right back to that first day, when she made me call him up. Even then, she seemed turned on. Even when I told her about his shady past; in fact, I think that just accentuated her fantasy. Then, after we checked into our hotels in Vegas, she asked if I had any pics of him on my mobile phone. When she saw them, she didn't comment, but I saw her pupils dilating like a cat eyeing up a bowl of cream. And what about that night she claimed she'd *bumped* into him and was doing me this amazing favour by drinking with him alone? How could I have been so naïve?

When I first saw their rings, I started yelling at them. Reece turned to Luke as though hoping he'd explain everything, and Luke turned to Reece as though hoping she'd explain everything. Then he made a hasty exit. Reece gaped after him. Then she started making pathetic excuses.

'It was a joke,' she kept saying, curling her fair hair around a trembling finger. 'Luke was going to marry me, then you.'

'That makes no sense whatsoever,' I snarled.

'Don't you remember, we were joking in the bar about polygamy. That's why we ended up going to the church – well, except you passed out, so we sort of laid you down in a pew and then you were kind of the passed-out Maid of Honour. The minister told us he'd never had an unconscious Maid of Honour before but he said there was always a first time for everything in Vegas.' She smiled a twitchy smile, as though hoping I'd laugh. I didn't.

'So you waited until I passed out and then you nicked my boyfriend and married him,' I said furiously.

'But I thought you and Luke were just friends,' Reece cried, tears trembling in her eyes, threatening to tip blue-mascara streaks down her cheeks.

She was right, of course, but that wasn't the *point*. She was my friend. She'd betrayed me. I would never have done this to her.

'And we didn't consummate it – we just had a drunken snog and then Luke carried you back to your room. He was joking that he was meant to be carrying his bride over the threshold, not you.'

'Oh, I'm sorry that I spoiled your honeymoon.'

'Julia, please don't be like this. I know you must be pissed off, but it really was just a spur of the moment crazy stupid drunken thing. I mean, marrying a random stranger in Vegas was always on *my* list of *Ten Things to Do Before I Die.*'

'Well, I'm glad you ticked *that* box,' I said savagely.

'Well . . .' Reece swallowed, as though wildly searching

for a retaliation. And then she found one. She couldn't have known how good it was. 'You and Ciaran – you went off on that helicopter ride! I didn't come after you and have a big go!'

For a moment I was speechless. I opened my mouth to say, 'But you and Ciaran had broken up.' But then Reece would only say, 'But so had you and Luke.' I opened my mouth to say, 'It was innocent.' But then Reece would say, 'So were we.'

And the truth was, I have spent months and months yearning after Ciaran. For God's sake, I'd been so awful and pathetic I'd even once lain in bed, listening to *them* making love and caressed myself. Thinking that I was some sad pervert.

I stood there, feeling the moral high ground slipping away from me like quicksand. She's right, I thought. No matter how awful this is, I have no right to judge her.

And then Luke came back in. He said in a solemn voice, 'Since we're bound until death us do part, maybe I should just jump off the balcony and make you all feel better.' He and Reece looked at each other and burst into nervous laughter. My anger reared up again: I wanted to punch the pair of them. Shaking, I hissed at them both to leave my room *right now*. I sounded as though I was possessed. They took one look at each other, then practically ran away.

The shower carries on spinning a curtain of icy water around me. I've cooled down. Shivers start to ripple over me but I sit tight. If I get pneumonia and die – well, good. I stare into the plume of water and see a vision of my funeral. Reece and Luke look sober and contrite. Then I picture them at the buffet afterwards, flirting with each other across the sausage rolls, then going into some room filled with coats and making love. I let out a cry and lift up my hands, breaking the water, splashing it over my face. I wish I could just find a switch that I could press and stop my emotions.

Finally I get out of the bath and rub myself vigorously. But my teeth keep chattering and my body keeps shivering. For the first time since I've arrived in Vegas, I feel cold.

14

I sit in my hotel room for another hour or so. I feel as though I'm sickening for flu. I'm aware that I haven't eaten for hours but I don't feel hungry. To eat would be a way of connecting with the world, a form of acceptance. I want to push the world away and tell it that I'm not happy with my lot in life, that I won't accept it, that I don't deserve this.

That's the trouble with heartache. It is selfish. It centres you solely in your own world; there's no room for anyone else's troubles.

I tell myself that I need to get some perspective, so I go out on to the balcony. I gaze down at a girl swimming lazily in the hotel pool. Then I see a man standing by a palm tree, talking into his mobile, gesticulating as though he's seriously pissed off with the caller. I sweep my eyes beyond the pool. I see an elderly woman getting out of a taxi, struggling to walk, her shuffling husband helping her. I see a little boy push his brother and they both burst into shrieking tears. See? I tell myself. Everyone there is in the centre of their own worlds. Everyone is struggling with something, whether it's love or work or health or family. Essentially, we're all the same.

I try to think of a past situation that affected me this deeply. I rewind memories, going back beyond Japan and Luke's betrayal, to the day I got fired from Charlton Cross. I remember how sick and upset I felt that day. And now do I care? Not really. Yet once, my job was everything to me. So now I try to reason that in a week's time, I'll have moved on a little. And in a month's time, maybe I'll be able to laugh at this. And I succeed in experiencing some Zenlike moment of peace in the present.

It doesn't last.

I stare down at my hand and notice a smudge on my skin ... *John Ruston*. Mum called, I remember in shock. After all that time in the shower, the number's washed away. I'll have to call her up and ask for it again. I feel my anger boil up once more. Bloody Reece. This was a special moment, one that I've been waiting for almost my entire life – and she's ruined it for me.

And then I just feel seriously fucked off again.

I go back into the room and pick up all of my chips; temptation whispers in my mind. I put them into my handbag, wondering if I should just go and blow the lot.

Then I notice something on my bedside table. My list.

It's travelled with me to quite a few countries by now

and it's seriously crumpled and blotched. My hands tremble; I'm close to tearing it up. This list was meant to be fun. It was meant to be fulfilling. But what has it actually brought me?

1. *Sleep with an Italian man* – I slept with Luke, the world's worst womaniser.
2. *Go scuba-diving* – I spent the whole time yearning after Ciaran.
3. *Stand on the top of a volcano* – ditto.
4. *Go up the tallest building in Tokyo* – and wasn't that romantic, sharing the view with Luke?
5. *Meet my favourite childhood author* – admittedly not the worst disaster, but it stirred up memories of my father, which only makes me feel more pained about the fact that I may never meet him; plus I sent Herbie French the world's most embarrassing letter, a ramble about my love life, just a few days before he died.
6. *Gamble in Las Vegas* – which results in a wedding.
7. *Kiss a girl and see if I like it* – and all I did was use poor Lucy and risk our friendship.

What did my mum say when I was younger?

Be careful what you wish for, or it might come true.

My heart booms; my hands shake. I tear the list into pieces, tearing and tearing until ...

I hear a knock on the door. Still holding the paper

403

pieces bunched up in my fist, I go and open it. It's Luke. His brown eyes look huge with boyish fear.

'Hey,' he says.

As I lift my fist, he recoils as though he's expecting a blow. Then I uncurl my palm so that the pieces scatter over his head and shoulders, drifting to the floor like confetti.

'I guess that's your way of saying congratulations,' he says in a shaky voice.

I glare at him. 'No,' I reply. 'It's my way of saying I hate you and I never want to see you again.'

'Please,' Luke says. 'Can I just come in?' He nods down the corridor, where a maid is trundling a trolley piled high with linen and cleaning products.

I sigh sharply and let him come in. To be honest, a part of me wants another fight. I still have more angry words burning inside me, wanting to be released.

'Look,' Luke pleads, 'it was never going to work out between us, Julia. I realised that a few nights ago when I saw that you would never get past the Jodie thing ...'

'Oh well, I'm sorry,' I spit out. 'I'm really sorry that your ex-fiancée and baby Winston got in the way there for a minute.'

'Please,' Luke says earnestly. 'I realise I'm a serious screwball. You don't need to tell me that. But that's the point. Reece *can* see past the Jodie thing.'

For a moment I can't quite digest his words. I thought that Luke had come in here to say a thousand apologies.

To tell me the wedding was just some joke. To tell me they were about to arrange a divorce.

Not to let me down gently.

'You were never going to forgive me,' Luke says. He laughs sadly. 'And now you're *really* never going to forgive me. But Reece and I – we're two of a kind. We've both got rich parents. We've both had it easy; I guess we've both been spoiled. We also both like to do crazy things. I honestly want to try to make a go of it with her.'

'You actually do want to be married to her?' I say.

'Yeah,' Luke says. 'I think so. I kinda feel that even though it was a drunken mistake, I don't want to run away again like I did with Jodie. I mean, look, I do love you, Julia, but I love Reece too, even though I've only known her for such a short time. And I think maybe she suits me best.'

A few minutes ago, I couldn't have believed this situation could actually get worse. But now it has.

'Listen to yourself!' I cry. 'Luke – you came to Vegas to get back with me. Then you say you're glad you married Reece. And now you say you love me. You don't have a fucking clue what love is!'

'Wrong,' Luke protests furiously. 'I just don't believe that love *has* to be an exclusive thing. I have a liberal idea of love, where you can love whoever you like in any way you want. I'm not into rat-race couples who want to own each other like possessions and spend their lives sharing mortgages and hire-purchase schemes. I don't believe that's love. Love is being free. But you – well, you're more conservative. So.' He pauses.

I press my lips together in disbelief.

'I'm sorry if we upset you,' Luke goes on. 'I honestly didn't think you'd react this badly. But if you had really liked me, you would have taken me back the moment I flew over here. That was a pretty big gesture. But you just wanted to make me suffer, Julia. You wanted me to keep chasing you, but you didn't really want me back.'

My eyes fill with tears. His logic is twisted and utterly immoral, but there is some truth in it. I don't think my heart ever would have opened its arms to let Luke back in.

'It's not just you, it's Reece,' I sigh. 'She's been my best friend for a long time even though we've been moving apart. But I can promise you, Luke, I would *never* have done this to her. I just wouldn't. Of course, for you and Reece, I'm just boring old Julia who doesn't get why it's all so hilarious.'

'No,' Luke protests. 'We don't think that.'

'You've been saying it all through this holiday,' I cry, my voice rising. 'And I'd like to remind you that *I'm* the one who organised this bloody trip. It was *my* list of *Ten Things*. You all just gatecrashed. Well,' I say, grabbing my bag, 'I'm going off to have a bloody good gamble. As for you and Reece – you can go and celebrate your honey-moon.'

'Don't be stupid,' Luke says. 'This isn't a good time to gamble.'

'But I thought I was boring old Julia,' I snap, opening my door. 'Now get out of my room.' He steps out into the corridor and I slam it shut. He tries following me as I stalk towards the lift, but I turn and give him such a fierce glare that he puts his hands up as though I'm carrying a gun. Then he lets out a sigh, turns round and goes back to his hotel room.

I get on to the Monorail and pick a hotel casino entirely at random.

As I enter, I see a handsome young man in his twenties wearing a burgundy velvet jacket. He's carrying a huge pile of chips in his hands. His smile is decadent; his eyes are filmed with the glazed sheen of an addict. As I swap more money, it strikes me that the reason they don't use real money in casinos is because it's easier to part company with chips. They look like plastic toys from a board-game; you can't quite take them seriously. The observation lingers in the back of my mind as though I'm trying to warn myself. I'm conscious that my desire to gamble isn't fuelled by fun any more. I feel *hungry* to get to the tables. I want to pour money into slot machines and spray it across poker tables as though I can flush away my pain.

It doesn't work.

Within two hours I've lost it all and I feel terrible. I take a break and go to the bar for an Apple Martini. Thank God I'm booked to leave Vegas tomorrow. I'm due to head to New York for a few more days so I can speak to Mum about John Ruston and Dad. And then ... well, we'll see. Maybe once I get away from Reece and Luke I'll find some perspective.

Another Apple Martini makes me feel both better and worse. It both blurs my pain and intensifies it.

I put down my empty glass. I really should leave now but I can't face the thought of my empty room. I hear Reece's voice, a mocking sing-song in my head, '*Julia, you're so booorrring ...*'

Suddenly a black, raging desire to gamble comes over me again. I go to the cash machine and get out a wodge of notes. I'm vaguely aware that so far tonight I've only lost my excess, my winnings. If I gamble any more, I'm going to risk the money I need to complete my list of *Ten Things*. But who cares about that? I wonder savagely. Who cares who cares who cares.

I spot the hunched back of the guy with the burgundy velvet jacket I saw earlier. It's a sign, I decide. I go and join his Blackjack table. As I slip into my seat, he doesn't even look at me. His eyes are fixed on the flow of cards.

The other players are a couple in their sixties. They say, 'Hi,' and give me apple-pie smiles. I smile back.

The dealer is in her twenties, with ebony hair tied back in a ponytail. I've learned from experience that dealers all have different personalities, which they impose on their tables. Some are fun and friendly and will chat and offer advice. This woman clearly falls into the other category:

no-nonsense. Her face is benign but closed-off; she means business.

Which is just fine by me. I'm not in the mood for small talk, either.

I convert a few hundred into chips, which she passes over without a word.

Time to place my opening bet. I put down $50. The guy in the burgundy velvet jacket lifts his eyes and smirks at me. The dealer opens her mouth to speak but he beats her to it.

'Hey, didn't you see the sign?'

Oh. I'm more drunk and distressed than I realised; I forgot to even look out for it.

'Minimum bets are five hundred dollars at this table,' he says. His voice is smooth as coffee. 'We're playing a serious game.' He nods at a distant table. 'Minimums are fifty dollars there.'

I really ought to move. I cannot afford an expensive table. But I'm tipsy and this guy is pissing me off. I'm going to bloody show him.

So I shrug and push out my chips. $500. Not so very much, is it?

The dealer deals me two cards face up. A six of hearts. A seven of clubs. Thirteen.

A platinum-blonde waitress comes up, smiling charmingly. I really should not have another drink at this moment in time. I open my mouth to ask for a Coke but somehow the words that spill out are, 'Apple Martini.'

OK. Back to the game. The dealer's looking impatient. Her card is a Jack, which means 10; her other card is hidden.

I tap the table, indicating that I want another card.

A Jack. Which equals ten points. My score is twenty-three. Which means in the space of thirty seconds I've managed to lose $500. I'll swear that the guy in the burgundy jacket is looking at me out of the corner of his eye, silently revelling in my failure. Great.

As I watch the dealer swivel my chips away from me, I have a sudden jolt of memory from last night. I've tried so hard to remember, and now I do, I only want to forget. I recall Luke putting his arms around Reece's waist and saying, 'So, hon, will you marry me?' in a jokey voice and I got jealous and tried to tug them away.

Bastard.

I put down $500 for another game. I'll show Luke and Reece and this bloody velvet-jacketed idiot.

This time, I get an ace and a six. An ace is cool. An ace can mean one *or* eleven. Seventeen isn't such a bad score. The dealer's face-up card is only an eight. I could damn well beat her.

Or maybe that's just my Apple Martini talking.

I tap the green baize for another card.

A Queen. Ten points. So if I make my ace count as one, plus six … plus a Queen, that's a score of seventeen. It's the same. It's probably best to stick at this point because if I get another card I'm bound to go over. My chances of beating the dealer are good.

Then she flips over her other card. An ace. Which means my seventeen is soundly beaten by her bloody eighteen *and I have just lost another $500.*

Now I definitely need another Apple Martini.

I should stop. I've lost $1000. But the dark feeling inside me has been replaced by desperation. There's no way I can fulfil numbers eight or nine on my list because I've just gambled the funds away – and this makes me mad. Not only have I lost my best friend, but my bloody trip is about to be ruined. I have to make this money back. I *have* to take the gamble.

I put down another $500.

The next game lasts thirty seconds. I get a total of eighteen, but the dealer gets twenty-one.

Fuck. I lift my eyes, suddenly aware that the old lady is looking at me. Her eyes are kind and filled with concern. I quickly try to compose my face, worried that my terror is scrawled over it. But I feel as though she's silently telling me to just stop.

But I can't stop now. *Luke*, I scream silently, *this is all your bloody fault. I've bet away my airfare to India. I now officially cannot afford to see my dear father*. Everything is screwed up. I have to win. I have to get back that $500. And then I'll stop, I really really will, even though I'll be down and broke. I cannot abandon my trip to India; I cannot let him go when I'm so close to tracking him down.

I put down another $500. As the cards come towards me, I pray blurrily that I get a good hand.

An eight and a six. Fourteen. OK, this isn't bad. It's probably too low to stick so I'll ask for another card. In fact, I may as well raise the stakes. I have one $500 left. I'll throw it in on this one last card and just go for it and pray luck will shine on me . . .

'Raise,' I say.

The dealer remains expressionless. Next to me, the burgundy guy is positively glowing with *Schadenfreude*. The old couple slip away from the table; they wave goodbye with worried eyes.

The dealer passes me a card. Everything depends on this now. Everything. If this card is less than a seven, I'll be fine and I'll have a good score. If it is a seven, I'll have Blackjack and I'll have something to salvage from this horrific nightmare. But for a moment I can't bear to even look at it. My whole body is shaking; my heart is jattering like mad.

OK. Time to face the truth.

I look down.

8. Find my father

1

From   Julia.rothwell15@hotmail.co.uk
To   ciaran.ohare111@yahoo.com
Sent   2.09.09

Hi Ciaran,

I hope you don't mind me emailing you – got your current email address off Reece. I just wanted to check that you are OK as I know that your time in Las Vegas maybe wasn't the best experience you've ever had! I also hope that you haven't been buried under an avalanche of work.

I am back in New York, staying with my mum and Anthony (who send their love, by the way).

It's fairly quiet here, but tomorrow I'm seeing my NY pal Lucy for a drink – you met her briefly.

Take care,
Julia

From   ciaran.ohare111@yahoo.com
To   Julia.rothwell15@hotmail.co.uk
Sent   3.09.09

Hi Julia,

Of course I don't mind you emailing me, you idiot. After all these years!
Are you kidding me? Las Vegas was the best time I've ever had in my
life. I'm sorry I fell apart and behaved in a pathetic manner. I swear
my liver is still processing all the vodka I drank. I was just having a
meltdown. But I'm glad to say that I'm feeling a lot better now. The
doctors say I'll be just fine; I've been fitted with a strait-jacket and it's
very comfortable – they even do them with Armani labels.

Seriously, I do actually feel as though my work is strait-jacket terri-
tory right now. They're firing loads of people as the recession
deepens blah blah blah. Of course, it just means that everyone has
got to do twice the workload for the same wage. I'm working sixteen
hours a day, I'm working weekends, I feel dead with tiredness. I
have no energy to even go to the bloody supermarket; I'm living off
McDonald's and takeaways – truly grim. I'm desperate to quit the
company but I won't be able to for another six months (besides,
then I get my bonus). So now I just have to save, save, save.

So what happened in Vegas after I left? Did you win a million? I
can picture you now, in a New York salon, enjoying your Botox
injections with Lucy whilst male slaves bring you chocolates on
trays lol. Is that number ten on your list fulfilled?

Seriously, it is great to hear from you.

Bye, darling,
Ciaran x,

From   Julia.rothwell15@hotmail.co.uk

To   ciaran.ohare111@yahoo.com

Sent   4.09.09

Hey Ciaran,

Thanks – it's nice to know that you still think I'm an idiot after all these years.

Actually, for once you're right. I am an idiot. I did something really stupid in Vegas. I was freaked out by Reece and Luke and all that happened, and in the heat of the moment I got pissed and gambled away EVERY LAST PENNY OF MY MONEY. It's all now sitting in the coffers of the Bellagio Hotel casino.

So I'm broke. And I'm stuck. I want to go to India and I've realised the only way I can go is to be a volunteer on an Aid programme. It means I'll get free board and it will be a really good thing to do. I feel so lame about throwing away my money that I want to serve some sort of penance. However, I do have to raise the money for my airfare.

I think I might end up working in a bar in NY or something. That film *Coyote Ugly* was on TV the other night – maybe I should strut up and down a bar in leather trousers throwing beer over men. To think I was on a six-figure salary, once upon a time. But I'm glad I gave up work. And you – you really ought to be eating better, Mr O'Hare. Buy yourself some raw carrots.

I don't want you to shoot the messenger, but there is something I need to tell you. Luke and Reece got married on a drunken whim. This isn't a joke. I know it sounds unreal and insane but it happened. I don't think they're very proud of it, nor are they very compatible – on the last day in Vegas Luke actually threw Reece into the Bellagio fountain, and I don't think it was for fun. But they are trying to make the best of it. I just thought you deserved to know the truth.

Take care,
Julia x

From   ciaran.ohare111@yahoo.com
To   Julia.rothwell15@hotmail.co.uk
Sent   4.09.09

Dear Julia,
It's fine, you don't need to worry that I'm going to shoot myself. I already knew about Reece and Luke. She phoned me the day after their delightful marriage. She sounded really drunk and spewed all this stuff about how maybe she'd made a mistake and she was sorry. I told her that this was the last conversation we were ever going to have and hung up.

As for your money – I am really so sorry to hear about that. When I was in Vegas, it struck me that there's a sort of whirlpool of decadence there that sucks you in. At the same time, in a funny way, I think that you gambling away all your money is good thing. Let's face it, Julia, you're not an idiot – you're one of the most brilliant and talented women I've ever met. But I think that your job limited you. I hope you don't mind me saying this, but I feel your trip has set you free. Maybe you crossed too many boundaries in Vegas

(Lucy?) but you were closed in by too many before. Maybe now you just need to find the right balance.

And I'm sorry if you're heartbroken about Luke, because I know he meant a lot to you. He treated you like shite and if he was here now . . . well, I'd do a lot more than throw him in the Trafalgar Square fountain, I can tell you.

But why India? Is that number eight on your list? You must tell me about the other things on it. I am intrigued. Well, better go. Work is mad, my boss is barking.

Take care,
Ciaran x

From   Julia.rothwell15@hotmail.co.uk
To   ciaran.ohare111@yahoo.com
Sent   5.09.09

Dear Ciaran

Reece and Luke are coming over tomorrow to visit me. I don't know how I feel about seeing them. When I picture Luke's face, I just want to punch him. As for Reece . . . I do remember in Vegas that you warned me that she was going off the rails. And I didn't really believe you. So much for my 'brilliant' mind (and yes, your sarcasm is painful Mr O'Hare!). But Reece and I have been friends for well over twenty years and I just feel I ought to carry on being a good friend to her. I need to try to understand why she's behaving like this and what she's going through.

I do wonder if they'll be consulting a divorce lawyer soon, though.
As for my *Ten Things* list – the reason I want to go to India is to
find my father. I know you asked me about him years ago and I
said I had no idea who he was. Well, that's not entirely true. I have
a few blurry memories of him. He bought me *The Lost Princess* as
a birthday present, which is why I wanted to visit Herbie French.
A man called John Ruston phoned my mum recently and said that
my father wanted to get in touch. I know it sounds wonderful but
I'm really scared – I don't understand why my father didn't himself.
I'm scared he's ill or that something terrible has happened to him –
why use a stranger to make that call for him? I don't even know
who this John Ruston guy is, nor does Mum.

Mum originally told me that my father didn't want to know me, but
now it turns out that every few years he calls her for an update on
me and Alexander. All this time and she's had some idea of where
he is, though she argued that he's been travelling all over the place
and she can never keep up with him. He doesn't even have a
mobile, apparently – he just calls from some random hotel or
callbox. I tried to get hold of John Ruston and got no reply either.
BUT this Ruston guy told Mum that he and my father were helping
out at an orphanage in Tamil Nadu, on the very southern tip of
India. So through a charity website I've managed to arrange a
placement in a children's home that's close by. I'm scared too that
by the time I do this bar job and raise enough money for my flight,
he'll be gone. But I have to take the risk. I try not to pray and hope
too hard, but I can't help it. I want to meet him so much.

Mum thinks it's a bad idea. She thinks he's a bad man.

What makes this whole situation so hard is that Lucy told a friend of hers, who works at a national paper in NY, about me visiting Herbie. They keep trying to contact me and offering me money to write about what happened. But I know that Herbie would have hated to have our private meeting splattered all over the press, so I've turned down the offer. They keep upping it and I'm feeling sick, knowing I could just take it . . . but I won't.

Mum doesn't get that at all. She thinks I'm mad.

God, I've rambled on for so long in this email, haven't I? I will leave you in peace now.

I know that it's past midnight over there in England. Over here, I'm typing this at seven in the evening. Soon my sunset will become your dawn.

Take care,

Julia x

From   ciaran.ohare111@yahoo.com

To   Julia.rothwell15@hotmail.co.uk

Sent   5.09.09

Dear Julia,

Your email really touched me. I recall you mentioned your dad a few times when we were together, but you always sounded as though you didn't care about him. And now I know the truth.

I can't imagine what it must feel like, not knowing your dad. Mind you, I didn't see much of mine when I was a kid. He had a very stiff upper lip. We weren't that rich but he was determined to give me a good education so he used every spare penny packing me off to boarding school. I remember that every time he dropped me off, when it was time to say goodbye he never showed a flicker of emotion. I'd stand and watch him driving away, fighting hard not to be a boy who cried. When he died, my mum told me he'd only ever said he loved her once during their entire marriage. But he showed it every day, in the little things he did for her. And I realised that all those times he'd dropped me at boarding school, it had killed him to let me go, and to sacrifice seeing me grow up, but he thought it was for the best.

There. We've both made confessions and at this rate we'll soon end up on *Jerry Springer!* No, worse – on *Jeremy Kyle.*

It's dawn now. Thanks for making it a spectacular one . . .

Take care,

Ciaran x

From   Julia.rothwell15@hotmail.co.uk

To   ciaran.ohare111@yahoo.com

Sent   6.09.09

Dear Ciaran,

I saw Reece and Luke. God!!! They are already seeing a marriage counsellor.

Do you know what was most infuriating of all? When we were in Vegas, Luke managed to win loads of money. The night after he married Reece, he also hit the casinos and he got $10,000 on the slots. So now he's bloody loaded. And he said that he would give me the money for my flight to India, and that we should all go together. He was very earnest – he says that he feels he's behaved like a cad and is having some sort of spiritual crisis and that if he and Reece go to India, they'll find direction from a guru and sort their mess out. The counsellor is also very 'supportive' (she apparently told Reece that they were the most 'challenging' couple she'd met in a long time, so maybe she just wants to get rid of them?). Reece doesn't seem very keen on going. She's trying to persuade him to go to a Tantric Sex Centre in Delhi instead.

Anyhow, it was kind of Luke to offer me the money. I did want to tell him where to shove it, but I have to swallow my pride because all that matters to me right now is finding my father. This may be my last chance. After this, I'll have to scrap nine and ten on my list (there doesn't seem much point in even telling you them, since they'll never happen) and come back to England.

Maybe in India I can just shake off Luke and Reece. I can't see them lasting long on an Aid programme, to be honest. I think they may find it 'challenging'.

I hope you're not working too hard. Thanks for sharing that story about your father too – it was very sweet. I wish I'd had a father like him.

Take care,
Julia x

From   ciaran.ohare111@yahoo.com
To   Julia.rothwell15@hotmail.co.uk
Sent   7.09.09

Dear Julia,

Don't take his money, please. He's obviously feeling guilty about the foul way he treated you. And so he fucking well should. There's something wrong about you accepting that money. And can you imagine the pair of them in India together? Reece will probably decide she wants to become a Bollywood star and Luke'll seduce every pretty Indian girl in sight. I don't think they should be unleashed on any children – they might do them permanent psychological damage.

Let me lend you the money. Really. There'll be no obligation and you can pay me back when you come home to England and you've started work. There'll be no pressure, I can promise you that.

Work is terrible. This morning I felt and must have looked so drained and the trains were late *yet again* due to a leaf on the line or some such nonsense that I slumped down on the floor and sat there, waiting – and some bastard mistook me for a homeless person and put some change in my cappuccino cup. Nice! I hope it's not a sign of my future.

Take care,
Ciaran x

From   Julia.rothwell15@hotmail.co.uk
To   ciaran.ohare111@yahoo.com
Sent   7.09.09

Dear Ciaran,

When you're not being horrible and calling me an idiot, you can be the sweetest guy in the world, you know that? It is so lovely of you to offer me a loan, but I can't take it. I know it sucks accepting Luke's money, but he owes me a stack of cash, one way and another.

Whereas you – you need to save up. I know what it feels like to be trapped in a job you want to escape from. I won't get in the way of that. I want you to leave your job and find happiness. Maybe you need to work out your own list of *Ten Things*. What would be on it?

Thanks again, you sweet star,
Julia x

P.S. Over here my sunset is looking like a good one.

2

I'm sitting on a plane to Delhi with Luke on one side of me and Reece on the other. In ten hours' time I will be in the same country as my father. I keep trying to picture his face. Does he have hair or is he bald? Does he still have the same crooked smile as in my photo of him? Right now, he may well be awake, looking up at the stars that I'm flying beneath, wondering how I am.

I don't think I'm going to be able to sleep a wink on this flight. After all my travelling, I've developed a theory that on the journey to a new place, you get a premonition of how you'll fuse with the energy of the country. It's like an intuitive foretaste. On the flight to Vegas I felt uneasy and look what happened there. This time I'm simply humming with anticipation. I'm convinced that this trip is going to be tremendous. That it's going to change my life. That's why I didn't even buy a return ticket. I'm prepared to stay here for as long as it takes to find my father, but I can't see beyond that point.

The rational side of me warns me not to start super-imposing superstition on to things ... but I just can't help feeling excited.

A member of the cabin crew stalks elegantly down the aisle, giving our row a disturbed look. I smile at her reas-suringly.

When we first got on to the plane, Luke and Reece had the window and middle seats, while I was stuck at the end. Then they had a massive row. Luke accidentally spilled cola all over his top. Reece complained that it was karmic retribution for him greedily stealing all the psychic energy in yesterday's tantric sex session. Now, Reece behaved like a spoiled brat in Vegas too, but Ciaran handled her well by calmly walking away. Luke, however, bickers and pouts and sulks, which only makes Reece bicker and pout and sulk in retaliation. The pair of them are like two toddlers throwing a tantrum. Now I know why your marriage guidance counsellor was so keen to get rid of you, I thought.

Honestly, the whole thing was so embarrassing. Passengers starting lifting sleep masks and yanking out earphones and complaining.

'I'll sit in the middle,' I said to the air stewardess, desper-ately trying to smooth things over.

Now Reece is sleeping. I stare down at her. If someone had told me at the start of my trip that Reece would end up getting married to my ex, I would never have believed them. And if they'd then told me that I'd still be friends with her, I would have said *no way*.

Yet here I am.

Ciaran thinks I'm crazy. Last night he sent me an email saying he thought I had the heart of Mother Teresa not to have murdered Reece by now. He can't understand how I can even speak to her. But Ciaran doesn't know about the history of my heart. I can forgive Reece because I still feel that I spent eighteen months silently betraying her by hungering after Ciaran.

Becoming aware of Luke's gaze on me, I turn to face him.

'Hey,' he says in a low voice, fingering his guidebook. 'It says here that Chennai is the sister city to Denver, Colorado. Apparently there are elephants wandering about in the roads too. Sounds awesome.'

'It does,' I agree. Though personally I have no interest in anything except for finding my father.

Ever since his marriage to Reece, Luke has started to look more careworn, and his body language, normally liquid and sprawling, is more tense. On the outside, he keeps joking and laughing the same as ever. But I reckon he's suffered a fair number of nights where he's lain awake and wondered what the fuck he's doing with his life, where he can't quite believe the tangle he's got himself into. He'll blame Fate, of course, because Luke could never see that the situation he's created might be his responsibility.

'In some parts of India they believe in polygamy,' Luke reads on. I smile and his eyes linger on mine, then fall to my lips. I look away sharply. Then I feel awkward.

'Thanks for lending me the money for my ticket,' I say softly. 'It really means so much to me. If I'd had to work for a month or two – well, I reckon my dad would have moved on and it would have been too late. If I do meet him, it will be down to you.'

'It's not a loan, it's a gift,' Luke says. 'Really, hon, I don't care about money. It's just a capitalist burden. Whenever I have it, I like to give it away.'

'I will pay you back as soon as I can,' I insist.

'Sure. You owe me,' he says teasingly, stroking a strand of hair away from my face and tucking it behind my ear.

I quickly reach for the newspaper inside the netted holdall in front of me. I find it disconcerting that Luke is flirting with me just as much as he did before he'd even ever met Reece. I keep trying to reassure myself that it's just his vivacious manner, that Luke isn't just about the worst womaniser I've ever met.

'Hey,' Luke glances over. 'That's you, isn't it?'

'What!' I peer hard at the newspaper. It's an article about Herbie French. The kind that makes me seize up with indignation. When Herbie first passed away, all of the articles were full of respect and awe; they spoke of him like a literary god. Then his ex-wife came along and started giving interviews about how cruel Herbie was, how he was a wife-beater, how he falsely accused her of infidelity and threw her out of his house without a penny. I have no doubt she's making it all up for attention. Most columnists agree but of course the more sensationalist papers have picked up the story and run with it.

'Julia, you're famous,' Luke repeats, jabbing the page with his finger.

Oh shit. Luke is right. There's a picture of me in the bottom corner of the article. It's a really lousy one; my hair is badly cut and I've got my classic I-hate-having-my-photo-taken look on my face. How the hell did they get hold of it?

'Herbie's ex-wife claims that Julia Rothwell, a random British fan who was invited to visit Herbie French after she wrote him an erotic letter, is vying for her share of the Will,' Luke murmurs, reading from the article.

'*What!* This is just outrageous,' I gasp in horror. Then my eyes bulge as I read on: '*Reece Wentworth-Jones, a close friend of Ms Rothwell, said, "Julia has had a life-long crush on Herbie but I'm pretty sure she's not contesting his Will – though I know she's broke right now so any money would come in handy."* Oh my God.'

'Yeah, they called Reece up when we were in New York,' Luke says casually. 'I told her not to say anything, but then she started to babble. And then she asked them not to print it.' He shakes his head, rolling his eyes.

I turn to Reece, ready to thump her awake – and then my eyes lock with those of the air stewardess as she sashays down the aisle. She gives me a look as if to say,

'If you dare cause any more trouble, you'll be out of this plane in parachutes within the next minute,' and I sit back, silently fuming. Reece has now officially gone from being the best friend I ever had to the wrost.

Chennai Airport is a crazy place. It's so jam-packed that when we get a trolley our luggage keeps getting knocked off by crowds or jolting off when we trundle over potholes. Then we spot a driver holding up a sign with scrawled writing: *Luke Julia Reek*, which makes us all chuckle and Reece the object of some teasing.

We drive out into a rural landscape. It's night now and I can see the silhouettes of palm trees rearing against the murky clouds, the moonlight glittering on the roofs of temples. Tamil Nadu is largely Hindu and it's known as 'The Land of the Temples' because they exist in such abundance.

Luke, who's sitting in the front, soon charms the driver with his sweet playful manner. He tells him that Vegas was marginally hotter than India is, but it's a tough contest. Out of the window, we see makeshift tents erected on the sides of the road. Reece makes a remark that it's like Glastonbury. I can't tell if she's joking or just suffering culture shock. I'm still smarting over that article, but I can't hold on to my irritation because the thought keeps leaping up: *I am now in the same country as my father*.

The Tamil Children's Home is a yellow building fringed by coconut trees. It takes in orphans and children whose parents are simply too poor to feed them or send them to school. When we arrive, the staff welcome us by placing garlands of yellow flowers around our necks. One woman, Misha, seems to be in charge of looking after us; she has curly dark hair and big, lustrous eyes. The people here are all incredibly friendly, whispering that the children are sleeping at the moment but we'll be introduced in the morning. I smile at them and say I can't wait. But then a sense of misery, blurred with the heaviness of jetlag, comes over me. Suddenly I'm conscious that I'm *here*. My search for my father has passed from fantasy to reality. There's nothing more that I want to do than whip out a photo and ask if they know him. But I can't – at least, not yet. In theory I've come here to look after children; they're putting me up for that sole reason. My father will have to wait a day or so. I need to earn their trust, get their help. But every second of delay pains me.

My bedroom is comfy but as I lie down I feel overwhelmed by my task and I shed a few tears of exhaustion. I find myself whispering a prayer to the kindly Hindu gods of India. *Please can you help me to find him? Please help me, please ...*

3

I feel as though I want to throttle Reece. The staff kindly let us have a lie-in and a few hours to settle in. Now it's 4.30 p.m. and we're due to meet the children. We're going to be broken into our duties gently by assisting with afternoon playtime. Luke's already gone out to meet them, but I'm feeling full of trepidation. I've been so engrossed in my quest for Dad that I've neglected to face the fact that I'm really not that great with children. What if they're all horrible brats? What if they ignore all my orders and get out of control? What if they hate me?

And Reece isn't helping matters. She's sitting in her room *putting on her bloody make-up*. As if anyone here gives a sod if her mascara looks good.

'Reece, *come on*!' I say. 'They're waiting for us.' I'm actually still pissed off with her from last night about the Herbie newspaper quote and now the layers of resentment are starting to build.

*   *   *

When we finally meet the children, however, my resentment is quickly forgotten. We're taken into a courtyard where about fifty brown faces gape at us. Misha warned us that some of the kids have never seen a white face before. A few of the little ones even burst into tears but most marvel at us. One minute I feel like an alien, the next a celebrity. Several of the kids come up and give me a hug, then ask, with wide-eyed awe, if they can have my autograph.

The rest of the day is completely manic. Children keep running up and telling me their names but soon I lose track of Krishna and Laksha and Absha and Kabi and Ganesh and Rajesh. I was half-expecting that the children here would be like victims in a misery memoir or the Eastern equivalent of Asbo kids. But these children are bright, vibrant, sparkling, sweet – and also exhausting!

'I'm Amirah,' one little girl with curly dark locks and very big eyes addresses me. She has a smile that wins my heart; dimples glint in her cheeks. 'Hello. You hello. I hello. Hello.'

Funnily enough, the only Tamil word I know is *Vanakkam*, which means 'Welcome'. So our language skills are evenly matched.

I fall instantly in love with Amirah, who has such a charming way about her. We all play a raucous game of tag, which the children adore. Then before dinner, it's time for worship of the *devas*, for chanting and prayers.

Finally we have a moment to gasp for breath. Luke and

Reece look somewhat shell-shocked, but in a good way. For the first time in weeks they've had to stop being selfish. In forgetting themselves, they look a good deal happier.

Dinner is rice with a simple, spicy vegetable curry. We help the children with some studying and their English. Then we help to put them to bed. They sleep on mats and it's so hot that few bother with blankets. Before closing her eyes, Amirah shoots me a secret smile and I can't help but smile back fondly.

We go to bed at eleven, exhausted, only to be up again at 6 a.m. Since I've been on my *Ten Things* trip, I've enjoyed the luxury of lie-ins to compensate for my years of early starts on screeching tubes. But this morning I feel exhilarated, rising early with the dawn misting scarlet on the horizon. It's bath-time.

This consists of three troughs in the courtyard. The water is splashed over the kids via buckets. By the end of the session, the children are clean and happy and we're all soaked through.

'Man,' Luke says, tugging at his damp T-shirt, laughing uproariously, 'this is such a hoot.'

Reece giggles in agreement.

As we walk the children to school, we pass by lush green fields, coconut trees and small huts with crouching roofs. Water buffalos drag ploughs through the fields. Women pass by in saris as bright as Sicilian corals, carrying baskets on their heads. Despite feeling disorientated by my exotic surroundings, I also feel at home. It must be to do with the fact that I'm doing something useful. The indolence and extravagance of Vegas didn't really suit my Protestant work ethic, nor did it meet my desire for fresh challenges. Here it seems that every second is spoken for, and every second is joyfully productive. The only downside is that it's hard to find time to even think about finding Dad. I carry my wish inside my heart and it whispers to me all through breakfast and teaching English and lunch and playtime and prayers and dinner and study – *find him, find him, hurry and find him*.

For a few days, I don't mention his name. I know now that the best time to ask is in the afternoons, after lunch, when the children are at school and playtime hasn't yet begun. It's the main time for us to rest and have a chance to share adult conversations with Misha and Ravi over coffee or *chai*. I plan to do it on Thursday afternoon, but the opportunity slips by. Even Luke asks me why I haven't made any enquiries yet and I make an excuse, realising how nervous I am.

The next day, afternoon comes round and we all sit at a table, under cover from the glare of the sun, sipping cups of Tamil's famous filter coffee. We're all chatting when Misha mentions a local school where she used to work. I immediately prick up my ears; Luke notices.

'Julia's dad was helping out at a local school here,' he interjects. 'She's hoping to track him down.'

'Luke,' I say in a terse voice, giving him a sharp kick

under the table. A moment later, however, I feel grateful to him, for Misha and Ravi look interested.

'What's his name?' Misha asks.

'Greg Hanson,' I say. They both look blank. 'What about the name John Ruston – does that mean anything to you?'

Now, *his* name makes an impact. Misha looks startled and Ravi's normally sweet expression becomes an angry frown. As they confer in tense voices, every muscle in my body becomes a taut wire.

'What is it? What's wrong? Please, you have to tell me.'

They glance at me, then carry on conferring. I quickly pull the photo of Dad out of my bag. It shakes violently as I hold it out before them. Misha takes it, then passes it to Ravi, whose frown grows deeper as he fingers his moustache. Misha gives it back to me quickly with an unconvincing Indian head waggle.

'I have never seen him before in my life – never ever.'

Too many negatives make a positive.

'Come on, please,' I beg in a desperate tone. 'I don't mind if it's bad news. Just tell me anything you know.'

Ravi exhales. 'John Ruston is a very bad man – and your father is his acquaintance. They are both wanted by the police here.'

'Really?' Oh God. I can hear my mum's voice echoing warnings. She told me he was a bad man and did I listen? 'What did they do?'

'This John Ruston,' says Misha, 'he stole some goods. And your father – well, he was with him.'

'So . . . right.' I flick a glance at Luke. He looks alarmed. I turn away from him. 'I'd still like to see my father even if he's not such a great guy. It's really important. Can you tell me where he is?'

Misha and Ravi look vague. Luke gently advises that I should just leave this alone. As if my heart gives me any choice in the matter.

'The school,' I persist. 'Can you give me the name of the school?'

'He worked at the Ganesh Children's Home,' Ravi says at last. 'But I do not know where he is now.'

'Thank you,' I say. I have the place. I can go there tomorrow! Then I become conscious of the heavy silence. Misha and Ravi are looking at me with faint unease; I become conscious that my father's reputation has now tainted me in some way, that they feel just a little suspicious of who I might be and what I'm doing here. 'I – I haven't seen my dad since I was this high,' I explain quickly. 'I just want to see him again – just once. And thank you so much for giving this information to me. Good night.'

As I get up to go, I feel dizzy and Luke steadies me. It's such a sweet, affectionate gesture that I lean against him gratefully. Then Reece comes dancing up.

'Hey you, hands off my husband!' she says; her light-hearted tone has an edge to it. 'What's up?'

I give Luke a look so he won't say anything to her. But Luke, being Luke, can't contain himself and he immediately starts to tell her. I walk away quickly, not wanting their verdict, their judgement.

So. That's it then. As I fled back to my room, Amirah, who ought to have been in bed, ran up for a hug. I pushed her away, unable to accept human warmth or give any back. Hearing my father being condemned made me condemned.

Now I'm in my room and I've shed some tears. I feel a strong sense of shame. I was so silly to believe in a fantasy fairytale in which my father wore a villain's cloak that hid a hero underneath. I wish I could just get on the first plane out of here and fly over to NY to see Mum. I'd give her a hug and say, 'You were right.' And we'd heal together and make a pledge never to have anything to do with him again. I toss and turn through the night as the darkness deepens and then eases.

As I begin to calm down, I also begin to wonder. I accept that my father is a bad man, but I'm still his daughter. Before I came, I had fantasies that we'd develop a wonderful relationship – he'd travel the world in his unfettered way and send me postcards, and every so often I'd get a crazy call from Morocco or Bali and we'd confide in each other. Now I realise it's unlikely that we'll be able to develop a long-term relationship, unless I fancy touring the various prisons of the world and getting to know how different cultures treat their criminals. But if I could just meet him *once*, just see him in the flesh, just look into his eyes – it would create such a sense of peace inside me. Then I could go away and get on with my life.

My reason whispers that this might be a bad idea. So does Luke.

The next morning, during breakfast, we have a brief chat. I tell him that I still intend to look for my dad.

'What?' Luke asks. 'Are you kidding me?'

'He might be bad,' I snap. 'But nobody is *all* bad.'

Just then, Amirah comes running up. Seeing me, she stops short and eyes me warily. I spread open my arms and she breaks into a smile of relief and runs into them. I cradle my cheek against the top of her head, giving Luke a pained look.

'He is my father,' I say emphatically.

'I'd have gladly never met my dad.'

I want to tell Luke that he doesn't mean that. I want to tell him that a vacuum is far worse than a troubled relationship. I want to tell him that he ought to treasure his relationship with his dad and try to make amends. But I have a feeling he wouldn't listen to me.

Luke gives me a playful nip on the waist and I shrug away from him, laughing. But as the afternoon goes on in a haze of heat and joyous, screaming children, my emotions gnaw away at me. I'm not sure if I can face seeing my father and being utterly disappointed by him. Perhaps it would be best to pack away my curiosity and accept that I'm lucky enough to have a loving mother and Fate gave me no more than that. Perhaps it would be best to protect my heart.

4

This morning I got an email from Ciaran telling me he'd resigned from his job. He said it wasn't worth waiting for the bonus – he's just glad to be free. He asked me whether I'd had any luck finding my dad.

The truth is, I'm in a kind of limbo. I did go out for a walk yesterday, looking for the school Dad had taught at. I was determined to go on my own so that nobody could talk me out of it or tell me not to be stupid. But I only ended up getting lost, my eyes streaming, my face drenched in sweat from the midday sun. On the way back, I kicked up the red earth with a feeling of relief, reminding myself that it would be a mistake to meet him. But once I returned, I felt sad and wished . . . in truth, I'm not sure what I wished for.

And then Ciaran's email came and it stirred something in me. Even though I'm not remotely qualified to be a banking support lawyer, the thought flashed across my mind: Ooh, I wish I could apply for his job. I feel hungry to be back in an office with a laptop and my mug of coffee and the buzz of a deadline and a male chauvinist to prove wrong with my star results. Now that I don't think I'm going to see my dad, I feel rootless. Which is just how I felt when I first lost my job – as though I was a piece of driftwood being tossed about by waves and the whim of the winds. A job would anchor me.

And then Amirah will come running up and sing to me, or Misha will pass me a cup of *chai* with her delightful smile, or the children will give me a hug and say they want me to stick around forever. And I'll think, I should stay. Just a little longer. For them.

Reece is less keen.

I'm standing outside the children's home, waiting for her and Luke to show up. We've got a day off and we've agreed to go to Mamallapuram, which is famous for its gorgeous beach and Pallava rock-cut architecture and caves. The taxi we've booked turns up early and the driver unwinds his window, smiling. He's chewing paan and it flashes red on his tongue. He spits on the dusty road, gives me a lazy smile, then says, 'So you pay fifty dollars extra waiting time, OK?'

I smile weakly. I understand why Indians want to haggle all the time when dollars are like gold to them and $800 is the equivalent of a year's salary – but Luke is the one who's paying. For the first few days here, he and Reece got spun into a whirlwind of philanthropic ecstasy. But then the novelty seemed to wear off. Let's face it, it is hard work, being here. Yesterday Reece claimed she had flu, but I smelled the distinct scent of *ganja* wafting from her room and then she went off for hours and came back with her hands beautifully decorated with henna from a beauty salon. Misha was very charming but I felt embarrassed, knowing that we're getting free board and lodging here in exchange for helping out, not for swanning around as we feel like it. Then Misha generously suggested we all have a day off, perhaps hoping we might come back to our work with renewed vigour.

Luke and Reece emerge wearing matching Armani sunglasses, sunhats and pouts so expressive they belong on a catwalk. I repress a sigh, knowing they've been arguing again. They slump in the back of the taxi. As we lurch through the crazy roads, veering wildly behind cows and other cars who ignore lights, road signs and any sense of etiquette, Reece sighs and says, 'I *have* to get out of here. I'm sick of this sun. Do you know what I feel like right now? A Starbucks ice-cool latte. I want British clouds and *Hollyoaks* and a McDonald's double cheeseburger with fries and a Toffee Swirl Oreo McFlurry.'

'Oh – so we flew thousands of miles to visit a new continent and get a good old quarter-pounder,' Luke says sarcastically.

'I'm not staying here. You can take the piss but it won't make change my mind. I want to go and audition for a Bollywood movie. I've heard they're shooting in Varanasi.'

What! I open my mouth, then decide it's best not to join in with the bickering. Then we pass an elderly woman, begging by the side of the road, her toothless mouth gaping desperately, one of her eyes milky with blindness. She certainly puts my problems into perspective, and I feel ashamed, knowing that actually I have everything: a flat, an iPod, food, a comfortable bed to sleep in.

But if they do go, I'll probably go with them, which means I definitely won't get to see Dad. I know I've pretty much given up on him but I still feel a pang, knowing I might never meet him.

When we get to the beach, the driver asks for a truly stupendous fee. When Luke passes it over, the man looks excited, thinking he's conned us. But I know Luke is just following his generous anti-capitalist agenda and I feel an affectionate warmth for him.

The beach is crowded and beautiful. The sand is powdery and cows wander amongst backpackers. There are stalls selling statues of Lord Ganesh and Natarava, and deer elephants carved in soapstone and granite and marble. People see our white faces and smile; one man comes up and presses some bananas into our hands, gabbling Tamil, then retreats, smiling broadly. We call our thanks, enchanted. This is one of the nicest things about India: the perpetual warmth of strangers.

'I'm just going to hang out on the beach,' Reece says, plopping her bananas down beside her. 'You guys can go off and be spiritual. Whatever.'

Luke puts his arm tight around me.

'Fine,' he says. 'I'll go with my other wife, then.'

I feel indignant when Reece gives me a hissy look, as though I'm some sort of brazen hussy.

Luke and I pick our way across the crowded beach to the famous shore temple. Immediately, we're accosted by guides, saying, 'We show you everything, for just one hundred rupees, we be your guide for day.' Luke says we're OK but gives one of them 200 rupees anyway, which is a mistake, as it results in a crowd of 'guides' multiplying around us, vehemently offering their services.

Giggling nervously, Luke and I escape into the temple, gazing at the stone carvings of *devas*. I can't help noticing that Luke stands very close to me. Since Vegas I've given up on love; every drop of energy in my heart has been focused on my father. Now I feel an unexpected yearning, a reminder of how it feels, to share a beautiful moment with a man. As though Luke picks up on my thoughts, he turns and looks at me. I quickly suggest we return to the beach.

Then we have trouble finding Reece; the beach is so crowed. I curve my palm over my eyes, scanning the shore when suddenly Luke cries: 'LOOK OUT!'

I turn and see *an elephant heading towards me*. Luke dives on top of me, throwing me out of the way. I feel the sand blow over me, feel his body warm on top of mine. A few Indians start to point and I quickly push him away, knowing that public displays of affection aren't appreciated over here.

'Wow,' Luke says, as the elephant moves at less than one mile an hour. 'I saved your life just in the nick of time.'

I think I probably had time to crawl out of its path but I smile at him anyway. The elephant has a decorated shawl on its back; its keeper is tugging him along, smiling and nodding at people. It's a deliciously surreal sight, one that I know I will treasure.

Reece behaves as though she can't find anything to treasure. When we find her, she declares that she's bored stiff. Travel isn't about the places you see, I realise, but your openness to letting a new culture seep into you, enjoying its flavour as it tingles in your bloodstream. And then I feel sad, because a part of me is in mourning for the friendship we once had, secretly hoping we'll go back to the intimacy of our old girly ways.

Reece is silent on the journey home and I feel Luke's thigh firm against mine.

Back at the children's home, Reece goes straight to their room. Luke follows me down the corridor. Outside my room, I turn and say goodbye to him but he doesn't reply. He just grins down at me. Then he spreads his palms against the wall, hemming me in between his bare arms.

'Don't you think you owe me something for saving you from being nearly trampled to death by an elephant?' he asks. His voice is playful, conscious of how outrageous his bargaining is, but there's a predatory glitter in his eyes.

He leans down—

'*Luke!*'

His breath hovers against my lips; I feel the hair on my skin prickle upright. He's behaving so badly, so dangerously, the outrageousness of it is a turn-on.

He holds his lips a millimetre from mine. I feel as though he's a snake offering me an apple, waiting to see if I'll take a bite. I move, meaning to push him away, but our lips brush and then we're lost. My arms curl around him. He pushes me hard against the wall. His hand splays against my thigh, pulling it up against his jeans. Our kisses become clumsy and ragged with desire . . .

And then suddenly he pulls back.

I realise that if he followed me into my room right now, I wouldn't be able to resist him. The thought makes me feel weak and terrible and excited all at once.

'We shouldn't be doing this,' he says, as though there would be nothing more delicious in the world than to do this.

Then I see the doubt in his eyes and I feel thrown. I wasn't expecting a sudden fit of morality from *his* side. He backs away and I blink, desperate to hold the mood.

'I can't come into your room,' Luke says. And now he sounds as though he means it.

I stare at him. The way he's talking, it's as though *I* came on to *him*.

'I won't tell Reece you kissed me if you don't,' he concludes.

It takes me a few seconds to translate the accusation in his voice.

'Wait – I didn't! *You* kissed *me*,' I object.

'Well, you didn't push me away,' Luke says in return. 'Anyhow, it's really trivial to argue about who started it. It's just not fair on Reece.'

He turns and walks away down the corridor. I stare at his back, throwing silent daggers of fury at him. He's playing a game, I tell myself. Then I wonder if the real truth is just that Luke himself doesn't even know what the game is or what the rules are. As I enter my room, I resavour the shivery pleasure of our kiss and kick the bed crossly. What did he say to Jodie when he found out she was pregnant? '*Well, Jodie, you were the one who spread your legs and forced me to put my sperm into you!*' Bastard, bastard.

The stupid thing about this is that I don't even really like Luke any more. Well – for about five minutes I was wowed, but this whole incident has reminded me of why I went off him. And men in general.

* * *

From   Julia.rothwell15@hotmail.co.uk
To   ciaran.ohare111@yahoo.com
Sent   12.09.09

Dear Ciaran,

I know I only emailed you this morning but in the space of just a few hours everything has gone completely pear-shaped. I don't think I'm going to get to see my father after all. It's all such a mess and I hardly know where to begin.

Luke kissed me.

I don't want to get back together with him. I don't know why I let it happen. I just got sucked in by his charm and I forgot what he's really like underneath. I'm trying very hard not to get mad at him now. I know Luke acts in a very spontaneous way without meaning any harm and he's very confused. But he and Reece are at crisis point – that must be why he kissed me. I think that subconsciously he was looking to lay blame elsewhere and now I've become the perfect scapegoat.

Anyway, they both got completely mad at me. They said I was ungrateful for borrowing Luke's money. Then they went to their room and had such a bad screaming match that the children here started crying and the staff had to ask them to keep it down. Then they just packed up their stuff and took off. Literally – I went down to the local market to buy some batteries for my iPod and a few sticks of incense – and when I came back, their rooms were empty. Reece didn't even say goodbye. Luke just left a note saying that he was sorry but he couldn't keep on supporting me or it would upset Reece. He said they didn't feel that being at the orphanage was helping their marriage (as if any place could possibly help their marriage!) and that they'd gone to Varanasi to visit the temples there.

The trouble is, they've left me with absolutely no money. I left New York with some debts and a bit of my overdraft (Vegas hangover) and now I literally have nothing. I just went out on to the streets and saw a load of beggars and I didn't give them a thing; an Indian guy was watching me and I'm sure he thought I was some rich mean Westerner. But if I ever want to get home I'll have to join them.

You see, it didn't really work out with going to see my dad. It's a bit of a long story. I love working with the children but I also feel my time here should come to an end. Of course, I can survive for now but I also feel a bit panicked as I don't have a penny to get a plane ticket out.

Well, that's my news. Tell me all of yours.
Julia x

From   ciaran.ohare111@yahoo.com
To   Julia.rothwell@hotmail.co.uk
Sent   24.09.09

Dear Julia,
I've applied for a fast-track visa. I sent my passport to Birmingham today and it will be ready tomorrow – I'm going to drive up to collect it. Then I'll catch a plane from Birmingham to Chennai, getting in at 3.00 p.m. on 27th September.

Don't worry about anything – I'll sort it all. I've got my redundancy money. We'll find your dad and then I'll bring you home.

See you soon,
Ciaran x

5

I'm standing in the Anna Terminal, Chennai Airport, along with about three hundred Indians who are all holding up signs. All I'm holding is a present for Ciaran, which elicits a few glances and smiles. It's 3 a.m. and I still can't quite believe that dear Ciaran has just hopped on to a plane and spent twelve hours travelling over to help me out. He truly is my hero, my lifesaver, my guardian angel. I thought he'd be mad at me for kissing Luke – but in his email he didn't even mention it. Maybe it is best to pretend it never happened.

The board says his flight has been delayed – but only by twenty minutes. And then there's a surge of people who come through Departures and I spot the curve of his dark head and my heart leaps.

He's looking absolutely knackered and his eyes have that dazed what-time-zone-am-I-in? haze to them. I have to call his name out a few times; he actually walks past me, then wheels back.

'Julia!' His face lights up.

I say a breathless, 'Hi,' then throw my welcoming present – a garland of flowers – over his neck. He touches them in surprise, then grins and pulls me into a tight hug that crushes them.

I have so much to ask but we get caught up in the trauma of his case going missing and then turning up on another carousel before we finally make it to the taxi. He slumps into the back, then turns and grins at me before being overwhelmed by yawns. I tell him to sleep and he says there's no need but a minute later his head is lolling against the seat in sheer exhaustion. I was dying to tell him everything but now I feel calm. Since I've been in India I've felt adrift, floating about in a sea of panic. Now I feel anchored with a sense of peace.

The feeling doesn't last.

I wake up the next morning and my euphoria fades. I sheepishly remind myself that although it's very wonderful of Ciaran to come flying all the way over here to help me, my cause is no longer a certain one. I'm not even sure if I want to meet my father now. I'm scared that Ciaran might be mad at me. Then I try to reassure myself he'll understand. And then we'll fly back home to England, sweet London town, and I can get back to normal life.

Ciaran booked into a hotel for a night as I felt the

lovely people at the Home had already suffered enough of a merry-go-round of people coming and going.

After I've walked the children to school, I head straight over to his hotel for breakfast. Ciaran makes me smile because he has no interest in Tamil's filter coffee, no matter how good its reputation; he has brought along his treasured box of Earl Grey. I also have to smile when I see the simply huge straw hat he's brought along to protect his head from the sun. Noticing my glance, he grins and confesses he picked it up at the airport at the last minute.

'So do you know where your dad is?' Ciaran asks, tucking into a mango.

'Kind of. Well, I have a lead but I'm not really sure if he's there,' I say, coughing uneasily.

'Right. Then let's follow it up.'

'I'm really busy with the children today.'

'They'll give you one afternoon off, surely?' Ciaran frowns at me and I realise I can't hide behind cardboard cut-out excuses. He is much too sharp for that and he won't accept any bullshit. So I tell him. I confess that I've been told my father's a bad man. I say I'm not sure if meeting him will do me more harm than good.

'But if you go home now, you'll regret it for the rest of your life,' Ciaran keeps saying. 'You should just try, just meet him once.'

I don't know if it's the heat or the jetlag or an inevitable sense of anti-climax, but I can sense that Ciaran is getting cross. He's got all togged up in his role of knight in shining armour and now I'm like some petulant princess who declares she doesn't need saving.

'I'm just not sure,' I say, fingering some stray jaggary crystals on the table.

'You have to see him!' Ciaran declares emphatically. 'You have to. We've come all this way out here. I'll support you, you can take as long as you like.'

'Oh, for God's sake!' I cry. 'First Luke pays for me and tries to control me – and now you. Just because you're paying it doesn't mean to say that you own me or you can tell me what to do.'

'Julia.' Ciaran looks aghast. He lays his palms out flat on the table. 'I didn't mean it like that at all. This is my gift to you. This is all for free.'

'I'm sorry,' I reply sheepishly. 'I just feel so embarrassed about being so broke – after all those years when I was loaded. And I'm sorry because I do know you didn't mean it like that. You couldn't be more different from Luke.'

Ciaran smiles, but I detect his guard has gone up in some way.

'Thank you so much for coming out here,' I say. 'Really.'

'Look,' he says. 'Why don't we just go to the school this afternoon when you have your break from the kids and see if he's there? You don't even know for certain if he will be. But it's up to you, of course.'

When we get to the school later that day, I feel strangely relieved when the lady tells us he's not there. The school is very similar to the orphanage I'm working at: a yellow building surrounded by palms. When we first arrived, the guy who greeted us couldn't speak English, and led us to a Mrs Kutty. She's wearing a beautiful pink and turquoise sari. Her hair is grey and curly and a pair of gold-rimmed glasses sit on her wrinkled nose.

'But tomorrow he will be back,' she says, flashing a smile of broken teeth.

My stomach explodes into butterflies.

'And is he … do you like him?' I ask in a shrill voice.

'Like?' She laughs and does an Indian head waggle. 'Oh yes. Very good man. He helps us. We love. The children love.'

Seeing the astonishment on my face, she guides me over to a classroom. On the walls are pictures the children have drawn. Then I see that half a dozen in the left-hand corner are of a particular man with grey hair in a pony-tail and blue eyes. In all of the pictures he is smiling. He is special: yellow suns smile on him, birds circle him, his stick hands hang on to smaller ones. I stare over at Ciaran and he gently places a hand on my spine, smiling at me.

'I just don't understand why Misha and Ravi would say such bad things about him,' I cry as we head back home. 'It was so unfair of them.'

I turn to Ciaran and as I do so, the brims of our sunhats collide and we burst into laughter.

'Calm down,' Ciaran says, touching my sunburned arm.

'Maybe he did offend them, but everyone has different sides to their character – so who knows? Let's just meet him and see how it goes. And let's stop here for some coconut juice,' he adds, pointing to a roadside café. 'I am absolutely boiling.'

We gulp the juice down in thirsty relief. I can't help feeling we've swapped roles: now Ciaran is the one who is calmly cautious and I'm the one brimming with insane excitement.

I don't calm down all day. I get so hyper playing with the children in the afternoon that for the first time ever, I'm the one who tires them out, and they go to prayers in a very quiet state. I flick a glance at Misha – I still feel fiery about her badmouthing my dad but I also feel it's best not to confront her; it wouldn't be fair on the children and I can't really draw any conclusions until I've met him.

I can hardly eat a grain of rice at dinner and I find myself rushing the kids through their homework so I can head over to see Ciaran. We sit in his room, under the whir of the air-conditioning, sipping more coconut juice which the concierge brought up, talking and talking. He lights up some incense we bought in the market, the sweet smell of sandalwood snaking in coils through the air. I'm feeling so pent-up about meeting my dad, I almost feel relieved when he changes the subject back to Luke and Reece; we have a giggle over what they must be up to.

'So, are you feeling OK about Reece now?' I ask him.

'Oh God, yes. I don't waste a second of my time thinking about her,' Ciaran says, and his tone is cool, devoid of anger. He gives me a very direct stare. 'I'm just sorry that I didn't dump her earlier, really – that I let the whole stupid thing drag on for as long as eighteen months. I'm sorry I even let her come on to me in the first place.'

'Oh, really?' I ask, feeling a flicker of surprise.

There's a pause. My surprise rapidly evolves into agitation. When Reece and Ciaran got together, I asked Reece to share all the girly details with me. I remember she was all bouncy and sunny and kept saying every other minute, 'You don't mind, do you, Julia? You don't mind?' and the more she asked, the more I had to say, 'No,' even though my heart was breaking. Each aspect of the anecdote she told me seemed like an instrument of torture, exquisitely shaped to precisely pierce my heart. Based on Reece's version of events, I composed a film in my head that I watched over and over: Reece sitting on the sofa, Ciaran putting a hand on her knee, Reece giggling shyly and trying to remove it, Ciaran grabbing her and kissing her . . .

'I thought you made the first move on Reece,' I say at last.

'Hmm?' Ciaran looks distracted, as though his mind is elsewhere. 'Oh God, no. I'm not that superficial, Julia, or some kind of cad like Luke. I mean, you and I had only just broken up and I was trying to get you back.' He smiles at me, as though it's such an absurd memory he can hardly believe it happened and I smile quickly too, removing hairs from my mouth as the breeze blows them in.

'No,' he carries on, 'it was quite funny, really. I was sitting in the lounge waiting for you, and she came in wearing her lingerie. I asked why she had her underwear on and she said it was her nightie – but I swear I'd never seen anything that covered so little. I could see everything and it was all so obvious I just sat there cringing. I didn't respond to her innuendos – her remark about her accidentally buying her nightie in a size too small and how utterly *embarrassed* she was that it revealed so much. So in the end she just took off her nightie and leaped on me. And yeah – I have to admit I did get turned on at that point. She made me feel better.' Ciaran takes a sip of his coconut juice.

I sit in silence, feeling quite shocked. Is Ciaran so bitter that he's rewriting history? But he seems genuinely matter-of-fact, even breezy.

'For the first few months,' he goes on, 'I was up front with Reece. I told her that I still had feelings for you and I wasn't committed to her, although, of course, I liked her. I told her it was a rebound fling. But she kept telling me I was being an idiot, thinking I might get back together with you. She said you had no interest in me and that it was never going to happen. She kind of drove it home.' He turns to me. 'I'm only telling you this because – well, because I know how it feels to be hanging on to your love for someone when it's over, so I know how bad you must be feeling about Luke.'

'Uh, yeah.' I'm still some way behind him in the conversation. Shit. I started to fall for Ciaran about three months after he and Reece were together. I yearned for him so badly I felt as if my heart was physically going to implode. *And I could have had him.* I could have saved myself from months of devastation. For a moment, my unnecessary suffering shocks me. But there's no way I would have tried to steal Ciaran back off Reece once she had him. No, I was doomed to suffer in silence. But God, this does shed a new light on things . . .

'You don't have to talk about Luke, if it's too painful,' Ciaran says.

'Uh.' I shrug. 'I'm fine.' Ciaran looks slightly surprised and I suddenly worry that I must come across as completely superficial. 'Well, OK, I'm devastated, of course, but . . .'

'Well.' Ciaran suddenly seems to draw away, crossing his arms in front of his chest. 'Just take your time. Don't get into any rebound flings.'

'No,' I say, feeling hurt. 'I wasn't planning to bother with romance at all, for the time being. I'm just here to see my dad.'

'And then what?' Ciaran asks. 'What's left on your list of *Ten Things*?'

'Oh, I've run out of money,' I laugh, shrugging. 'But it's fine. Just seeing Dad will be enough.'

'Out of curiosity – what else was on the list?' Ciaran persists.

'Well, number nine was going to be swimming with

dolphins,' I say. Then, seeing the look on his face: 'Yes, I know it's a cliché but I've read reports about the amazing experiences people have – and I just think it could be quite beautiful, quite cleansing.'

'Hey, I'm not laughing,' Ciaran protests, even though he is. I nudge him and he laughs some more. 'OK, OK. But what about number ten?'

I flush violently, remembering my original number ten: *Tell Ciaran O'Hare that I love him*. But I think we're past that now. Ciaran has been the best friend in the world to me and there's no way I'm going to blow it. The things he's been saying seem to me to be his way of showing that he's put his feelings, and our past, behind him. And I think he's right. Romance has only ever brought me misery on this trip. I don't even value sexual love that highly any more, and I certainly don't believe in the concept of The One. Friendships, however, are something I still have faith in. Having a laugh with someone; looking out for them; Reece may have gone but my new friendships with Ciaran and Lucy are ones to utterly treasure.

'Come on,' he prompts. 'Tell me.'

'Um – it was bungee-jumping,' I improvise quickly.

'Really?' Ciaran asks in amazement. 'But I thought you were scared of heights!'

'Er, I was,' I agree. 'But I . . . that's exactly why I felt it would be a good idea to confront my fear and do it anyway.' I yawn and check my watch, rather keen to change the subject.

'Hey, you should get some sleep,' Ciaran says. 'It's a big day tomorrow.'

Now I wish I hadn't looked at my watch. I'd be happy to spend the whole night just chatting with Ciaran. But I stand up and we pause by the door as though not sure how to say good night, then settle on a hug. The warmth of his skin clings to me as I walk down to the orphanage, making me smile as I slip into bed.

Then I stare at the ceiling. Right now, my dad will have returned to his school and have been told that his daughter arrived today, looking for him. And that she will be back tomorrow. How does that make him feel?

6

'Yes, he is here today,' Mrs Kutty says.

I can hardly believe it's so simple. All the way to the school, I was convinced that at the last minute something was going to go wrong and Fate was going to snatch my dad away from me again. That we'd arrive and Mrs Kutty would say he left last night, or had been arrested, or had simply heard I'd turned up and run away to avoid me.

'He waits for you.' Mrs Kutty points to a courtyard.

I turn to look at Ciaran. I'm so nervous that I swear my anxiety has seeped into him, for he gives me a thrilled but jittery smile. As I'm about to go, he takes my hand and squeezes it hard.

'Go easy,' he says.

I'm not even sure what he means by that and I'm too overcome to consider it. I walk down the corridor, hearing the sounds of distant children screaming and playing. And then I walk out into the sun-beaten courtyard and see my father sitting on a step, smoking a cigarette.

He looks up at me, nods and stands up. I go over to his side. I'm shaking violently from head to foot.

'I'm Julia,' I say.

'I'm Greg.'

I feel very strange. He looks so different from his photo that you'd barely know he was the same man. He's more muscular and his dark hair has become grey and is tied back in a ponytail. In the photograph, he possessed the softness of youth, an air of mischievous fun. Now there's something hardened about him, in the thin line of his lips, in his menacing posture. Then I look into his eyes and I see they're just the same: a dancing blue, fanned by laughter lines.

I thought there'd be an instant connection between us. I thought we'd hug and stare at each other in ecstatic wonder. But he's maintaining a distance; there's a wariness in his eyes. A sense of anguish is starting to grow inside my stomach like an ugly weed. I remember my mother's words of warning and wonder if I've made a terrible mistake.

'Well, it's good to see you,' I say, working hard to keep my voice steady.

'Hey.' He shoves his hands in his pockets. 'I don't have long.' Then, seeing my face, he says: 'Sorry.'

We sit down on the step, a careful space between us so that there's no danger of touching. Oh God. This is horrific. I thought that with two and a half decades to catch up on, there would barely be time to cover everything. Instead, the air becomes sticky with silence. I ferociously try to think up an icebreaker, but my shocked mind is a blank.

'So,' he says at last, his voice thick with awkwardness. 'What have you been doing with your life?'

'I went to uni. I got a First.' I pause, wanting to sense some paternal pride, but he just nods, staring into the distance, as though he's barely listening. 'I got a very good job in a bank. I got promoted. And then last year, with the recession and everything, I got fired,' I say this bit very hurriedly, 'and then I decided to explore the world and go travelling.'

'I couldn't do nine to five,' my father says. 'So you're your mother's girl.'

I flinch. Doesn't he see that these are just things I've done? There there is so much more to me than just a potted history of my career path? Then he flicks me a quick glance and a jolt of recognition shocks me.

I realise that the reason I have always been drawn to his blue eyes in that photo is because they are exactly the same colour as mine. This is the man without whom I wouldn't be breathing. Without whom I wouldn't have gone to school, kissed a boy, become best friends with Reece, met Luke, loved Ciaran, be sitting here now under this baking sun. The man who has created me in many ways even with his absence, yet who barely seems interested in our first conversation in almost thirty years. I feel hate and love fighting a battle in my heart.

'You really have no interest in me being here, do you?' I burst out, hearing the emotion lacerate my voice. 'You really don't want to know.'

He's supposed to disagree vehemently with me. Instead, he stares at his feet, knobbly creatures encased in straw sandals.

'I called up your mum from time to time because I wanted to know how you were doing. But I felt it was better to do it from a distance.'

'From a distance?' I feel a hot pain behind my eyes, threatening to crack into the humiliation of tears. 'But you're my dad.'

'Sometimes,' he says, his voice soaked with sadness, 'sometimes the longer you put something off, the harder it is to do ...'

But I'm not some cheque you have to pay into the bank or a letter you have to post, I feel like shouting. A silence falls into the cracks between our words. I want to retain my dignity, to just get up and walk away, but part of me desperately wants to feel that he loves me. Just a little.

'I met Herbie French, you know,' I blurt out. 'I'm the first person in twenty years to have met him.'

He pulls a fresh cigarette from his box, clicks his lighter, blows out smoke, then raises an eyebrow.

'Is that right?' he says, with faint amusement in his eyes. 'He was working on a new book called *The Mermaid*

Who Hated Fish,' I carry on in a high voice. 'He told me that he was married and loved his wife but he lost her and so he became a recluse. I don't think he ever forgave her or life for taking her away from him. But even though he was crabby I felt he was . . . a good man.'

My father's eyes start to moon; his mouth opens slightly.

'The *New York Times* even wanted to interview me about it all, but I refused.'

'How the hell did you get to meet him, if he was a recluse?'

'I kept going back and back. I made this kite and I tied a note to it and it flew into his grounds. And in the end . . .' I smile at the memory. 'I broke in.'

Now there's wonder on his face, admiration in his eyes. As if to say, *That's my girl*. But now I feel even more mad at him. Why should I have to prove myself to him? Why can't he just love me because I'm sitting here now, next to him?

'Yeah, I'm not just some nine to five bore,' I say.

He nods, blowing out smoke.

I mean to punch his arm gently, with affection, to make contact. But in my passion I do it hard. Immediately, he spins to his feet, his hand curled up into a fist. I stare at him in shock. I realise he's reacted on autopilot, a response that has been wired into him after years in prison. But this rationale doesn't detract from my pain.

I'm about to get to my feet, when he sits down next to me again and tells me he's sorry. His voice sounds choked. And then suddenly his arms are tight around me. I tense up, shrinking as his body shakes against mine. Then I realise that he's crying. My body becomes liquid and I start to cry too. He clutches me so tightly that I have to wriggle and gasp, 'You're hurting me.'

'Sorry, sorry.'

'No, no – it's just that you're so strong.'

He breaks away and wipes his eyes. When he hugged me, his cigarette went out. Now he quickly relights it and blows out a shuddering stream of smoke.

'When you were a kid, I always used to read you that book,' he says in a shaky voice. 'I loved it so much. And so did you. D'you remember?'

'I . . .' I frown. 'I did love that book. But I thought that— I mean, am I remembering it all wrong? I remember that Mum chucked you out of the house and *then* I found the book. So how could you have read to me?'

'Don't you remember?' His eyes fill up again when I shake my head. 'We made a pact. You knew that your mum was going to throw me out and one day when you were crying and begging for me to stay, we made a pact. I whispered to you to leave your bedroom window a little bit ajar. Those were the days that your mum lived in that crappy little bungalow in Cheam. I still remember the awful suburban feel of it all. Nine to fivers everywhere. And I'd come along and creep in the garden after your mum had put you to bed and I'd read you a chapter in whispers. And then I'd go.'

'Oh my God, I remember,' I cry. 'And I thought it was all a dream.'

'I always felt gutted that I wasn't able to read you the last chapter. But I had to flee the country before we got there.' He sighs ruefully, then shrugs as though to say, *c'est la vie.*

'I still have that very copy,' I say. I turn to face him. 'Why did you do that stuff? Why did you put yourself in prison?'

He stares at me and his blue eyes make me shiver again.

'I've always had a bit of a problem with authority. I had rubbish teachers at school and I had a brain, I can see that now, but nobody to help me develop it. So I got restless and to be honest, I like the thrill of crime, being able to use my wits, planning a job. And I wanted money. Pretty much all the problems in this world come down to a lack of it. The irony of it all is, I did love your mum, yet what I did for that love destroyed it. I wanted to be a good husband and dad, and give you everything, but I went about it the wrong way. It began like this. I was working as a security guard and the guy there said we could make a bit on the side by dealing hash. Well, I thought it was just a laugh, an easy way of making a few extra quid and getting a few spliffs out of it for myself. If you'd told me then where I'd end up, I'd have said you were being silly. But a lot of our tragedies are created by small stepping-stones.'

My father stands up and paces; gesticulates with his

hands as he goes on. 'You go down a certain path and by the time you stop to look back, you realise you're in too deep and it's too late to change anything. Suddenly you're a criminal. And I never got used to that label.' He sighs. 'Even in jail, I thought, I don't belong here. I'm just a guy who made mistakes – I'm not like the others here. And then one day I realised that half of them were thinking the same. I mean, back at school, when I was a kid, I thought I'd end up having a normal life. Instead, I became someone that society hates, not one of the lucky ones, the conventional ones. An outcast.'

'But, but – you have done good, haven't you? Haven't you?' I say. 'Mrs Kutty says you've achieved so much at this school.' I reach out and touch his hand and he holds it and I feel like I might cry again.

'Well, even that went wrong. I came here on a false passport and I wanted to try and help this school. But I got so frustrated by the lack of funds and decided I was going to raise money myself, to get them all books and proper equipment.'

'John Ruston.' I read his mind.

'Yeah – Ruston. I always seem to attract the wrong people,' my father admits. 'That's the trouble with life. Habits become patterns, patterns become ruts.' He laughs and blows out some smoke. 'Bloody idiot, I was, trying to raise the money by dealing. What was I thinking?' He squeezes my hand. 'The kids got their equipment, I'm glad to say, but we pissed off a few people on the way and I'm in serious trouble now. I need, in fact, to get out of here before they come after me.'

'You're *leaving*?' My voice breaks in horror.

'Yeah.' He lets go of my hand, fiddling with his cigarette packet. 'I'm sorry, Julia.'

'I just – we've only just . . .' I feel too choked up to speak.

'I know. But look at it this way. If you'd come just one day later, you'd have missed me and we'd probably never have met.' He looks into my eyes. 'So there's a kind of kismet there.'

'But,' I wail, my tears prickling again, 'I've been here in India for *ten days*. I could have come to find you earlier. We could have had ten days, a week.' I shake my head at the unfairness of it all.

Then I feel his hand cup my shoulder. My dad's hand.

'Sometimes you just have to keep cool about the little worries, and wait to see the bigger picture. There's no point in kicking against these things. It's life.'

I stare into his eyes and see the jaded wisdom in them. And then he smiles at me and touches my hair.

'Look at my little princess, all grown up,' he says. 'It's going to be hard saying goodbye to you, but we'll keep in touch, right? I'll call you. I promise you, I'll call. This won't be the end of it.'

And when I tell him I don't want him to go, he hugs me tight to his chest. I breathe in the smell of his cigarette smoke and deodorant, the sweat in his cotton shirt and the perfume of his skin. I feel his callused palm stroking my hair. And I want this moment to last forever.

7

The Bharatanatyam dance is traditionally performed by women. It is a spiritual dance, an act of devotion, the embodiment of music in visual form. Ciaran and I sit side by side in the Hindu temple, watching the beautiful dancer sway in time to a *sarangi*. The atmosphere is vibrating with spiritual energy and I can feel it humming inside me – and yet it doesn't quite penetrate my heart. It feels as though there's a kernel of sorrow right in the centre. It's sad and ironic: I thought that finding my father would satisfy this longing that's ached inside me for so many years. But now that I've met him the pain is only more poignant. I feel cheated that, having found him, he's been taken away from me so quickly. Sometimes I feel angry at Fate for its bad planning. Sometimes I feel angry with him for all the wasted years we might have been in touch. Time is the one thing you can never get back.

The dancer arches her body gracefully. The Bharatana-tyam is also known as the fire dance, and her movements flicker and swirl like a dancing flame.

Suddenly I feel my mobile, which is on silent, pulsing through my canvas bag. I pull it out and my heart leaps. My God! I thought it would be months before he called up. Without even thinking, I eagerly press my thumb down on the green button and cry, 'Hello?'

About fifty heads turn to look at me. Ciaran gives me an embarrassed nudge. The dancer stares right at me. Muttering flustered apologies, I quickly escape outside.

'Julia?' My dad's voice is affectionate. 'How are you?'

'I'm good. I was just watching a Bharatanatyam dance.' My voice is breathless, my heart beating hard. 'How are you?'

'I haven't slept for two nights.' He laughs lightly. 'I've just been lying awake, thinking about you – getting over the shock of it.'

'Wow,' I say carefully. Since our meeting, I've lain awake also, feeling scared that I laid too much on him, expected him to give too much, forgot how much he needed to process. So I'm just going to be sweet and light today. Let our intimacy grow step by step.

'You know, seeing you was one of the best things that's happened to me in a long time,' he says. 'For years, I would call up your mum to ask how you were, but to meet you . . . well, I thought I could never offer any inspi-ration to you. I thought I'd only screw you up. But you came all the way to India to find me – and if you hadn't I might have died not having seen you again.'

I remain silent. I have a feeling it's easier for him to say all this on the phone rather than face to face.

'I'm just really proud of you,' he says. 'You've made such a success of your life. You've had your job and you've travelled and you've damn well met Herbie French!' We both laugh. And then he sobers, his voice cracking: 'You've done it all so right.'

I feel touched, yet it's as though he's putting me on a pedestal and for one weird moment our ages and roles have been reversed.

'I'm unemployed now,' I say, and laugh softly.

'Well, what I've learned in life is that there are no real boundaries. You can do whatever you want. Don't let anyone tell you don't deserve your happiness – you should always fight to protect it. Ignore anyone who puts you down. And do whatever you like.' Then he laughs self-consciously. 'Maybe that's what got me into trouble.'

'I like your philosophy,' I say shyly. 'But where are you, by the way?'

'Somewhere hot. And I've gotta go, my princess. I'm sorry this is so short, but I'll keep calling.'

'I love you,' I suddenly blurt out.

There's a silence. Then he says, 'I'm going to read Herbie now, for the first time in twenty-odd years,' in a voice so tender that I don't mind that he doesn't echo my words.

I turn the phone off and smile. I feel a bit embarrassed

about going back into the temple, so I wait for Ciaran to come out. I don't mind waiting. I'm happy to just stand here, watching the sunset fade, with this feeling of new peace in my heart.

By the time Ciaran and I have got the bus back to the Tamil Children's Home (and nearly been killed on the way as the bus veered round a herd of mooing cows), the sunset has become moonlight. The air is warm and the full moon is beautiful. We sit on the steps in the courtyard, talking quietly so that we don't wake the children.

'Well,' Ciaran says. 'I'm wondering if it's time to move on from here. What do you think?'

'I agree,' I say sleepily. 'So can you, er, lend me the money for our flights back to England?'

'No,' Ciaran says, giving me a strange look.

'Oh right. Sorry,' I say hastily, flushing. I suddenly feel mortified: how could I even ask Ciaran when he's done so much for me *and* he's no longer holding down a steady job *and* I've been so cheeky to even forget that. That's the trouble with being broke. Back when I had money I could never have envisaged just how desperate it feels, that silent clawing feeling inside.

Ciaran reaches into his pocket and pulls out a crumpled sheet of paper. It looks as though it's been printed from the internet. He passes it to me. My eyes flick over it, the occasional word jumping out: *Kauai . . . island . . .*

hotel ... sea ... dolphins. I can't quite digest it. Then my eyes pick out our names.

Mr C O'Hare Flight Chennai (MAA) to Kauai (LIH)
Ms J Rothwell Flight Chennai (MAA) to Kauai (LIH)

And then I twig.

When I look at Ciaran I realise he's spent the last few minutes fighting back a huge smile which now erupts on his face.

'We're going swimming with dolphins,' he says. Then he rolls his eyes and sighs. 'How cheesy is that?'

And then I do something even more cheesy. I'm so over-whelmed that I burst into tears.

'Oh Ciaran,' I mumble, salt and snot flowing over my face in a most undignified manner. 'Thanks so much.'

I know that I'm over-reacting wildly – but it's just the kindness of his gesture. The love in it. Whether it's romantic or friendly or sexy or brotherly doesn't even matter at this point. I had thought that Ciaran had already proved that he's the most incredible friend I've ever had by coming out here and helping me find my father, but now I rather think he's excelled himself.

The trouble is, Ciaran gets all embarrassed by my crying fit. He makes a sarcastic remark that it really isn't that big a deal. He pats me on the shoulder, says good night and warns me that I'd better pack because we're flying out tomorrow evening. Then he calmly walks off to bed.

I sit and dry my eyes. I wish he would come back so I could hug him and tell him how amazing he is. But he'd only get even more edgy. So instead I smile up at the full, milky moon, lace together my fingers and say out loud, 'Thank you – *thank you.*'

9. Swim with dolphins

and

10. . . . ?

1

I'm sitting in a boat next to Ciaran and six other eager dolphin-seekers. I'm trying hard not to gush and fill the air with inane compliments.

When we flew over on the plane yesterday, we had a lovely journey – even though our flight here to Kauai, which is at the top of the Hawaiian island chain, lasted for simply *hours* with a stopover in LA. I couldn't help comparing it to the flight to India, during which I'd had to endure the company of newly-weds Reece and Luke: twelve hours spent tied up in emotional knots. By contrast, Ciaran and I chatted and watched movies and shared comfortable silences. At some point his head dropped on to my shoulder and his snores gently reverberated against my collarbone. I wanted to stroke his hair but I resisted.

But when we got to the island, I started raving about everything. 'Oh my God, that waterfall is the biggest I've ever seen!' 'The sea is crystal clear – it's just exquisite!'

'God, those mountains look like something out of a picture postcard!' And I had to conclude every observation with a *thank you*. Poor Ciaran started playing his Mr Darcy routine. The more I thanked him, the more he became boyish and reticent with embarrassment. So now I'm playing it cool and pretending that I'm not completely bursting with excitement *that we're about to go swimming with dolphins*.

I cannot describe how perfect this day is. The water is a sparkling aquamarine. The landscape is so exquisite, we could be floating in Paradise. If heaven exists, then I swear it will mimic this place.

The only slight problem is that, so far, there haven't been any dolphins.

On the way here, Ciaran and I had a small and rather sweet-natured argument about this trip. You see, there are two ways to swim with dolphins. The first – and admittedly more sensible option – is to go to the Big Island (Hawaii) and swim with the captive dolphins. The second is that you go out in a boat, have some fun snorkelling and exploring the sea, and hope that the dolphins come by and want to play.

Ciaran rolled his eyes and said, 'So basically we could hang around for ten days and they might just wave a fin in our direction, that's what you're saying?'

Then I explained to him that I'd done my research and this was the way I wanted it to be.

I'd read up about dolphin encounters and people

reporting feelings of bliss, of childlike awe and a sense of overwhelming freedom. It seemed hypocritical to me to enjoy a sense of liberation with a creature that has been locked up. So I told him that I wanted to swim with the dolphins on their own terms.

'I think I'm going to be depressed if we get rejected by the dolphins – can you imagine?' Ciaran said dolefully. Then he nodded. 'But I like your integrity. We'll do it your way.'

Now we're doing it my way and I feel a little disappointed. I thought that my integrity, as Ciaran put it, would be rewarded. Part of me expected the dolphins to circle together in a group and say, 'Julia's the nice one who didn't want us to be locked up, so she's got bonus karma points' – and then seek me out. We've all been snorkelling for the last two hours and we've seen some green sea turtles: known as the *honu*, Hawaii's oldest residents, they have speckly golden-brown shells, cute waggly flippers and curved heads with beady eyes. But no dolphins.

I half-expect Ciaran to say *I told you so*. But he's very mature and gracious. Actually, as we climb on to the boat and head back, I think he's mildly amused. I suspect he's still secretly finding this whole dolphin excursion a bit kitsch for his tastes, for he makes a little joke about the dolphins being AWOL because they're having a group therapy session. 'They must need it after all the emotional weirdos who offload their stress on to them,' he says, and gets some offended looks from the group while I try not to laugh. I'm in such an optimistic mood right now, that I don't mind: another day of waiting will only build the anticipation.

'D'you want to go out to dinner tonight?' Ciaran asks as we head back to the hotel.

'Yes, please.'

'Great.' He won't look me in the eye. 'Well. See you in the foyer – around seven?'

'Great,' I echo him breathlessly.

We're staying in adjacent rooms, in a lovely little hotel overlooking the mountain greenery.

When I take a shower, I can't help it: as the hot droplets tingle over my skin, I keep picturing Ciaran in the shower next door. I see the water running over his face, caressing those shoulderblades, wetting the dark hairs on his chest, trickling over his thigh . . . I quickly tell myself to calm down and primly twist the shower knob to cold.

When I go to pick my clothes for dinner, I find myself pulling out my red dress. I've worn it in Venice and Vegas. I'm convinced it's not a lucky dress. But then again, it is the sexiest thing I own.

Half an hour later, I stare at my trembling reflection in the mirror. I feel relieved. I haven't worn make-up in quite a while and I've got too used to sloppy ponytails. Now

I feel reassured that I scrub up OK. Then I remind myself that I look incredibly dressed up – and what if Ciaran is just wearing jeans and a T-shirt?

I take off the dress and pull on something casual. But it just doesn't satisfy – I ache to look my best for him. So I put the red dress on again, take it off again. I end up sitting on my bed in a paroxysm of anguish. I'm conscious that Ciaran cares for me deeply or we wouldn't be here. And I think there is an attraction between us as well as a tender affection. But beyond that, I'm not sure of anything. Ciaran is a closed book. His emotions aren't there on the page; they're hidden in the white spaces. I still have no idea if he booked this trip simply to cheer me up, or because he just wanted to travel.

We're both adults; we're both aware that there's an electricity tingling between us. But what if he thinks a one-night stand might be fun for old times' sake? Or perhaps he just wants a holiday romance? And I'm not sure I could do that; if I had one more taste of him, I'd be thirsty forever. Our dive in the sea today brought back memories of Sicily that lapped against me in the waves, left a tingle on my skin like a film of salt. Sicily was weeks ago, and so much has happened since then and yet I still yearn for him as much as I've always done. I have to be very careful to protect myself; I got over Luke and healed myself, but I'm not sure if I could ever get over a heartbreak caused by Ciaran.

Maybe friendship is better. Friendship is easy. Friendship

is simple and sweet. I ought to signal that by wearing my jeans and T-shirt.

I find myself putting on the red dress.

Ciaran sits opposite me, studying the menu hard. I'm staring at mine but all I can think is how I want to eat him up. He's wearing jeans but he put on a preppy olive shirt under his smart black jacket. In fact, we both look ridiculously overdressed compared to the rest of the tourists in their coloured shirts and shorts. But when Ciaran saw me in the hallway, he told me I looked beautiful, and boy, did I feel glad I'd taken the plunge.

He asks me what I'm going to order and I accidentally flip my fork on to the floor with a clatter. Ciaran immediately steals another one from an empty table. My self-consciousness is making me clumsy. It's weird: it feels as though Ciaran and I have never been on a date before. As though this is the first time.

If this is a date.

Finally, we order. The food looks exquisitely sumptuous: I'm going to have Ginger Panko Island fishcakes and I love the look of that lemongrass crème brûlée for dessert. Since I've been with Ciaran, my stomach has happily digested everything I've eaten. I feel like joking that my nutritionist ought to bottle him and sell him to her patients.

'This is so heavenly,' I begin and then stop myself. 'Sorry. I won't keep gushing on about everything forever.'

'I like it,' says Ciaran, and he actually beams. Then

something wicked flashes in his eyes. 'I remember the days when you were a hardened career woman, Julia. And now you're soft as marshmallow. What has this trip done to you?'

What have you done to me? I ask silently.

'Oh, I shall go back to being a career girl, no doubt,' I say, embarrassment sharp in my voice. 'Even though I've loved every minute of this trip, I still feel that I need to have a dynamic, busy career. But this time I want to have some work-life balance.'

I dread that Ciaran will say something chauvinist or persuade me that I should party forever.

'I'm a long way from feeling that,' he says instead. 'Right now, I never want to step into an office again. But I think it's great that you want to go back to work. Then you can repay your loans to me – just kidding,' he jokes as I hit him with the menu. 'Genuinely, I think it's a good idea. Whatever makes you happy. And hey, on the internet this morning I saw a report saying the recession is over. Here's to a bright future!' He raises his glass and I chink mine against his, and as we drink we smile at each other.

We eat, but I barely know what I'm tasting. I'm vaguely aware of people dining, getting up and swaying to the music, but it all blends with the distant shush of the sea. It feels as though I'm in a bubble with Ciaran and the volume and brightness are turned up to the highest pitch. I'm conscious of his fingers curling against his knife and fork. The dark hair on his chest bristling up from under his shirt; the stubble prickling his chin. The dimples in his cheeks when he smiles. The tiredness still etched under his eyes but the sparkle in his pupils. His knees brushing mine under the table. His scent quivering across it.

The more we drink, the more our eyes linger on each other. Until finally we just sit and stare at each other with naked intensity.

And then my mobile rings. It's really not the moment to answer it. Yet I think I want to burst the bubble because I'm too overwhelmed by it. I don't even look at the number, so when I hear her voice, I suffer a momentary shock.

'How are you, honey? I've been meaning to get in touch for *ages*. I've been wondering what's up with you . . . are you still in India? You have to tell me *all* your gossip.'

'I'm – I'm in Kauai,' I blurt out.

'Really?' she bubbles away. It is as though our friendship never ended. 'Why are you there?'

'I'm with Ciaran,' I say honestly. 'We're swimming with dolphins. How are you and Luke?'

I see Ciaran's eyes close in dismay as he realises who I'm talking to; at the same time I hear Reece babble something about a quickie divorce. Then Ciaran says firmly, 'I need to speak to her. For old times' sake.' I pass my phone over and he switches it off, then passes it back to me.

I think I rather love him for doing that.

'Let's dance,' Ciaran says.

A live band is playing and there are several beautiful female islanders doing the *hula* dance at the front, swaying and writhing with rhythmic grace. A few of the tourists are trying to copy them and they look quite foolish. The other diners are jiving in their own style and they look much more natural.

Ciaran and I stand a few inches apart, gazing at each other. Then he starts to sway and tap his feet. I'm amazed at how good a dancer Ciaran is. His style is old-fashioned and as smooth as Sinatra; his olive shirt sets off the dark of his hair and eyes. I sway opposite him, a little stiffly at first and then, as the music seeps into me, with more abandon. Ciaran smiles at me, puts his arm around my waist and we do a few ballroom steps in a mock-classic style. I twirl and then spin back to face him, our bodies almost but not quite touching, our eyes on each other's lips.

Somehow, it feels more intimate than sex.

And yet, for all this intensity, when the evening is over we end up outside our hotel rooms looking terribly British and awkward. If it was anyone else, I wouldn't mind risking a kiss. But to make a move – well, that would be like putting all my emotions down on the table on top of one gambling chip. This is Ciaran, who means everything to me, whose friendship I want to last forever.

'So . . . good night.'

'Good night.'

A burning silence.

'Are you still wearing those blue pyjamas?' Ciaran asks teasingly.

'I . . .' I laugh, blushing. 'I know they're pretty naff, but they're . . . yeah.'

Suddenly the mood is broken. My pyjamas – and my lack of sexiness – are clearly a source of comedy to him. I quickly say good night and he steps back, nodding and smiling, and goes into his room.

The moment I get into my room, however, my body screams with frustrated desire. One minute, I feel cloudy with euphoria as I savour our dance, the next I feel furious with myself for not bloody following him into his room. When he teased me about my pyjamas, I should have told him I now wear sexy burgundy lingerie. I feel as though he was testing me with that question, trying to suss out whether I'm still lame in bed, whether I prefer calculators to condoms. When I close my eyes, fantasies blaze. Ciaran and I kissing, stumbling backwards together. Me unbuttoning his shirt, pulling it down his back. His tongue in my mouth. His hands on my body. Tasting his sweat, his body, his kisses.

I grab my purse and remove a coin. Fate can decide this one. *Tails I go to his room, Heads I don't.* I toss it, catch it, and then frown. This is silly. I'm getting as bad as Luke. This is my life. *I'm* in charge of my destiny; *I* have to make my own decisions – and face the consequences. I stare out of my window. I can hear the sea, its salty whispers against the shore. I breathe out and step back from my desire. There's no hurry. This isn't some business deal I'm trying to close. This is something that is developing at its own pace. We have a week here. There's plenty of time.

I put the coin back into my purse without looking at it and slip into bed.

2

Dolphins are self-aware – a complex cognitive capacity which only humans and great apes share. They're so intelligent that baby dolphins develop their own distinct style of whistles, which means that dolphins can actually whistle out each other's names across the waves.

These are some of the facts that our tour guide passes on to us as we head out in the boat again, hoping to get lucky. The sea is blue and the sun is bright but I don't feel quite as high as I did yesterday. Sighing, I swivel round so that my legs are dangling over the edge of the boat, the waves caressing my feet. I haven't told Ciaran this, but Reece kept calling this morning and in the end I picked up.

Our conversation was brief and tense. She asked if she could come out to Kauai and join us. I said I didn't think it would be a good idea. She then played the blackmail card, reminding me that Luke had funded my India trip.

I felt guilty then, and awkward. I didn't want to openly admit to Reece that something was developing between me and Ciaran, though I'm sure she's guessed. So I asked her to call back later. I can't let her ruin this holiday, so I'm just going to be strong and tough with her and tell her she can't come. But the thought of the call hangs over me like a dark cloud ...

'Hey!' Ciaran suddenly nudges me.

I realise that everyone in the boat has fallen silent. *They're here.*

The dolphins have crept up on us with playful stealth. Suddenly I feel the water churning around my feet and I don't dare move. I just breathe very gently. For a dolphin is hovering right under my feet.

And then we touch. I feel a thrill – he wants to make contact. A second later, the dolphin has dived back into the waves.

I turn to Ciaran breathlessly. My heart is beating with happy speed. He looks thrilled – but thrilled only for me. I experience a brief disappointment, for I wish he could enjoy this for himself. But it's soon forgotten in the mood of dizzy joy that fills the boat. The guide tells us to be gentle and within seconds the five of us are pulling on snorkels and slipping into the water.

We all remain silent, scared we might frighten them away. The pod of dolphins outnumbers us: there are about a dozen of them. They dip and dive at a teasing distance. Then one of them does a backflip, spraying water over us. We all laugh: it feels like a glorious invitation to play.

Our group fragments. Ciaran and I swim over to a mother with a smaller dolphin which I think is her baby.

The baby approaches us. He's carrying a large green piece of seaweed on the tip of his nose. He lifts the seaweed up, lets it bob in the water, then dives down under, then captures it back on his nose. Then he whistles up a small stream of water, as though crying, *Isn't this fun?*

Ciaran and I turn to each other and smile. I'm tingling all over, aware that the universe doesn't give gifts, moments like this, very often.

What's just as beautiful as the dolphin is the look on Ciaran's face. He's no longer a detached observer. His face is soft, his eyes mesmerised. He's enchanted.

I can't resist a compulsion to swim closer, to touch the baby dolphin. Ciaran grabs my arm to hold me back and the mother dolphin swims closer in a protective arc. I'm scared she feels threatened and I've ruined the moment and they'll swim away. Then she ploughs right past me and our eyes meet. In that moment, magic sparkles. I see in her eyes no sense of threat, just something wise and kind and infinitely benign. It's as though she knows what I'm thinking and she's telling me not to worry. Not to worry about a thing. It touches me to the very core of my heart.

And then she circles away, her baby following. She does a backflip and her beautiful baby echoes her.

I feel myself starting to cry. I've done an awful lot of

crying on this trip, but these tears feel different. There's no wrench in my stomach, no wracking of my ribcage. I remember how, when I was a child, my mum first took me to the beach. I'd never seen the sea before and I burst into tears. She thought I was frightened, and that was partly true – but they were also tears of joy and wonder. The tears I cry now are like the tears of a child. They're sweet and cleansing; they open up my heart and allow love to pour in.

Then I turn to look at Ciaran and see he's blinking hard too.

The dolphins are leaving now. They dance away into the sunset, flipping their fins as though saying goodbye.

I feel something in the water and jump, thinking it's a jellyfish. Then I realise Ciaran is threading his hand into mine. I laugh awkwardly and accept it. And he squeezes it, sharing the moment – just as he did all those months back in Sicily, when we watched the volcano – only this time, my anguish has been replaced with joy.

With my other hand, I wave goodbye to the dolphins.

I turn to Ciaran and in his eyes I see a blaze of emotion. He too, has been opened up, his heart peeled raw. I see in his pupils the softness of love, dancing glints of lust. Cupping my face in his palms, he leans in and brushes his lips against mine. They taste of sea-salt and sun and bliss. I feel like a teenager, curious and innocent; I feel as though we've never kissed before. He comes closer, his body slicing warm through the cool of the waves. And then something seems to break inside him. He kisses me hungrily, showering kisses over my lips, my hair, my neck, before returning to my lips. I hear him groan and I feel a sense of wonder that he can want me this badly, and a sharp, happy desire cuts through me – and then, the next thing I know, the water's engulfing us and we both emerge, laughing and spluttering. We were so engrossed, we forgot to tread water.

We also become aware that everyone else has returned to the boat and is watching us patiently. The tour guide makes a pointed cough. When we climb back on, however, both scarlet-faced, nobody seems to really mind about our passionate display. I can feel a complete change in the mood of the boat, that the collective heart of the group is happy and open.

Back in my hotel room, I mooch about. I ache to be in his arms, but stretching out the anticipation is also pleasurable. When we came back to the hotel, he kissed me again in the corridor and I felt an unexpected desire to be apart from him. I recognised in myself the same compulsion as Dad when he pulled me into a hug and then moved away. It's as though your heart expands so much that it has to quickly contract again to find balance. But as it all sinks in, I sit on my bed and think, *Ciaran loves me*. A sense of wonder comes over me. We'll go to dinner tonight, and then we'll go to bed together and then we'll be together forever.

And you know what I do then? I sit down and write a joyful letter to Herbie, even though I know he'll never get to read it, just because I feel so high. I fold it up and hide it in my bag.

My mobile is sitting on the desk and it's then I notice that there are a number of missed calls. There are three logs of Reece's number; two from an unknown number. Which could just be Reece trying to hide her caller ID. A text beeps up that I have a voicemail message. As I dial to get it, I feel a sense of irritation as my dreamy bubble bursts. I'm having such a fabulous time here; trust Reece to interrupt it. But on a practical level, I do have to be firm but gentle and tell her she can't come out here. Plus, she is still living in my flat. We have issues to resolve and discuss.

Then I decide I won't worry about this headache. I'm going to be selfish and save this time for me and Ciaran alone. I'll call her back tomorrow.

When the message comes through, however, I'm jolted to find it's not from Reece.

'Hi – this is Henry Edmundson from Edmundson and Goldberg, Attorneys at Law. I'd be grateful if you could call me in relation to the recent death of Herbie French. We're in charge of administering Mr French's estate and we have some matters we'd like to discuss with you.'

'Ciaran, something strange and exciting's happened,' I spill out as we sit down to eat that evening.

'Really?' Ciaran asks, taking my hand in his. He smiles. I don't think I've ever seen Ciaran smile as much as he has since we swam with the dolphins. His face looks light and clear; there's a bloom of happiness in his cheeks; he's never looked more handsome.

Then I drag my attention back to business. 'I had a call from Herbie French's lawyers.'

'Oh no,' Ciaran jokes. 'Did they find out that you murdered him?' Then he twigs. 'Oh wow – he's left you something in his Will.'

I nod.

'Well, that is bloody fantastic.' He squeezes my hand tightly. Then, picking up on my mood, he asks, 'What?'

'It's just – so *annoying*.' I break my hand away from his, fiddling with a fork, and let out a long sigh. 'His lawyers want me to fly over for a night and they've asked that it happens right away. I don't want to leave you now when we've just . . .'

'Well, you should go,' Ciaran says at once, but I see the disappointment in his eyes.

'I asked them to delay it but they said they need me to urgently sign some documents. Apparently it's all been rather complicated and his ex-wife has been obstructive, trying to mess things up.'

Ciaran remains silent and I press my lips together, feeling churned up. Why is it that life flings us so much crap and then all the good things happen at once? I suppose Ciaran could travel with me, but then we'd lose out on this amazing holiday that he's paid so much for and I'd feel horribly guilty.

'Well, if it's only for one night, that's nothing,' Ciaran says, and his smile is back. 'We can go to the internet after dinner and get you on a flight tomorrow. You can see them, stay the night at your mum's and then come back. I'll be waiting for you. So will the dolphins.'

'Oh, Ciaran, thank you!' I cry. 'And when – when I get this Will thing done, if Herbie has left me any money, *I'll* treat *you* to a holiday and some flights and a whole load of dinners.'

Ciaran leans across the table and gives me a kiss, holding my face tight in his hands. When he breaks off and sits down, we both pause for a breathless moment. Then he chuckles.

'What?' I ask.

'Nothing.'

'What!'

'Well, what if Herbie just gives you something really awful in his Will? Like an ancient egg-timer?'

'Oh God, yes,' I laugh. 'I'm trying not to get too excited about it all.' Although my voice is literally manic with excitement.

There's a local temple that I want to visit. One of the waiters tells us about a ceremony there where you write down your hopes and wishes, then the priests burn them in the sacred fire, chanting to bring their fruition. Ciaran suggests that since we have a little time before the evening ritual begins, we should go for a brief walk on the beach first.

I feel such an ache that we're about to be separated just when we've got together. At the same time, it makes everything all the more special. The beach is beautiful, the sunset spraying her scarlet love across the sky and sea. We take off our shoes, the sand pearly beneath our feet. I breathe in the sweet salty air and smile at Ciaran. The wild thought comes into my mind: If he asked me to marry him right now, I'd say yes.

'What are you smiling at?' Ciaran asks, stroking my cheek with his finger.

'Nothing.' I look up at him from under my lashes. 'I'm just happy. I've been waiting a long time to be with you.'

We walk a little way in silence. Ciaran guides me to a secluded area, circled by some bushes and palms. We sit down and he puts his arm around me and though it's a relatively innocent gesture, I feel heat flood through my body. I wonder if we're about to begin something that may mean we don't make it to the temple this evening . . .

But Ciaran breaks off when I lean in to kiss him. His expression looks earnest as he asks: 'How long, then? What was the moment when you realised that you'd made a terrible mistake in dumping me?'

'Ciaran!' I push him gently. 'No, you're right. It's the biggest mistake I ever made in my life. But sometimes you have to lose someone before you realise how much you care about them. I didn't appreciate you, and I'm sorry for that.'

And do I dare admit to him that my love came rushing back just a few short months after he got together with Reece? That I have hungered after him for *two entire years?*

'So you can't remember when you wanted me again? Is it that unmemorable?' Ciaran asks. I'm shocked by the hurt in his voice. I suddenly realise that he needs reassurance. It's always been so obvious to me in my little world that I love him, that I forget how hard I've fought to conceal it – and how successful I've been in doing that.

'It was in Vegas,' I say quickly. 'The Shark Tank. When we stood and hugged – I just wanted to kiss you better.'

Am I doing a terrible thing by lying to him? But I'm just too embarrassed to admit the truth. He'll think I'm some crazy obsessive; he might be turned off me.

'What about you?' I ask tentatively.

'It was Vegas too,' Ciaran says.

Phew. I said the right thing.

'Maybe it was a bit before the Shark Tank,' Ciaran says. 'And in the helicopter, I did come close to kissing you, but it seemed wrong when you were kind of with Luke and I was screwed up by . . . everything. And then in India – well, I held back as you told me you'd kissed Luke again and I thought you were still getting him out of your system. D'you remember that night when we sat down and I told you about the dolphin holiday – and you cried? Well, the reason I walked off so abruptly was because I had to stop myself from kissing you.'

'Really?' I cry, overwhelmed. He leans over and kisses me greedily and we fall back on to the sand. He presses my body tightly to his and groans.

'What about last night?' I whisper. 'Did you want me then?'

Ciaran cups his hand tightly against the small of my back.

'I spent the whole night wondering whether to just ram myself through your hotel door and climb into bed with you.'

'You would have been very welcome,' I whisper in a trembling voice.

We kiss again, until our breath becomes ragged. Then Ciaran breaks off, staring at me with glazed eyes.

'I think maybe we should go to the temple now,' he says.

'Oh, right.' My desire simmers down; humiliation starts to heat up. 'Is this about my blue pyjamas?'

'What?' Ciaran asks, looking bewildered.

'I'm . . . might still have those blue pyjamas, but I am different now,' I declare, giving him a wanton look that projects rather more confidence than I'm feeling inside.

Ciaran smiles and places his hand against my belly, immediately creating a swirl of tingling warmth beneath my skin.

'Oh, I'd love to see those blue pyjamas,' Ciaran says in a low, melodic voice. He leans in and kisses my neck, biting the skin lightly and immediately I feel excited and relieved, reassured that he still wants me. 'It's just . . .' He tilts his head to one side, his eyes caressing my face. 'I feel that I've waited so long for you, I want to draw it all out for as long as we can. I want it to be really special. You've got a flight early tomorrow and . . . I think we should go to the temple tonight, and then I want to spend all night holding you, and then you can go to New York. And I'll wait for you, and when you come back – well, then we'll have all the time in the world. We can just lock ourselves into a hotel room and we won't come out all day or night.' The look in his eyes says the rest.

I tell him that it's a wonderful idea and I can't think of a better plan.

We stand in the temple together, watching the orange flames turn wishes and dreams to ash. I fancy that I can see them wisping off into the air, snaking their way to fulfilment. Then an elderly man shuffles up, barely able to walk, and adds his piece of paper to the wooden basket. I sense that he wrote down his last wishes, his last regrets. I find myself thinking of people I have loved and lost. The sudden sense of mortality makes me shiver and I move a little closer to Ciaran. He looks down at me and immediately takes my hand.

As I walk up to the fire with my letter to Herbie, I feel

strange: hot and prickly all over, almost feverish with anxiety. But when I throw the letter into the basket with the others and watch the priest toss them into the flames, there's an immediate sense of relief, of cool exhalation.

Then I turn back and see Ciaran standing there, smiling at me. And I feel as though he can see into my heart and knows everything that's in my letter without me having to say a word. I walk up to him and we hold hands and stroll out of the temple together – and I don't think I've ever felt closer to anyone in my life.

3

The next morning, Ciaran accompanies me in a taxi to the airport. It's dawn and the sky is a tender blue. The island is very quiet, the roads are virtually empty and the atmosphere feels magical. Palm trees wave gently in the breeze; flowers are uncurling in anticipation of the sun's first kiss. I gently stroke Ciaran's chest through his shirt and I feel his fingers combing my hair. I close my eyes, breathing in his scent deeply. It's like gulping in a visceral memory of last night; I feel my heart burst with intense happiness. Then the taxi curves a corner and through the window we both catch a glimpse of a distant plume of water spurting up from the ocean: a dolphin playing. We both break into smiles. Then Ciaran leans down and gives me a kiss, clutching me tightly.

At the airport, I check in. For the first time in my life, the wait seems to pass so quickly. We don't want to let each other go. We kiss and say goodbye and then kiss some more.

'I ought to be flying with you,' Ciaran moans.

'I know, I know, maybe we should have got you a ticket too – but I can't waste any more of your money,' I say regretfully.

'It will only be one night,' he sighs. And then he holds me and a breeze swirls in, tinted with salt and sweet memories.

We kiss. He groans faintly, and the sound shivers through me, reverberating with his hunger to share our first proper night together. I whisper into his ear, 'I'll be with you tomorrow night, Mr O'Hare.'

He whispers back, 'And then we'll do everything. I love you.'

It's weird being back in New York after Kauai. Even after a week I've become acclimatised to a slow pace of life. Being in a yellow taxi cab makes me feel as though I've drunk twenty cups of coffee. The tooting startles me. The buildings look as though they've been washed in grey city dirt.

I find a text on my phone from Ciaran. *Missing you already. Planning exciting things with your egg-timer? X*

The taxi pulls up at Mum's.

It's just typical: within twenty minutes of us having shared a hug, she's nagging me. Firstly, about money and what on earth am I doing swanning around Hawaiian islands when I ought to be looking for a job?

'Mum – Ciaran treated me, OK?' I assert crossly, whilst trying to focus on putting make-up on for my meeting with the lawyers. 'He really likes me.'

'That's what you said about Luke,' she sighs.

I pull a face at her but her words start to drip-feed insecurity into me. She's right: I did say that about Luke. But Ciaran is different. Isn't he? Then I turn away and savagely paint on some red lipstick. I swear all of this bickering is because she wants to ask what happened with Dad in India but is too proud to do so. It's probably better not to bring it up because whatever I say, she'll tell me what a bad man he is and put herself in a bitter mood.

Then Anthony calls out that the limo from the lawyers has arrived early. I dash upstairs, clean my teeth, go to the loo and yank on my coat, run a quick comb through my hair, wishing I'd had time to wash it as it's a tad greasy, and then hurry down into the limo. I'm heartened by the look on Mum's face when she sees it – even she has to be impressed. I send Ciaran an excited text: *I'm on my way to his house – oh God!! Miss you too xx* and he texts back *Call me as soon as you hear.*

When the limo pulls down the familiar country roads to Herbie's house, I smile nostalgically. At the gates, I see that the guy on duty is *that* guard. To think that he once threatened me with the cops for trying to see Herbie! When he spots me, I can't resist flashing him a smug grin. He smiles back with equal loathing.

As we drive into Herbie's grounds, I'm dismayed to see that the long grass has been cut back to a spruce green. It already feels as though the character is seeping out of the house.

I'm greeted at the door by a tall man with woolly grey hair and a goatee beard, his slate eyes glinting behind his wire-rimmed glasses. He introduces himself as Mr Edmundson – Herbie's lawyer.

'Would you like to take a look around the house?' he asks pleasantly.

'I'd love to,' I say. I feel flattered to be given a tour but another, jumpy part of me just wants to sit down and *hear what he has to say.*

I force myself to get a grip as he guides me into the living room. It's elegant in a very old-fashioned way, with blue wallpaper and heavy walnut antique furniture and lamps made from swirling gold. But it also makes me feel sad, for lingering in the air is both the presence and absence of Herbie.

'I've heard that the house is going to be preserved as a museum,' I say. 'I hope it is – I think that's a lovely idea.'

'Well, there are all sorts of rumours floating about in the press, as I'm sure you're aware,' Mr Edmundson says dryly and I bite my lip.

Then we head upstairs. In Herbie's bedroom there's a four-poster bed covered in old blue silk and a chest of drawers, and—

I cry out in delight.

'My kite!'

There it is, yellow and ragged, sitting in the corner. I feel quite moved to think that Herbie had treasured it. On the chest of drawers, his things are still laid out, neat and precise. A small pair of nail scissors. A notepad with a batch of freshly sharpened HB pencils. A comb with strands of grey hair in it. And that comb suddenly and unexpectedly just really gets to me ...

Mr Edmundson passes me a handkerchief and waits patiently as I wipe my eyes.

'Shall we go downstairs now and discuss my client's wishes?' he asks gently.

Downstairs, Mr Edmundson opens up his briefcase and rifles through some documents with his delicate, manicured hands. I can't help noticing a piece of paper that looks familiar. Oh God – is that *my* handwriting? It looks like the letter that I wrote to Herbie a few days before he died, in which I asked him for love-life advice and whether I should choose Luke or Ciaran. How embarrassing. The lawyers must have had a good old snigger at that.

'Ms Rothwell,' he says finally. 'I'm delighted to inform you that Mr French has left you a gift.' He passes me a brown A5-sized envelope. The flap is open: I peek inside. It's a book. I pull it out.

And then in an instant I completely forget to be embarrassed and my heart leaps in shock.

'You're the first member of the public to see the new book,' Mr Edmundson says, smiling.

I stare down at the cover, my heart pounding. My God, this is such a privilege – just wait until I tell Ciaran about this! The cover is decorated with a mermaid and the title reads *The Mermaid Who Hated Fish*. Then I turn it over, reading the brief blurb on the back: *There's a mermaid who lives at the bottom of this sea, and her name is*

'Julia,' I say out loud. 'That's a coincidence.'

'No,' says Mr Edmundson. 'You inspired him to rename the character. He changed her from Melissa to Julia.'

Melissa? What an irony, considering she was my enemy at Charlton Cross. And to think that Ciaran and I joked about an egg-timer; I want to giggle with the shock of it all.

'This is simply the most amazing gift anyone has ever given me,' I say instead.

I smooth my hand reverently over the cover. It's then I notice something peeking out from the inside cover. I open it up and my heart jumps a second time. It's a thick, creamy envelope, with my name curling across it in calligraphy.

'You might like to read Herbie's letter alone, in private,' Mr Edmundson suggests.

'Yes, of course,' I say, resisting the urge to tear it open in wild excitement.

'Finally . . .' Mr Edmundson begins, sifting through his papers.

'There's *more*?' I cry in disbelief.

'Oh yes.' He smiles. 'Now, Herbie has made a provision in his Will that you will receive all future royalties from the worldwide sales of *The Mermaid Who Hated Fish*. This includes an advance from his publishers, Alfred A. Knopf, which has been negotiated by his agent, Simon Trewin, who will retain ten per cent commission for the duration of the contract. The advance will be $250,000 to be paid in three instalments, one now, one on hardback publication, the last on paperback. If you'd like to sign these contracts, we can ensure the funds will be transferred to your bank account right away.'

I know I ought to be screaming and jumping up and down. But I just sit and blink like a confused reptile.

Mr Edmundson frowns. 'His former wife did try to contest the Will but she accepted that you will receive royalties from the book when she gained control of his property.'

'So he did leave her something in the end,' I say.

'No,' Mr Edmundson says. 'He left her with nothing. It was her lawyers who managed to wrangle something for her. She wasn't too happy about you gaining the rights to the book but there was really nothing she could do. It was set out in stone in his Will.'

'I'm just . . . I'm amazed. I only met him once, you see.'

'Well, you were the only person he'd met in twenty years, so you were bound to make an impression,' Mr Edmundson says in a rather back-handed compliment. 'Now, would you like to sign this contract?'

After I've submitted a wobbly set of signatures in a

daze, Mr Edmundson wraps everything up briskly. As we go into the hallway, he tells me that Herbie's ex-wife is planning to sell the house to a company that will knock it down and build a gas station.

'You're kidding me!' I cry angrily.

'His fans are all incensed,' Mr Edmundson says, with a faint shrug. 'But there's nothing that anybody can do about it.'

'Well, hey, maybe they can have a little shrine dedicated to Herbie in between the leaded and unleaded,' I say. Then I see the look on Mr Edmundson's face and I realise that I don't want to sour this trip, to walk away with a bad feeling when I've just received something so special. So, as he leads me to the front door, I turn around, drink in the hallway with its little table and Herbie's coats hanging on the hooks, and his pipe on the table and I say a silent goodbye.

When I get into the limo, the driver – who is clearly curious – asks me how it went. I just smile. I still feel devoid of an emotional response. I can't even call Ciaran.

In the middle of New York, it suddenly hits me. I let out a huge whoop. The driver swerves.

'I'm really sorry!' I cry, clamping my hands over my mouth. 'I'm just – just – you know.'

The driver smiles at me. 'He gave you a nice present, right?' He winks at me, rubbing his finger and thumb together with an envious expression.

'I'm – I'm in his new book!' I cry, hugging it to my chest.

The driver's face falls. 'Oh, right,' he says. 'Great. Yeah.'

I call up Ciaran, dying to share my news, but there's no reply so I leave a jumbled, frantic message on his voice-mail.

Back home, I tell everyone my news in a joyful gush. Mum cries; Anthony gives me a hug. I call Lucy and she screams down the phone at me for about five minutes. Up in my room, with the door closed so that Mum can't hear, I secretly give Dad a call. He's so proud of me that I shed a few tears. I'm so happy I even think about calling Reece but in a moment of commonsense I desist.

My joy keeps lapping over me in waves. Every time I think I've calmed down, it hits me again and I have to do a little jiggle in the hallway or whoop or say a prayer of thanks. I keep thinking about all the places I can take Ciaran. I head out to the shops and feel like buying every-thing I see for him. In the end, I just settle on a Cormac McCarthy novel, a tie and – grin – an egg-timer. Back home, I try calling him again but there's still no reply.

I end up going out for a drink with Lucy and raving on and on about how wonderful Ciaran is.

'When I get back, I'm not going to tell him about the book,' I say to her. 'I'm going to hold up the egg-timer and put on a sad face and see how long I can fool him.'

'I wish I could be there to see his face,' Lucy laughs.

Then she raises her glass in a toast. 'I'm just glad you proved me wrong about him. I can't believe I told you to go with Luke. Normally I always get it so right – but there's always a first.'

I get back to Mum's around 1 a.m. Upstairs in my room, I pick up the copy of *The Mermaid Who Hated Fish*, clutching it tightly. My letter from Herbie is still sitting in the covers. I'm dying to read it, but when I was out shopping, it struck me that it would be a deeper gesture of love to open it with Ciaran and read it together.

At 2 a.m., I wake up and check my mobile again. Nothing. I suddenly feel wildly, irrationally worried about what's up with Ciaran. Maybe he's become a celibate Hindu priest and decided to join the Kauai temple. Maybe he went swimming and a psycho seaweed wrapped itself about his throat and killed him. Or maybe . . . maybe he's just had too much thinking time. Maybe he's decided that he only kissed me in the height of all that dolphin euphoria. Maybe now he's calmed down he's realised that I'm just plain old boring Julia.

I sit up in bed. My curtains are slightly open and I can hear the traffic from below. New York: the city that never sleeps. Tonight I share their spirit. My brain will simply not switch off.

I pad into the kitchen and get a cool drink of water. Then I splash some on my burning forehead. *Just what is the matter with you, Julia?* I ask myself. In its tender early stages, love makes you so fragile, I muse. Along with the blossoming of happiness it also sprouts thorns of insecurities, fears of attractiveness, of being worthy enough to deserve it.

And I feel my agitation growing. The stirrings of past disappointment; echoes of Luke. This was the reason I was scared of getting together with Ciaran. I didn't want to end up in this situation: hurting, vulnerable, having to second guess what he's feeling.

I go back to bed and stare at the clock. Two-thirty a.m. Oh God, I want to get on to a plane right now. I just want to *know*. Even if he's gone off me, I want the truth. Maybe I should pull my boots on over my pyjamas, race to the airport and see if they have a flight—

Then I remember the wise words of advice I learned in India – from my own father.

Sometimes you just have to keep cool about the little worries, and wait to see the bigger picture. It's not easy but I try to pull back from the situation. I remind myself that I should detach until I have full understanding, not fret until I can see the full picture.

I'm sitting in my seat on the aircraft, staring out of the window when a jaunty man with an auburn beard, dressed in a spruce pale-grey suit, comes and sits down next to me.

He proceeds to spend the next fifteen minutes telling me all about the beautiful Hawaiian woman he's coming over to marry, and how she has become his redemption. He shows me a picture; she looks about sixteen. In the past I might have been judgemental but I know now that love has a sense of humour; even the most ill-matched couples can bring each other happiness.

'So why are you in New York?' he asks.

I let out a long sigh. 'I got an inheritance. A big one. I won't need to work again for years,' I say flatly.

'Well, why do you look so sad?' he asks, patting my knee.

Because all the money in the world doesn't mean a thing without Ciaran, I answer silently, staring miserably out of the window.

Ciaran didn't text me this morning. Nor did he take my call. And though it's a tiny thing, I know that when it comes to love, the tiny gestures are significant. They add up to big gestures in the end. I've learned that lesson from Luke. It's no use trying to whitewash over those prickles of intuition that warn you something is wrong; you really have to listen to them.

As the plane rises into the air, I watch the city fall away. I wonder if I'll end up spending my money zigzagging from country to country, trying to run away from this sadness.

4

He's not here.

I feel as though a hand has reached out and is squeezing my heart into a tight, hot ball. Despite the missed calls, I was certain that he'd be here at the airport to meet me. He knows when my flight gets in. But I've hung about for thirty minutes and I swear I've scoured every centimetre of Departures. I'm carrying my overnight bag in one hand and in the other I'm still clutching on to this bloody egg-timer. I've stopped picturing how funny his face will be when he spots it; it's grown sweaty in my palm.

He's not here.

And then I see her. *Shit.*

Oh God. Oh no. *She's* here.

This is so fucking predictable. She has bloody gate-crashed my trip *yet again*. I don't believe this. I check again to see if it really is her – and then she spots me and comes running up and flings her arms around me.

517

'Reece,' I say blankly. She clings on tight but I cannot summon the enthusiasm to hug her in return.

'How are you?' She grabs my hand, tugging me out. 'I've got a taxi waiting, I thought I'd come and meet your flight.'

'But Ciaran said . . .' I trail off as Reece picks up my overnight bag and then hurries forward to the taxi. I pause, standing very still as the shock hits me, staring beyond the frills of a nearby palm tree, across to the blue ribbon of sea on the horizon.

'Reece,' I say. 'How did you know that my flight was coming in now?'

'Ciaran told me,' she says in a light-hearted voice. 'I got here yesterday and he said your flight was coming in and I offered to meet you. I said I was madly happy to be meeting my lovely best friend Julia.'

'But—'

'Come on!' She indicates that the taxi driver is waiting, and dumps my bag in the back seat. I slip in beside it, my elbow nestling into my bag, and the driver sets off. I can't speak for a few minutes. I can't bear to ask her; I just can't bear it. I press my trembling fingers to my forehead. My visions of a reunion with Ciaran, of a long deep kiss, of the feel of his arms around me, are quickly turning to ashes.

'Are you OK, Julia?' Reece touches my arm.

I stare over at her. She looks different. Reece always used to be so baby-faced and pretty; we all joked that

she looked about twelve. Now, for the first time, she looks
... not old, but jaded, somehow. Her eyes have a glassy
look and her blond hair is a bleached straggle. My eyes
fall to her left hand. Her wedding ring has gone. *She's
just friends with Ciaran*, a voice inside me whispers desperately. *Remember how badly he slagged her off. There's
simply no way that ...*

'So what did Ciaran say?' I ask.

'We ...' A slight blush tickles Reece's cheeks and I
freeze. She shrugs girlishly. 'I think it's so sweet that he
organised some dolphin-swimming to cheer you up,' she
concludes evasively.

I feel as though I've been punched in the stomach. I
tell myself that I don't believe her; she's just bullshitting
me. And then I see her pull a BlackBerry out of her pocket.
Reece doesn't own a BlackBerry. In fact, it looks all too
familiar.

'Ciaran gave this to me,' she says. 'He said he was
overworked so he passed it to me to look after so he
wouldn't have to bother with any more calls or emails
on this trip.'

So that's why he hasn't returned my calls, I think with
a second's relief. And then: But why would he give Reece
his phone when he knew I had such big news? When he
knew I was coming?

And—

There he is. There's Ciaran – in a taxi on the other side
of the road, going in the opposite direction. I gape out

of my window and into his. He stares at me, starting. Then his taxi passes by and he's gone.

'Reece, what is going on?' I ask sharply. 'This is all so crazy – well, actually it's not. It's completely fucking predictable that you'd just turn up here, like you've gate-crashed half my bloody trip – but what are you playing at this time? Why did you come to the airport and not Ciaran?'

'Ciaran's really tired, Julia,' Reece says, as though I'm a bit slow. 'We had a very late night last night.'

I stare out of the window. I feel as though I'm going to be sick. Claustrophobia overwhelms me in waves of sickly heat. I open the door, the road spinning beneath my arm, before I manage to get out the corresponding words: 'Please – stop.' The taxi veers on to the bank; the driver complains at me. I get out and grab my bag. Reece hangs on to the strap and asks me what I'm doing. I take her hand, uncurl her fingers, shove her away and pull my bag out. She looks shocked and indignant. I storm off and leave the taxi behind, until my smart shoes are ploughing through soft white sand.

Bastard, is the word that keeps repeating in my brain. *Bastard bastard*. I could *punch* him, I really could. I slump into the sand next to my bag, not caring that people are giving me odd looks and sand is spraying into my jeans and shoes. I hold my head in my hands and I tell myself to be cool and logical. Reece could be stirring things up; Ciaran did get fed up with her; Ciaran has done amazing things for me ...

But she has his BlackBerry. There's no getting away from that.

Ciaran, I yell back in his defence, desperately hunting for ammunition, has brought me here on this holiday at great expense.

Ciaran's really tired – we had a very late night last night. Reece's words echo in my mind.

I've got it all wrong. I have read too much into everything. He cares for me, I have no doubt, but not enough to resist avoiding my calls and shagging Reece whilst I was away. This is reality. This is not a happy ending – this is real life.

I am too shocked even to cry. I feel as though my heart is dust. I'm never going to find love, I think dully. Like I always feared – it's just not in my destiny. I stare at the waves, tossing in turbulence, and remember that first disco where Reece got the guy and I got the cast-off. And now, all these years on, it's still the same old story. And it always will be that story. Even though I don't think Reece and I can ever be friends again, I can already see the past echoing in the future. I'll meet a guy but he'll just be on the lookout for something better. He'll go for someone like her.

I stand up. I'm still carrying this stupid egg-timer and now it's got sand in it. I consider throwing it into the ocean—

And then I turn and see Ciaran in the distance, walking towards me.

5

He comes storming up to me and puts his arms around me. He leans in to kiss me and I lean up, aching to respond, when I find myself superimposing Luke's features over his face. I've been here before. I'm not about to play the fool again.

'Ciaran.' I push him away weakly. Suddenly I feel exhausted; I just want to curl up on my own under the covers and sleep for three days. 'No ... no ... it's over. Go back to Reece.'

'Reece? I didn't know she was coming,' Ciaran says.

'Then how did she find out we were here?'

'You bloody told her,' he points out, looking confused. 'She gave me the impression you'd invited her. God, I had no wish for her to come. I thought you'd had a moment of complete insanity to let her join us out here. I also suspected she was probably bullshitting me.'

He goes on for a few more minutes, saying he has no interest in Reece and he can't believe I'm even questioning him. I don't say a word. I just stay dull and numb and silent. But I'm listening with my ears pricked up, waiting for him to make a slip. And then I'll pull it like a thread and the whole story will unwind in full. It'll be something along the lines of *Well, Reece and I just had a bit too much to drink and then you weren't here, you'd gone off to the lawyer's and deserted me* ... I've been here before. This is just like Luke and Tokyo.

Ciaran keeps on talking, trying to persuade me with a desperation that can only prove his guilt. *Yeah, yeah, yeah*, I say silently. And suddenly I don't think I can even be bothered to listen any more.

I'm too idealistic, I realise. My lack of romantic experience in my twenties has turned me into a naïve teenager. I knew that Luke was trouble but I thought I'd found redemption in Ciaran. Someone to prove to me that the male sex are worthy. That love is not just a golden ideal in books and films. I feel a painful shudder inside my chest when I realise that the deep emotions that Ciaran stirred inside me over the last few days weren't real. Then I think sadly: Well, I'll always treasure the illusion even if it was a lie.

'For God's sake!' Ciaran shouts, and I suddenly become aware that his indignation has climbed the scale to soprano anger. 'Are you even listening to me?'

And then I too feel angry. I boil with it. Just because

I won't believe his lies – how dare he get stroppy with me!

'Don't you shout at me,' I cry. 'Reece has your bloody BlackBerry!'

'She does?' Ciaran asks in amazement. Then he blinks. 'So that's where it went. The stupid cow must have stolen it. I thought I'd lost it.'

I frown, longing to believe him.

'You know, every phone number I have is on that BlackBerry,' Ciaran says. 'And no, I don't have a photographic memory, I don't know your number by heart. If you don't bloody believe me, you can go to the hotel and speak to the receptionists. They hate me.'

'They hate you?' I ask in a small voice. 'Why?'

'Firstly because I accused their maid of stealing my BlackBerry. Secondly, because you can get a call log from the phone in my room, whereby I was trying like mad to remember your mum's number and kept on calling random New Yorkers and then got told to fuck off about thirty times in a row. You saw me in the taxi! I'm sorry that I was late for your flight but the whole Reece thing was a total headfuck because I was pleading with her to give me your number and she refused. She kept saying we ought to be together. So by the time I'd given up on her stupid game, she'd already left to chase after you *and* taken the taxi I'd booked, and so I followed on late. So that's the dreadful morning I had and I was so – *damn looking forward to seeing you*,' Ciaran says in a trembling voice. 'But if you are really going to believe Reece and her demented lies over me – well then, you must have a very low opinion of me, Julia.'

I stare at him with an open mouth. He blinks hard, waiting for a response. But I can't quite speak. Hope is whispering in my heart. I'm trying hard not to be naïve and just believe any story, but yes, I think this actually makes sense. I think he's telling the truth.

But now he's walking away from me.

'Ciaran,' I shout.

I hurry after him, trying to grab his arm, but he keeps on walking.

'Ciaran, please – look, I'm sorry. I know you're different from Luke, but I still . . . I just . . . I'm sorry. Reece is just – she's dreadful. I think she's been dreadful for quite a while, but I don't think I realised it.'

Finally, he stops. He stares at me with a look that I can't quite fathom, it seems to contain such a medley of emotions: love and hate, sweetness and anger, exasperation and affection.

'This isn't just about Reece,' he says, his voice thick with emotion.

'I know that,' I say quickly, although I don't know entirely what he means. In fact, all I want to do now is just express my apology: hug him tight and smother him in kisses and caresses.

'Don't you realise,' Ciaran suddenly cries, his voice nearly a yell, 'how long I've been waiting for you? I've been in love with you for so long.' He trails off, his voice breaking with humiliation and sadness. Then: 'It's never been there for you, has it – that's why you dumped me. And you're right – I have behaved like a bastard. I had no interest in Reece last night and I never really have. If you want to know the truth, Reece *did* come on to me that first night eighteen months ago, but I only ever dated her just to get back at you. I thought I'd make you jealous, I thought you'd be mad at me. And you didn't even notice or care. And it's the same now. You won't even believe me over something so obvious – you don't even trust me. It'll always be the same – you're right that it will never work. I'll always love you more than you love – or even *like* me. I'm just fucked, right?'

He starts to walk off again and I stare at his back, my mouth agape.

I run after him again, spraying up sand, and grab his arm. He yanks it away, looking at me, his eyes stinging hurt. I open my mouth and I'm so overwhelmed by his revelation that I start to laugh. It's terrible, utterly inappropriate, utterly unromantic – but I think I'm in mild hysterics.

'Oh, thanks,' Ciaran snarls. 'I'm so glad I amuse you, Julia.'

I manage to get a grip on myself.

'It's just, what you said about dating Reece to get back at me . . . You did that and then you fell in love with her, right?' I ask, sober now, my voice quiet.

'I—' Ciaran begins, then bites his lip. 'I – well, no. I kind of hoped I might fall for Reece, but it never happened.'

'You dated for a year and a half!'

He turns and looks at me, straight in the eye.

'I dated her to be close to you. I mean, don't get me wrong, I'm not a complete bastard – I did feel very fond of her. Reece is fun. I felt very *protective* of her. But the whole time, I was hoping I'd get over you, or get you back.'

'But the other night,' I persist, my heart thudding very hard, 'the other night you said that you fell for me in Vegas. You said it happened in the helicopter.'

'Well, I felt like a prick,' Ciaran cries. 'It just sounded so – I mean, you said you fell for me in Vegas so I thought I'd say that I fell for you then too.'

But that's my story, I think in delirious confusion. I'm the one who lied about Vegas. I frown at him. I do believe him now when he says that he's not interested in Reece. But I can't help wondering whether the whole I've-always-loved-you tale is just some sort of spin, to make me feel good and convince me that he cares.

'But you were so *rude* to me,' I object. 'All the time you were dating Reece, you were so mean. We stood at the top of Mount Etna and you told me you thought I should throw myself in.'

'Well, of course I did! I was in love with you!' Ciaran bellows.

'Well, I'm sorry,' I bellow back, 'but it's not exactly the

type of thing you find in the middle of a greetings card.'

'Well, you told me you hoped I'd drown when I was scuba-diving!'

'Because I was covering up my feelings,' I say shakily. He gives me a look and I chew my lip. 'So you dated Reece and ... you liked me.'

'Why d'you think I put up with her treating me like shit?' Ciaran says, getting het-up again. 'I go to Sicily and she bloody gets off with our scuba-diving instructor right under my nose. Then she didn't even bother with a condom and does a pregnancy test. What guy would hang around after that? I wanted to see *you*. I knew she was doing it to provoke me – because deep down she knew I cared for you.'

'Oh no.' I laugh incredulously. 'Reece would never think that.'

'Have you ever wondered why she is so jealous of you?'

'Reece isn't jealous of me,' I say in shock. 'She's blonde and pretty and everyone fancies her ...'

'Reece is very jealous of you,' Ciaran says firmly. 'Why do you think she's here now, Julia? Just open your eyes and see it all, will you? She's scared of losing you as a friend and scared of losing me even though she's never loved me, because I'm *someone*. She's a best friend from hell and you just haven't woken up to it. She's terrified of seeing us get together and leaving her on her own, so she's making one last attempt to destroy everything. She did it to you with Luke, and it didn't matter then because he didn't deserve you. But please, please, Julia – don't let her do that with us.'

'She hasn't been a great friend to me recently,' I admit. 'We've known each other for so long that I suppose I didn't really want to face up to what she was doing.' In fact, if I look hard at the picture Ciaran's placed before me, Reece has put on a fluffy front whilst scheming hard to ruin my love life. But I can't bring myself to hate her any more. Reece isn't important right now. Ciaran's words are still singing inside me, creating shivers of delirious joy.

'So,' he says, 'do you think,' his voice is small and his face boyish with vulnerability, 'that we might have a chance?'

'You're an idiot, you know that?' I tell him. 'Haven't you noticed that I've loved you for so long too?' I burst out laughing. 'It's just so crazy that neither of us realised. And all this time, you loved me too.'

But Ciaran isn't smiling.

'You don't have to do this, you know,' he says.

'What?'

'Pretend that you've liked me all along. You don't need to feel guilty or try to make me feel better.'

'But – but it's *true*,' I falter. 'I genuinely did change. It happened after I stupidly dumped you and you started dating Reece. I realised then how special you are. You're not going to believe me, are you?' I can hardly believe the irony of this moment. Never in my fantasies did I imagine that I'd have to *persuade* him to believe in my love.

'All I need to know is that you can trust me, and that there is still a spark between us. Reece hasn't ruined it, has she? It is still there? I just want us to have a second chance, to get it right this time.'

I stare up at him. I don't think I've ever felt so happy or so exasperated in my entire life. Then I realise that this yin-yang of emotion is the colour of my love for Ciaran. Reaching up, I give him a long, deep kiss. He holds me tight and kisses me back, then pulls my head against his chest and strokes my hair. And we stand there, peaceful together, the sea shushing gently in the background.

'What the hell is that thing in your pocket?' Ciaran suddenly asks, frowning.

'It's an egg-timer,' I laugh. I'm much too dazed and high to even attempt to trick him. 'Oh, Ciaran, Herbie left me the most wonderful gift. He's put me in his new book and I'm to get all the royalties, which means that I can treat you to so many holidays that you will *have* to believe how much I love you.'

When I open up my rucksack – still ditched in the sand after my swift escape from the taxi – and pass the book to him, Ciaran gazes down at it in excitement.

'I'm so proud of you,' he says huskily.

'And look – there's a letter. I wanted you to open it with me,' I say, my voice tender. I pass it to Ciaran and watch as he cuts open the envelope with his nail. He then does a double-take.

'It's empty. No, it isn't.' He pulls out a small scrap of paper which has been folded over and passes it to me.

I open it up. Herbie's handwriting is shaky: *Dear Julia, I will reply to your question on the understanding that you won't bother me again with your romantic issues, which I am ill-equipped to advise on.*

I'd choose Ciaran.

Epilogue

'What about eating a chocolate-encrusted scorpion?' I suggest.

'Um, pretty weird, but a possibility,' Ciaran says, and writes it down.

'I was actually joking.' I laugh, nudging him.

'Well, I'm open to everything,' he tells me. 'OK, I've got three so far. Go skinny-dipping in the South of France. Learn how to play the ukulele. Make love on a train, cross-country. I need seven more.' He doodles lightly on his notebook and gives me a slightly dirty look. I take a big gulp of my Earl Grey tea, blushing and wondering if Ciaran thinks it's time to take a break from the list.

We're sitting in my flat on my new big squishy mustard-yellow sofa. I stare over at the fish-tank, now drained of any water. When Reece came out to India she forgot to ask anyone to feed Cameron and Ashton, and apparently got home to find them floating on the surface of the dirty water. She moved out of the flat whilst we stayed in Kauai. Even though I know that it's for the best, I still feel a little sad sometimes. I miss the friend I used to have.

Then my eyes sweep around the living room. I appreciate the new black and white picture hanging on the wall, the spotless carpet, this sofa. It is rather nice living with a boyfriend who has a strong sense of cleanliness. I turn to look at Ciaran, who is chewing on his pen. Only he could make pen-chewing look so sexy. Every time, he always gets me: when he suddenly grabs me in the middle of the street and gives me a hug. When he's cooking me a lovely roast dinner and winks as he pulls it out of the oven and waits for me to take a taste so he can revel in my pleasure. When I wake up in the mornings and find him staring at me and then leans down through the sun-dappled shadows and kisses me. Or sometimes, not even him: his coat. His shoes. His box of Earl Grey sitting on the kitchen table. My heart will just thump and I will feel so lucky to have him and I pray to God that I get to keep him.

The nice thing is, Ciaran's just as insecure as me. Every so often he'll look at me with worried eyes and ask if I'm thinking of dumping him again. And I have to hold him so tight he can hardly breathe and kiss him like mad and tell him how much I love him for him to calm down again.

We're working on a new list of *Ten Things*, only this time the list is for Ciaran. We were both planning to go back to work and be sensible and save our money, but then the thought of having just a *bit* more fun was too irresistible ...

'Of course,' Ciaran breaks off, 'before we get on to my list of *Ten Things*, we've got to finish off yours completely.'

'Eh?' I ask in confusion. 'I've done all mine.'

'No,' he argues, 'you've only done nine. Have you forgotten about number ten?' He breaks into a triumphant smile. 'Well, I'm going to make it happen. I got your tickets for bungee-jumping.'

'*What?*'

He stares at me and I feel the full force of his love, how earnestly he wants to make me happy. But – *bungee-jumping*? What on earth is he thinking?

'You know. In India, you said it was the last one on your list ... What?' He breaks off when he sees me laughing.

'Oh shit. Can you get a refund?' I ask. 'I mean, it's just that bungee-jumping isn't actually number ten on my list ...'

'So what was it then?' Ciaran asks.

And then he looks into my eyes, and I see a smile of ecstasy spread across his face, I know that finally, he believes in my love for him.

Now you can buy any of these other **Review** titles from your bookshop or *direct from the publisher*.

FREE P&P AND UK DELIVERY
(Overseas and Ireland £3.50 per book)

Unsticky	Sara Manning	£6.99
Changing Grooms	Sasha Wagstaff	£6.99
Things I Wish I'd Known	Linda Green	£6.99
The Stepmother	Carrie Adams	£6.99
An Offer You Can't Refuse	Jill Mansell	£6.99
The Other Side of the Stars	Clemency Burton-Hill	£6.99
The Sisterhood	Emily Barr	£6.99
Left Bank	Katie Muir	£6.99
The Best of Times	Penny Vincenzi	£7.99
Bad Behaviour	Sheila O'Flanagan	£6.99

TO ORDER SIMPLY CALL THIS NUMBER

01235 400 414

or visit our website: www.headline.co.uk

Prices and availability
subject to change without notice.